MR 9/2 R
JR

7/05

WHEN THE DEAD CRY OUT

Hilary Bonner is a former showbusiness editor of the *Mail on Sunday* and the *Daily Mirror*. She now lives in Somerset, and writes full time. She is the author of seven previous novels, *The Cruelty of Morning*, *A Fancy to Kill For*, *A Passion So Deadly*, *For Death Comes Softly*, *A Deep Deceit*, *A Kind of Wild Justice* and *A Moment of Madness*.

HILARY BONNER

WHEN THE
DEAD CRY OUT

 St. Martin's Minotaur ♞ New York

www.minotaurbooks.com

Library of Congress Cataloging-in-Publication Data

Bonner, Hilary.
　　When the dead cry out / Hilary Bonner.—1st St. Martin's Minotaur ed.
　　　　p. cm.
　　ISBN 0-312-33946-1
　　EAN 978-0-312-33946-3
　　1. Police—Great Britain—Fiction. 2. Married women—Crimes against—Fiction. 3. Missing persons—Fiction. 4. Policewomen—Fiction. 5. Journalists—Fiction. I. Title.

PR6102.O56W47 2005
823'.92—dc22   2005046456

First published in the United Kingdom by William Heinemann

First U.S. Edition: July 2005

10　9　8　7　6　5　4　3　2　1

FOR MUM
July 25th 1908 – December 18th 2002
With love and gratitude

Grateful thanks are due to:

Police Diving Supervisor DC Brian Bolt, and Detective Sergeant Pat Pitts of the Devon and Cornwall Constabulary; Detective Sergeant (retired) Frank Waghorn; all at Rolex UK; and Home Office Pathologist Doctor Huw White for their expert advice without which this book could not have been completed; and Kirsty Fowkes, whose editorial input was also invaluable.

Prologue

The morning began much the same as any other for Karen Meadows. It was a typical summer's day on the English Riviera. Sky grey, the air warm and damp.

As usual the recently promoted detective superintendent breakfasted alone, apart from her cat, in her apartment overlooking the sea. She had lived there, a mile or so from the centre of Torquay, for nine years. Her brain was full of work because that was pretty much all she let it be full of. Her heart was full of nothing much because that was how she liked it – or at least that was how she told herself she liked it. Her eyes no longer took in the view across the bay which was glorious in even the dullest of weather.

Breakfast took the form of three mugs of strong tea, dash of milk, no sugar, consumed on the run as Karen never seemed to have time to do anything properly in the mornings, and two menthol cigarettes. She kidded herself that the peppermint taste made them healthier than the other kind. Not that she wasted a lot of time worrying about her health. She was too busy to allow any such preoccupation, and there was nobody else it mattered much to, she reflected bitterly. She showered and dressed in between smoking and drinking her tea.

Karen Meadows had always had good taste in everything except, on one or two unfortunate occasions, men. Her home was very stylish, simply decorated in shades of cream and pale greys and blues, and furnished almost entirely with antiques of a standard considerably higher than might be expected of a woman whose sole income was her police salary, which was down to her off-duty passion for browsing junk shops and antiques fairs and auctions. Unfortunately her housekeeping skills did not match her talent as either an antiques collector or an interior decorator. Sighing at her own inadequacies she sifted through the teetering pile of clothes at the foot of her bed beneath which a pretty little Victorian nursing chair, worthy of far better treatment, was totally buried. Karen had no idea how anyone as organised and in control as she knew she was in her work could be so disorganised and untidy at home. It was her constant dream that one day she would wake up and find that she had become effortlessly tidy and ordered overnight.

Meanwhile she was forced to delve through the debris on the chair, and then to search her overstuffed wardrobe, much of the contents of which had fallen on to the floor, in order to somehow unearth a pair of baggy cream trousers that were barely creased at all, a denim waistcoat and a beige linen jacket which was actually supposed to look crumpled, the main reason she had bought it in the first place. She found one of the grey satin designer trainers she had decided were the only shoes that would possibly do that day underneath the bed, and the other, for reasons which defied her, on the worktop in the kitchen. She fed Sophie the cat on the remains of last night's old Marks & Spencer's chicken because she had run out of tinned cat food, located her various keys with the customary difficulty, then gulped down the last mouthful of her final mug of tea, some of which she slurped on to her jacket thus necessitating a panic-stricken dash to the bathroom for an emergency mopping-up operation.

Yet, miraculously, when she ultimately emerged from her flat she looked as good as she almost always contrived to and considerably younger than her forty-one years. Her glossy dark hair, cut into a geometric bob, framed a good strong-boned face, albeit one which had a tendency, no doubt accentuated by her job, to look severe. And the clothes she wore, as ever casual and giving the impression of being thrown together – even though every day she agonised over her appearance, rather tragically she thought, and not without difficulty considering the problems she invariably had finding anything at all – suited her well and added to the impression of youthfulness that she had about her.

Certainly the way she looked totally belied the chaos which

had, as usual, engulfed the start of her day. And as she headed for the lift, an ancient convoluted contraption which managed to provide at least a hint of real or imagined danger almost every time she used it, Karen looked confident and in control, though admittedly not a bit like most people's idea of a police-woman.

She flashed a big smile and paused to speak to an elderly woman neighbour who was taking out a plastic bag of rubbish.

'When you've finished, Ethel, give my place a going-over, will you?' she remarked cheerily.

'For you, darling, anything,' replied the old lady. 'I'm expensive though. You'd never be able to afford me, not in your job.'

'You never know, Ethel. Perhaps I'll join the villains instead of trying to catch 'em.'

'May as well, dear. They'll probably make you a peer then, like that Jeffrey Archer.'

Karen could still hear Ethel chuckling as she stepped into the elevator, closing the latticed iron outer gates behind her. Briefly she leaned against the ornately mirrored walls of the inner cage and closed her eyes for just a few seconds. She felt tired. Terribly tired.

It was the same every morning. And it never used to be like this. Karen was a natural high flier, capable, in charge of herself, personable, warm, funny. That was her image, that was the personality she put across and had lived up to throughout her life. She liked the way the world perceived her. She liked the way people reacted when she walked into a room. She didn't want that perception to change because without it she was convinced she would be lost.

She didn't want the world to know that she was plagued with self-doubt, that what went on inside her head was as far removed from the image she put across as was the chaotic way she lived from the way she would like to live. That would never do. Karen's state of mind was a very private thing. She never spoke of her dementia-ridden mother in a nursing home whom she increasingly saw less and less. In any case the guilt, justi-fied or not, was abiding and nothing anybody said could ever help. She never spoke of the regrets she felt that she had not married and had a family and that she had probably now reached an age where that was no longer likely to happen. She never let on that she had ever wanted a child. Nobody who knew her would ever have suspected that Karen Meadows was anything other than a happy, successful, fulfilled woman. The police force had made her believe that to show any other side of herself would be seen only as weakness. And that would never do. Karen refused to give away anything about her true self. She believed that if she ever allowed her contained outer shell to crack open even a little she would fall straight through it flat on to her face.

So inside the lift she pushed herself upright again, pressed the ground-floor button, and shook her head quite ferociously in order both to clear it and to deny the troubled thoughts it contained. The temperamental old lift shuddered into action, incomprehensibly bouncing an inch or two upwards before lurching dramatically downwards in such a jerky fashion that Karen was forced to lean against one of its walls again to ensure that she didn't lose her footing.

The banter with Ethel had been fairly typical of Karen Meadows. It was automatic for her to respond to people in that way. She lived her daily life on a kind of personality autopilot. She didn't know how else to do it. It wasn't contrived. It wasn't altruistic. After all, it worked for her, too, as well as for those around her. She knew that by the end of a halfway good day she would probably be believing in her own image again, almost as much as did all those she encountered.

As she made her way out of the building and across the parking area towards her car she lit a third cigarette and inhaled deeply. Tomorrow she would give up, she told herself for the umpteenth time.

Her mobile phone rang just as she was about to unlock her car door. She dropped the car keys as she rummaged for it in her big shoulder bag, overstuffed like the wardrobe. Swearing to herself she went down on one knee to pick up the keys with her left hand as she finally located the phone in the bottom of the bag and pushed the speak button with her right one.

'It's Phil, boss.'

Detective Sergeant Cooper's voice was pitched slightly higher than usual. He sounded excited.

'Those divers out off Berry Head, the ones exploring that old Nazi E-boat that's been in the news. They've found something; bones, parts of a skeleton, inside the hull.'

Karen stopped scrabbling for her keys at once. Cooper wouldn't have called to tell her they'd found the remains of some poor German sailor. In any case that was pretty unlikely after getting on for sixty years in the depths of the Atlantic Ocean.

'Go on,' she encouraged.

'It was wrapped in tarpaulin and wound around with heavy chains. So we can pretty well forget any thoughts either of one of the original crew or any sort of freak accident at sea. Looks almost certain some bastard just threw it into the sea from a boat.'

Karen remained motionless on one knee, oblivious to the small sharp pieces of gravel digging into her skin through the thin cotton of her trousers. Her mouth felt dry when she opened it to speak again. Her brain was buzzing. She ran her tongue around her lips. The sharp moment of suspense, albeit so brief, while she considered the possible meaning of what she had been told, made it difficult for her to formulate the words she wanted to say.

'Anybody taken a guess at how long the skeleton may have been there?' she asked eventually, aware that her voice was perfectly calm. Karen always managed to sound calm whatever she was feeling inside. It was one of the many tricks she had developed which made up her persona.

'No way, boss. But the divers did say that it had been pretty securely wrapped in the tarpaulin, and also that it had drifted or been swept inside the hull of the E-boat where it was wedged in such a way that it's been protected from the currents and the fish. So it could well have been there much longer than you'd normally reckon possible from its condition.'

Karen thought quickly. She always did. That was what made her so bloody good at her job.

'You said parts of a skeleton? What about the head?'

Phil Cooper would know at once what she was getting at. If the head were intact that might mean teeth still existed. Dental records gave swift irrefutable identification. DNA might

5

be obtainable but it was not always as straightforward as people assumed, and certainly not when only bones were left of a corpse.

'Most of the torso and the arm and leg bones are there apparently, but the tarpaulin had worked loose around the neck freeing the head to all the destructive elements of the Atlantic Ocean,' Cooper replied. 'Nothing of it left at all, they don't reckon. Sorry, boss.'

Karen grunted. Her brain was still buzzing as if a swarm of honeybees had crawled inside it. She closed the fingers of her free hand around her dropped car keys and rose slowly to her feet.

'Are they certain it's just the one body?'

'I think I can guess what you're getting at, boss.'

Karen had been pretty sure that he would, but she had no time for the niceties of game playing.

'Well?' she inquired sharply.

'Seems so. The amount of bones, and even the way the skeleton was bundled up, suggests a single adult corpse only. We don't have an expert opinion yet, though.'

Karen grunted.

'Where's the skeleton now?'

'On its way to the morgue at Torbay Hospital.'

'Meet you there in fifteen.'

She snapped off her phone without waiting for a reply. Her heart was pumping very fast, as if she had been exercising hard. When she opened the car door and slipped into the driver's seat she was aware that her mouth was drier than ever. Her hands on the wheel trembled very slightly. Her eyes gleamed with excitement. Apart from any other considerations, this was what she had joined the police force for. Until Phil Cooper had called, her day ahead was to have been devoted entirely to paperwork and admin, the aspects of her job which held no appeal for her at all. Now she could cast that aside with a clear conscience, for once.

She gunned the engine into life and swung her sleek convertible sports car out of the car park. It was one of the new MGs. Her long-time journalist friend John Kelly, a devotee of the original MGBs, whom she was sure she would encounter very soon as he had a nose for a story that would shame your average bloodhound, was derisory of what he called 'the pale imitations'. But then Kelly, who always seemed to be in trouble of one sort or another, was barely qualified to speak as his most recent series of misadventures had led to him being banned from driving for the foreseeable future.

The sky was beginning to lighten a little as Karen pulled into the main sea front road, so out of habit she reached up with one hand, unfastened the hood and swung it back – a trick she had taught herself as soon as she acquired the car. Karen was not the type who had either the time or the inclination to pull into a lay-by and stop in order to lower a car hood. Her hair shifted only slightly with the draught caused by the vehicle's forward motion. She had one of those cuts which rarely moved out of place. It was, she sometimes thought, possibly the only intrinsically tidy thing about her and she was extremely fussy about her hair, washing it daily and fussing over it constantly. If Karen's hair didn't look right, she was inclined to feel unable to function at all.

She reached into the glove compartment for a pair of dark glasses and coasted to a halt at the first set of traffic lights, the determined upward tilt of her jaw and the inexplicable aura of excitement she now exuded from every pore making her appear particularly attractive.

She was quite unaware of the admiring glances of the driver of the car adjacent to her. But Karen's image, maintained always in such a fragile manner, was firmly reinstated, both in her mind and that of others. She had already forgotten the empty blackness of her early morning mood, which was, in any case, not for public consumption. Neither did she remember how tired she had felt just a few minutes earlier. Her brain was on overdrive. The adrenaline raced through her system making every nerve-end tingle with anticipation.

It couldn't be, she thought. Not after all this time. Not after twenty-eight years. It really couldn't be. Could it?

Part One

One

On a sunny afternoon in June twenty-seven years earlier, Karen Meadows, then a gawky thirteen-year-old, had been on her way home from school. As she approached the little street just off Braddons Hill Road, high above Torquay, where she had lived all her life she broke into an easy long-limbed trot. She was late for tea, again, and likely to be in trouble, again.

It was her own fault that she was in such a hurry. She had no idea why she had lingered so long in the cloakroom gossiping, nor why she had detoured to look at the sea after that. The truth, of course, was that she wasn't particularly keen on returning home at all. But her head was still at the stage of adolescence where she merely accepted her home life for what it was and she had yet to begin to work out the psychology of her own behaviour. At that moment she just wished she wasn't so late. She didn't want another row with her mother.

She quickened her pace as she rounded the final corner of her journey, the trot developing into a full-out run, the school bag which hung from her right shoulder flying out now behind her and banging against her backside as she ran. Her mouth was set in a determined line. She hammered her feet on to the paving stones, pushing her body forward, all her energy focused into the urgency of the moment. She wasn't looking where she was going at all.

And so it was that she found herself enfolded in the arms of a rather large policeman into whose ample body she had cannoned at full speed.

'Whoa, not so fast,' he said, pushing her gently away. She stood for a moment panting, the remaining breath knocked from her body by the force of the impact with the policeman. As her breath and her wits returned she became aware that the street where she lived looked rather different from usual.

It was lined with a varied assortment of police vehicles. Parkview, the small private hotel next to the big semi-detached Victorian villa where Karen lived with her parents, was cordoned off with yellow tape as was a considerable stretch of the pavement outside and part of the road itself. Men in overalls appeared to be digging up the garden. Just outside the cordoned-off area a young man in a vivid green suit with flared trousers was standing alongside another young man who held a camera which was pointed at Parkview. As Karen tried to take it all in two more men came through the front door of the hotel carrying transparent plastic bags containing what appeared to be bundles of clothes. A hand-drawn sign just behind the policeman Karen had collided with read 'Crime Scene. Keep Out.'

Karen realised then that the policeman must be on some kind of sentry duty. Another uniformed officer stood at the far side of the cordoned-off area, within which, she suddenly became aware, lay the entrance and driveway to her home.

Pulling away from the policeman she started to tremble with anxiety. What had happened? Parkview seemed to be at the centre of the activity. And the thought of what that could mean made Karen all the more anxious. Was her mother all right? Karen was just a kid, still at school, but she already knew that it was her place to worry about her mother considerably more than the other way round.

Margaret Meadows was a charismatic, pretty woman with a mercurial mind and, on a good day, a natural facility to lift the moment with her zest for life and her easy laughter. She was also prone to bouts of depression which were both deep and debilitating. But Karen and her father referred only to her mother being bad with her nerves, and no one outside her immediate family knew about this at all as far as Karen was aware – because people like the Meadowses didn't talk about such things.

Karen loved her mother deeply, absolutely adored her, as did almost everyone who came in contact with Margaret Meadows. There was something quite captivating about her. Maybe it was partly her vulnerability which made her so irresistible. Certainly she was the most emotional of women, which in her case meant not only that she gave more love than most people have in them to give, but also that the emotional demands she made on her only child at such a young age were quite mind-blowing.

Most of the time Karen coped. She had had plenty of practice already. But sometimes she was overwhelmed by the various grown-up pressures which engulfed her. And when she was afraid or overly excited she invariably found it impossible to speak. It wasn't a stammer. She didn't stammer. It was more than that. The words just would not come. Karen understood all too well the true meaning of the expression to be struck dumb, and it terrified her. As she grew older she was to incorporate into her veritable armoury of defence mechanisms a strategy for overcoming what had been a real handicap in her youth, and for remaining calm and in control while she did so, or at least appearing to be calm. At thirteen that was not the case.

And so Karen was rendered speechless by the scene which confronted her that day, and by its possible implications. The question she wanted to ask was too big to be put into words. Her face turned red with the effort. The only noise she could manage to get out from between her lips was a kind of strangled moan.

'What is it, girl?' asked the policeman kindly, bending over her and putting a hand on her left shoulder. 'Don't upset yourself.'

Karen just looked at him. Eyes wide.

'That's not where you live, is it?' he inquired, looking slightly puzzled and gesturing at Parkview.

Karen managed to shake her head. She pointed to the villa next door.

'Ah,' said the policeman. 'Well, you shouldn't have anything to worry about then. Are you going to tell me your name?'

At that instant Karen couldn't tell him her name. She wasn't even sure she could remember it, let alone say it. She had to know though, she had to ask the question she dreaded. Eventually she somehow managed to get the words out.

'Mum. M-my mum. Is she all right?'

'Well, I expect so, darling, but you're going to have to tell me your name or at least her name before I can be sure, aren't you?'

'M-Margaret Meadows.' Karen spat out the words, using all the willpower she could summon up.

'Ah, Mrs Meadows. Yes, of course. Laurel House. The trouble's next door to you, girl. Your mother's fine. Just fine. A bit upset by all the commotion, but then who wouldn't be?'

'Can I go in?'

'Yes, course you can. Just walk along with me, all right.'

The policeman lifted a line of taping behind him so that he and Karen could duck underneath. Karen, by nature a very observant girl, was beginning to function at least halfway properly again. She noticed that several of her neighbours were watching the proceedings, most of them covertly. Mrs Stephens on the corner was outside cleaning her windows, but her head was all the time turned towards Parkview. Mr Johnson, the retired schoolmaster who lived opposite, was washing his car very slowly, a job that his wife normally did. Karen looked up and down the street. The curtains twitched at the Beverleys, but upstairs at Hillden House the bedroom windows were wide open and old Mr Peabody was leaning right out staring openly at all that was going on.

A grunting noise behind Karen attracted her attention back to the policeman accompanying her, who, having also straightened up on the inner side of the tape barrier, was standing with one arm behind him pressed gingerly into the small of his back.

'*Anno Domini*,' he muttered. 'Don't ever grow old, darling. That's my advice to you.'

Karen was interested in neither the policeman's back trouble nor his age, which in any case seemed to her to be so great that it was quite beyond her comprehension. She peered anxiously up at him as they walked together towards the gateway to Laurel House.

'What's going on?' she asked eventually, in what she knew was rather a squeaky voice. 'What's happened at Parkview?'

'Nothing to worry about. We're just making some inquiries, that's all.'

'But you're digging up the garden?'

'I think I prefer you when you can't get your words out, missy.'

The policeman smiled down on her. Normally Karen enjoyed the company of people who were good-humoured and seemed to take things calmly. It wasn't what she was used to, after all. But on that day she had other things on her mind.

Abruptly she turned her back on the big affable policeman, flung open the wrought-iron gates to her house and ran as fast as she could up the driveway to the front door.

She needn't have worried about being late for tea. Her mother was always unpredictable. For some weeks now a full high tea had been laid out for Karen's return from school and Margaret Meadows had given her daughter a lecture on how hurt and offended she was should Karen have been even a few minutes late home. It was the kind of emotional pressure Karen was used to from her mother, and sometimes it had the diverse effect of making her be deliberately and rather perversely late.

But on this day Margaret Meadows had done nothing about tea. Karen's heart sank. It seemed that her mother was bad with her nerves again. She was sitting morosely at the table in the kitchen, her head bowed, and did not look up as Karen entered the room.

'Are you all right?' Karen asked automatically, although seeing her mother like that really made the question redundant.

Mrs Meadows made no attempt to respond.

She remained in exactly the same position as Karen walked quietly forward and sat down opposite her at the orange Formica-topped table – a legacy of the mid-sixties, the last time the old house had been decorated or changed in any way. Margaret Meadows still did not look up. Her wispy blonde hair was a mess and had fallen over her face hiding it from view. Karen dropped her shoulders slightly and bent her head to one side so that she could see her mother's face, or at least most of it. As she had expected, Margaret Meadows' eyes were red and puffy and her cheeks were damp with tears and smeared with mascara and eye-liner. Her mouth hung open and slack. Lipstick was smudged all around it. Karen knew well enough that her mother, who never rose before she left for school, also never emerged from her bedroom without make-up. Today she would have been considerably better off without it, as it happened, Karen thought.

Aware of her daughter's scrutiny Margaret Meadows lowered her head even more until her upper body was bent right over and the top of her head was almost touching the table. She was wearing a vibrant pink cardigan over some kind of flimsy floating dress, clothes that seemed totally out of place. But she always dressed like that, a cross between Marilyn Monroe and a Barbie doll, Karen had once heard Mr Peabody remark in the newsagent's. Mr Peabody had a rather acerbic turn of phrase and was invariably as direct in everything he did and said as he was in his blatant appraisal of the police presence around Parkview.

Karen preferred to think about Mr Peabody, or anyone or anything at all that might be a distraction, rather than thinking too much about the state her mother was in. It was one of her ways of coping. None the less she accepted that, somehow or other, it was her job to deal with this. Her father never took any notice at all. He would return from work in an hour or so and if his wife was still crouched over the kitchen table in tears he would just walk away and leave Karen to it.

Still somewhat distracted, Karen noticed that Margaret Meadows had found a screwed-up paper hankie tucked some-where into her clothing and, conscious at last perhaps both of her daughter's presence and of the likelihood of smudged residual make-up, was now scrubbing ineffectively at her face with it. Karen reluctantly prepared to turn her full attention back to her mother. At that moment she would actually much rather have been with Mr Peabody or the fat policeman or her teachers at school or almost anybody who wasn't totally neurotic, as she had once also heard Mr Peabody remark about her mother. It had been the first time Karen had ever heard the word, but she had somehow understood at once that it was just another way of describing her mother's bad nerves. Although how Mr Peabody knew anything about all that was a mystery to Karen, given that everything that happened within the somewhat crumbling walls of Laurel House remained a carefully guarded family secret.

Almost at once Karen felt terribly disloyal. Her mother wasn't bad with her nerves all the time. Her mother could be lovely, the loveliest mother anybody could possibly have. It was just that Margaret Meadows couldn't always cope, and increasingly often Karen wasn't sure that she could either. She knew that too much was asked of her too often, but she didn't know how to put this into words that her mother would understand, and she knew that even if she did it wouldn't do any good.

Karen continued to study this person she loved who was capable of causing her so much distress without having any idea that she was doing so. A half-empty mug of tea was on the table in front of Margaret Meadows. It looked extremely unappetising; a film had formed on the top of it so it had surely gone cold. The teapot, in its brown and orange patterned cosy, was alongside.

'Do you want me to freshen that up for you?' asked Karen. She had a habit of repeating the exact expressions she heard uttered around her by people much older than her. Sometimes they sounded rather strange emitting from young teenage lips. But much about Karen belied her youth. She had grown up very fast indeed. She'd had to. That had just been the way things were.

Her mother shook her head, still not looking up. With one hand she began to make a gesture downwards which she then seemed to think better of. Karen sighed again and leaned further sideways so that she could peer beneath the table. It was as she expected. A whisky bottle stood on the floor by Margaret Meadows' feet. There was just an inch or so of amber liquid left in it.

Karen straightened up and then stretched forward across the table so that her head was close to her mother's bowed one. She could smell the whisky then, on her mother's breath and from the mug too, she thought. She couldn't understand why her mother even bothered to attempt to hide the bottle, but it was something she always did. Karen really had no idea why. She reached under the table, picked up the bottle and put it in her school bag. Out of sight out of mind, she thought to herself.

Aloud she said sternly: 'I may be shutting the stable door after the horse has bolted, but I think you've had more than enough of that.'

Her mother did not protest, she rarely did, neither did she respond. She was quite used to being treated like this by her daughter, quite used to her daughter's rather quaint phraseology and use of old sayings. Not that her mother drank often, Karen reminded herself, well, not very often. And only when she was bad with her nerves. It was just that when she did she was inclined to empty the bottle.

'Look, Mum,' Karen continued. 'Why don't you go upstairs and have a nice lie-down?'

There was still no response. Wearily Karen leaned back in her chair and found her gaze wandering idly around the big kitchen, a huge cavernous room in a huge cavernous house, which had about it none of the cosiness traditionally associated with kitchens. In spite of its size there was no big cooking range, just a small gas cooker. A line of orange Formica-finished units ran along one dark brown painted wall, another unfortunate legacy of the mid-sixties which contrived to make the north-facing room seem particularly dark and drab. The orange-topped table also wasn't big enough for the kitchen. It was, however, quite big enough for the three people who lived in the oversized Victorian villa.

Some houses have a warm feeling about them which hits you as soon as you enter. Some houses give you the feeling that nothing bad has ever happened in them, that they have by and large been happy houses. Laurel House was just the opposite. When Karen went to bed at night she always pulled the bedclothes right over her head. That way she could pretend she was somewhere else.

She had no idea whether or not her parents had intended to have more children, whether they had planned to fill some of the six bedrooms on the three storeys of Laurel House with lodgers, or whether they simply liked the idea of living in a big house. If the latter was the case they had made a mistake quite equal in size to the vast dimensions of their coldly austere home.

Karen knew that her parents had lived in Laurel House ever since their marriage three years before she was born. Yet there was still not enough furniture to half-fill the place and all the rooms were shabby. There was no central heating and in winter the house was freezing. Karen always assumed that her father, who did something or other he never talked about in local government and dressed in the same grey suit for work every day until it wore out when he bought another identical one, just never made enough money to run the house properly. And her mother never worked at all, of course. Margaret Meadows, with her charm and looks, would probably have obtained a job quickly enough had it ever occurred to her to do so. But she was possibly as aware as anybody else that she would never have been capable of holding one down.

One bitter cold winter's evening when the three of them had been huddled shivering around an inadequate fire in the vast loftily-ceilinged front room with damp stretching in ever increasing patches on either side of the chimney breast, Karen had asked her parents why they didn't sell the big old house and buy something smaller which would be easier and cheaper to maintain. Typically, her father, who always had an air of terminal weariness about him, had simply got up from his broken-springed armchair, which twanged every time he shifted himself in futile attempts to find a comfortable position, and walked out of the room. He didn't glance at either his wife or daughter. With the resilience of the young to all that is inevitable and unalterable Karen had long before accepted that her father had for whatever reason given up caring about anything much, including her and her mother. Colin Meadows, in his mid-forties then, was not an old man, but he gave the impression of being so, and a beaten one at that.

She also accepted that all too often she had to be the strong one in this family. So, squaring her shoulders, she rose to her feet, retrieved a mug from one of the orange Formica cupboards, returned to the table and poured herself a cup of tea out of the teapot. She took one mouthful and instantly spat it back into the mug. It was disgusting. Even the tea from the pot which had been encased in its cosy was stone cold.

Obliquely Karen wondered then just how long her mother had been sitting at the table like that, emptying her bottle of whisky. And she wanted very much to ask her if this latest attack of bad nerves had in any way been brought on by the goings-on next door at Parkview. But she was afraid to mention anything that might make her mother worse.

'Shall I make a fresh pot?' she inquired instead. 'It would do you the world of good, I reckon. Nothing like a nice hot cup of tea to perk you up, is there, Mum?'

At last Margaret Meadows looked up from the table. Her face was pale and pinched beneath the make-up smudges which her inveterate scrubbing with the paper tissue had done little to remove. Her eyes flicked pink and nervous in her daughter's direction, her lips trembled. Her voice, when she eventually spoke, was flat and low but the words came out clear and unhesitant. She did not sound at all drunk. But then, she never did.

'They've taken Richard,' she said. 'The police have taken Richard.'

Karen's heart jumped. She knew who her mother was talking about at once. Their neighbour Richard Marshall, the proprietor of Parkview. Karen did not speak. Instead she sat staring at her mother, taking in the shocked expression in Margaret Meadows' red-rimmed eyes. Her mother had obviously been knocked sideways by the police action. There were so many questions Karen wanted to ask her, but again she didn't dare.

For a few seconds Margaret Meadows stared bleakly back at her daughter, then she suddenly threw her upper body forward on to the table, knocking over her mug of cold tea, and began to weep noisily and copiously. Her body shook with great heaving sobs. Meanwhile, in that curiously objective way she had developed, her highly observant daughter noticed that her mother's tears were flowing so abundantly that they were running on to the tabletop and diluting the brown puddle of tea into which Margaret Meadows had lain her head.

Karen knew that there was nothing she could do for the moment. Eventually her mother would stop crying and then Karen would help her back to bed. It was an all-too-familiar routine.

Meanwhile all she could do was carry on as normal. Squaring her small shoulders she stood up, trotted upstairs to her parents' bedroom, and picked up the various items of clothing, lying around on the bed and floor which obviously needed washing. She then went into her own bedroom and changed out of her school uniform into the jeans and T-shirt she wore around the house, after which she took her soiled school blouse into the big bathroom where the washing machine was plumbed in and loaded it and the dirty washing from her parents' room into it. It was what she did every evening.

By the time she returned downstairs to the kitchen her mother was no longer sobbing so dramatically. Instead she was sitting upright in her chair again and was once more dabbing ineffectively at her tear-stained face with a tissue. Karen took a cloth from the sink and began to mop up the spilt tea from the table.

It was not the first time she had seen her mother in this kind of state, not by a long chalk. And neither, she knew only too well, would it be last. Often nobody had any idea what brought on her mother's attacks of bad nerves. On this occasion Karen had little doubt that it had been, as she had suspected from the beginning, the goings-on next door at Parkview.

There was so much Karen did not understand, and yet there were muddled half-formed memories inside her head, like pictures torn haphazardly from an album, which made her feel very frightened and would not go away. As she wiped up the spilt tea Karen stared at her mother. Margaret Meadows did not even seem to notice. Karen wished her mother would talk to her, explain things. But she never ever did. Karen would just have to sort her troubled thoughts out the best way she could, just like always. But sometimes, as she struggled to make sense of the crazy adult world around her, that was very hard to do. All she knew for certain was that she mustn't tell anyone about her fears. The Meadowses were very private people. And if nothing else, Karen had been brought up to understand and respect privacy. Appearances were all. You didn't talk about what went on behind your own locked front door. Not to anyone.

Not even when the police were digging up the garden next door. Not even when you had a fair idea what they might be looking for – not even when you were battling with thoughts and images too crazy and terrible even to think about.

Two

The young man in the green suit, of which he was somewhat misguidedly extremely proud, had watched idly as the tall gangly schoolgirl disappeared inside Laurel House. With one hand he brushed his hair from his eyes. It was 1976, and he sported a thick head of dark hair which, in accordance with the fashion of the time, hung over his collar at the back and flopped over his forehead at the front. He was also misguidedly proud of his hairdo.

The young man's name was John Kelly. He was a reporter in the last year of his indenture with the local weekly paper, the *Torquay Times*, and as he surveyed the scene, he reflected that maybe he should be talking to more of the neighbours, but he somehow didn't want to yet. Charles Peabody, whom Kelly knew because the older man compiled crossword puzzles for his newspaper, had already given him the benefit of his view on the goings-on of the day which had been predictably opinionated and based on little more than pure speculation.

John Kelly preferred to focus all of his energy on Parkview, going over and over in his head what may have happened there.

He removed a cigarette packet from the pocket of his jacket, which he carefully smoothed down as he did so, lit up and then passed the packet to the photographer accompanying him. It looked as though he might be on the biggest story Torquay had ever known, and thanks to a tip from a police contact Kelly was on the scene first, before the national boys or the local evening and morning papers.

Kelly knew the story behind all this police activity better than most. He had written it enough times for the *TT*, but most of it had ended up on the spike as he supposed he'd known it must. For legal reasons. Now the police had finally taken action all that would change, and what had merely been a ferocious chain of gossip throughout Torquay could, he hoped, finally be printed.

Richard Marshall and his wife Clara had run the Parkview Hotel for several years. They had two small daughters, Lorraine, aged six, and five-year-old Janine. Marshall was a big, handsome, personable man with a quick wit and an easy way with people. He had been well enough liked until a year previously.

Then, suddenly, Clara Marshall and her daughters had disappeared. Their absence caused little comment at first. Marriages broke up all the time, even in the seventies. Most mothers leaving the marital home would want to take their children with them, and Richard Marshall had always had a plausible explanation for everything, as was his wont. The gossip had grown only gradually, gaining momentum, of course, when Marshall had moved another woman into his hotel home with what his neighbours considered to be quite indecent haste. By the time the police finally began to investigate, the level of gossip was such that there could be nobody in Torquay who did not at least suspect some kind of mystery concerning the disappearance of Clara Marshall and her children. And for many suspicion had grown into a horrible sense of certainty about their fate.

Kelly, whose mother was the head teacher of the primary school the Marshall children had attended, was one of those who had come to believe that murder had been committed. Kelly's own inquiries over the past few months had revealed no sign of Clara or the girls. He was a local paper reporter whose resources and time were both very limited. But he knew that the police had now checked bank, social security and national health records to no avail. Clara Marshall and her daughters appeared to have vanished off the face of the earth. The finger of suspicion pointed firmly at Clara's husband, Richard. But gossip, conjecture and assumption were not evidence. They did not solve a crime, nor indeed did they even prove that one had been committed.

And one way and another it had been a whole long year before the police had made their move. Now Kelly had been told that the Devon and Cornwall Constabulary was about to launch the biggest missing persons inquiry the West of England had ever known. Now. A year later, when the trail was surely cold. Kelly took several short fast puffs on his cigarette. He feared that it may already be too late. Too late not only for Clara Marshall and her girls, but too late to prove anything against anybody.

Kelly didn't like that. The whole thing was a mess. And his mother, whom he adored, was deeply upset by it. She had reasons for feeling that she could have saved the Marshall girls from whatever had happened to them. Kelly thought she was wrong to blame herself in any way. None the less this story was personal to him. If Clara Marshall and her daughters had indeed been murdered, then he wanted their killer brought to justice every bit as much as the police did.

Impatiently he threw his half-smoked cigarette to the ground, and extinguished it with the toe of one shoe.

'C'mon, Micky,' he said to his photographer companion. 'I don't see any more mileage here. We know they've taken the bastard to the nick. Let's take a trip down there, shall we?'

Meanwhile, at Torquay Police Station, Detective Chief Inspector Bill Talbot strode into the interview room wearing a confident expression, which did not reflect his inner feelings at all. This case was already the most frustrating he had experienced in his career.

Squeezed behind the little wooden table in the centre of the small bare room sat Richard Marshall, totally impassive, features in repose, his disconcertingly clear pale blue eyes alert but giving nothing away. This was far from Talbot's first confrontation with Marshall. None the less he was once again struck by the man's immense physical presence. It wasn't just his size, although Marshall – six foot three or four, and seventeen or eighteen stone, Talbot reckoned – was indeed an extremely big man which was evident even when he was sitting down. His shoulders were huge, stretching the fine fabric of his well-tailored navy blue blazer. Even his head, with its shock of thick dark brown curly hair, was big. And his face, although Talbot had to reluctantly accept that Marshall was a good-looking man, was broad and fleshy. He had a big nose, a bulky fore-head, and lips so full that although there was nothing remotely effeminate about him, his mouth would almost have been better suited to a woman were it not quite so wide. But it was more than all of that. Marshall had a way of filling a room and dominating those in it. He returned Talbot's gaze steadily, unflinching, confident. Even if that wasn't how he felt it was the way he came across. He looked every bit as if he might be about to conduct an interview with the policeman rather than the other way round. The muscles at the back of Talbot's neck had tightened quite painfully. Indeed, he was aware of every fibre in his body tensing up in anticipation of the task ahead.

Marshall was good, very good. He also had experience of police investigations. He had a criminal record. He had served six months in jail for his part in a time-share scam concerning property in Spain. Marshall had been the front man, and Talbot had no doubt he would have been very good at it too. He was so smooth. A number of people, mostly elderly folk, had lost a lot of money, in some cases their life's savings, because of that unpleasant little operation. Marshall had also been suspected over the years of being involved in other cons and always seemed to be somehow or other skimming along on the edge of the law. Talbot considered him an unsavoury charac-ter in every way. It was, however, a quantum leap from anything the Detective Chief Inspector knew about Richard Marshall to murder. None the less, Talbot firmly believed that Marshall was capable of such a deed and that he also had both the gall and the ability to stand up to the most ferocious of police investigations.

Marshall had been arrested in connection with the disap-pearance of his wife and children, but he had yet to be charged. There was not enough evidence for that. In fact there was no evidence at all worth mentioning. Talbot was hoping to God that either Marshall would break, which as it happened the man gave no indication at all of doing, or that some hard evidence would turn up – like a body. And fast, too. Clara Marshall and the girls had been missing for just a week less than a year exactly, and Talbot knew that there was going to be criticism of the police for not acting sooner. In fact there would still have been no operation in place had not Clara Marshall's partially estranged father finally arrived in the town two weeks earlier in search of his daughter.

The Detective Chief Inspector's big fear was that even now there was little or nothing to act on and that he was going to have to let Marshall go. Talbot's divisional commander, Chief Superintendent Raymond Parish, was notoriously cautious when it came to detaining suspects without their having been charged, allegedly because he had been involved in an incident as a young officer when a man had died in custody during what was later ruled by the court to have been an illegal period of detention. In 1976 there was no statutory protocol governing the length of time for which you could lock people up while still trying to finalise a case against them, but there were rules of thumb consistent with the ancient laws of habeas corpus. And DCI Talbot was well aware that Parish would not want to let him keep Marshall without charge for very much more than twenty-four hours. Talbot, who was pretty good at working the system, might be able to stretch that a bit, but he certainly would not be able to detain the man for more than one night without formalising his arrest.

Doing his best to cast aside all doubts, Talbot sat down next to Detective Sergeant Mike Malone and Detective Constable Janet Parkin. Marshall was alone on the opposite side of the table. He had not even asked for a solicitor.

'Right, switch on then, Mike,' said the DCI briskly, gesturing to the big double tape recorder, with its giant spools, which sat on the table before him. Malone did so and then announced the interview for the record, listing the officers who were present in the small brightly lit room.

'I want to go over it all again, Mr Marshall, every detail, from the beginning,' said Talbot.

'What, again?' The big man's response was weary, but it was the weariness of someone dealing with a tiresome irritation rather than that of an anxious suspect.

'Yes, again.'

'I've told you everything.'

'Do so again, please.'

Marshall sighed. He raised his eyes so that he was looking at the ceiling rather than at the three police officers before he began to speak. His voice was calm, with that hint of weariness still about it, and his manner patiently tolerant as if he were addressing a rather dim child of whom he was none the less quite fond.

'On the last Sunday in June last year my wife told me that she was leaving me. It was not unexpected. We had not been getting on well for some time. I also suspected that she was having an affair.

'She quite suddenly confirmed my suspicions and said that she was leaving me for another man. He was an Australian over here on an extended visit. He was little more than a back-packer, it seemed. There was no way they could look after the children, she told me. She planned to start another life with her new boyfriend.'

Marshall paused, and stretched out his long arms, hands palm upwards as if begging for understanding. 'There was nothing I could have done even if I'd wanted to. Clara was always a very determined woman.'

There was a pause. 'Go on,' prompted Talbot.

'I persuaded a neighbour, Mrs Meadows next door, to look after the girls. It was June, one of our busiest months. We were full at Parkview. Clara did all the cooking. She abandoned us to total chaos. I didn't have the time or energy to think about anything except somehow keeping things going, keeping all the balls up in the air. All I did was concentrate on the practicalities. I set about finding somebody to stand in for Clara, while at first trying to provide meals myself. And I didn't do a very good job of it. I'm no cook. The guests were not very forgiving, either.

'Then two days later Clara turned up again. She said she couldn't live without the girls. She begged me to let her take them. With all that was going on I didn't see how I could look after them, so I agreed that she could have them. You can't know how much I've regretted that since, but I wasn't thinking straight. I was just taking it all a minute at a time. And she is their mother after all. Fathers aren't the same, are they?'

Again outstretched arms and this time a sideways inclination of the head asked for understanding. None of the police officers responded. Marshall continued without prompting.

'I have not seen my wife and children since that day. Neither have I heard from them. And that's all I know.'

'Is it, Mr Marshall?'

'I've told you again and again that it is.'

'Yes. But are you telling the truth?'

Marshall shrugged. 'I'm sick of this,' he said. 'I'm trying to co-operate. I want this cleared up as much as you do. But you lot don't seem prepared to listen. You're as bad as all the local gossips. You've made up your own minds about what happened to Clara and the kids and nothing I have to say makes any difference, does it?'

Talbot ignored the question.

'You were having an affair at the time of your wife's disappearance, Mr Marshall,' he continued quietly.

'Yes, I was. But only out of a kind of retaliation, really. I loved my wife. I didn't want to do anything to harm our marriage.'

'Mr Marshall, you have a reputation as a womaniser. You have been married three times – or very nearly . . .'

Marshall half-smiled. He actually looked almost pleased with himself. When only in his twenties he had married his second 'wife' while still wed to his first. He actually had a conviction for bigamy as well as for fraud. But at his trial he had escaped with only a suspended jail sentence after a doctor had given evidence about the state of stress he was allegedly in and, rather more remarkably, both women had spoken in his defence. Talbot looked the other man up and down appraisingly. Women, in particular, always seemed totally taken in by Richard Marshall, he reflected, for reasons which baffled DCI Talbot.

'We have no cause at all, except your version of things,' Talbot continued, 'to believe that your wife was ever involved with anyone else. But you had a string of affairs during your marriage, didn't you?'

'I wouldn't call them affairs exactly.'

'All right. You moved Mrs Esther Hunter into your home just one month after Clara disappeared, did you not?'

'After Clara left.'

'Don't play word games with me, Marshall. Answer the question.'

'You know I did. You also know why. Her husband found out she'd been seeing me and chucked her out. She just turned up on my doorstep. What was I supposed to do? Send her away? Anyway, I needed help in the hotel. I just couldn't manage and I couldn't afford the wages I was paying out.'

'Very gracious, Mr Marshall.'

The big man smiled again and reached up with one hand to straighten the knot of his tie. It didn't need straightening. Talbot found his gaze drawn to it. He was pretty sure the striped green-and-red tie was from a rather prestigious guards regiment and that Marshall, although he had been called up for National Service as a younger man, had no right to wear it. Which was typical, of course. Marshall dropped his hand on to the table again and leaned forward until his face was just inches away from Talbot's. He was almost conspiratorial.

'The truth, Detective Chief Inspector,' he said. 'Just the truth.'

Instinctively Talbot pulled away, then mentally kicked himself. 'Two days after your children were last seen you were spotted taking your boat out of Torquay Harbour,' he continued resolutely. 'You motored around the bay towards Berry Head, then out to deep water, where you seemed to hover for some time.'

'I was fishing. I used to go fishing most evenings when I could get away, and take the children with me whenever I could. They loved it. . . .'

Suddenly there was a catch in Richard Marshall's voice. It was the first time he had shown any emotion at all.

Talbot did his best to grasp the moment.

'I put it to you that you murdered your wife and children and that you went out in your boat that night in order to dump their bodies at sea.'

Talbot could see Marshall's body tensing at last. Just as his had done earlier. The other man's hands, once more clasped before him, were trembling. For a moment Talbot hoped he might be about to break through his composure after all. But no. Marshall was a tough cookie.

30

You could almost see him physically and mentally taking a hold of himself.

'Don't be ridiculous,' he said.

They came to Laurel House at ten o'clock the following morning, a Saturday, arriving in the middle of a summer thunderstorm, so that they stood in the hallway dripping water from their sodden raincoats all over the threadbare carpet. Karen's mother was sober, thank God, and no longer in a state of near-hysterics, but she was still in bed, of course, recovering from her excesses of the previous day. Her father was playing golf. It was what he did when he wasn't working. 'At least it gets me out of this damned house,' he would shamelessly announce.

So it was Karen who answered the front door to Detective Sergeant Malone and Detective Constable Parkin, took their wet coats from them and escorted them into the big shabby sitting-room. She ran upstairs to get her mother, and once she was sure that a protesting Margaret Meadows was safely installed in the bathroom in order to apply her obligatory layers of make-up, Karen ran downstairs again to make DS Malone and DC Parkin tea while they waited.

Then when her mother finally surfaced, somewhat to Karen's annoyance looking perfectly well-groomed and together and behaving quite charmingly, Karen was asked to leave the room. Karen didn't think that was very fair, and therefore had no compunction whatsoever about putting her ear to the keyhole so that she could listen. It was not the first time Karen had put her ear to a keyhole in that house. Almost always she seemed to hear something she would rather not have heard. And yet again she was afraid of what she might learn. It didn't stop her, though.

The woman detective constable seemed to do most of the talking. It was she who asked Margaret Meadows if she had looked after Lorraine and Janine Marshall around the time of Clara's disappearance.

'Yes, I did,' replied Karen's mother. 'Richard came to me in a terrible state the night she left him. He said he didn't know what to do. Begged me to take the girls until he sorted himself out.'

'And how long were they with you?'

'Not much more than a day really. It was a Sunday night when he brought them to me. I kept them until the Tuesday morning. Karen took them to school on the Monday. . . .'

'Karen?'

'My daughter. She let you in.'

'But she's only—'

Karen's mother interrupted swiftly. There had been just a note of criticism in the policewoman's voice. Karen recognised it at once. She was used to it, or something like it, almost every time her mother and father spoke to each other. And her mother was always quick to defend herself if she thought she was being criticised in any way.

'She's thirteen. Almost fourteen. All right, she was only twelve then. But she's always been very grown-up for her age. She'd already babysat for the Marshalls once or twice before . . . before Clara went away. In any case, I was having one of my bad spells. . . .'

Karen remembered it well, remembered eating her breakfast that morning while listening to her parents rowing over the Marshall girls. Her mother had made a rare early-morning appearance in the kitchen, but she had been clad only in her dressing-gown, had clearly had no intention of getting dressed, and had paid little attention to Janine or Lorraine who had sat white-faced and silent at the table. Lorraine had been tearful, but nobody took much notice, least of all Karen who had spent her childhood accepting family rows and disruptions as the norm, and merely assumed that the Marshall girls would do the same.

The girls' primary school had been next door to her grammar school and as she had neared it with her young charges Karen remembered rounding on a still-snivelling Lorraine.

'Shut up or I'll give you one,' she'd unsympathetically shouted at the little girl who had immediately shied away from her, lower lip trembling uncontrollably. At the time Karen couldn't have cared less. She hadn't wanted to be seen by any of her schoolfriends with wailing little ones in tow. Any curiosity she might have felt about the girls being so unceremoniously dumped at Laurel House, and certainly any compassion for their predicament, had been totally negated by the sheer irritation of having the unwanted responsibility for these two small children thrust upon her.

Karen pressed her ear closer to the keyhole. Her mother was still talking. 'I did pick them up from school in the afternoon. And I really wasn't well. The last thing I needed was two small children to look after, as well as Karen.'

Karen screwed up her face and thought hard. When had her mother ever looked after her, she wondered. Probably not at all really since she'd been a baby, and she had gathered that even then it had been her maternal grandmother, now dead, who had done most of the looking-after.

'But that's what neighbours are for, isn't it?' Margaret Meadows continued. She paused then, as if waiting for a reply. When none came she started to speak again.

'Then early on the Tuesday Richard came round and took them back. He said his mother was on her way from Bournemouth, that she was going to look after Lorraine and Janine until either Clara turned up again or he could make some permanent arrangement to look after them himself.'

The detective constable's voice was edgy when she eventually spoke again.

'So did Clara turn up again?'

'Yes.' Margaret Meadows paused once more. 'Well, he said she did. Months afterwards I asked him if the girls were still with his mother. He said Clara had come back for them.'

'Did you see her?'

'No.'

'So did you believe him?'

'Yes, of course.' The meaning of the words was clear enough, but Karen could detect the note of uncertainty in her mother's voice. 'Well, yes, I did. But I know other people didn't. And nobody's ever seen her since, have they? I thought that was what all this was about?'

The last sentence was also a query.

'Indeed it is, Mrs Marshall, indeed it is,' replied DC Parkin. 'Did you ever meet Richard Marshall's mother, by the way?'

'No.' Margaret Meadows sounded puzzled, as if she hadn't

thought about that before. 'No, I didn't. I don't know if anyone did. . . .'

Her voice tailed away. She seemed to be trying to think things through and didn't like the route along which her thoughts were taking her.

DC Parkin and DS Malone left soon afterwards. Margaret Meadows remained in the sitting-room. She was not given to observing life's social niceties if it didn't suit her. Karen beat a fast retreat to the top of the stairs allowing the two police officers to let themselves out of the house.

Afterwards she sat on the stairs, nearly at the top where they turned at right angles into the landing. Her mother did not know it, but she had been crouched in exactly the same position – curled up, hugging her legs to her chest – and exactly the same spot on that June Sunday evening the previous year when Richard Marshall had brought his little girls round. In bed earlier than usual because of a bad cold, Karen had been lying uncomfortably awake, sniffing, sneezing and coughing away, when she had heard the doorbell, followed by a voice. At first she wasn't sure who had arrived, but she made herself concentrate and then realised that this was the voice of their nearest neighbour. She was familiar enough with his voice, and with him too, although hardly at all with his wife who always seemed to be rather overshadowed by her much larger husband. Richard Marshall was a big noisy man who always had plenty to say for himself if you met him in the street or at the shops, but Karen had never heard him sound like this before, so low and urgent. She had somehow known at once that this was no ordinary visit. Indeed, apart from one fateful afternoon, she had never seen Richard Marshall at Laurel House before. And so, her curiosity aroused, she had crept her way from her bedroom along the landing to the staircase in order to find out what was going on. Karen had done a lot of that sort of thing as a child. It was the only way she ever got to find out anything, because nobody ever told her.

From her vantage point she had peered down at the little scene being enacted below. The hall at Laurel House was badly lit and both Richard and her mother were standing in such a way that Karen couldn't see their faces. Janine and Lorraine were each holding one of their father's hands. One of them was crying, but Karen was not sure which. She could not see their faces either.

'All right, I'll do what I can, but at least come in for a moment so that we can talk about it. I can see you're upset,' she heard her mother say.

'You're not wrong about that. But I can't stay. I really can't. I've too much to do.'

He had opened the door then and seemed to be on his way out, pausing only when her mother said: 'You haven't brought any clothes for the girls, Richard, not even any nightclothes.'

'I'm sorry. I'm just not thinking straight. I'll sort some stuff out for them and bring it round early in the morning. They'll need their school uniforms, of course, but they can sleep in their T-shirts. They often do, anyway.'

'All right, but how long do you want me to keep them? You know what Karen's father is like. He's out now at one of his quiz nights. God knows what he'll say when he comes home and finds your two here.'

'It won't be for long, I promise.' Richard's voice had been wheedling. 'Just till I manage to sort something out. A couple of days. . . .'

Karen had sneezed then. She had been trying very hard to stifle it, but had finally been unable to do so.

'Karen, Karen, is that you?' Her mother had turned and leaned forward around the staircase so that even in the poor light Karen could see her upturned face. 'Go back to bed, you silly girl, or you'll never get better. It's only Richard from next door.'

Karen had scurried off, knowing full well she'd be told no more even if she bothered to ask. But she sensed that there was some kind of crisis. The girls, Janine and Lorraine, had been quiet and withdrawn throughout their brief stay at Laurel House, and Karen was at an age when she was in any case totally disinterested in children younger than herself. She had made a point of ignoring them as much as possible, something she now regretted, being of such an intrinsically nosy nature, because she thought she might have missed the opportunity to learn something. Something important perhaps.

But just the way in which Richard Marshall had delivered his children that night, and the whole sorry little episode, had stuck in Karen's mind. And so she listened with great interest at the door when the police interviewed her mother, listened while her mother told them about Richard's visit that night. Told them about looking after the little girls. Listened to hear if she would tell them the rest of it. But she didn't. Not any of it.

It was quite apparent that the police didn't know what Karen knew. They couldn't know, or their whole approach would have been different, Karen felt sure. Her mother's secret was still safe. Which she supposed was a good thing, although somehow she wasn't quite sure.

Karen remained there for several minutes, resting her chin on her knees, silent, unmoving. She felt more than a bit wobbly.

Eventually her mother wandered aimlessly out of the sitting-room. Her eyes were blank. Karen could not read any expression in them. This was not unusual. Margaret Meadows invariably retreated into a world of her own whenever threatened by anything she might regard as remotely unpleasant or even merely unwelcome. She drifted towards the kitchen, apparently not noticing her daughter on the staircase.

Karen watched her mother's retreating back. She wanted so much to talk to her, yet again to ask her the questions she was bursting to ask. But her mother would never talk to her about anything that mattered, so she certainly wouldn't discuss this. She expected her daughter to behave like an adult, but only treated her like one when it suited her.

This infuriated Karen. One minute it seemed to be assumed that she knew about everything that had been going on. The next moment she was expected to forget that she knew anything at all.

But Karen knew all right. And how she wished that she didn't.

She tightened her grip around her legs and buried her whole face in her knees. She wanted a family like everybody else she knew seemed to have. She wanted a mother. A proper mother. Not this beautiful drifting creature who blew hot and cold with the wind. This woman who was sometimes a friend, sometimes a big sister, sometimes someone from another planet, and certainly never the kind of mother Karen longed for.

She was, however, all that Karen had. And Karen would never do anything to hurt her. Anything that might lead to losing her. Karen would never ever tell.

Talbot had kept Richard Marshall in custody overnight. And once more, shortly after Malone and Parkin reported back, he decided to conduct another interview with Marshall himself.

'Margaret Meadows says you told her that your mother was coming to pick up your girls. But your mother says you never even asked her to do so and she did not know that they and Clara had disappeared until several months after they were last seen.'

Marshall didn't miss a beat. A night in a police cell had not shaken him one jot. But then, Talbot had not really expected it to.

'I told Margaret that I was going to ask my mother to come to pick up the girls, not that I had already asked her,' he responded quickly. 'I'd managed to get help in the hotel, though at a tremendous price. I was therefore at least able to look after them until I could get my mother down here and so I went next door to get them. But then Clara came back and asked for them before I even got round to calling my mother.'

'You never told Mrs Meadows any of that.'

'Why would I? I told nobody anything more than I had to. I was emotionally drained by it all. My wife had walked out on me. My family had broken up. I didn't want to talk about it. I barely knew Margaret Meadows. . . .'

'You knew her well enough to dump your children on her.'

'I was desperate.'

'So did she never ask you about them afterwards?'

'I don't remember. I didn't see her often.'

'She says you just told her that Clara had come back for them.'

'Perhaps I did then. It was the truth, after all. But I never said any more than I had to. I didn't see it was any of her business or anybody else's.'

'It is now, Mr Marshall, it's the business both of the police and of the public. Make no mistake about it.'

Marshall shrugged.

'And what about your mother? Why didn't you tell her straight away that your wife and children had left you? Isn't it rather curious that you failed to tell your own mother?'

Marshall shrugged again. 'I can be a bit of an ostrich,' he said. 'I think I was hoping Clara would come back, bring the girls back. I've been hoping that all this time in spite of everything.'

He looked directly, challengingly, at Talbot. 'In spite of what you think, that's the truth, too.'

He paused as if waiting for Talbot to respond. When the DCI showed absolutely no signs of doing so he sighed and continued.

'The fewer people I told the less real it all seemed. Anyway, my mother and I have never been close. . . .'

'Who are you close to, Mr Marshall?'

Marshall looked blank.

Talbot persisted. He was beginning to think his only hope was to break Richard Marshall although he knew that was a big big ask.

'Were you close to your children?'

'Of course. I love my kids. I still love my kids.'

There was a note of aggression in Marshall's voice then.

'At best you let them go very very easily then, didn't you? I wouldn't let my kids go that easily. No way.'

It was Talbot's turn to pause, to wait for a response, and Marshall's not to make one.

'At worst you killed them.'

Marshall still didn't respond. Talbot got up from the table and walked to the little window.

He had his back to Marshall when he spoke again.

'What was it like?' he asked conversationally.

'What was what like?'

'Killing your own children, of course.'

Again Marshall didn't miss a beat. He continued to sound calm and to speak in a manner of overly deliberate patience, even though such an horrific scenario had been put to him.

'I didn't kill my children. My wife returned and took them away with her. Find my wife and you will find Lorraine and Janine.'

Talbot took a deep breath and persisted. He could think of no better plan. He walked across to Richard Marshall and leaned over so that his mouth was close to the other man's ear. When he spoke again his voice was little more than a whisper.

'How did you kill them, Richard?'

There was no reply.

'Did you strangle them? Did you suffocate them with a pillow? Which one did you murder first? What did you see in their little faces? Were they afraid? Did one of them see you kill the other? Perhaps you hit them over the head with something? Perhaps you used a knife on them? Was there blood? Did you watch your daughters' lifeblood pour out of them? What did you do with their little bodies? I think you wrapped them up and took them out in your boat and dumped them, along with their mother, probably. That's what I think. Why don't you tell me, Richard, why don't you tell me how you murdered your own daughters?'

Talbot fired the questions one after the other. Rat-a-tat-tat. Like bullets from a gun. His voice grew louder as he proceeded. He became aware of Malone and Parkin, who were also present yet again, fidgeting with discomfort. He didn't care. He was going for broke.

But Richard Marshall did not flinch. Neither did he speak. He remained absolutely still, staring stonily ahead, his eyes more blank than ever.

'Suspect refuses to answer,' barked Talbot at the tape recorder, as he sat down once again opposite Marshall and drew in a big intake of breath.

'Right,' he said, speaking very quietly again. 'Let's change direction a bit here and look at the facts. We have removed a large amount of clothing from your house which belonged to your wife and children. Indeed very little of their clothing, if any, seemed to have been taken. Your wife also left some valuable jewellery behind. How do you explain that?'

'Clara left with one suitcase. I have no idea what she took

or what she left behind. She took all she wanted, I suppose. Presumably she didn't want her jewellery. I had given her almost all of it and that could have been the reason she didn't want it. When she came back for the children she did take another couple of bags of things with her. More than likely they'd already grown out of most of the stuff that she left.'

The man was perfectly controlled. Talbot's earlier aggressive line of questioning did not seem to have rattled him at all.

'Extremely plausible, Mr Marshall,' said the DCI.

Marshall raised his eyebrows and leaned back in his chair, still appearing to be quite composed. 'The truth very often is, Detective Chief Inspector,' he replied laconically. 'Very often indeed.'

Three

Nobody in Torquay Police Station noticed, but the rain was pouring down outside throughout Bill Talbot's second long interview session with Richard Marshall. John Kelly and photographer Micky Lomas, standing morosely on the pavement, were getting a good soaking. It really was a filthy day for the time of year, and their vigil had already been a long one.

Apart from hurried calls of nature, taken in turn, usually combined with dashes to the sandwich shop up the road, they had left the station for only a few hours, in order to grab some much needed sleep, since taking up their position there the previous day.

Kelly checked his watch, wiping the raindrops off the face in order to do so. It was just past 9.30 p.m. Other journalists had come and gone during the course of the day, but none were there now. After all, they had no idea when, or even if, Marshall would step outside the station again. Nor did they even know for certain that Marshall was still inside.

There were all sorts of other lines of inquiry the various news teams on the case could convince their desks that they should be on, lines of inquiry which did not necessarily involve getting soaked to the skin. Kelly glanced at the sky. The weather was so dreadful that day had turned into dark night rather early for the time of year. All he could see was blackness, certainly no sign of any stars or a moon, which indicated that the leaden cloud which had hung over Torbay since before dawn that morning was still solid above. Certainly the rain, which had subsided into light drizzle for a couple of hours around lunchtime and cleared totally for just an hour or so in the early afternoon, now seemed heavier than ever.

But the young Kelly was already showing signs of the

tenacity which would later lead him to the top of his profession in Fleet Street. He was determined to stand his ground. If Marshall was charged neither he nor anyone else would get anything other than a brief official statement from the police. But if he was not charged, then Kelly was determined to give himself every opportunity of being the first journalist to confront him. Already John Kelly did not give up easily. Not on any story as big as this one, and certainly not on this one. Not with his mother to contend with at home, he didn't.

Kelly's dossier on Marshall was burning a hole in his notebook. Kelly was a local boy and he had homed in on the gossip right at the beginning, spurred on of course by the peripheral involvement of his mother, as head teacher of the Marshall girls' primary school. Angela Kelly had known the two little girls well and had been extremely fond of them. She had known Clara Marshall too, and Richard, although a little less well, before all the fuss began. She was that sort of teacher. She made it her business to know about the children in her care and their families. Kelly's mother had been involved from the start. And Kelly's mother had taken the Marshall business very very personally. Which was why it was so personal to Kelly, too.

Kelly hunched his inadequate raincoat, a showerproof job which had been leaking all day, around his shoulders and looked down at his watch again. If Marshall was inside, which he was somehow quite certain he was – he was sure the man hadn't been released yet and he didn't think the police would have taken him anywhere else – and if there was not enough evidence to charge him, which Kelly's police contacts had already indicated to him was likely, they would not be able to keep him much longer.

Kelly was aware of Micky Lomas shuffling his feet disconsolately next to him. He knew he was more or less blackmailing the photographer into staying, because Micky didn't dare leave as long as Kelly was prepared to keep up the vigil, in case Kelly got words and he had to confess to no picture. Micky had not uttered a word of dissent, but left Kelly in no doubt that he was extremely fed up.

The reporter deliberately did not look at Micky. Maybe

another smoke would put the snapper in a better mood. Kelly slipped a hand inside his coat pocket and fished out his cigarettes. The packet was sodden. He opened it carefully and passed it to Micky who took out a cigarette which promptly disintegrated in his fingers. The cigarettes were sodden, too. Micky impatiently tossed the one in his hand on to the ground and stood on it rather aggressively.

'Sorry,' muttered Kelly.

Micky just grunted, and from inside his state-of-the-art, thoroughly waterproof jacket, complete with hood, withdrew a dry packet of cigarettes which he threw at Kelly who, to his relief, caught it smartly while wondering what Micky's reaction would have been had he dropped the cigarettes on to the wet pavement. Well, Micky might feel hard done by, but at least he was wearing proper heavy-weather gear, Kelly reflected as he lit up. Photographers always did and reporters never did. Kelly had no idea why, and made a mental note to pay Millets a visit as soon as his next pay cheque came through. He glanced sideways. Micky was also wearing waterproof trousers and thick-soled boots. Kelly's own feet were clad in inadequate city shoes as ever, and from about the knees down, the trousers of his green suit, of which he had been so proud only the day before, were wet through.

Kelly didn't have gloves either. And, summer or not, the thorough drenching he had now received meant that he was very cold indeed. He cupped his hands over his cigarette, wondering if the faint glow might warm his chilled fingers just a little.

And as he did so the doors of the police station opened and out stepped Richard Marshall. He was quite alone.

Kelly snatched his cigarette from his mouth and threw it on the ground. By his side Micky Lomas leapt into action with admirable swiftness. The young photographer moved smoothly forward, raising his camera to his eye as he did so, and had rattled off several frames of Marshall before the older man had time to blink.

It was Kelly's turn then.

'Have you been released, Mr Marshall?' he called out. 'Can you tell us what is happening, please?'

Marshall, whose attention had been focused on the flash of the camera exploding before him, swung on his heel and turned to face Kelly. It was impossible in the half-light outside the station to read the expression in his eyes. His body language said shock and aggression. His fists were tightly clenched and his head jutted towards Kelly.

Involuntarily the reporter took a step backwards.

Then he watched Marshall relax, unclench his fists and slide one hand into his pocket.

'Yes. I've been released,' Marshall replied quietly. 'The police have no grounds to hold me, no grounds whatsoever.'

'So you are not going to be charged?'

'What with?' asked Marshall.

He stepped forward then, catching the full effect of the lights outside the station, and Kelly could momentarily see the big jowly face quite well. Marshall was smiling, his eyes crinkled at the edges. His voice was ironic, his expression friendly.

Like Bill Talbot inside the station earlier Kelly decided to go for broke.

'With the murder of your wife and children,' he said bluntly.

Marshall's eyes stopped crinkling, but the smile did not slip. Kelly had heard that he was a cool customer, and he was now learning just how cool.

'I have nothing more to say to you, young man,' he said.

Then a taxi pulled up by the kerb giving Kelly's trousers a further soaking as it did so, and Marshall, his eyes crinkling again with what appeared to be genuine amusement, swung away from him and walked towards it.

'Mr Marshall, please,' continued Kelly, gallantly ignoring his latest misfortune. 'My readers want to hear your side of the story.'

Marshall turned again.

'No, they don't,' he said mildly. 'They want to see me crucified.'

Kelly persisted. 'They just want to know what happened, that's all.'

'So do I, young man, so do I,' said Marshall obliquely.

'Look, would you do a proper interview with me? In depth. Something to put the record straight once and for all.'

44

Marshall managed a small hollow laugh. 'Dream on, young man, putting the record straight on this one is something that's never going to happen.'

It was a totally ambiguous remark. Kelly studied the Devon and Cornwall Constabulary's prime suspect carefully. Marshall was just so controlled for someone who may have murdered his entire family and spent a whole day and night and part of the previous day either locked up in a police cell or being questioned repeatedly. He had also been, by and large, perfectly pleasant in his manner, not at all what you might expect. Or at least, not what you might expect unless you knew the kind of spell he was capable of putting on people, particularly women.

A few weeks earlier Kelly had sought out Marshall's latest mistress, Esther Hunter, the woman he had moved so quickly into Parkview, at the hairdressing salon she ran down by the harbour.

He remembered vividly how she had reacted when he had asked her if she was aware of what people were saying about her man and if it worried her at all.

'Of course I'm aware,' she had responded sharply. 'How could I not be? And no, I'm not worried about any of it because it's all a pack of wicked lies. Clara has gone off to live a new life and that's all Richard and I want to do. That and be left alone. Now get off my premises.'

Esther Hunter, Kelly felt, was a nice enough woman, kindly, and quite beyond reproach before her involvement with Marshall. Kelly believed absolutely that she did not accept for one moment that her lover could possibly have murdered his family. She was simply besotted with him.

The reporter watched in silence as Richard Marshall opened the door of the taxi. He lowered himself into the back seat and then, with the door still open, addressed Kelly again.

'I don't actually want to talk to anyone about any of this any more,' he said as mildly as before. 'Not you, not the police either. In fact I've seen enough of the police over the last few days to last a lifetime. Hence the taxi home. There was no way I was going in a police car, even though they did offer.'

He smiled wryly. It was a measured appeal for sympathy and understanding. Kelly had none of either for this man whom he honestly believed to be some sort of monster. He was, however, impressed by the way Marshall handled himself.

No wonder the police had got nowhere, he thought to himself, as he watched the taxi splash its way up the road. And in that moment he had a dreadful feeling that they never would.

It was past midnight before Kelly made it home. To Micky Lomas's further annoyance the reporter had insisted on following Marshall back to the Parkview Hotel and taking up a vigil in the street outside. To be honest Kelly had not expected any kind of result. Rather childishly perhaps, he admitted to himself, he had just wanted Marshall to know that he was there. Waiting and watching. But after standing in the rain for another two hours or so, even Kelly had had enough.

As he opened the front door to his house his mother hurried into the hallway from the sitting-room.

'Still up?' he inquired.

'I wanted to know what has happened,' she said. Kelly was not surprised. He knew how much the Marshall affair was playing on his mother's mind.

'They've let him go,' replied Kelly shortly.

'Oh my God,' said Angela Kelly. 'Oh my God.'

She backed away from her son, still staring at him but not really seeing him, he thought, and retreated into the sitting-room again.

He stood for a moment, dripping water on to the hall carpet, before shrugging out of his sodden raincoat which he draped over the hall-stand. His precious green suit, he feared, was ruined. He looked down at it sorrowfully. Then he took off the jacket, peeled off the trousers which stuck damply to his legs as he did so, and arranged them also on the hall-stand, forlornly hoping that they might dry without too much damage.

He ran upstairs, pulled on a sweater and a pair of jeans and returned downstairs to join his mother. She glanced towards him as he walked into the sitting-room, failing, it seemed, to notice that he had changed his clothes already, just as minutes earlier she had failed to notice that he was wet through. All of which was out of character for Angela Kelly.

She was sitting in the old leather armchair by the window.

'Make us a cup of tea, John, will you?' she asked.

Obediently he went to the kitchen and returned with two steaming mugs. His mother wrapped her hands around her drink, nursing it as if she were cold and it were warming her.

'It's my fault, John,' she suddenly blurted out.

Kelly had already heard that from her. It was worse now, of course. Now that Marshall had been released.

'Oh, don't be ridiculous, Mum,' he responded.

'I'm not being ridiculous, John. Lorraine Marshall told me her father had killed her mother. She actually told me, and I did nothing about it. Absolutely nothing.'

'That's not true. She didn't tell you that. And you didn't "do nothing" about it.'

'I may as well have done.' Angela Kelly put down her mug of tea on the table by her side, quite uninterested in drinking it, apparently, even though she had asked for it. Kelly noticed then that the previous year's school photograph was also on that little table. It should have been hanging on the wall in the hall with the others. His mother had obviously been sitting looking at the picture until he arrived home. The Marshall sisters were side by side, sitting cross-legged in the front row. Kelly knew exactly which they were. His mother had pointed them out to him often enough. Two pretty girls, both with dark brown hair and pale blue eyes like their father, smiling for the camera, just as they had been told to do, no doubt. They looked almost doll-like in their grey and maroon school uniforms. Kelly felt his mother's eyes following his gaze.

'Can you imagine that any father could kill two innocent little children like that?' his mother asked, her voice high-pitched, almost as if she were on the verge of hysteria.

'No, Mum, I can't,' he said. 'Neither could anyone else, and neither could you. You shouldn't blame yourself and you don't even know for certain that you have any reason to do so.'

'Oh, but I do, John. I do blame myself. And I do know. Really I do. Sometimes at night, I dream, sometimes it's so vivid it's actually like I can see him attacking Clara and those poor dear girls.'

The words came tumbling out. Sighing, Kelly prepared

himself to listen yet again to the same old story. His mother had been torturing herself over the past few months, and this had reached crisis point in the previous few days, since the police had finally decided to launch a missing persons inquiry and had eventually arrested Richard Marshall.

'I just don't understand why I didn't go to the police at the time,' she said. 'I'll never forgive myself. I could have saved those two little girls.'

'Look, I keep telling you, we still don't even know for certain that they're dead,' protested Kelly.

'Now you're being ridiculous,' responded his mother.

Kelly slumped back in his chair. She was almost certainly right, of course. And the girls' mother was almost certainly dead, too. Kelly had never met Clara Marshall or her daughters. He knew them only through his own mother who, although apparently more distressed by the fate of the children, also always talked fondly and regretfully of Clara Marshall whom she described as a quiet but warmly attractive young woman, totally devoted to her little girls.

He said nothing more. After a bit his mother spoke again. Her eyes were very bright.

'She told me her father had murdered her mother, and I did nothing about it,' she repeated.

Kelly fished in his pockets for cigarettes, then remembered that he didn't have any. The packet which had drowned within the folds of his inadequate raincoat had been his last. This really was turning out to be a bad day, he thought.

'Look, Mum,' he began patiently, beginning the diatribe of reassurance that he had already uttered many times. 'Lorraine Marshall told you in school that her father had "got rid" of her mother. You said that she was upset, but if parents are having marriage difficulties of course their children are upset. You had absolutely no reason to suspect murder, for Christ's sake. And you did do something. You went round to see Richard Marshall that evening.'

Angela Kelly grunted in a derisory fashion. 'Yes, I did, didn't I? And he spun me this yarn about how Clara had run away with an Aussie backpacker and how his heart was broken, and I swallowed it hook, line and sinker. Then when the children didn't come to school the next day and he called to say their mother had taken them away with her, I swallowed that too.'

'He's an operator, Mum. Richard Marshall has a history of conning people. You may be a head teacher, but you're not infallible, you know. And anyway, when you realised there could be something seriously wrong you went straight to the police. . . .'

'Yes, six months after the children disappeared. Six whole months after. And even then only when all the gossip started. I should have thought it through. I should have done something about it at the time. I shouldn't have been taken in by the dreadful man.'

'Look, the police interviewed Marshall then, didn't they, and he convinced them too. He is very plausible.'

But Bill Talbot also had regrets, Kelly knew that. Bill Talbot wished he had listened to the likes of Angela Kelly much earlier. Talbot was well aware that the investigation had taken far too long to get going, but until Clara Marshall's father had stepped in, the police had really had nothing more than gossip and hearsay to go on.

The reporter reflected on all that for a moment, until he was interrupted by his mother's voice again.

'It's worse than that, John, and you know it,' she said, going off on a now familiar tangent. 'I told Marshall what Lorraine had said in school. I told him that she had said that her father had got rid of her mother. I honestly believe that he went and got the girls from Mrs Meadows the next day and killed them because of what I'd told him. I believe that absolutely and nothing will ever make me change my mind.'

Kelly didn't bother to reply. He finished his tea and went to bed. He had no idea at all how to help his mother. Indeed, he didn't think anybody could help his mother. She blamed herself, and that was that.

In the morning Angela Kelly made no further mention of the previous night's conversation as she served breakfast to her husband, also a schoolteacher, and to her son.

Adam Kelly was a good solid man who had no time at all for anything fanciful. He'd apparently gone to bed early the night before and left his wife to do her fretting alone. Indeed, Kelly doubted that his mother had shared any of her true feelings about the Marshall case with him. She saved that for her only son, he thought wryly.

He studied her carefully. Her eyes were red and swollen. She looked as if she had almost certainly been crying during the night. He noticed then that there was a brandy glass upside down on the draining-board and that the bottle of brandy, normally kept for medicinal use only in their house, stood on the worktop alongside. Kelly was further alarmed. He didn't suppose for one minute that Angela Kelly had consumed more than a measure or two, but he had never before known his mother to drink spirits at all – except occasionally as part of a hot toddy if she had the flu or a bad cold. It was all getting very worrying. He did hope she was not going to dwell on the Marshall case for much longer. But he already feared that she would.

Leaving her and his father at the kitchen table he walked into the hall to make a check call to the police station. The policeman who answered the phone was a young man Kelly had been to school with. The first bit of luck he'd had in days, thought Kelly wryly, still mourning the demise of his beloved green suit.

'No, there's no plans to bring him in again that I know of,' said PC Joe Willis morosely.

Kelly was already well aware that almost everybody even remotely involved with this case was affected by it in some way. And it only took a little bit of prompting to make PC Willis considerably more forthcoming.

'Off the record, Johnny, the old man is tearing his hair out. You daren't go near him. A woman and two little girls have disappeared off the face of the earth, somehow or other we don't even get to investigate formally till a year later and the trail's as cold as a dead man's willy. And if you ask me, Johnny boy, that's the way things are going to stay. We've fuck all to go on. The search at the house has produced zilch.

'If that bastard Marshall did what we all think he did, if he really murdered his wife and kids, well, you know what, Johnny? He's got away with it. That's what I reckon.'

Kelly put down the receiver glumly. That was the news he had expected but not what he had wanted to hear. Apart from anything else, his dossier on the Marshall affair, so meticulously compiled, was never likely to see the light of day now. Certainly the *Torquay Times* wouldn't print such legally dangerous material.

But this was much more than a story to Kelly. This was a murder that had happened on his doorstep involving people who were very nearly neighbours. The two little girls had been his mother's pupils. This was a case that had shaken an entire town to the core. It seemed to be all anyone talked about, in the shop, in the pub, on the street.

The whole of Torquay was under a shadow because of it. The pupils at his mother's school were tearful and upset, he knew, as they became caught up in all the stories and rumours about what had happened to their little classmates.

And as for his mother – well, she was the sort of old-fashioned headmistress who felt that all the children in her school were her responsibility. She had made it quite clear how much she blamed herself. Kelly didn't see that changing, either, and it frightened him.

Part Two

Four

Twenty-seven years later both Karen Meadows and John Kelly could remember it all so vividly. Twenty-seven years later Richard Marshall remained a free man and his wife and children had never been found – dead or alive.

The policewoman and the reporter both had different takes on the affair, and had been touched by different aspects of it in different ways. But the disappearance of Clara Marshall and her children, and all that surrounded it, was not something that anyone even remotely involved was likely to forget.

The worst fears of the people of Torbay back in 1975, and a year later when the police missing persons inquiry was finally launched, had been realised. The mystery had remained unsolved. The police hadn't been able to pin anything on Richard Marshall then or since. He'd never been brought to justice for the dreadful crime of which everyone involved had always been convinced he was guilty.

But now a body had been found at sea, preserved by freak circumstances, at least to the degree of still being recognisable as human remains. And Karen Meadows, as she turned off the sea front on to the Newton Abbot road on her way to the hospital, reflected on how this could change everything. She was tensed up, almost trembling with anticipation, and afraid of even beginning to hope that this discovery in the old sunken Nazi E-boat might lead to justice at last.

At the junction she badly fumbled a gear change. She really must relax, keep cool. But that was easier said than done. The Marshall case had already had a profound influence on Karen's life, as it had on Kelly's and almost everyone's who had ever been involved in it. For a start she thought, in a perverse kind of way probably, considering the aura of failure that had always surrounded the police investigation into the Marshall affair, that it was the subconscious influence behind her later decision to join the police force. Neither of her parents had ever discussed her future with Karen when she was growing up. Curious perhaps, but nothing much was ever discussed between the three of them as far as she could remember.

So when a school careers teacher asked her what she wanted to do with her life Karen had been as surprised as the teacher when she heard herself reply: 'I want to be a police officer.'

In that curiously objective way of looking at things that she had developed as a very young child Karen had carefully followed the inquiry which had turned out to be so ill-fated, watching all the goings-on in her street, tuning in to the television news bulletins, reading all the newspaper reports, and listening to local gossip, and she had been intrigued. Rather precociously perhaps for a schoolgirl she had lain in her bed at night going over in her mind how she would handle the investigation. She must already have had ambition too, she reflected. After all, she always imagined herself in charge of things, leading the operation. And she supposed she rather liked the idea of being part of such a team. Perhaps she had seen the police force as some sort of substitute for the kind of family she would so much liked to have belonged to.

It was her personal involvement with the Marshall case which had had the biggest effect on her, however. Throughout her life, as the years had passed and Clara and the children continued to be unheard of while Marshall remained a free man, Karen, a bit like Kelly's mum back in 1976, never ceased to wonder if it would have made any difference had she told anybody what she had known all that time ago.

It was too late now anyway, she reflected, managing her next gear change rather more smoothly. She had always felt that her mother held the key to something, although she was not entirely sure what, but any information Margaret Meadows may have kept close to her chest for twenty-eight years was now going to stay there. Karen's mother had vascular dementia. Her mind which had been so troubled throughout most of her life had now more or less entirely departed. She had been at the Old Manor nursing home just outside Torquay for two years. It was Karen who had had to make the decision to place

56

her there and she had been consumed with guilt ever since. She still felt she should be looking after her mother even though it was quite impossible, even though she had done more than her fair share of looking after Margaret Meadows, even though Margaret herself was at least partly responsible for her own sorry state. The condition from which she suffered, which caused the brain to suffer an oxygen deficiency, had been brought about in part by her excessive drinking habits.

Whatever the cause, Margaret Meadows would never now be any sort of witness in a murder inquiry, even if she might once have been an important one.

There was something else, too. Karen couldn't stop seeing those frightened little faces of the Marshall girls inside her head, just as she had seen them all those years ago. And they had been frightened. Both of them. Very frightened. She had no doubt about that now, and it still haunted her sometimes. But back in 1975 Karen had been completely unmoved by the little girls' plight. Almost unaware of it, in a curious, detached, early teen sort of way. She didn't entirely blame herself. She had been just a thirteen-year-old kid herself, struggling to survive in a totally dysfunctional family. Yet she couldn't help wondering still what might have revealed itself if she had shown just a little more concern for, or even interest in, Janine and Lorraine. Or indeed, if her mother or father had done.

As it was she could recall all too clearly just about her only contribution on what could well have been the last day of their young lives.

'Shut up or I'll give you one.'

Karen winced at the thought. These were deeply disconcerting memories. Sometimes she was not sure that her extreme youth and difficult family circumstances were excuse enough for her behaviour during that tragic last encounter with the Marshall sisters.

The traffic slowed to a crawl along the Newton Abbot road. Karen lit another cigarette and tried to think about the present, not the past. She knew she was not the only one in the Devon and Cornwall Constabulary who had special reasons for wanting to solve the mystery of the disappearance of Clara Marshall and her children.

The unsolved case had been a blight on the local force for more than a quarter of a century. It still rankled with many of the older officers and even the very youngest and newest had inherited its burden and were familiar with every sorry detail. The fact that two children were presumed to have been murdered made the case a highly emotive one, all the more so because their own father was the prime suspect.

Bill Talbot, the Senior Investigating Officer, had always blamed himself, Karen knew that. He had no real reason to, that Karen could see, but like almost everybody who worked on the case he had been driven half-mad with frustration because he believed passionately that Richard Marshall was guilty of a dreadful crime.

Karen drummed her fingers impatiently on the steering-wheel. The traffic lights in front of her had changed three times while she had remained virtually stationary. Leaning out over the door and peering around the edge of the windscreen so that she could get a view of the road ahead past the line of vehicles in front of her, she could see that the traffic on the far side of the lights was jammed solid. No wonder nothing was moving. She took another pull of her cigarette and cursed the holiday season. It was August bank holiday week, and half the world seemed to have descended on Torbay. The entire economy of the West of England might rely on the tourist industry, but all it ever seemed to mean to a police officer was more trouble.

Eventually she arrived at the hospital. She was told that the examination of the remains was just beginning. Hastily she donned the regulation white paper suit. The fact that this particular body was barely even that made no difference to procedure. It was just as important as ever for there to be no opportunity for a flash lawyer to imply that any kind of contamination had taken place. None the less Karen regarded getting booted and suited as an even greater nuisance than usual. Not so very long ago police observers had been allowed to wear their own clothes without any protective overalls as long as they stood well away from the operating table. Not any more. She broke into a sweat as she struggled to pull the plastic galoshes on over her chunky trainers. For what seemed like for ever she couldn't get them past the thickly cushioned heels.

'Amazing bloody performance for a fucking skeleton,' she muttered to herself, succeeding at last with one frantic pull.

Phil Cooper, Karen's favourite detective sergeant, was already there, standing alongside the county pathologist Audley Richards, a taciturn character as precise in his work as his small neat moustache. Karen respected Doctor Richards, but had never managed to attain with him the easy bantering relationship which she had enjoyed with his predecessor. And Karen, of course, was impatient. It went with her territory.

'Is it a man or a woman?' she asked at once, gesturing to the bones on the mortuary table. That was, after all, the so far unasked question which had been foremost in her mind since Phil had called that morning.

Audley Richards peered at her over his half-moon spectacles. With his thinning grey hair and aquiline nose, he looked more the part than any other doctor she had ever encountered.

'Patience, Detective Superintendent, patience,' he murmured. 'I will be giving you my full report in due course.'

Karen clasped her hands behind her back, forcing herself not to rise to the bait. Sometimes she thought the pathologist deliberately set out to irritate her.

'C'mon, Audley,' she said. 'You can tell me that straight away. That skeleton is in pretty darned good nick, considering. I reckon you knew its sex after one glance.'

Richards smiled without humour. 'The shape of the hips indicates that these are the remains of a woman, and although the extra rib is not intact you can still see the start of it quite clearly.'

Karen felt a dryness in her mouth. This was the most important news of all. Had the skeleton been a man, or had it not been possible from its condition to immediately ascertain its sex, then the assumption she had already jumped to might have had to be dismissed after all. Or at least put on hold. As it was, the medical confirmation that these were the remains of a woman led instantly to her next question.

'So how long has the skeleton been in the sea?' she asked.

Audley Richards sighed dramatically. He glowered at her over his glasses.

'I'm a pathologist, not a psychic. I do not have a crystal ball,' he instructed. 'Months or even years rather than days – but that's as far as I'm going to be able to go. For anything more accurate than that you'll need to establish the isotopes of these bones, and that's a job for the experts in forensics.'

Karen had known that would probably be the answer. She was also aware that this was a new technique, as far as she knew conducted by only one forensic laboratory in London, and a technique which was still regarded as experimental and was certainly not at all precise. It would also take several weeks after the skeleton was delivered for any results at all to be achieved.

Audley Richards had turned his back on her in a rather determined way and seemed engrossed in his examination. She gave in then, standing in silence for another fifteen minutes or so, until he had finished. It seemed like much longer than that before he turned to her.

'Right,' he said. 'We have here the skeleton of a youngish woman. Height, five foot four or five. No signs of any deterioration through age. From her bone formation I would estimate that she could be anything between twenty years old and forty. But these remains do not tell us a great deal more than that.'

Karen felt her heart thumping very loudly inside her chest. Audley Richards was not in the habit of giving anything away until he was absolutely sure of his facts, and on this occasion it seemed he did not have much to give. But the skeleton lying on the mortician's table before them could be Clara Marshall, it really could.

'Any idea how she may have died?'

Knowing Audley Richards as well as she did, Karen didn't really expect a meaningful reply to that either. Not yet, anyway. And she was right.

The pathologist shook his head. 'There are no signs of any damage to the remaining bones. No new fractures. No old fractures, either, come to that. In view of the circumstances in which she was found it is almost certain that she was murdered, but exactly how I have no idea, and from the condition of this skeleton alone I do not see that changing.'

He pointed to the upper part of the skeleton. 'As you can see the head is missing. It looks as if the tarpaulin disintegrated quite early on around that area of the body for some reason. Most of the neck bones are missing too. I couldn't even tell if she had been strangled. To be honest, Karen, I don't think we are going to learn a lot more from these remains.'

'So there are no immediate means of identification at all?'

'No. We don't have a head, so we don't have teeth to check with dental records. No old fractures, so checking with medical records won't help either. It will almost certainly be possible to extract DNA from the bones, of course, but you'll also need DNA from a close relative to compare it with. Catch-22 in a situation like this when you have a mystery corpse which might date back a bit.'

It was Karen's turn to smile grimly then.

'I think I might know exactly where to find that relative, actually,' she said.

'You have a crystal ball now, Superintendent, do you?' inquired Richards loftily.

'For once, I don't think I'm going to need one,' Karen replied.

'Well, don't forget that the DNA you get from bones is not the stuff you take as samples for police records. It's mitochondrial DNA. And mtDNA only passes directly down the female line. So you would have to have DNA samples available from this victim's mother or grandmother, or from any children she might have.'

Karen mentally kicked herself as she and Phil Cooper left the hospital building together. Like most police officers she had never quite got to grips with all the various idiosyncrasies of DNA. And the possible victim's relative she had had in mind was not in the direct female line. Indeed not female at all. So that was the end of that avenue, she thought.

She glanced at Cooper. He was in somewhat better shape than she had on several occasions seen him following an autopsy. Karen had learned to harden her heart and soul concerning post-mortem examinations. She never flinched, whatever gory business was being conducted on the mortician's table. Phil Cooper was often unable to conceal how much the proceedings affected him. The burly rugby-playing policeman was known to be a bit of a softy and he had a very human side when it came to watching corpses being carved into and dismembered.

But this autopsy had not been like that. The dead body was just a pile of decaying old bones. There was no emotion to cloud the judgement of the two police officers. No nasty retching feelings in the stomach to control. Nothing to stand in the way of an analytical assessment of the known facts, of solid methodical policing, in fact. Except of course the legacy of the past, thought Karen.

'So shall I do that, then, boss?'

Phil Cooper's voice came from the distance. Karen realised she hadn't heard a word he'd said.

'Do what, Phil?'

'Get Search and Recovery down there, the dive team. See what else they can come up with. Maybe they can find some teeth for us. Maybe there are signs of another body.'

Cooper was ahead of her. He may not have been around back in the seventies, but he knew all about the Marshall case. He, too, would have been wondering if they had finally found the body of Clara Marshall. And, if so, had her children been dumped in the sea with her? And was it stretching probability too much to consider that their remains, too, might have been protected in such a way within the sunken German E-boat?

'Yes, Phil,' she replied. 'Thank you. That's the logical next step. And have we warned those treasure hunters off?'

'Marine archaeologists, boss.'

'What?'

'Marine archaeologists. Not treasure hunters.'

'Whatever they're called. I don't want them anywhere near that wrecked boat till we've done with it. It's a crime scene.'

'Right, boss.'

Audley Richards had delivered quite a blow when he had effectively scuppered her belief that a DNA match might swiftly be obtained. But Karen was determined that somehow or other the identity of this mystery skeleton would be revealed.

She walked with Cooper to the car park. But he had managed to park a little closer to the pathology department than her and as, by then alone, she approached her car over by the road, Karen was not at all surprised to see John Kelly standing quietly alongside it. Kelly was still a journalist, one who had come almost full circle. After a chequered career – he had been a Fleet Street high-flyer before falling from grace somewhat spectacularly – he was back in his old Torbay stamping ground, chief reporter now of the *Evening Argus*. His hair had thinned and turned grey with the years, and he had a very slight paunch. Nowadays he favoured Marks & Spencer's sports jackets, often worn with jeans, a combination he still considered to be quite trendy and daring, having long ago discarded any more extravagant fashions like those he had been so proud of in the seventies. Kelly had travelled a long way along a bumpy road. Surprisingly, perhaps, his attitude to his job had not changed a bit. He drove himself just as hard and remained as easily excited by a big story as he had ever been. In addition, Karen knew he had always followed very closely the case she thought they might, just might, be about to reopen and, anyway, it was typical of him to be there when there was the scent of anything unusual about. Kelly almost invariably seemed to be ahead of the game, when it came to stories if nothing else.

It was also typical of Kelly to pick a location for his approach to her which would give him the best chance of at least a word or two. Karen might walk away from her old friend had he tried to approach her within the hospital itself or while she was with Cooper, but not if confronted by him alone and discreetly.

'Fancy seeing you here,' she muttered without a great deal of enthusiasm.

'And thank you for the warmth of your greeting.'

She smiled, giving in a bit.

'Might have known you'd be first on the scene,' she said.

'I'll take that as a compliment.'

'Still like to know how, though.'

'A reporter must never reveal his source.'

'Thank God for that.'

She laughed briefly. They both knew she had been Kelly's source often enough. They went back a long way. They had that sort of relationship.

'So, is it Clara Marshall?'

'Well, that's getting to the point of it, Kelly, I must say—'

'C'mon, Karen,' he interrupted. 'There can't be anyone who was in Torquay when Clara and her children disappeared or who knew anything about what happened then who won't think that as soon as they hear about the body.'

'I know.' She ran her fingers through her hair, turned her face towards the sun and screwed up her eyes. The day was getting warmer by the minute, which made a change that summer. Karen's head was in a whirl. All those memories chasing themselves around in her brain. It was so hard to keep a grip on this case, to maintain the professional approach. And yet she knew she had to be more in control than ever if she was to have even a chance of handling it properly.

'So, is it?'

Karen shrugged. 'Don't be ridiculous, Kelly,' she said. 'If it were her you know how long she'd have been in the water. No immediate identification is possible.' She thought about Audley Richards' remark and allowed herself a little self-indulgence. 'I don't have a crystal ball, you know,' she continued.

'There'll be DNA, though. You'll be able to find out for certain eventually.'

Kelly's voice was sharp and edgy. Karen stopped looking up at the sky and turned to face him, studying him closely. He looked tense. Pinched. Much as she felt herself. She wasn't overly surprised. She knew Kelly had worked on the case at the time. She didn't know any more. She had no idea if he had any other involvement. But she was aware that everybody who'd ever been near it seemed to have been touched in some way.

'Not necessarily, Kelly,' she said quietly. And she explained briefly what Audley Richards had told her.

Kelly nodded glumly. He didn't say anything. Instead he produced a packet of cigarettes and offered her one.

She shook her head. 'I prefer these,' she said, taking out her own packet of menthols. 'Anyway, I thought you'd given up.'

'Many times,' he said. 'Christ, Karen, it's the only vice I've got left. Give a guy a break.'

'I just hope we get a break.'

'It's time, Karen.' He was suddenly very serious. She noticed that his fists were clenched by his sides. 'It's time. It really is. We've all lived with this too long. Richard Marshall has had all the luck so far. It's time the luck changed.'

Karen knew what he meant. And John Kelly's words were still ringing in her ears when, twenty minutes or so later, she walked into her office.

She picked up her desk phone at once to make a call to Scotland. Then she thought better of it. It was far too early. It really was. But as she replaced the receiver the phone immediately rang, and she picked it up again at once.

'It's Bill,' said a quiet voice.

Karen smiled. 'You didn't take long,' she responded. She had expected to hear from retired Detective Chief Inspector Bill Talbot sooner or later – but not quite this soon.

'I still have one or two good contacts.'

'I'll bet you do.'

'So is it true?'

'Depends what you're asking about. It's true we've found a skeleton, or parts of a skeleton to be exact, off Berry Head. But we've not been able to identify it yet nor can anyone even say how long it's been in the water.' She paused, savouring the moment, knowing the effect her next words would have on him. 'Audley Richards reckons it's a youngish woman, though, about five foot four or five.'

At the other end of the phone she heard Bill Talbot's sharp intake of breath.

'Clara Marshall was five foot five,' he said straight away.

Karen was not surprised. She would have expected her old boss to remember every salient detail of the case which she knew had bugged so much of his career.

'Thanks, Bill,' she said quietly. 'I thought you'd know that.'

'So what do you think?' Talbot asked sharply.

'Same as you, I expect. But I'm trying to be led only by science.'

'I don't know whether I want it to be her or not.'

'No. But if it is, then maybe we could get that bastard at last.'

'You know how I feel about that.'

'It wasn't your fault, Bill.'

'I'd heard the gossip around the town. At the little girls' school. Everybody had. We should have moved earlier. But you know all about that. One big cock-up.'

'With the benefit of hindsight, yes. But how many times have you and everyone else been over it all for almost three decades? Marshall was always so bloody plausible. And how many cases have there been in history of men murdering their entire family like this, for God's sake? A tragic murder and then a suicide, yes. But not this. It's just so unusual. And we always look for precedents, don't we? Policemen and lawyers, that's what we do. As for gossip? Well, it would be just crazy to act on gossip, which is so often malicious, too. Crazy. And if nobody has been reported missing by their family it's rare to say the least to launch a missing persons inquiry. A vicious circle, I know. But that's how things were on this one. And do remember, there's nobody who's ever touched the bloody case who doesn't have regrets, Bill.' Karen paused. 'I know I do.'

'It was all history by the time you even came into the job, and you were just a kid when it happened. How could you have any regrets, Karen?'

'I guess it just always seemed close.' Karen didn't want to go into that. 'I lived next door to the Marshalls, remember,' she continued.

'Of course I remember. Your mother took the kids in after Clara disappeared. We interviewed her. Yes, I do realise, Karen, you lived it too.'

'I used to babysit Lorraine and Janine sometimes, never for long and only two or three times that I remember, for an hour or so when their mother went shopping or something. Did you know that?'

'No.'

'Only for pocket money. I was at that stage when I didn't

really like little kids around me. Well, it makes no difference, anyway.' Karen shrugged, made an effort to pull herself together.

'No, I don't suppose it does. Look, do you fancy a jar or something later on? Go over things if you like, I might be able to help.'

Karen sighed. Bill Talbot had never been able to let go of this one, and she doubted he ever would. On the other hand, maybe he could help. He knew more about the case from the very start than anybody else in the world, that was for certain.

'It'll have to be a hell of a lot later on. This is going to be a long long day.'

'How about if I come round the Bell about eight, eight thirty?' Bill Talbot was suggesting a pub close to the nick, somewhere pretty much on the spot. 'You pop over when you can. I'll just stay there. Time makes no difference to me nowadays, I've nothing else to do.'

Karen had never been able to imagine Bill Talbot in retirement. This was not a man who had been looking forward to the golf course or cultivating his roses. This was a man who had lived for his work. She considered for a moment the workload she knew faced her now that the skeleton had been found. And there were already other cases on her desk.

'All right,' said Karen. 'But make it tomorrow night, will you? I think today is going to be impossible.'

'No problem,' said Bill as he hung up.

Karen replaced the receiver very slowly.

How could she have any regrets? Little did Bill Talbot know.

Five

Throughout the rest of the day Karen was immersed in the complex business of setting up a modern murder investigation. And a murder investigation with a bit of a difference. One that involved a corpse that was at least a quarter of a century old. Paperwork and meetings with fellow officers kept her at Torquay Station until well past 10 p.m. when she gratefully beat a retreat home to her bed.

The following day dawned horribly. It was a truly ghastly morning. Wet, windy and cold. More like November than August.

'It would be,' muttered Karen as she dragged herself over to her bedroom window. 'It just bloody well would be.'

She peered out at the sea. Summer or not, it looked iron grey and extremely uninviting. There were big breakers even quite close in within the bay. Karen had made plans to visit the crime scene, and her first inclination was to change her arrangements. She had no wish to be aboard a boat in these conditions. But a combination of professionalism and bloody-mindedness forced her to proceed according to plan. Stoically she rummaged in a drawer for her thermal underwear and pulled on a tracksuit.

Three mugs of tea and two menthol cigarettes later, telling herself yet again that she really would give up smoking the following day, Karen put on a fleece and a hooded water-proof over her tracksuit and set off for the harbour. There a police dive boat was waiting to pick up her and Phil Cooper and take them to what passed for the crime scene. It was difficult to see quite how an old wartime wreck at 50 metres was a modern crime scene, but that was indeed what it had now become.

In spite of the inclement weather Karen decided to walk

along the sea front to the harbour on the far side of the bay. There was, after all, never anywhere to park in Torquay once the tourist season was in full flow. Averting her eyes from the uninviting heaving grey mass of the sea, Karen concentrated on the matter in hand. She considered what she and Phil might achieve from their trip out to Berry Head. She realised there would be little to see, and although she was an amateur scuba diver she had neither the skill nor the inclination even to attempt the kind of diving necessitated. But Karen was the sort of detective who liked to see everything for herself and was hands-on to a degree not always considered proper in a senior investigating officer. Karen always liked to do, or at least sit in on, as much of the interviewing of prime suspects as she possibly could – to the irritation, she knew, of many members of her team. Reports on pieces of paper, or in e-mail form half the time nowadays, did not get through to Karen in the same way. She liked to feel the very texture of any crime she was investigating all around her and that meant being there, right on the spot. That was how she got her head around things. And that was why she wanted to visit the place where the skeleton had been found, even though it would be 50 metres below them, under the sea.

Phil Cooper was already standing on the jetty waiting to board. He was wearing bright yellow oilskins, and he raised one yellow arm in greeting. His face broke into a crooked grin. Cooper's nose had been broken long ago in some rugby scrum or other. His floppy brown hair was blowing in the wind. The busted nose contrived to make him more good-looking rather than less, Karen thought. For a fleeting moment she was struck by how attractive he looked, much more so, and much more at home somehow, dressed like that than be-suited at his desk.

Karen waved back and hurried forward, dismissing such thoughts as quickly as they had arrived. She was Phil Cooper's senior officer. He was thirteen years her junior and he was the married father of two little girls upon whom he doted and whose photograph, along with one of his pretty red-headed wife, he carried tucked in the back of his battered wallet. Karen knew that because they always seemed to drop out every time he attempted to remove any money. On purpose maybe. Phil took every opportunity to show off his family.

She did a double take when she saw the vessel waiting to take her and Phil out to the scene about a mile off Berry Head, just where the shelf of the seabed dropped from around 30 metres to 50. It was what she knew the professionals called a rigid inflatable. To her it was a rubber dinghy. This was going to be a bumpy ride. Gritting her teeth she quickly removed her light waterproof in order to don the set of oilskins and the life-jacket provided by the two police divers crewing the boat. She removed her trainers and replaced them with rubber boots, hoping that conditions were not going to be as bad as these precautions suggested, and then clambered aboard.

It took less than twenty minutes to reach the crime scene, but the ride was every bit as bumpy and as wet as Karen had expected. There, to her relief, a larger hard boat, the *Blue Rose*, a fishing vessel chartered from Brixham she was told, stood at anchor. The inflatable was moored alongside and all aboard transferred to the *Blue Rose* where they were greeted by the diving supervisor, Brian Stokes, a uniformed sergeant from Newton Abbot, whom Karen recognised by sight.

'What puzzles me, Brian, if that body has been down there as long as we think it may have been, is how it's remained undiscovered for so long. There's so much diving goes on off Berry Head, and all divers like shipwrecks.'

'Yes, but this one was designated a war grave, ma'am, because the bodies of the crew were never recovered at the time,' Stokes responded. 'So it was a restricted area. Now that doesn't always stop divers, but also, this particular wreck was fairly inaccessible and 50 metres is a bit deeper than most sports divers will go. Deeper than they should go, anyway. My guys only get around nine minutes' bottom time and they're diving on surface demand too, which makes it a lot safer because if they do have a problem and need to make extra decompression stops, at least they won't run out of air.'

Karen nodded. She understood police diving procedure and the high standards that were adhered to. All the men and women were only part-time divers and had other jobs in the force, but they were trained to the very highest level.

'I read about this E-boat, of course,' she said. 'She went down towards the end of the war, and some historian has worked out that there could be some important papers aboard, if they could possibly have survived, that might give information about what happened to Hitler, what he was planning if things went wrong. Isn't that it?'

'More or less, ma'am. Bit far-fetched if you ask me, but these marine archaeologists were called in and given permission to go down. And, of course, they had the same sort of equipment as we use. I've got two men down there at the moment, by the way, and the team that went down earlier today found a load of antique gold jewellery, Nazi booty presumably.'

Karen expressed polite interest and concentrated on the scene around her. She was a West Country girl. She liked being on water, although she preferred rather pleasanter conditions. Mercifully, however, the rain had eased a little, and peering out towards the horizon she could see that the ominous black clouds she had studied so assiduously earlier were beginning to lift. The *Blue Rose*, a sturdily built vessel, was moving only relatively gently in the swell. Although, of course, it might just seem that way in comparison to the turbulent bounce of the RI, Karen thought.

She turned to face the coast, just a grey mass in the distance, and leaned against the iron rails surrounding the deck of the *Blue Rose*. Whatever anybody might be doing aboard a boat this far out to sea could not be properly seen from the shore, that was for certain, not even with binoculars.

Karen shivered. But not with the cold. Although conditions were still pretty unpleasant, she was warm and dry enough within her oilskins. No. Karen shivered because the trip out to sea had done exactly what she had hoped it would do. It had taken her back to that fateful day twenty-eight years ago when she believed even more fervently than ever that Marshall had disposed of his family in this cold cruel place. But would she ever be able to prove it? Would anyone ever be able to prove it?

They stayed out at the site for about an hour, watching proceedings. There was not much to see. The two dry-suit clad divers who had been down below when Karen and Cooper had arrived emerged after half an hour or so and that was the big excitement of the visit. They had, however, found nothing pertaining to the body, although they reported the discovery of still more gold jewellery which they had yet to bring to the surface.

Another team of two divers was duly despatched, but eventually even Karen had to agree, to Phil Cooper's relief she suspected, that there was no further purpose in the senior investigating officer staying out at sea any longer. She had a big and important operation to run, and she wasn't going to be able to do so bobbing about off Berry Head, that was for certain.

The rigid inflatable had bumped and bucked its way almost back to Torquay when Brian Stokes came on the portable radio from the *Blue Rose* asking to speak to Karen.

'The boys have found something,' he said. 'A gold watch. Definitely well post-war, we reckon. It was mixed up with the other stuff.'

Karen's heart rate quickened.

'Let's get back there,' she commanded.

Standing next to her, Phil Cooper uttered the smallest of moans, virtually imperceptible. Karen heard him, though. She had good ears. She turned to look at him. She had already noticed, to her amusement, that the big man was not actually nearly as at home at sea as might be expected from looking at him. In fact his ruddy complexion had turned quite pale.

'You all right, Phil?'

'Never better, boss,' he replied with a wan smile.

Back at the site the watch had already been safely installed in a transparent plastic evidence bag which Brian Stokes promptly handed to her. There could be no conventional forensic evidence on an item which had been at the bottom of the ocean for one year let alone twenty-eight, if indeed that was the case, but at the very least the watch had to be protected from further deterioration.

Karen studied it closely. If it had been dumped in the ocean at the time, as she suspected, it was in rather better condition than she would have imagined it to be, but then gold lasts for centuries underwater and this appeared to be a solid gold watch. Indeed, it was a gold watch of a very particular make and style. Karen couldn't believe it. He heart was really racing now.

'It's a Rolex, Phil,' she breathed.

Cooper was leaning over her shoulder, peering at this unlikely find which had been retrieved from 50 metres below the surface of the ocean.

'Not again, boss,' he muttered. 'That's extraordinary. Could be just the stroke of luck we need.'

'Yes, well, the only bugger who's ever had any luck in this case before, is that jammy bastard Marshall.' She thought of Kelly and his last words to her the previous day at the hospital. 'It's time,' she said. 'It's time the luck changed.'

She held the plastic bag up in order to catch the best of the light. A shaft of watery sunlight had broken through a patch in the clouds. The tarnished watch gleamed. Karen willed it to speak to her, to tell her who its owner was, at least.

Phil was right. This could be lucky, very lucky indeed. But was it too much to hope for that history would repeat itself so effectively? For a few seconds Karen reflected on that other case, so familiar to everyone within the Devon and Cornwall Constabulary.

Five years earlier a body had become caught in fishermen's nets off the South Devon coast and freakishly retrieved virtually before any deterioration had set in. But nobody had a clue who the dead man might be, and therefore DNA was of little help. A Rolex watch was, however, found on the corpse and it turned out that this could be identified positively because each Rolex watch has a unique case number. Rolex were able to supply the name of the German jeweller who had sold the watch. That had not actually taken the matter any further as the jeweller had been unable to tell from his records to whom he had then sold the watch, but Rolex UK then turned serious detective. They had looked inside the watch and found a repair number. This had led directly to the dead man and subsequently to his murderer who had even moved into his house.

Lightly Karen ran a finger over the watch within its plastic protector. She remembered the procedure, even though she had no idea exactly how to do it. You had to look between the lugs inside the watch with the hands at the six o'clock position. There was some corrosion naturally, and she doubted the hands would even turn.

The watch had a date indicator on it. Karen squinted at it. It would have been extremely helpful to have been able to tell the date on which that Rolex finally stopped. But the figures had worn, certainly too much to be ascertained with the naked eye.

Karen handed the watch to Phil Cooper and gave instructions to return to shore. On the way she made a phone call on her mobile. Bill Talbot answered swiftly, his tones as clipped and businesslike as ever. Retirement really did not seem to have changed him very much.

'We've found a watch on the sunken E-boat, a gold Rolex,' she began without preamble. 'You don't happen to know if Clara Marshall had one, do you?'

The reply came fast. That was Bill Talbot. Karen could hear the excitement in his voice, too. Talbot sensed a breakthrough at last. And Talbot wanted this one desperately, had done for nearly thirty years.

'She did. It was a present from her father. As you know we found almost all of her jewellery, left behind in the house. We asked her father if he could see anything missing, anything distinctive that she might have with her. He told us about this Rolex watch he'd given her. Apparently she never went anywhere without it.'

This was exactly what Karen had wanted to hear, and yet there was an unreality about the whole proceedings. And it was more than that. It was as if Clara Marshall were crying out from the deep, crying out to be heard, to achieve justice at last.

Back at Torquay Police Station Karen immediately picked up the phone in her office to dial Scotland again. This time she completed the call. The man she was trying to reach was Clara Marshall's father.

She did not even consider sending the Scottish police around to his home, despite the fact that police officers did not normally deliver the kind of news Karen had for Sean Macdonald by telephone. But then the Clara Marshall scenario was rather different from usual.

After all these years Karen knew that Macdonald no longer harboured even the most remote hope that his only daughter was still alive. Karen also knew that the only hope he clung to any more was for confirmation of her death and perhaps even the possibility of properly burying her remains. Other than that, like her, like Bill Talbot, like so many frustrated men and women, Sean Macdonald just wanted her killer brought to justice.

Karen had got to know him well over the years. Driven by a sense of guilt he could never quite conquer, Sean Macdonald, who had been estranged from his daughter at the time of her disappearance, had visited Torquay twice a year every year for twenty-seven years – once to be there for the anniversary of when she had last been seen at the end of June and once for her birthday. Karen reckoned the visits were a sort of pilgrimage for him, and Macdonald, who never wore his broken heart on his sleeve but instead behaved with dignity and restraint at all times, was much liked and had become accepted in the force. She knew there had been real anger within him, a cold fury which she had actually once witnessed firsthand as a child, albeit from a safe distance, but that this had been tempered over the years by a kind of grim acceptance. Everybody who knew about the case and about him, which was most of them, still treated the now old man as a very special visitor. Bill Talbot had nurtured him, spent time with him whenever he could. Karen had inherited Mac from her former boss and had continued the relationship. There really had seemed to be little alternative. And indeed, she had come to actively enjoy the company of the elderly Scotsman, particularly when she discovered that he shared her love of antiques and liked nothing better than to lose days hunting through junk shops looking for lost treasures. Karen had even once travelled to Edinburgh to visit one of the city's antique fairs with Mac. One way and another she was absolutely sure that Clara Marshall's father would rather hear what news there was from her than from strangers.

She leaned back in her chair and stretched her long legs, waiting for a reply. Eventually she heard Sean Macdonald's crisply modulated highland tones, but realised at once that she was just listening to an answerphone.

She waited for the bleep, all the while wondering what kind of message she should leave. But suddenly there was a click and the real Sean Macdonald came on the line.

'It's Karen,' she announced.

'Karen. How are ye, lass?'

'I'm fine, Mac. You?'

'Och, I'm well enough.'

There was a pause. Karen hesitated. It had been reported in the newspapers and on the news that morning that a body had been found off Berry Head and there had already been considerable speculation over the possible identity of the corpse. The Marshall case had always been big media business. But Mac didn't sound as if he knew anything. She simply felt that he was waiting for her to go on, to tell him whatever it was she had called to tell him, because fond as she was of the Scotsman, it had been some time since they had spoken, and she knew he had sensed that she was not calling him merely to exchange niceties about his well-being.

'You haven't seen today's papers then . . .,' she began tentatively.

'No, I've been on a fishing trip. Trying to get away from all that. . . .' Mac's voice trailed off. She could feel his suspense.

'We've found some human remains at sea off Berry Head—' she went on.

Mac interrupted her. He was obviously unable to contain himself.

'Is it her?' he blurted out. 'Or one of the children? Can it be, after all this time?'

Karen's voice was gentle when she spoke again.

'It's impossible to be sure yet,' she said. 'There isn't a lot to go on—'

Karen had chosen her words carefully, but Sean Macdonald was an intelligent man. He knew what she was getting at well enough. He knew there would be damn all left of someone thrown into the sea nearly thirty years ago. Indeed, the skeleton they had found had, due to having been wrapped up in the way that it was and protected by its unique resting place, been considerably more intact than might reasonably have been expected. Except for its missing head, of course.

As if reading her mind Sean Macdonald cut in.

'Teeth,' he said. 'What about dental records? What sort of state are the teeth in?'

'Actually we have yet to find any teeth. The head was the least intact part of the skeleton.'

Well, it was the truth, she was just being a little economical with it. She didn't feel the necessity to share with Mac at that instant the brutal details, to tell him that the head had disappeared into the depths of the ocean and the bellies of the marine life to which it was home.

'DNA?' Macdonald asked then. Everybody knew about DNA, but they usually didn't realise that even DNA could not always deliver.

She explained the mitochondrial DNA scenario to him. 'No chance of Clara's maternal grandmother being alive, I don't suppose?' she ventured.

'She'd be well over a hundred if she were,' replied Mac flatly. 'And Clara's mother was an only child just like Clara. I'm afraid you're dead right, Karen, we've got no one in the female line to make a comparison with.'

'There is something, though,' said Karen. 'Our divers found a Rolex watch out at the site. I understand that you gave—'

'Yes,' Mac interrupted straight away. 'I gave Clara a gold Rolex for her twenty-first birthday present. She always wore it. Can you tell if it's hers?'

'It's possible. I need to ask you a few questions. Can you remember where you bought the watch?'

'Of course. I don't spend that sort of money on gifts very often. I am Scots, you know!'

It wasn't the first time she had heard Mac joke his way through various events surrounding his daughter's disappearance. It was his major defence mechanism, Karen thought. She waited.

'I bought it in Inverness. There was a famous old jewellers there, Gavin of Inverness. Closed down about twelve years ago when old Gavin retired. It was an 18-carat Rolex Oyster. They told me it was the best ladies' watch money could buy. It certainly should have been. Over five hundred pounds back in 1965. I believe they're around seven thousand now. . . .'

His voice tailed off.

'Thanks, Mac. We may well be able to prove quite quickly that the watch is the one you bought and gave to Clara.'

'Can you really do that?'

'With a bit of luck,' said Karen, and she explained to him about the previous Rolex watch murder, about case numbers and service records.

'We'll get on to Mr Gavin, too,' she said. 'In case by any miracle he still has any records.'

'Right,' said Mac. 'And if you do prove that it's Clara, will that be enough to go after Marshall? Will you be able to get him at last?'

'I don't know yet, Mac. But I'll give it my best shot, I promise you that.'

'I know you will, lassie.' Mac paused again. 'I'm coming down,' he continued. 'I'll get a flight first thing tomorrow. I want to be there. And, and . . . I want to see her, I want to see my daughter. . . .'

'That's up to you, Mac. I'd never dream of stopping you. But we are talking about a skeleton that's been underwater for nearly three decades, if indeed it really does turn out to be Clara—'

Mac interrupted again. 'It's her. I know it's her, lass. So do you, I reckon. You can feel it, just like I can.'

As he spoke Karen realised that the Scotsman was quite right. She did feel that it was Clara who had been found. She had from the start. Even before she knew that the skeleton was female. It could be just a kind of wishful thinking, though, and she certainly wasn't going to respond to Mac's statement.

'Either way,' she continued, still gently but firmly. 'It's not a pretty sight and, well, it's not intact. I've told you.'

'You half-told me, lassie. The head's missing, I presume.' It was Mac's turn to make his voice gentle now.

Karen grunted, a muttered affirmative.

'And was it removed before or after her death?'

'Can't say for sure yet, but we think afterwards and we don't reckon that had anything to do with cause of death. Almost certainly the sea and all the life it contains was responsible for the disposal of the head.'

'I see.' Mac sounded dispassionate enough. Karen supposed that over the years he had become hardened to whatever eventualities there might be. Probably he just wanted to know. Knowledge can be strangely comforting, even when it is unwelcome. Knowledge can at least give some rest to a tortured soul. And there are few more tortured than the loved ones of someone who seems just to have disappeared off the face of the earth.

Karen was wrong about Sean Macdonald. As he put down the phone he was aware of his whole body trembling. He tried to collect his thoughts. It wasn't easy. He was, in many ways, no better prepared for learning that his daughter's body may have been found than he had been when he first realised what may have happened to her. He was not at all dispassionate. If anything the loss of his daughter and grandchildren had grown more difficult rather than easier to bear as the years had passed. The pain had increased rather than lessened.

For almost three decades he had craved news, wanted desperately to know exactly what had happened to Clara. And for many years now he had indeed sometimes kidded himself that even to know that she was dead would be a relief, her and those two lovely little girls, but it wasn't a relief at all.

Karen's phone call had been devastating, and no less so because of the passage of time.

Mac was an old man now, into his early eighties. His once handsome features bore deeply etched lines, and it was not ageing alone that had been responsible for that. He lowered his head into his hands, closing his fingers over his ears. The wild shock of hair that had not thinned with the years but merely turned totally white fell forward almost like a screen. He might have been grateful for that had there been anyone else in the house to see his face. But there wasn't. There wasn't really anybody else left in the world for Sean Macdonald any more.

He could feel the tears welling up, and he was not a man

who wept easily. Indeed, he was the sort who still didn't really think that men should cry. Inside his head he could still hear Karen Meadows' words.

'It's not a pretty sight, it's not intact, we have yet to find any teeth.'

The picture this conjured up was a vivid one for Sean Macdonald. He had last seen his only daughter almost a year before her disappearance and he remembered it only too well.

Clara had wanted money. Officially to bail out the hotel again. In practice, Mac had been sure, to pay off whatever debts her husband had accumulated in whatever was his latest madcap scheme.

Mac had never liked Richard Marshall. And when he'd found out that he had been a bigamist and a fraudster he had liked him even less. Clara, however, would never hear a word against the man she had married.

'You don't understand, Dad,' she told him. 'Richard's first wife was a monster. And he never really committed fraud. He always intended to sort out those Spanish time share deals. He was just juggling money to keep his business afloat. Then he got desperate, that's all.'

Clara had always had an answer for everything as far as her husband was concerned. The result had been a terrible row, the worst there had ever been between this father and daughter. Indeed, possibly the only proper row they'd ever had – which had made it worse, much worse, and probably accounted for the consequences being so serious and long-term.

Clara had travelled to Scotland specifically in order to acquire money from her father, Mac had felt back then, adding to his distress and his determination not to comply. Not that time. Not again. Rather pettily, he now thought, he had resented the fact that he never seemed to see his only daughter unless she wanted something.

'I'll not give another penny to that waster you've wed, to that smooth-talking con man you can't see through. Though it grieves me more than you'll ever know, Clara, there'll never be another penny from me for you or my grandchildren unless you leave that man. Then, I promise you, you'll never want for anything.'

Mac had known as he spoke that he had made a mistake, that he had handled it badly. He had known, too, that if his wife, Clara's mother, had still been alive, she would have steered him clear of out-and-out confrontation. Sally Macdonald had been a calm, sensible woman with an inner strength you just never quarrelled with. She had been a natural mediator, a peace keeper.

Mac was different. He was a man of unswerving loyalty and devotion to those close to him, a man who loved fiercely, who cared deeply, and who had little leaning towards compromise in such matters. His words had come from the heart, his intention had been to help, not to hurt. The result had, however, been inevitable.

Clara had been her father's daughter. She didn't take kindly to being threatened.

Her response had been swift and every bit as uncompromising as her father's.

'If you turn your back on my husband, then you turn your back on me, Dad,' she had told him. 'I'm going home to Torquay now, and I promise you one thing. You will never see me or your granddaughters ever again.'

Mac had just let her go. Watched her defiantly flick her long light brown hair over one shoulder as she walked out of the big old granite house on the outskirts of Inverness where she had been brought up, a house that he and Sally had hoped to fill with children – but that had not been destined to happen. Clara, a slight, pretty girl with big round hazel eyes like her mother's, had been the only one. Sally Macdonald's mental strength had not been matched by her physical state. She suffered ill health throughout her all-too-short life. Before and after Clara there had been a series of miscarriages brought to a halt only by Mac's decision that they would never try again for another child. Enough was enough. Sally had died aged only forty-seven, eight long years before his fateful confrontation with his only daughter. Now it looked as if he were going to lose all that remained of the woman he had adored, his only daughter, and his grandchildren.

Mac had felt as if a stake had been thrust into his heart. But he didn't show his feelings, of course. Mac was a dour

Scot. Strong. Unbending. To give in, to tell her he'd accept any bloody man in her life as long as he didn't lose her, to tell her he'd gladly give her everything that he had, that would have been a terrible display of weakness. That would never have done.

And so Mac had stood holding open the front door as Clara had walked briskly down the garden path. It had been mid-October, and the borders which framed the two small lawns on either side of the path were still planted with the straggly remains of summer bedding plants. Sally Macdonald had always looked after the garden, and she had loved the colourful blaze of busy lizzies, petunias and geraniums. Sean tried to carry on in every way just as his wife had liked it. Things didn't work out quite like that, though. The garden never looked the way it had in her time. That year, at least, Mac had managed to get the bedding plants in, but by October they had degenerated into the kind of mess Sally would never have allowed. And so, it seemed, had his relationship with his only daughter.

Clara did not look back. She did not say goodbye. She just stepped into the waiting cab, called to take her to the railway station, without even a backward glance.

Mac had wanted to cry out: 'Don't go. Please don't go. Not like this. Never like this.'

The words wouldn't come. He had watched Clara's departure in grim silence. Mac was a stubborn man. He heard nothing from his daughter after her return to Torquay, and neither had he expected to. Clara had also inherited his stubbornness.

At Christmas he had almost relented. He had written a conciliatory message on a Christmas card to Clara and enclosed a healthy cheque, not the sort of money she had been asking for but a nice present all the same, with instructions for her to buy something nice for herself and the girls. Then he had ripped the envelope up and thrown the whole lot into the fire.

None the less, he had looked every day at his post and hoped for a card at least from Clara. There had been nothing. Mac had spent Christmas alone. He had friends. There had, even then, been women friends. Mac had been a red-blooded man in those days, solvent and not unattractive. There had always been women in his life. But he had almost masochistically enjoyed spending Christmas in solitary misery, bemoaning his estrangement from the daughter he adored.

It was Clara's birthday in early May. Mac had gone through the same routine. He'd written a letter and a cheque and put them in an envelope. Then he'd ripped up the lot. The little girls' birthdays were in July. They had been born just a week apart, Lorraine in 1968 and Janine in 1969. Mac sent them a card each and a postal order for ten pounds and this time he posted both. But he neither expected nor received acknowledgement.

Several times between July and the following Christmas Mac considered telephoning Clara. He wanted a reconciliation more than anything else in the world. Under any terms. He was prepared to give his daughter anything she wanted. Indeed, anything her dreadful husband wanted too. But making the first move was very difficult for him. Twice he actually forced himself to make the call. On the first occasion he got the Parkview Hotel answering machine. On the second Richard Marshall answered. Both times Mac hung up. By then, however, he was reassured by at least hearing Marshall's voice and learning that the family were still at Parkview. It had occurred to him that they could all have moved on and he might really have lost touch with the daughter he loved. Presumably they had coped with their money problems. Marshall had probably conned some poor old ladies again, thought Sean uncharitably.

All the while he hoped that his daughter would make the first move, that she would contact him. But there was no word. Finally, the second Christmas, Mac could stand it no longer. Again he bought Christmas cards and wrote Clara a cheque, agonising for days over the amount. He was not prepared to send anything like the five thousand Clara had originally asked for to bail her and Richard out of trouble. In Scotland in 1975 you could very nearly buy a castle for that. But he did want it to be a substantial amount. Eventually he settled on one thousand pounds. Still a great deal of money back then. And twenty per cent of what he had been asked for. Mac was a percentage man.

This time he actually posted the cards and the cheque and he also sent Clara a letter, regretting their quarrel but not apologising, of course, in which he inquired after her welfare and that of the children and expressed a wish to see them all again so that they could talk.

Again there was no word. But in his January bank statement Mac noticed that his cheque had been cleared, which somehow made him uneasy. It wasn't Clara's style. He had half-expected the cheque to be returned. Clara, even Clara in need, could very easily be that stubborn. But it was out of character for his daughter to accept such a large sum of money without acknowledgement, particularly under the strained circumstances, Mac thought. She must really be very desperate indeed, he reflected. And he didn't like to think of that, whoever she was married to.

Eventually, a couple of weeks later, he phoned again. Once more Richard had answered the phone. The conversation had been brief and to the point.

'I'd like to speak to my daughter, please.'

'Sorry, Mac, she doesn't want to speak to you.' Richard's voice had been level enough.

'Then I'd like to hear her tell me that.' Mac had forced himself to respond equally levelly.

'No chance. I've just told you. She never wants anything to do with you again.'

Mac, of course, had snapped. Instantly. He had been much less controlled in those days. Clara's disappearance had changed him, more than the passage of time, he thought. After that it was as if nothing mattered that much except a pursuit of some sort of justice, and he had been forced to accept that there was no point in being anything other than calm about it or he would just go mad.

Back then, unaware that he was probably already dealing with a major tragedy, he had lost his temper and shouted down the phone.

'In that case I won't send her any more cheques. I'm sure you're well able to take care of your family, a big man like you—'

Marshall had slammed the phone down on him. Mac didn't

try again. Instead he cursed himself. He really had done a good job of trying to mend bridges. A really good job.

He had not attempted to contact his daughter's family again until her birthday in May. Once again he sent a card and a cheque for a thousand pounds. Once again he waited hopefully to hear anything from her. Once again he heard nothing yet once again the cheque was cleared.

By then becoming increasingly uneasy, Mac phoned several times more. Mostly he got the answerphone. Twice he got Richard who told him the first time that Sally didn't want to speak to him and the second time that she was not there. She and the girls had gone to stay with some friend in Kent that Mac had never heard of, although he had to admit that wasn't so surprising given the lack of communication between him and his daughter.

'I've no idea when they'll be back,' Marshall had told him.

A thought had suddenly struck Mac. It was term-time.

'What about school?' he asked.

He was quite sure that Clara would not willingly have taken her daughters anywhere during the school term. Her choice in men had never risen to Mac's high standards for her, but she was a good and responsible mother.

'I've no idea, she's in charge of all that,' Marshall had grunted back.

Mac had asked him to tell Clara that he'd called.

'No point,' replied the other man. 'She doesn't want to know.'

Two weeks later, midway through June, Mac could stand it no longer. He packed a bag and set off for Torquay, flying from Edinburgh to Bristol where he hired a car.

And he remembered all too well the look of horror on Richard Marshall's face when he'd opened the front door of Parkview to his father-in-law.

'She's not here, I told you. She's away.'

'Still?' Mac had been grim-faced. Determined.

For a moment he'd thought that Marshall was about to slam the door in his face. Richard Marshall was a big powerful man, younger too. But Mac, although of only average height and slight of build, was a tough sinewy character who during the war had been a sergeant in one of Scotland's most élite regiments and had seen action in some of Europe's cruellest battlegrounds. He had survived against the odds on more than one occasion and had virtually no physical fear. He simply stuck his foot in the door of the Parkview Hotel and took a pace forward.

Marshall faced up to him for just a few seconds, then stepped back. His shoulders dropped. His features crumpled.

'You'd better come in,' he said.

Mac had done so, thinking that Marshall was behaving like a typical bully, retreating at once when forcefully challenged.

Marshall led the way into the small dining-room where Mac knew, from a much earlier previous visit, breakfast was served to guests. He had looked around him. It was impossible to tell how many guests, if any, were presently booked into the little hotel. But the lace-curtained room somehow did not have the well-cared-for look about it which Clara, like her mother before her, specialised in. There were flowers in the small vases on the table, but they were all wilting. It was mid-afternoon. The breakfast tables had still not been properly cleared or wiped down and the windows looked as if they could do with a good clean. Mac began to wonder just how long his daughter had been away.

Marshall had beckoned to him to sit down. Mac did so. Keeping his cool. Using his head for once. He wanted to learn from Marshall, find out what was going on. There was no point in antagonising the man.

'Look, you may as well know,' began Marshall. 'She's left me. Taken the girls and gone off with this Aussie. I don't even know where they are.'

Mac had been amazed. This was the last thing he had expected to hear. Clara had given no indication of any intention of leaving her wayward husband, just the opposite really, and neither had she given any indication that she had anyone else in her life. But then, he had to admit, she wouldn't have done, would she, not to him? None the less, even allowing for his daughter's inherited stubborn streak, he couldn't believe she could have put on such a convincing devoted wife act to her own father had she really been involved with another man.

'Why didn't you tell me this? Why the charade? When did she leave?'

The questions poured out of him without his being able to control them. Marshall just shrugged, made no attempt to reply.

'I'm fucking talking to you,' Mac stormed. His distress displaying itself in temper as usual. He never learned. He always regretted it later, but the more he hurt inside, the more upset he was, the more he shouted. 'Why didn't Clara tell me she was leaving you? That's what I want to know.'

Marshall had half-smirked. 'What, and give you the satisfaction?'

His words hit Mac hard. There was so much truth in them, and truth, Mac always felt, was a rare commodity with Richard Marshall. This time the other man was spot on. Mac had told Clara he would support her, give her anything she wanted, if she left her husband. It would be just like her to leave the bloody man and not let him know. Marshall was right. She really wouldn't want to give him the satisfaction.

Mac had stood up then and left. The worst scenario had happened. His daughter had moved on without leaving a forwarding address, and she had taken his grandchildren with her. If Richard Marshall was to be believed, he too had no idea where she had gone.

If Richard Marshall was to be believed. Mac had reflected on that as he had climbed into his hire car and started the engine. He had never believed a word Marshall had said before, and had almost invariably been proven right not to, so why was he believing the man now? And just the fact that his cheques had been cleared did not necessarily establish his daughter had ever received them. She and her husband had always had a joint account, as Mac knew well. He had paid enough money into it over the years, after all.

On an impulse Mac switched the engine off and got out of the car again. For a few moments he leaned against the vehicle while he looked up and down the street, hoping that there might be some neighbours about. The street was deserted. Equally impulsively he headed for the big Victorian villa next to Parkview and rang the bell.

A tall, very thin girl in her early teens had answered.

'Hello,' he said, making his voice as gentle as possible. 'I'm looking for your neighbour, Mrs Marshall, Clara Marshall. I just wondered if you'd seen her lately.'

The girl had looked frightened and said nothing.

'It's OK,' Mac had reassured her quickly, and followed up with a lie. 'It's just that there's nobody in next door and I wondered if you knew when Clara might be back, or if she was away or anything?'

Still no reply.

'I'm her father. I've come all the way from Scotland to surprise her.'

Still no response.

Mac sighed. 'It's all right, lassie, honestly. Look, is your mother in?'

As if on cue a voice, very slightly slurred, called out from somewhere within the house.

'Who is it, Karen?'

'It's no one, Mum. Just a man who's come to the wrong house.'

The girl's voice, when he eventually heard it, had surprised Mac. She looked so frightened and unsure of herself. But when she finally spoke and addressed her mother she had sounded almost as if she were the parent reassuring her child. Certainly as if she were the one in charge.

He had looked properly into her eyes then, and noticed for the first time how intelligent they were. Something was bothering the girl, though. And he suspected it was not unconnected with those slurred tones he had heard. Mac backed off at once.

'I'm sorry, lassie, I'm intruding,' he said.

'My mother isn't well. She suffers with her nerves, you see. The doctor's given her some very strong pills.'

The girl had sprung to her mother's defence instinctively and at once even though she really had no need to do so. Mac liked that and thought how brave she was. Her swift response had told its own tale. He reflected briefly on what this child might have to put up with within the walls of that big old house. But he had no time for other people's troubles. He had

88

enough of his own. He tried again to get at least a simple question answered.

'Look, I just wondered if you had any idea where my daughter, where Clara Marshall, might be.'

The girl shook her head.

'She's not there,' she said suddenly. 'She doesn't live there any more. Why don't you know that if you're her father?'

Mac had been badly taken aback. If it were true that his daughter had moved out of the marital home and started a new life, why indeed didn't he know that? There was no easy answer. He didn't have a clue where Clara might be and it was all his own stupid stubborn fault.

He took his leave of the girl he was to encounter again many years later when she was a senior police detective, and decided to try another house across the road. And there he struck lucky, if that was the word.

The man who answered the door to him did so swiftly with something of a flourish, as he did everything. Charles Peabody was not a man to mince words, either. When Mac inquired whether he knew his daughter, or had any idea where she might be, Peabody introduced himself in such a way that the Scotsman felt he was supposed to know who he was, and then proceeded to pass on what scant information he had and to give his opinion in a pompously forceful manner.

'If you want to know the truth, nobody's seen nor heard of Clara Marshall or her girls for nearly a year,' he announced. 'And it's high time somebody did something about it, I say. Richard Marshall's already moved his bit on the side in. And her a married woman, too. It's not right. It's a scandal, that's what it is.

'As for your daughter, well, there's all sorts of stories around in the town about what might have happened to her. She's your girl, Mr Macdonald, and I don't want to alarm you. But there's plenty round here who'd put nothing past Richard Marshall, nothing at all.'

In spite of his professed intention not to alarm Sean Macdonald, Peabody displayed little restraint or sensitivity.

Obviously not the man's style, thought Mac obliquely, as he felt a cold chill run through his body. He didn't need

Charles Peabody to spell out the stories which were abundant in Torquay. He didn't actually need anything spelled out. He had to admit that for some time now, ever since that Christmas cheque had been cleared without acknowledgement, there had been nasty lurking doubts in the back of his mind concerning the welfare of his daughter and her children.

He had dismissed them as fanciful. Richard Marshall might be a small-time villain and a man he strongly disliked, but to turn him into anything else was merely being self-indulgent, he had told himself.

Now he allowed all those thoughts, his doubts, to overtake him. He had no more time for neighbours' tittle-tattle. He wanted the truth.

He said thank you and goodbye to Mr Peabody in as calm a manner as he could manage, and as soon as the other man closed his front door he half-ran across the road back to Parkview where he hammered noisily on the door, his heart pumping like a piston engine.

Marshall didn't respond quickly enough. Mac began to shout then. 'Come on, you bastard. Come on. Answer this bloody door before I knock it down.'

Eventually Richard Marshall had opened the door. But only a crack. The security chain remained in place.

'What do you want?' he asked nervously.

'I want to know where my daughter is. I want to know what you've done with my daughter, you bastard.'

'You're mad. I've told you. She's left me, I don't know where she is.'

'I think you do know, you bastard. You fucking bastard. I think you do know. And I'll not rest till I get the truth, I promise you that.'

'You're mad, and you've been listening to gossip. I saw you, running around to the neighbours.'

'If you've harmed a hair of my daughter's head I'll kill you, I promise you, you fucker,' screamed Mac.

'You and which army?'

Marshall, perhaps given confidence by his security chain, had returned to his normal arrogance, which had always so infuriated Mac.

The Scotsman lunged crazily forward trying to reach through the narrow gap between the door and its frame. He went for Marshall's throat. He wanted to throttle the bastard. Although how he thought he would succeed in doing so through a crack in the door he had no idea. He was not thinking, of course.

Marshall pulled sharply back, threw his substantial weight behind the door and smashed it shut. Mac only just got his hands out in time.

He pulled himself together. Stepped back. Tears were coursing down his cheeks. He wiped them away with the back of one hand, struggled to regain control. He was trembling from head to foot. Mac was a strong man physically and mentally. But suddenly he had collapsed. His whole world had collapsed. He turned and lurched along the path. At the gate he stumbled, reached out and held on to a gatepost for support. As he did so he noticed the girl from next door. She was standing on the pavement just behind the fence. He had little doubt that she had been watching and listening.

'What the hell do ye think you're doing?' Mac yelled. 'Just get the hell out of here, now.'

The girl had obeyed at once. Her eyes wide with fear she took off at a run through the big gates into the house next door and up the driveway, her feet barely touching the ground, she was moving so fast.

Fleetingly, Mac was ashamed of himself for rounding on a mere child. He hadn't been able to help himself, though. His tears were still falling in spite of his efforts to control them, and Mac was a proud man. A man's man. He had never been able to stand anyone, not even his late wife, seeing him cry. And yet there he was on a public thoroughfare blubbing like a baby.

He couldn't help that either.

Suddenly, with devastating clarity, he had been overwhelmed with a terrible knowledge. He believed beyond any doubt at all that he would indeed never see his daughter and her children again. Just as Clara had told him.

But he believed now that she was dead. That they were all dead. And that Richard Marshall had killed them.

That evening and throughout the night, spent in the Grand Hotel on the sea front, torturing himself in a place that he knew had been a great favourite of his daughter's, Sean Macdonald struggled with the terrible revelation that had overwhelmed him.

In the morning he went to Torquay Police Station to report that his daughter Mrs Clara Marshall and her two little girls Lorraine and Janine were missing.

Six

At Torquay Police Station twenty-seven years later Karen sat in thought for a few moments following her phone call to Sean Macdonald. She had not been surprised by his reaction. She knew exactly what the potential of this freak discovery would mean to him.

Neither she nor anybody else could bring Clara Marshall and her children back. But perhaps they really could bring Richard Marshall to justice at last. She'd make sure she gave it her best shot, that was for certain; and so, she was sure, would all of her team. This was so much more than just another case. Karen leaned forward in her chair, ready for action again, and buzzed Phil Cooper who appeared swiftly in the open doorway of her office.

'Right, Phil, I have a list for you,' she began briskly. 'One, we need to establish that the Rolex belonged to Clara. Get somebody to track down this retired jeweller, Gavin, in Inverness. Mac says he a bought a Rolex for Clara from him.' She passed Cooper the piece of paper on which she had written the details. 'It's a very long shot that he'll still have any records, but you never know. Meanwhile get the watch to the Rolex HQ in Kent, and get it to them today. Tell them we need them to do their stuff again, just like they did on that other case. Tell them we need to know where that watch was sold. And we need to know fast. If we're going to pick up Marshall I want to get on with it. He probably knows what we've found off Berry Head, it's already been in the papers and on the news. I don't want him doing some sort of disappearing act. He's just the sort of bastard who'd be capable of making himself disappear permanently. If we can prove quickly that watch was sold by Gavin, and the date, then that would establish near enough one hundred per cent that it was bought by

Mac. We're there then. And we'd have really strong circumstantial evidence against Marshall at last. At least we'd have a body, even if it's only a damaged skeleton.

'Two. Find out where Marshall is, or Ricky Maxwell, as I believe he calls himself nowadays. I want to be sure that when the moment comes we can get to him right away.

'Three. Make sure Torbay Hospital have arranged for the skeleton to be despatched to that lab in London where they establish the isotopes of bones. I'm not going to wait for the results before picking up Marshall and hopefully charging him, but it would be good to know for certain more or less how long those remains have been in the water well before we go to court.

'And four. This investigation is top priority again. Get the team sifting through this lot.' Karen gestured at a dozen or so cardboard boxes piled against the far wall of her office, records of the initial investigation that had been brought out of storage the previous day. The case had never been formally closed, as indeed no unsolved murder case in Great Britain ever is, and virtually each year had added at least some new information, though none of it, so far, ever of much use.

'Tell the guys they're looking for anything, anything at all that may have been overlooked before and could give us a new lead,' Karen continued. 'There might be something that is relevant now, because we've found that skeleton, that wasn't before. And when they've finished with this lot there's plenty more paperwork we haven't dug out yet, and then there's bits and bobs on computer, too, that have been added more recently.'

'Consider it done, boss.'

Karen could see that the sergeant was really buzzing. They all were. This was the big one for them. They all wanted to get Marshall so much.

She followed Cooper as he hurried out of her office – he on the way to the incident room, she on the way to the coffee machine.

Back in her office clutching her paper cup of something that certainly had the colour of coffee even if maybe not the flavour, Karen allowed herself to reflect on her own involvement all those years ago. She had been little more than a child when it had all happened. What could she have known really? There were things, though, things that had bugged her for nearly thirty years.

She cast her mind back, trying to sort out her jumbled thoughts.

It was about a month before Clara Marshall disappeared that Karen was sent home from school early because of a power cut. At about 2.30 in the afternoon she had arrived at Laurel House to find the front door locked, which was unusual in mid-afternoon. Puzzled, Karen had rung the doorbell. And she'd had to do so twice more before her mother had finally opened it.

Margaret Meadows had been wearing one of the flimsy floral dressing-gowns she specialised in, and nothing else, her daughter had thought. Not even underwear. She looked on edge, and glanced quickly over her shoulder at least twice as she let Karen in.

'You're ever so early, dear, I wasn't expecting you yet,' she muttered nervously.

Karen explained what had happened at school, all the while studying her mother curiously. Something was wrong, but she couldn't work out what. Her mother picked up on it, and presumably felt she needed to explain her attire.

'I-I was about to have a bath, dear,' she said, with a hesitant, slightly apologetic smile.

Karen followed her into the hall, without further comment. She was, however, watchful, just as always. She had never known her mother take a bath in the middle of the afternoon. Margaret Meadows had a routine, whether she was drinking or not. Once she finally got out of bed, which was usually around mid-morning and sometimes not until midday, she always bathed before putting on her make-up. Karen had never yet known her to face the day ahead without going through that routine.

She was still studying her mother with interest when Richard Marshall came bounding down the stairs, white shirt undone, his jacket, a dark coloured blazer of some sort, with shiny gold buttons, slung casually over one shoulder, his shock of dark curly hair tousled.

'I don't think you'll have any more trouble with that tap, Margaret,' he said obliquely.

'Oh. Uh. Thank you, Richard.'

Karen turned to face her mother. Margaret Meadows had blushed crimson. She bowed her head slightly as if trying to hide her face behind the blonde veil of her hair. Then she looked up and put on a bright smile which was not reflected in her eyes.

'Richard's been fixing that dripping tap in the bathroom, dear,' she told her daughter, obviously feeling another explanation was called for. 'Wasn't that nice of him?'

Karen may have had to grow up beyond her years, but she still had the directness and simplicity of thought which goes with youth.

'We didn't have a dripping tap in the bathroom,' she said flatly.

'Of course we did, darling.' This time Margaret Meadows' smile was indulgent. 'You just haven't noticed. Other things on your mind, I expect.'

Margaret had then turned towards Richard again. 'Oh, these young girls,' she said.

It had been Karen's turn to blush then. She could cheerfully have slapped her mother. Did the woman think she was stupid or something? Didn't she realise Karen was pretty damned sure she knew exactly what was going on? Why was she trying to make Karen look like a fool?

Richard Marshall pulled on his jacket. He was smirking too, or so it seemed to Karen. Although he had at least had the decency to attempt to fabricate some sort of reason for having been upstairs with her mother, his attitude was that of a man who simply didn't give a damn.

He hadn't even bothered to comb his hair, after all, or to finish dressing properly. He looked thoroughly pleased with himself, and he actually reached forward and ruffled Karen's hair.

'Well, if you can't enjoy yourself at her age, when can you?' he asked of no one in particular, while beaming at her in a horribly patronising fashion.

Karen had felt her blush deepening which seriously annoyed

96

her. She remembered how even then his demeanour was that of a man who thought he was invincible, a man who thought he was untouchable. Which was perhaps why he had dared just a short while later to do the dreadful deed she was so sure he was guilty of.

It would never have occurred to Richard Marshall back then that he would get caught out in anything that he did, Karen felt. She hadn't known then that he had already served time in jail. Had she done so she would merely have been forced to wonder at how little effect it had had on him. She pulled away from him, shaking her whole body as if to rid herself of his touch, and hurried into the kitchen, leaving him and her mother alone in the hall to make their farewells.

It was the only time that Karen ever caught the pair of them together and she had no idea whether or not they had been having a full-blown affair, or if this had been a one-afternoon stand. True to form in the Meadows household the incident was never mentioned again and Karen told nobody about it. Certainly she knew better than to mention it to her father. Neither did she tell the police, and her failure to do that was later to haunt her even though it never even occurred to her at the time.

Whatever the extent of her mother's relationship with Richard Marshall, Karen was quite sure that something had been going on and, in spite of her youth, equally convinced that she knew what the two of them had been doing the day she came home from school early.

But if she had ever had any doubts at all, these would have been assuaged the day a major missing persons inquiry was finally launched and Richard Marshall was arrested, almost exactly a year after his family's disappearance. Karen had been forced to prop her mother up during yet another drinking binge combined with a bout of depression, and Margaret Meadows had made it quite clear that this latest attack of bad nerves, as the family described her condition back then, had been brought about by Richard's arrest. She had been distraught for days, which even at the time had confused Karen considerably.

After all, it was the talk of the town that Richard had installed

Esther Hunter at Parkview less than a month after his wife and children disappeared. Everyone, it seemed, including Karen and all her schoolfriends, knew all about it. Esther Hunter was not only a hairdresser with her own business but she was also married to a popular Torbay builder who was a town councillor. She was well known locally, as, of course, was her husband. Her liaison with Richard, so unfortunately soon, it seemed, after the disappearance of Clara and the girls, was a big local scandal and it was that, as much as anything, which had focused attention on the strange events surrounding the Marshall family. Indeed, his indecent haste over Esther was generally seen to be Marshall's motive for getting rid of his wife and children.

Karen's mother knew all about Esther Hunter. Karen never saw her mother alone with Richard Marshall again and was pretty sure there was no longer an affair going on between them. She would have noticed, she felt certain. She was, after all, a pretty good spy. She didn't miss much. So why had her mother been so distressed to learn that, in her words, 'the police have taken Richard'?

Karen had not understood then and, to tell the truth, she did not understand now. She did know all about the mesmerising effect Marshall seemed to have on the women in his life. He turned them into blithering idiots, it seemed to her. And she remembered well enough that although the police had not found grounds to charge Richard Marshall back in 1976, and he had been released after little more than twenty-four hours and had been able to return to the Parkview Hotel and Esther Hunter, their investigation had not stopped there. Bill Talbot himself had visited Karen's street, high above the bay, on at least two occasions and talked to various neighbours. And naturally he had come to see Karen's mother. Her involvement, albeit peripheral, was already on record. But Karen, although not privy to the interviews, was certain her mother had told him no more than she had the two officers whose visit she had listened to at the keyhole.

Karen also remembered being embarrassed and made to feel uneasy just by the sight of Richard Marshall and Esther Hunter together at that time. She could not avoid bumping into them occasionally, even though she would have preferred not to. Marshall remained as bold and brash as ever. Karen invariably blushed when he spoke to her. On the other hand, Esther Hunter rarely said anything. Once Karen dropped a shopping bag at her feet and Esther, a small fair woman with a big gentle smile, had helped her pick up the spilt shopping. Karen remembered her appearing to be almost as shy and awkward as she herself felt. And Karen had blushed terribly, of course.

'It's all right, don't worry, I drop things all the time,' Esther had reassured her. Karen remained unable to reconcile this rather homely image of Esther Hunter with that of local legend, the scarlet woman who had, without a care, stepped into the abandoned shoes of the wife whom her lover had almost certainly murdered.

Then, just a few weeks after Richard Marshall had been released without charge, two things had happened. He and Esther took off without any farewells and without leaving a forwarding address, abandoning a debt-ridden Parkview in the hands of a local estate agent, and Karen's father left her mother. How much that had been caused by her mother's relationship with Richard Marshall, Karen did not know. Neither did she know if her father was even aware of the affair, if that was what it had been. He could not, however, have failed to notice Margaret Meadows' descent into alcoholic depression at the time of Marshall's arrest, and she had made little or no attempt to conceal what had sparked it off. Then, when Marshall had moved Esther Hunter into Parkview almost a year earlier there had been a similar bout of booze-fuelled depression, accompanied by loud drunken ramblings concerning Richard's 'betrayal', and even references to that 'whore next door'. You would have had to have been a fool not to realise what it was all about, and while Karen's father had been all manner of things, he certainly had not been that.

Karen eventually learned that her father had met another woman and was setting up home with her in Plymouth. She more or less picked that up from a mixture of local gossip and, as ever, from overhearing conversations, mostly on the phone between her mother and someone she guessed was a solicitor. Nobody actually told her anything. One day her father was living with her and her mother at Laurel House, and the next he was not. But then, communication was not a high priority in the Meadows household.

And when she asked her mother where her father was, the reply was fairly typical.

'Thinks he's found a better offer, darling, but don't worry, he'll be back.'

Colin Meadows never did return, however. For the first year or so of her parents' estrangement he would turn up about once a month to see Karen, but she could not even remember a conversation with him worthy of the name. There was always a present, usually a book token, once a sweater at least a size too small, and once, out of the blue, and far more gratefully received, a quite acceptable secondhand bicycle.

Then her father was killed in a car accident, along with the new woman in his life. And, strange though it may seem, Karen could not really remember how she reacted. Indeed, she could barely recall any reaction at all and she thought she must just have blotted it out. She remembered her mother telling her the grim news in quite a matter of fact way. It was the only time Karen ever heard her mother mention her father after he left home, except to pass on the arrangements for Karen's meetings with him, which had in any case gradually become less and less frequent. Karen did not go to her father's funeral, and could not even remember if she was given the opportunity to do so. Certainly nobody, least of all her mother, ever talked to her again about her father or the manner of his death, and she did not feel it was right, somehow, to ask. Instead Karen took her feelings inward. Something she did throughout her childhood and adolescence. Something she still bloody well did, she thought wryly.

She was aware that she had never grieved for her father, and she didn't know any more whether or not she had ever loved him. She didn't think she could have done. Not really. She had loved her mother, though – and still did, painfully so, a love now dogged by guilt – with all her faults and paradoxes. And maybe that is why she had never given anything emotionally to her father nor he to her. It almost seemed like a disloyalty to her mother.

Margaret Meadows, as was her wont, reacted unpredictably to the unexpected death of her husband. She inherited Laurel House outright – Colin Meadows had failed to make another will following his estrangement from his wife and in any case his new partner had died with him – and the old Victorian villa, short on tender loving care as it had been for so long, was a big house in a sought-after location and turned out to be worth a considerable amount of money.

Margaret Meadows sold the place at once and, in a way which might have seemed quite out of character, proceeded to handle her financial affairs extremely sensibly. She invested part of the proceeds of the sale of Laurel House in order to provide an income, and the rest she used to buy a small but pretty cottage in the village of Kingskerswell, where she and Karen then lived until Karen left home for college. Karen found herself observing, in that peculiarly detached way she had as a child, while her mother turned her entire life around. Margaret almost totally stopped drinking, joined the Women's Institute, took up jam making and ballroom dancing and found a charming widowed farmer to escort her around. She never married again, in spite of being asked to do so regularly by the farmer, and indeed it seemed as if the death of her husband gave her both the freedom and the will to live her life to the full.

The depressions became fewer and further between and, no longer fuelled by excessive alcohol, seemed to be controllable. Karen remembered thinking that her mother might have made a rather fine actress. Certainly her ability to reinvent herself as a totally different human being proved to be considerable and, while her performance as a stalwart of village life was worthy of an Oscar, Karen never quite believed in it, even though it seemed to keep her mother happy. Indeed, those years at Kingskerswell were among the happiest in Karen's life too. The changes both in her surroundings and in her mother's behaviour were extraordinary.

One thing did not change. They still never really communicated, never talked about anything important. Certainly Richard Marshall, and the mysterious disappearance of his wife and children, was never mentioned.

*

Throughout the rest of that day Karen found her thoughts returning to the past. The very act of reopening the investigation into the disappearance of Clara Marshall and her children, which although never officially closed had effectively ended years previously, was a journey down memory lane. And by and large not a particularly pleasant one.

Caught up in the buzz of it all, some time around six o'clock Karen suddenly remembered that she had arranged to meet Bill Talbot in the pub. She felt, however, that there was nothing further to learn from Talbot at that moment, and after such a long and traumatic day she really couldn't face what she feared was sure to descend into a morose drinking session while Talbot relived his and the Devon and Cornwall Constabulary's failings in the Marshall affair. So she called him to put off their meeting, pleading pressure of work which, as she suspected she would not be ready to leave the station until at least ten o'clock again that night, was actually more than just an excuse.

The following morning brought a potential breakthrough. Just before 11 a.m. they got word back from Rolex. A brief report was faxed over from their UK headquarters in East Grinstead, which a beaming Phil Cooper brought into Karen's office. The watch, serial number 765323, had been sold by Gavin of Inverness. Predictably, Mr Gavin no longer had any records of his business, certainly not going back to the sixties. But it was beyond all reasonable doubt that the watch had been bought by Sean Macdonald and given to his daughter Clara. Its discovery adjacent to her body in that old sunken German E-boat was, Karen felt sure, already sufficient to identify the remains they had found.

Karen punched her desk with the clenched fist of her left hand.

'At last, Phil, at last,' she murmured.

'I know, boss.'

For a second or two Karen felt the past overwhelming her again. Then she gave herself a mental shaking. They actually had some evidence, at least enough to establish at last that they were dealing with a murder. They had something tangible after all this time, they had a victim. They had a body. This was no time for any kind of self-indulgence. This was the moment for which she and so many others had waited so long, this was a moment to be grasped with both hands. She must concentrate absolutely on the present and on ensuring that some kind of justice was finally achieved on behalf of Clara Marshall and her children.

Karen turned her full attention to the sergeant once more.

'And Marshall? Do we know where he is, yet?'

Cooper's smile had broadened even more. 'We certainly do, boss. Just got confirmation. He's running a marina in Poole, not far from Bournemouth where he came from, of course. He calls himself Ricky Maxwell nowadays, like you said. Changed his name not long after he moved away from Torquay with that hairdresser woman, if you remember, boss.'

Karen shot him a withering look. 'Do you really think I could have forgotten, Phil?'

'Sorry, boss.'

Karen grinned.

'Bit of an unfortunate change of a name really, wasn't it? Maxwell. Later to be made notorious by Robert, one of the greatest villains in corporate history.'

She got to her feet and strode purposefully towards the door, gesturing for Cooper to follow her.

Outside in the incident room she called for attention, but she hadn't really needed to do so. All eyes were on her as soon as she walked in. She was acutely aware of the quite heady atmosphere of suppressed excitement in the room.

'Right, boys and girls,' she began. 'We have every reason to believe that we have at last found the body of Clara Marshall. And we all know who our prime suspect is, do we not?'

A murmur of assent rippled around the room.

'OK!' Karen continued. 'We also know where to find him. So . . .' She paused. A little bit of dramatic effect was all part of man management, she reckoned. 'Let's go get the bastard, shall we?'

Her words were greeted with a brief cheer and a chorus of muttered 'yes'es. Everybody in the force wanted Richard Marshall. The loudest shout of 'yes' came from Phil Cooper. Karen shot him an appreciative glance. She liked his enthusiasm. Liked everything about the man, in fact.

'I need two of you guys, Tompkins and Smiley.' She deliberately chose two of the older detective constables, long-serving
men who were all too familiar with the history of the Marshall
case. Then she turned to Cooper. 'I'll want you as well, Phil,
plus two uniforms. Find out who's available and make sure
they're young and fit just in case we need muscle. It wouldn't
really be Marshall's style to resist arrest, but I'm taking no
chances. The rest of you, just carry on. Let's dig deep on this
one. Marshall's well capable of escaping our net. I don't want
him to be given the opportunity to do so. So let's make sure
we miss absolutely nothing – and I really do want all those
old records gone through with a tooth-comb.'

This brought about the obligatory moans from the detectives assigned to the dreary task of dealing with the moun-
tainous paperwork already compiled for the case. But Karen
had the feeling they didn't really mind that much. Not if the
end result was locking up Richard Marshall.

By the time she set off for Poole along with her designated
team, Karen was wound up like a spring. She was excited and
she was also nervous. It was so important that no mistakes
were made, that nothing was allowed to go wrong. Her mouth
felt dry. Cooper, a man known for his healthy appetite,
produced a packet of ham sandwiches, no doubt prepared by
his wife, and offered her one. Karen shook her head. She
suddenly realised she had eaten nothing that day but she wasn't
hungry. And she knew she would not be able to eat until
Richard Marshall was safely in custody. However, she gratefully accepted a few mouthfuls from the bottle of water Cooper
passed to her. As she replaced the cap, her mobile phone rang.
It was John Kelly.

'Any news?' he asked.

'Sorry, John, I'm in a meeting. I can't talk right now. I'll
call you back.'

She quickly pushed the end button on the phone.

Kelly was not only that rare creature, a journalist whom she
as a police officer could rely on, he was also one of the few
men in the world whom she trusted. She was not, however,
prepared to take the slightest risk with this operation.

She didn't want anybody outside her team knowing what

was about to happen. The muscles at the back of her neck were so stretched and tense that they ached. This was a big big day for Karen Meadows.

For a moment, though, she was overwhelmed by a feeling of great sadness. So pleased had she been to have obtained some constructive information on the Clara Marshall case that she had not really considered what it actually meant.

There had been little doubt, almost from the beginning really, that Clara Marshall was no longer alive, and as the years had passed and there had been no word at all of either her or her children, any possibility of a different outcome had become less and less likely. But having little doubt and knowing were two different things. Maybe Karen, deep inside, had clung to some forlorn hope. And maybe Mac had too, even though the down-to-earth Scotsman would certainly deny it.

Either way, suddenly they were dealing with facts. With evidence. With reality. And it was a blunt and brutal reality. Clara's body had been found. It had been wrapped in a tarpaulin, bound in chains, and dumped at sea. Almost certainly the bodies of her children had been dumped along with hers. It was equally likely that they would never be found, that they had already been destroyed by the ravages of time and tide. Only freak circumstances had kept Clara's remains in any discernible condition.

Clara was dead. The only logical conclusion any police officer could have drawn from the case had finally been proven correct.

They were on their way to a result. A much longed-for result. But when she actually thought about the young woman whose tragic fate had cast a shadow over Karen's entire career and that of so many others, her sense of anticipation left her. As did the triumph she had felt earlier.

This case was about the destruction of young lives. About the most horrible kind of murder.

They arrived at Heron View Marina in Poole at about two in the afternoon, pulling off the main road and driving into the impressive marina complex in the exclusive Sandbanks area, where houses with harbour views invariably sold for two million pounds or so. Looking around her at the waterside hotel and the blocks of luxury flats overlooking rows of moored boats, almost all of which absolutely screamed money, Karen reflected that it seemed Richard Marshall had fallen on his feet yet again. She planned to do her best to change all that.

The sun was shining, and the water also shone, as did the sleek vessels slotted neatly around an extensive framework of jetties.

The girl in the marina office, next to the chandlery on the far side of the hotel, seemed rather startled by their arrival, perhaps understandably enough.

'We're looking for Ricky Maxwell,' announced Karen, using Marshall's assumed name.

'Ricky?' The girl appeared to have been stunned into a kind of stupidity.

'Yes, Ricky Maxwell,' replied Karen curtly. 'That is what I said.'

'Ricky?' the girl repeated. 'Oh. Y-yes. Yes. He's out there.'

She gestured towards the far end of the framework of jetties. Karen narrowed her eyes and peered into the distance. The sun was shining directly into her face. She could not see anybody where the girl was pointing.

'He's fitting a new battery on *Wessex Lady*,' said the girl then, as if that explained everything.

'*Wessex Lady*,' she repeated almost impatiently. 'The big Fairline at the end. You probably can't see him from here.'

Karen nodded and turned to leave the office. At least it did not seem that Richard Marshall had attempted to do a runner yet. But then, she would not really have expected him to. Not yet, anyway. Not a cool customer like him.

'Can I help at all?' asked the girl rather forlornly.

'No thanks, love.' It was Phil Cooper who bothered to reply. Karen was now focused on one thing, and one thing only.

'Phil, come with me,' she said. 'And you, Tompkins. And you, Richardson,' she instructed, nodding towards the larger of the two young police constables whose services Cooper had acquired. Then she spoke to the second uniformed man: 'You stay here with the car, Brownlow, just in case, and Smiley, you stay here too. Just watch and wait. Take no chances. Right?'

Without waiting for any response, and in anticipation of instant obedience, she took off along one of the jetties, her little entourage following in her wake. Once on her way out across the marina Karen was quickly able to spot *Wessex Lady.* The blue and white motor yacht was moored at the very end of the last jetty, as the girl in the office had indicated. But as they neared the vessel there was still no sign of anybody about. However, the boat's canvas hood had been opened and partly pulled to one side, there was a tool-box on the cockpit floor and the trapdoor to the engine compartment stood open.

Then, just as Karen was taking all this in, the top half of a big grey-haired man emerged from the engine compartment. He was directly facing Karen and her team and he saw them at once. He was carrying a large battery in both arms. Karen stared him straight in the face and was aware of a trapped expression flashing across his eyes, but it was gone so quickly that she was not even sure whether or not she may have been mistaken.

'Richard Marshall?' she began formally.

'Maxwell,' the man replied, his voice laconic. 'My name is Ricky Maxwell.'

Karen studied him for a moment, aware at once that the horrible fascination she had always had in him was still there. She had not actually met Marshall since her childhood, since she was fourteen, in fact, when he had finally moved away from Parkview with his girlfriend. Fleetingly, she wondered if he would recognise her. She had recognised him at once. But it was different that way round. He had been a grown man in his late thirties when she had last seen him, while she had been just a young teenager. Also, his photograph had frequently been in various newspapers, and she had seen it often enough in police files to be reminded regularly of his appearance.

Not that she really needed any reminding. Richard Marshall's face was engraved upon her soul. She continued to stare at him levelly. He returned the stare without blinking. He had always been a cool customer, she thought.

She knew that he must by now be well into his mid-sixties, but he still looked good, she reflected grudgingly. His hair was iron-grey but remained thick and curly, his skin tanned and healthy, his tall broad physique trim and well-preserved. His face, although generally regarded as handsome, had always been jowly, but had altered remarkably little with the passing of the years. Nothing about him suggested that he had ever been troubled much by guilt or remorse, but Karen was well enough aware that this was a man who had never displayed any kind of conscience.

Marshall even had about him still that self-satisfied expression she had always found so infuriating. It was more than self-satisfied. It was smug. Even at that moment, surely already aware that the small group confronting him were police officers, he contrived to look smug. It was unbelievable. More than anything Karen wanted to wipe that smug look off his face. By God, she did.

'Call yourself what you like,' she responded sharply. 'I'm Detective Superintendent Karen Meadows of the Devon and Cornwall Constabulary. You will always be Richard Marshall in my nick, and I'm arresting you on suspicion of murder.'

To her immense satisfaction the Marshall mask slipped. Finally. And Karen knew from Bill Talbot, and indeed from her own childhood memories, just how unusual that was. For once, he no longer looked smug at all. It occurred to her that watching his facial expression change that way might well be the only good moment experienced by any police officer in the whole Marshall investigation, spanning almost thirty years. Obliquely Karen thought that she would quite like to meet up with Bill Talbot now. She couldn't wait to tell Bill about this moment.

A look of panic began to spread across Marshall's face, which Karen found even more gratifying. He took another step up from the engine compartment, still holding the battery in both hands. He was towering above Karen now. Suddenly he lifted the heavy battery so that it was almost level with his chin. Involuntarily Karen flinched. It seemed that he might be about to throw the thing at her.

She sensed Phil Cooper moving forward to her right, while PC Richardson, on her left, leaned forward and grabbed hold of the railing around the boat. Karen realised that Richardson was about to attempt to jump aboard. In spite of her initial sense of fear concerning what Marshall might do, she used both hands to indicate to the men that she wanted them to hold back.

Then, her eyes never leaving Richard Marshall's face, she began to caution him. 'You don't have to say anything. But it may harm your defence if you do not mention when questioned something which you later rely on in court. Anything you do say may be used in evidence.'

Marshall stared right back at her. His eyes remained as unusual as she remembered them; clear, very pale blue, and just like those of his two little daughters. Suddenly an image of those two small frightened faces all those years ago flashed unwelcomely before her. She still believed that she, and she personally, had let those children down. She knew she was not alone in that. It didn't help. She could feel tears pricking – and that certainly would not help. She had a job to do. There was so much that could never be put right, but at least she could do her best to seek some sort of justice for Lorraine and Janine and their mother. She made herself concentrate all her intentions on what was happening now. On Richard Marshall.

He no longer looked panic-stricken, but rather more as if he were calculating the odds against him. She told herself again that it wasn't Marshall's style to do a runner or to resist arrest. As a natural con man he was far more the sort to bluff, to rely on his wits to get him out of trouble. Karen got the feeling he was quite methodically working out which course of action to take next.

Still holding the battery at chin level, still staring directly at Karen, Marshall took a further step up on to the deck of *Wessex Lady* until he was standing in full view in the cockpit, towering above her.

Fleetingly it occurred to Karen what a strong man he still must be. And at the same time she thought, not for the first time, how terrifying it must have been for his wife, so much smaller than him, and his little children, to have been faced with him in a violent mood.

Marshall took a pace forward as Karen finished the caution. She had to motion again for the officers accompanying her not to react. Her eyes never left Marshall's face. Eventually she was rewarded with a look of resignation. Very slowly, and in a totally controlled manner, Marshall began to lower the battery on to the deck in front of him. He did not speak.

'In lay terms, you're nicked,' said Karen, in the same laconic voice Marshall had used earlier. Marshall did not reply.

'I want you to move very slowly off the boat,' Karen instructed.

Marshall did so, still without comment. His face was very slightly flushed, his eyes downcast now. He looked sullen more than anything else. Karen quite liked that. This was, after all, a man whom she was quite sure had literally got away with murder for twenty-eight years.

When he was eventually standing on the walkway alongside her, pointedly avoiding her gaze now, she half-turned to Phil Cooper.

'Right, cuff 'im,' she instructed. And she could do nothing to prevent the slight note of triumph which crept into her voice.

Seven

As the handcuffed Marshall was led to the waiting cars the young woman from the marina office, looking quite distraught, ran after him, calling out: 'Ricky, Ricky, what's going on?'

Marshall glanced at her only briefly, then looked away. He said nothing. But maybe there was something in that glance that the girl recognised. Certainly she backed off straight away.

Phil Cooper, standing alongside DC Smiley, watched her with interest until, with one last anguished look at Marshall over her shoulder, she retreated out of sight into her little office. He returned his gaze then to Marshall as, in the custody of Karen Meadows and the other three police officers, he was loaded into one of the two waiting cars. The detective superintendent sat in the front of the blue saloon alongside DC Tompkins, the driver, while Marshall was sandwiched between the two uniformed men, PCs Brownlow and Richardson, in the back.

Cooper felt as if his eyes were riveted to the car as it moved slowly across the marina car park and then turned left out on to the main drag. He didn't have the personal long-term involvement of his superintendent, but like almost everybody in the Devon and Cornwall Constabulary, certainly everybody in Torquay, this case really mattered to him, as Karen had realised at once. Cooper had two little girls he doted on. Ever since the skeleton of Clara Marshall's body had been discovered, Cooper had found that when he thought about Marshall's children, which he could not help doing a lot, he pictured them inside his head with his own daughter's faces. It was not pleasant, not pleasant at all.

Phil Cooper, like all his colleagues, was also very aware of how important this one was to the Devon and Cornwall Constabulary. It was pretty devastating for police officers to have been sure for all this time that a man was guilty of treble murder and to have been unable to do anything about it.

Well, they'd got him now. And it was all their jobs to make sure that Richard Marshall remained well and truly got, as it were.

The detective superintendent had asked Phil and DC Ronald Smiley to stay behind and make some check calls around the marina and in the Poole and Bournemouth area. Phil Cooper knew well enough what was required. He and Smiley needed to build a profile of Marshall as he was today.

They needed to talk to people who knew Marshall, particularly anyone who might have any kind of new take on the man. And the obvious place to start was with that girl in the marina office.

Any kind of invasion by a team of half a dozen police officers is likely to be disruptive and distressing, at home or in the workplace, but Cooper had taken careful note of the girl's reaction as Marshall had been led away. She had looked both shocked and upset. And considerably more so, Cooper somehow suspected, than would have been the case had Richard Marshall merely been her employer.

Cooper knew well enough of Marshall's reputation as an inveterate womaniser. And by all accounts a highly successful one, reflected the detective, the very thought of which made him uneasy. The young woman looked to be in her early to mid-thirties, certainly a good thirty years younger than Marshall but that, Cooper reckoned, would not stop a man like him.

Gesturing for Smiley to accompany him he led the way back into the marina office. The young woman was standing just inside, by the window. Cooper had been unable to see her but he guessed that she too had watched the unmarked police car containing Richard Marshall leave the marina complex and turn on to the main drag en route for Dorchester, and then on past Honiton and Exeter to Torbay.

As Cooper and Smiley entered the office she quickly turned away, walked over to her desk and sat down, sweeping back her long bright chestnut hair with one hand. She was unusually tall, but she had quite a small tight-lipped face, Cooper observed. She also had a slightly sulky look about her, without which, the detective sergeant thought, she would have been rather pretty. The young woman contrived to stare straight ahead while ensuring that she did not look directly at either of the two police officers.

'If you'll excuse me, miss, I think we'd better have a word,' began Cooper, in the deceptively deferential manner he was inclined to adopt at the beginning of an interview. As he spoke he pulled up the one other chair in the little room, leaving Smiley to perch against a box of what seemed to be engine parts.

Cooper at first merely checked details, like the young woman's name and the precise nature of her job. And as he questioned her an intriguing, but not entirely unexpected, scenario began to emerge.

'My name is Jennifer Roth and I'm Ricky's personal assistant,' she said.

Cooper resisted the temptation bluntly to ask straight away if that was all she was. Instead he stuck to the gentle approach. He was that sort of policeman. He believed that softly softly got the best results. It certainly seemed to work for him, anyway.

'And perhaps you could explain to me exactly what that entails.'

She nodded. 'Ricky runs the marina and I run the office, answer the phone, do all the paperwork, send out invoices, pay the bills.'

Jennifer Roth had a very educated voice. Definitely public school, and with more than a little of the inborn sense of superiority which came with the territory, Cooper suspected, despite its having been shaken somewhat that day. He wondered fleetingly about her background.

'I see. And how long have you known Ricky and worked for him?'

'I've worked here for about four years now. I got the job quite soon after Ricky took over here.'

'Did you know him before that?'

Jennifer looked uncertain and said nothing.

'Did you know him before that?'

113

'No,' she said.

'So how did you get hired?'

'I answered a newspaper advertisement,' Jennifer replied quickly enough, but she still seemed unwilling to meet Cooper's eye and her face was distinctly flushed.

Cooper studied her for a moment or two.

'You seem a little upset,' he said gently. Jennifer looked up, meeting his gaze at last. She looked as if she didn't know how to respond. She opened her mouth as if she were about to say something and then closed it again, remaining sullenly silent.

'Are you upset?' he asked, a little more firmly.

She shook her head.

'I think you are,' Cooper persisted.

'Well, a bit, maybe. But wouldn't you be if your boss had just been taken away in handcuffs?'

Cooper bowed his head slightly, acknowledging her point. He was pretty sure it was more than that. But Jennifer Roth seemed to be warming to her theme, or perhaps she just felt this was ground that she could safely explore.

'I mean, what do I do? There are cheques here that need signing. It's Friday. Half the world will descend on us tonight wanting to go out on their boats for the weekend. Ricky does all the basic maintenance work, he's not a qualified mechanic but he's very knowledgeable and he gets the boats ready for most of the owners. Makes sure everything's in working order, and calls in extra help if needed. That's his big Friday job. What am I going to say to them?'

'That's up to you,' responded Cooper. 'We are investigating a very serious matter here, you do realise that, don't you?'

Again Jennifer Roth looked as if she didn't know what to say. Cooper waited until she eventually spoke. He had learned over his years of questioning people that if you presented them with silences which lasted long enough, the vast majority would say something as if somehow compelled to fill the vacuum. And very often he found it a most effective technique.

'Well, I assumed so,' said Jennifer Roth. 'You wouldn't have taken him away in handcuffs if that wasn't so, would you?'

'Absolutely right. And have you any idea what this serious matter is?'

Yet again Jennifer Roth hesitated.

'No,' she said eventually.

'Are you quite sure of that?'

'Quite sure, I've just told you,' Jennifer snapped the reply. She looked petulant more than anything else now. Petulant and sulky.

'We have just arrested the man you know as Ricky Maxwell on suspicion of the murder of his wife and children.'

'Oh.' Jennifer Roth closed her eyes and leaned back in her chair.

'Is that all you have to say?'

Jennifer opened her eyes. Small, vaguely blue eyes, matching the size of her features. Cooper thought he could see panic in them. He wasn't quite sure. Hers was a very strange reaction, not easy to assess.

'I don't know what to say.'

'You don't seem surprised.'

'Of course I'm surprised. Shocked is more the word. I'm shocked.'

Cooper studied her appraisingly again.

Her face was even more flushed. But if that was panic he had seen in those small, now veiled, eyes she gave no further sign of it. She seemed quite calm. Cooper waited to see if she would say any more, ask him any questions, even.

'Is there nothing you want to know about this?' he said after a bit. 'Aren't you curious?'

She half-shook her head, half-nodded. She was confused, you could see that clearly enough.

'No, I don't think so.'

'You haven't even asked when this happened, have you?'

'No. No.' She leaned back in her chair, tipping the two front legs slightly. She looked even more sulky and petulant. Certainly unwilling to co-operate. Then she sighed, in a resigned sort of way.

'OK. When did it happen?' she asked, her voice heavy with exaggerated weariness.

'Twenty-eight years ago,' Cooper replied, and he could not have explained why he was so sure that she already knew the answer. But he was sure. Quite sure, even though she responded only with a slight nod and said nothing more at all.

Abruptly he swung on to another tack.

'So how well do you know Ricky?' he asked.

'I don't know, really. Quite well, I suppose.'

Cooper sighed. His patience was running out. He wasn't sure whether Jennifer Roth was being deliberately obtuse, or whether, perhaps, she wasn't the brightest young woman he had ever encountered.

He took an oblique approach.

'Could you give me your address please, Miss Roth.'

The young woman hesitated just for a moment.

'Flat 5, Heron View Court, Poole,' she said eventually.

Cooper studied her thoughtfully. This was really a result. It was not only the address of one of the luxury apartments in the marina complex, it also had another significance. Cooper had somehow already suspected it, had a gut feeling, but he knew better than to rely on gut feelings and hunches, indeed always thought that hunches were at best a policing myth and at worst a dangerous alternative to a properly conducted investigation.

Somewhat ostentatiously he took his notebook from his pocket and flicked through it, as if checking something. He actually had no need to check anything. But it was several seconds before he looked up and spoke again. Several seconds which he hoped had been at least a little uncomfortable for Jennifer Roth.

'Same address as Richard Marshall,' he remarked expressionlessly.

She glowered at him then, suddenly displaying a flash of raw defiance.

'Ricky. Ricky Maxwell. That's his name.'

'That's the name he chooses to use in order to put his past behind him. A past that involves the murder of three people.'

'I don't believe it,' she said. 'It's just not true. I've never believed it.'

'A moment ago you said you knew nothing about it.'

'I'm in shock. I didn't know what to say. I was trying to think what would be best to say.'

'I'll tell you what it's best to say, always best. The truth. And my advice to you is to stick to it rigidly, Miss Roth.'

There was still defiance in her. She was, he thought, tougher than she looked. She rounded on him indignantly.

'Why are you speaking to me like that? You don't have any right. I'm not being accused of anything. I've never committed any sort of crime in my life. I just know that Ricky is innocent and I don't want to say anything to make things worse for him. That's all.'

Cooper more or less ignored the outburst. 'How long have you been living with Ricky?' he said, putting lightly ironic emphasis on the assumed name.

'Almost four years,' she answered quickly enough.

'So, more or less ever since you've been working here.'

'Yes. Right from the start. I came here to live with Ricky. That's why I moved here.'

'And a very nice address too, if I might say so. Marshall owns the place, does he?' Cooper glanced through the window at the apartment blocks alongside the marina. In this area, one of the most expensive in the UK, the flats with views out across Poole Harbour must be worth a cool half million, he reckoned.

'Yes.' Jennifer Roth's response was brief at first, then she seemed unable to stop herself saying more. 'Ricky made a lot of money on a property he owned in London,' she said defensively. 'Anyway, it's not one of the flats at the front. . . .'

Her voice tailed off. Cooper raised his eyebrows and studied her appraisingly, wondering why she had felt it necessary to explain Marshall's ability to own an expensive apartment, because even the ones which didn't actually have a harbour view would still be worth a great deal of money in this highly sought-after location. Maybe she knew all too well that whatever funds Marshall had used to buy the apartment had not come his way through totally honest means. Cooper himself would happily have bet a month's salary on that.

'So how long have you known Richard Marshall, and how did you meet him?' he persisted.

Jennifer Roth's face creased into an angry frown. For a moment Cooper thought she was going to tell him again that

Marshall was now Ricky Maxwell. But she didn't, although there was an edge of irritation to her reply.

'We were introduced by friends. It was quite a while ago, I can't remember when, and in any case I don't see what it's got to do with anything. We became closer over the years, and eventually it just seemed to happen that I came here to live with him.'

Cooper appraised her, allowed himself a little self-indulgence for a moment.

'You're a great deal younger than him, Miss Roth. Perhaps you could tell me what attracted you so much to him?'

'I could, Detective Sergeant, but I won't. It's none of your business.'

Cooper was aware of the until now impassive DC Smiley struggling to suppress a laugh, and didn't entirely blame him.

Fairly swiftly after that Cooper concluded the interview. He had learned at least one fact, although he did not know what importance it might have, which was that Marshall and Jennifer Roth were having a relationship. But he did not see much chance of learning anything else. Not with her attitude, he didn't – an attitude which would need to be dealt with if she was to be of any further use at all in the investigation, Cooper reckoned. So he decided at least to fire a final salvo before beating a tactical retreat.

'We will be talking again, Miss Roth,' he told her solemnly. 'It may not be me, it may be some of my colleagues, but we will be talking to you again. And, if I were you, I would really think about how you are going to handle this. For your own good, Miss Roth, I would strongly advise you to decide to be as helpful as you possibly can in future. This is a murder inquiry. You have been living with a man whom we believe has committed the most foul and brutal kind of murder.'

Jennifer Roth stood up then, and with surprising speed moved around her desk towards Cooper so that she was standing just a few inches from his chair, looking down at him. Cooper didn't like that. He quickly stood up too. Jennifer Roth really was tall, though. A little over six foot, he thought, certainly taller than him. Cooper was a broad shouldered, well-muscled man, a sportsman, a rugby player. However, he stood a bare five foot eleven, and Jennifer Roth was still looking down on him.

'But he didn't do it, you ridiculous pompous man,' she said. 'Don't you understand? Ricky has never hurt anyone in his life. He couldn't. He's a lovely gentle man. For almost thirty years he's been chased around the country by you people. He had to change his name because of the mud that's stuck to him.'

She paused. And when she continued her voice had risen several octaves.

'He didn't do it, you bastards,' she shouted. 'He didn't do anything. He loved his wife, and he loved his children. He didn't do it.'

And with that she slumped to her knees on the floor of the marina office, and buried her head in her hands. Her shoulders began to shake and she started to weep loudly, her whole body contorted with sobbing convulsions.

When Karen Meadows arrived back at Torquay Police Station Sean Macdonald was sitting in reception. Waiting for her.

Karen was up to her eyes in work. Her adrenalin was on overtime. But she invited him into her office at once. Sean Macdonald, like her, like all of them, had waited a long time for this day.

The Scotsman looked pale and tired, but he was fit and well-preserved for his age. A neat white beard complemented his full head of white hair. His eyes were still sparkling bright and yet so dark that the irises seemed almost black against his pale papery skin.

He gave Karen a small smile as he sat down in one of the armchairs in her office and she took the other one next to him.

'You've been to get him, haven't you?' he began quietly.

She nodded. But she was mildly surprised. Marshall had been safely delivered to the custody suite at the back of the building, driven straight into the private yard there and smartly escorted in by PCs Brownlow and Richardson. Mac couldn't have seen him. And she was sure nobody at the station would have told Mac about the arrest. She'd have them keelhauled if they had. But she had total confidence in her team not to do anything that might jeopardise this case, and in any event the front office clerks would probably not even be aware yet of what was going on.

'How do you know?' she inquired, genuinely interested.

Mac's smile widened. He still had a lovely smile, warm and gentle. But you could see the pain in his eyes: it was etched into the little lines at their corners and ran away from the sides of his mouth, too.

'I've longed for this moment for nearly thirty years,' he said quietly, enunciating each word in that precise way he had, his cut-glass Scottish accent pure and sharp as the first fall of snow on the mountains of his beloved Highlands.

'Night and day, ever since she went . . .' The voice tailed off. There was a catch in it. His smile faded away, slipping into the folds of skin around his mouth, disappearing into the leathery contours of a face that in itself told so much of the tragedy that had overshadowed his long life. He seemed to be struggling to regain control before continuing.

'It's been with me, all of it, all this time, at the back of my mind all day long regardless of what I am doing, and in my dreams every night. And I mean every night. It's always there.'

He looked at her. His eyes were even brighter now. She thought a tear or two might be forming.

'But you know that, lass, don't you?' he said gently.

She nodded. Mac lowered his eyes. But she could see that he was blinking rapidly. She had never seen Sean Macdonald break down, not at any stage since Clara had disappeared. He was a tough dour Scotsman, unaccustomed to showing his feelings. She did know just a little of what he had gone through for all those years. She really did. He was right about that.

'It's like an instinct with me, all of this,' Mac went on. 'When I got here and they said you were out, I just thought: "Yes, they've gone to get him. At last they've gone to get him." And I was right, wasn't I?'

Karen nodded again. 'Yes, Mac. You were right.'

'And he's here now? He's in this building?'

'Yes. He's here. In one of our cells by now, probably. Locked up where he belongs at last.'

Mac took a deep breath, drawing in a big gulp of air very slowly, almost as if it hurt him to do so. His voice was even softer when he began to speak again.

'I can feel him here,' he said. 'I can feel his presence. I knew he was here.'

He reached out, touched her hand with his.

'Can you keep him locked up? Can you do that, Karen lassie? Is he going to go down? Is there going to be justice for my lovely girls at last?'

'Oh, I do hope so, Mac. By God I do.'

'You're a good person, Karen Meadows, and a very fine police officer,' Mac said suddenly.

She was totally taken aback.

'I know a whole lot of people who would disagree with you on both counts,' she remarked wryly.

'And they'd be wrong. You're special, Karen. You're special because you care.'

Karen was afraid she was going to blush. This conversation continued to take her by surprise. She decided not to be clever or flippant. Mac had, after all, opened his heart to her, and she knew that wouldn't have come easily to him. Strange how when you got a result you had longed for, when something you really wanted finally happened or something you hated finally stopped, that was when you weakened. That was when the cracks began to show. It certainly seemed to be that way, and she thought it might be that way for her too – which was why she had to be so careful. She still felt a certain guilt, a certain responsibility. Still felt there were things she could have said, told the police all those years ago that may just have made a difference.

She forced herself to concentrate on the present again. She had, after all, been only a child when it had all happened. Now she was a senior police officer, and she was also in charge of the entire operation. She could not afford to allow any cracks to show. Not today. Not ever. That was her lot. But she could not stop herself sharing at least some of her feelings with this man whose life had been more or less destroyed, she knew, by what had happened to his family.

'Well, I do care about this case, that's for certain,' she admitted.

'I know, lassie. Be watchful, though, won't you. He's like an eel, that man. You grab hold of him, take him in your grasp, and he just slips away. He's done it all his life. A catalogue of crimes, some small, one truly terrible, and he's always got away with it. I know he went to jail once, but that was a light sentence. He should have got at least six years, not six months, for ruining all those people's lives, stealing their life's savings.'

Sean Macdonald spat the words out. His grip on Karen's hand had tightened so much now that it hurt. Obliquely she thought how strong he still was for his age.

'He mustn't be allowed to get away with it again, lassie,' he said. 'Not now. Not when we are so close after all this time. He mustn't be allowed to get off. . . .' Mac's voice tailed off again. 'To have him arrested at last, just when I'd almost stopped hoping. If he got off now, well, I don't think I could take it, Karen, I really don't think I could.'

Karen understood exactly how he felt. The Scotsman was not alone.

'I don't think I could either, Mac,' she responded softly.

Mac stayed for just under half an hour. He would remain in Torquay until after Marshall was charged, he told Karen, and when he left the station she was even more determined than ever that Richard Marshall would be charged and brought to justice.

There were, however, one or two hurdles to be jumped. Notably the Chief Constable and the Crown Prosecution Service. Both had to be convinced that this time the case was a goer – that at last Marshall could be charged with murder, and that the charge could be made to stick.

However, the evidence, although damning, remained circumstantial, and Karen felt that it was vital to continue to press the investigation and make every possible effort to strengthen the case against Marshall. Anything which could be gleaned from the man himself might prove of immense importance. So even though Marshall's coolness under questioning was legend, Karen decided that she would interview him herself. At least she would have nobody but herself to blame if no progress was made, she thought caustically.

Also, she somehow felt that she knew the man, knew what made him tick, knew how he would react. And she couldn't help hoping, although aware that this was an extremely long shot with Richard Marshall, that she might be the one to make him break. She felt so close to it all and had been involved, albeit peripherally, with the case for so long that it seemed strange to her, almost hard to believe, that she had never previously questioned Marshall. So strong was her sense of involvement that it seemed even more difficult to believe that, until earlier that day in Poole, she had never actually met Richard Marshall since she had lived next door to him as a child.

The sense of anticipation developed into nervous excitement as she gave instructions for Marshall to be taken to an interview room. DC Tompkins and PC Brownlow were already there when she arrived.

Marshall didn't look up, didn't speak, and in no way acknowledged her entry into the room. She studied him in silence for at least two minutes. Two could play at that game, she thought. Marshall looked sullen more than anything else. If he was nervous or afraid he gave little sign of it. In fact, Karen was afraid that she might be experiencing more nerves than he was. Either that or he was an extremely good actor. Karen hoped that it was the latter. At least that would give her an outside chance of making a breakthrough of some sort, she thought.

With one hand Marshall was playing with a wayward strand of his curly hair. With the other he drummed a silent rhythm on the table. He looked bored. Disinterested. He watched her as she watched him and eventually he gave a little tired sigh and said: 'Can we get on with it then?'

His voice was clear and controlled. He really was hard to fathom, she thought, and it was disconcerting. Particularly when you considered his Houdini-like history in his dealings with the law. The expression in his eyes gave little away. His fleshy but still handsome features displayed mild irritation more than anything else.

He was still wearing the blue overalls he'd had on when they'd arrested him. Apart from what looked like a freshly acquired oil stain they were very clean. He sat in as relaxed a way as it was possible to sit in an upright wooden chair, which he had turned slightly away from the table so that he could stretch out his long legs.

Karen noticed that his blue canvas boat shoes were also pristine. She looked at his hands. They too were clean and well cared for, the nails clipped short, but in a very manicured kind of way. His fingers were long and sinewy. They were strong hands. Hands which may have strangled a woman and two little girls. Or maybe he smothered them. Could he have used a weapon? A blunt instrument to batter them to death with, a knife to plunge into them? Karen shivered. She still feared that the truth would never be known. She tried to feel confident about this impending interview. But she didn't. Not any more. Just looking at Marshall had made her doubt her ability to get through to him at all. She tried to put that out of her mind, but it wasn't easy.

Bill Talbot had always said that Richard Marshall was inhuman, that the man did not feel and think the way most human beings did. Talbot had once told her that he thought Marshall experienced no guilt because his whole morality was different from that of the vast majority of the human race. He had been able to live with his terrible crime because he was so easily able to justify his own behaviour to himself, able to justify everything. Bill Talbot reckoned that Marshall believed he was the centre of the universe and that his own survival was all that really mattered, that he was the most important person in the world, and probably the cleverest. Marshall had a pretty low opinion of the police and their investigatory efforts, that was for certain; Karen could see that clearly enough in every aspect of his demeanour as he sat opposite her in the interview room.

And in view of their complete lack of success so far, twenty-eight years after the event, Karen had to agree that he had a point.

Bill Talbot also reckoned that Richard Marshall was completely unbreakable. Karen hoped that he wasn't right. She tried to make herself believe, really believe, that she was the one who could make him talk. She was so aware, in spite of the new evidence, how much still rested on this interview.

'We'll start when I say. And we'll stop when I say,' she told Marshall sharply. 'You are no longer in control of anything, Mr Marshall, so let's get that straight from the start, shall we?'

'Maxwell.'

'No. You have been arrested as Richard Marshall. That was your name when you committed the crime we have arrested you for, it is still your legal name and it is the name you will be charged under. I've just told you, you no longer call the shots, and you may as well get used to it.'

Marshall shrugged, held out both hands palms upwards.

'What's in a name, anyway?' he inquired.

There again was that laconic note in his voice that she had first noticed in Poole. His lips curled in a mocking smile. She had an almost overwhelming urge to slap his face and wipe the smirk off it.

'Right,' she said, briskly motioning to PC Brownlow to switch on the double tape recorder – an extremely neat state-of-the-art digital affair now, very different from the big clumsy machines which had been in operation when Marshall had last been arrested.

'Interview with Richard Marshall, present DC Tompkins, PC Brownlow and Detective Superintendent Karen Meadows.' She glanced down at her watch. 'Interview begins 5.15 p.m.'

Then she looked up at Marshall, squared her shoulders, and dived straight in, going for the shock approach.

'You should know that the remains of a body almost certainly identifiable as your wife Clara have been found,' she announced.

If Marshall was shocked he gave no sign of it at all. Instead he leaned further back in his chair and the smile widened.

'Really?' he remarked almost lazily. 'I saw something in the paper, actually. Pure speculation. You don't believe what you read in the papers if you've got any sense, do you?'

He looked and sounded extraordinarily sure of himself. But then, Karen reminded herself, if Marshall had killed his little family, as she was so sure that he had, then he would know full well where he had dumped their bodies, and he would be as certain as anyone could be that no body was likely to be found after all that time in the depths of the Atlantic Ocean.

He was, however, wrong about that, which was Karen's trump card. Freak circumstances had preserved at least one of those bodies, trapped it and kept it to some extent intact. Freak circumstances had also thrown up from the ocean bed that Rolex watch which could be traced beyond any reasonable doubt to Clara Marshall. Freak circumstances had at last presented the Devon and Cornwall Constabulary with that stroke of luck John Kelly had said was their due at last.

It was going to give her a lot of pleasure to relate all this to Marshall. Sometimes you held back from telling your suspect much about your case against them. Karen believed this was a situation in which it was right to tell him everything. Indeed she felt it was her only hope of breaking him, if there was even the remotest prospect of that, she thought, as she stared into his mocking eyes.

'On this occasion the newspaper reports have been spot on,' said Karen.

Marshall's eyes narrowed. You could almost see his thought processes. 'You've been able to positively identify a body that would therefore have been in the ocean for twenty-eight years,' he responded eventually, his voice casual but his words chosen with infinite care.

'Yes, we have, as a matter of fact,' Karen responded equally casually, making a big effort to remain calm.

Marshall flinched, she was sure he flinched. It was almost imperceptible, though. For a fleeting moment she thought she saw fear in those pale blue eyes, then it was gone. This man gave so little away.

She explained it all then, briefly but succinctly. And when she told him about the watch, the watch that was almost definitely Clara's and which had been found by her body, she noticed that he turned his face away, perhaps so that she could no longer see his eyes. She paused several times to let him speak if he wished, wondering if he could be tempted into some indiscretion. He wasn't, of course. He remained, outwardly at least, as cool as ever.

When she had finished he still did not speak until she actually asked him what he had to say. Marshall shrugged his big shoulders then, and turned to her again, the mockery back in his eyes – if, indeed, it had ever left. He really was a smug bastard.

'So?' he inquired. 'Even if it's Clara's watch it doesn't necessarily mean you've found her body. And if it is her body, well, I still have no idea how it got there. I didn't put it there. I never touched any of my family. I wouldn't ever have done such a thing. Not ever.'

'Mr Marshall, you were seen taking your boat out of Torquay Harbour at night, right after Clara and your girls were seen for the last time. We have witnesses to that. Now your wife's body has been found at sea, and I promise you absolutely that it is her and that our identification of her will almost certainly already stand up in any court in the land, and that we are confidently expecting further confirmation. I therefore put it to you also that any jury would accept the quite reasonable deduction that you killed Clara and the girls and that you dumped all three of their bodies at sea.'

'No. I didn't.' Marshall didn't bat an eyelid. His voice remained steady. 'You'll never shake me, you know. I didn't do it.'

Karen could feel the frustration already building up in her. He was an infuriating man. No wonder the case had bugged Bill Talbot so much, she thought.

'So it was all just a coincidence, was it?' she inquired, matching his earlier sarcasm with her own.

'Yes, it was,' he replied easily. 'Just a coincidence.'

Karen leaned forward across the table.

'I don't believe in those sorts of coincidences, Mr Marshall,' she said. 'And neither will a court of law.'

Eight

Karen interviewed Marshall solidly for almost two hours. At the end she reckoned she was probably considerably more exhausted than he was. Her prime suspect appeared to have remained singularly unmoved by all that was happening around him. He did not budge an inch. The passage of time had not changed him, it seemed. Although initially shaken by his arrest, he had settled back into what she had been told had always been his approach to any investigation into the disappearance of his family.

Marshall continued to waver between a kind of arrogant contempt and a laconic sarcasm. His confidence never seemed to falter. He even waived his rights to a solicitor throughout.

'I am innocent, why would I need a lawyer?' he inquired.

Karen decided that the only hope was to keep up the pressure in an attempt to wear Marshall down. She might be wearied by her verbal contest with him, but one advantage she did have over the man was that she was not alone. She could step down and ask others to take over. She decided on a policy of continuing to interview Marshall, with the minimum number of breaks allowed, for as long as the law permitted, using various members of her team in succession.

Then somewhere around 10 p.m., after munching a couple of chocolate bars to replenish her flagging energy, she resolved to have another go herself.

To her immense irritation Marshall's face positively lit up when she entered the interview room, breaking into a sardonic grin which stretched from ear to ear.

'Ah, Detective Superintendent,' he began, addressing her before she could him and thus yet again giving every appearance of being in charge, something he was extremely good at, Karen reflected.

'I've been puzzling about you all day. Finally I've got it. Karen Meadows. How could I ever have forgotten? Little Karen Meadows from next door. The lovely Margaret's daughter.'

The grin became a leer. His voice took on a husky note.

'And what a woman that Margaret Meadows was.'

His eyes were fixed on Karen's. They were both mocking and challenging.

DC Tompkins, who was already in the interview room, was also staring at Karen. Involuntarily she glanced towards him. But as usual Tompkins' expression gave little away. Karen turned her attention back to Marshall. She could see that he remembered every bit as clearly as she did the fateful day on which he had been upstairs with her mother when Karen had unexpectedly returned home early from school. She was also sure that he would have realised that she knew, had known for all these years, that he and her mother had had some kind of an affair. And he probably also realised that she had told nobody.

It was bad enough for Karen that she was now heading the Marshall investigation while aware that she had kept quiet about the affair for nearly thirty years. It was even worse to be aware that Marshall knew that, too. She had always told herself that nothing that had gone on between him and her mother could be relevant, but she actually knew from long experience that it may well have been, because you never could tell when you were investigating a crime. Sometimes the most inconsequential piece of information later proved to be crucial.

He appreciated all of that, the bastard. She was quite certain. Richard Marshall was a very perceptive and intuitive man – which was perhaps one of the reasons why he had gotten away with all that he had over the years.

'Oh yes, oh yes, what a woman!' Marshall repeated, still challenging Karen with his eyes.

Karen had a quick temper which had caused her trouble more than once in her career. She felt the rage rising in her and struggled to contain it. It was quite a struggle, too. Only the knowledge that it was Marshall's intention to make her lose her temper stopped her from doing so.

She did not, however, feel able to sit down and interview him again. In any case she reckoned it would be a waste of time for her to do so now. Unfortunately, Marshall had already won this session on points, and the best thing for her to do was walk away from it, she reckoned. But not without issuing a broadside or two.

She turned to DC Tompkins, still sitting patiently waiting for her, a typical police detective in his nondescript brown suit, his long, thin, slightly morose face as taciturn as ever. Yet she knew all too well that he would have taken in everything that Marshall had said.

'I suddenly have some other business to attend to so I'm sending someone else in to join you,' she told him obliquely and then continued with a blatant lie. 'Actually, we have received some more new information that I need to deal with right away.'

She swung round to face Marshall again.

'You can play all the games you like, sunshine,' she said, and there was low menace in her voice. 'It doesn't much matter what you tell us. I doubt you'd know the truth if it hit you full on. But we don't need you to say a damned thing any more. We've got enough on you to keep you locked up for the rest of your life. You can mock, you can laugh, you can kid yourself you're the cleverest bastard that ever walked the earth. All that's academic now. This time you're going to be charged. What I'm doing now is tying up every loose end there is because I'm not having you slip the net this time.

'You're going down, Marshall. Make no mistake about it. Finally your luck has run out.'

She was aware of DC Tompkins looking at her in mild surprise and it was rare indeed for the veteran detective to visibly display a response to anything. But she just hadn't been able to resist making her little speech. Without waiting for a reply she turned on her heel in order to leave the little room.

But as she opened the door she paused and glanced back over her shoulder.

'Do you understand what I'm telling you?' she inquired, almost mildly, of Marshall. 'Don't even think you're getting bail. This is it. I intend to make absolutely sure that you never step foot outside a prison again. It's over, Marshall. It's really over.'

And for the second time that day she was sure that she could see fear in his eyes.

She found she was still trembling with suppressed rage when she returned to her office. It had been extremely gratifying to wipe the smirk off Maxwell's face, but she was well aware that it had been self-indulgent, too. Once again she had probably not behaved in the way a police superintendent probably should have done. She just hadn't been able to help it.

Worse though, most of what she had told the man was unmitigated bullshit. Yes, it was her intention that everything she had said would come to be the truth. But although she thought the case against Marshall was now a strong one, it was a long way from copper-bottomed. She was not even one hundred per cent certain that she would be able to charge him. At least not yet. First of all she had to convince the Crown Prosecution Service and the chief constable. And the very thought of confronting Harry Tomlinson, not her favourite top cop by a long chalk, made Karen feel extremely weary.

She reached for the bottle of mineral water on her desk. It was warm and flat. She pulled a face. It was, however, liquid, which at that moment provided relief enough. Her mouth and throat were so dry they felt as if they had been sandpapered. Tension was responsible for that as much as the muggy heat of the day, she suspected.

She checked her watch. It was almost 11 p.m. She was exhausted. And still hungry in spite of the chocolate. She reckoned she might as well go home and try to start really early the following morning. There was, in any case, little more that she could do. Tomlinson could wait until the next day. He was probably off at one of his myriad politically motivated dinners, and in any event there was just a chance that, between them, the team might have worn Marshall down a bit by the following day. Not much of one though, if the bastard ran true to form, she reflected grimly. But as she prepared to leave the station she called through to the incident room and gave instructions for the pressure to be kept up on Marshall throughout the night.

'I want Marshall given absolutely the minimum rest,' she ordered. 'I want a team available to interview him continuously, every minute that we're allowed. Tell them to push. Really push. Our best hope is still to break the bastard. But also tell them to be sure to keep within the rules. Stick to the book. I don't want him getting off on some blasted technicality, that really would be the end.

'And it would be just our luck and Richard Marshall's.'

She leaned back in her chair and considered any other last-minute things she had to do before leaving. Oh God, she thought, Phil. The detective sergeant had also had a long day and had been trying to call her all evening to relate it in full.

He had already told her briefly about Jennifer Roth, but she had not had time to listen to the full account of his Dorset investigations.

Swiftly she dialled the number of his mobile phone.

'I'm in heavy traffic, I'd better not talk,' he said. 'I might get arrested.'

Karen didn't even manage a giggle.

'Where are you?' she inquired.

'On the Newton Abbot road, nearly back, but I think there may have been an accident or something.'

'Have you eaten?'

'Sandwiches.'

'Fancy telling me all about it over a pint and a curry?'

'I do.'

Phil hadn't hesitated. And she knew that it wasn't just that he always seemed to be hungry, either. There couldn't be a police officer alive who worked harder or longer hours than he did. Except her perhaps, she thought. It was a bonus that they enjoyed each other's company. Not for the first time she reflected on how lucky she was to have him on her team.

'See you at Akbar's as soon as you can make it, then,' she said. 'I'll be about fifteen minutes.'

Karen left her car in the station car park. The ten-minute walk to the restaurant would do her good and she felt like having a decent drink. She thought she might well get a taxi home.

The atmosphere at Akbar's was restful and relaxing. All dark red plush upholstery and similar wall coverings blending into one in the subdued lighting. Karen arrived first, but Phil joined her not long after, before she had even got around to ordering herself a drink. Although he was obviously tired, he also seemed excited. You could see that he was pumped up.

'You look how I feel,' she told him. 'Marshall's being impossible, of course, but at least he's inside. I don't know whether to collapse or cheer.'

'That's just how it is, boss. We're all the same, you know, even the really young guys. Everybody wants Marshall. Nobody will relax, though, until he's charged, and even then not really until he's convicted. That's the trouble with this one. You can't quite believe it, can you?'

Karen grunted. 'It's been a long haul,' she said, as she ordered two pints of lager and passed Cooper the menu.

'Thanks, boss,' replied the DS. 'You've no idea how much I'm looking forward to a square meal and a few beers.'

'Oh yes, I have,' said Karen. 'I really have.'

By the time they had finished their main courses, chicken masala, chicken tikka, and a selection of vegetable curries, Phil had told Karen all about his inquiries and given her a run-down on Jennifer Roth.

'She's a piece of work, boss, I'm telling you,' he said. 'At first she just seemed shocked rigid. But as soon as I started to push her she changed into something I hadn't expected. Like a trapped animal she was. She's a snooty bitch, too. And she won't have a word said against Marshall. Not a word.'

'Yup. Well, that much is par for the course. God knows what he does to the women in his life but they all seem totally taken in by him.'

Karen tried not to think about just how much her mother may have fallen into that category. She called for another two pints of lager, their third each.

Cooper held up a hand to stop her. 'I'd better not, I'm driving,' he said. 'The days when you could tell the pointy hat brigade you were in the job and they'd go away are long gone.'

Karen grinned. She knew that as Cooper was thirteen years her junior those days must be mere mythology to him, but she could remember them for real.

'Where've you parked?' she asked him. 'My car's at the nick. I'm leaving it there. To hell with it, Phil. You don't arrest Richard Marshall every day of your life.'

Cooper grinned back at her. 'You're right, boss,' he said. 'My motor's in the car park round the corner. As long as I get there early in the morning it'll be all right overnight. I'll have Sarah give me a lift in. In which case, how about a whisky chaser?'

'Done,' said Karen, and ordered two large ones.

They stayed in the restaurant until past 1 a.m., demolishing two more whiskies each.

'Do you ever think about how the law was in the old Wild West, boss?' asked Cooper casually at one point, when the booze had definitely kicked in.

Karen giggled. 'Can't say it's a major preoccupation, Phil,' she confessed.

'Yeah well, those cowboy lawmen could get away with murder, and did, didn't they?' Phil went on. 'If they'd got a fucking Richard Marshall in their territory they'd have shot him or lynched him straight away. Now, I'm not saying that's right, boss, no, I'm not. But you got to admit it wouldn't half save a lot of unnecessary bother.'

Cooper, whom Karen knew was not a big drinker at all, was obviously feeling no pain having downed the best part of three large whiskies. He was very very serious and spoke with careful deliberation. Karen became almost overwhelmed by an irrepressible urge to giggle. Eventually she could contain herself no longer. And her suppressed mirth came out in the form of an explosive snort.

Still apparently very serious, Cooper made a show of wiping his face with one hand and then the lapels of his jacket.

'Sorry, Phil, did I get you?' Karen asked, in between hoots of laughter.

'Think you did, boss. It's all right. I just don't know what I said that was so funny.'

The laughter really kicked in then. Uncontrollably.

'That's it, that's it,' she spluttered. 'You really don't, do you?'

Cooper looked bewildered. 'No, I don't, boss,' he said, downing the last of his whisky.

'You are quite wonderful sometimes, Phil, particularly when you've been drinking,' she continued through giggles. 'Oh, and when we're off duty I do wish to God you wouldn't call me "boss". That makes it even funnier, if you see what I mean.'

'No, I don't see, really, boss—'

'Oh Phil, please.'

'Right. All right. OK. Here goes. K-A-R-E-N. Karen.'

Phil beamed at her.

'Thank you,' she said.

'Did that sound all right, boss?' asked Cooper then.

She shot him a sharp look.

He grinned broadly. She pretended to throw the remains of her lager over him. It was all very childish. But it really felt good to unwind and play the fool.

'Go on, Karen,' he said, now using her name quite naturally. 'You may as well chuck it and finish the job.'

She knew it wasn't that funny. Cooper was right. None of it was that funny. But fuelled by alcohol, weakened by weariness and fired up with tension it seemed absolutely side-splittingly hilarious.

They completed their meal and paid their bill in hopeless fits of giggles. And they were still giggling when they climbed a little unsteadily into the taxi Karen had ordered. Karen's flat was almost on Cooper's route home to Paignton, so she asked the driver to drop her off first and then go on.

At West Beach Heights she turned to Cooper. 'I really needed that, Phil, it was a great release. Thank you.'

'I know, boss,' he said. 'I mean Karen. And thank you, too.'

He turned to her directly then, his grin cracking his face wide open yet again.

'You're great company. D'you know that?'

'Not sure that I do, Phil.'

He put one hand on her arm. He was deadly serious again.

'We must do it again some time.'

'Yes, we must.'

Very deliberately Karen kept her voice light, but something made her touch Phil's hand with her free one.

'I really enjoyed myself,' she said quietly.

'Me too.'

They stared at each other for a few seconds, and for just a fleeting moment Karen considered asking him upstairs. At once she dismissed the thought, mentally giving herself a sound smack.

'Good-night then, Phil,' she said, pulling her hand and arm free, drawing away from him and opening the door of the cab.

''Night, boss,' said Phil, and the return to the more formal mode of address seemed to Karen to indicate the sergeant's realisation that that rather curious moment of special contact between them, whatever it had really been, had passed. But then, as she stepped out and was about to shut the cab door, he leaned quickly forward and kissed her briefly on the cheek.

'Sweet dreams,' he said.

And then he was gone. She could just make out his head in the back of the cab. He didn't turn round once. It was almost as if that brief kiss hadn't happened.

She watched the cab until it disappeared towards Paignton round the first corner of the sea front road. Then she swung around and walked briskly into the building. She stepped into the old erratic lift which did its usual shaking and juddering act, but for once did not even consider its idiosyncrasies. Her head was buzzing.

Attempting to pull herself together she gave herself a telling-off for even considering inviting Phil Cooper in. A much longed-for arrest and a skinful of alcohol were no excuse for such reckless stupidity. In her much younger days Karen had once come close to losing her entire career because of an unwise romantic liaison. Indeed, only the innate decency and judgement of that most unlikely of creatures, a tabloid journalist in the form of one John Kelly, then a top Fleet Street man, had saved her.

She shook her head, partly to clear it and partly in disbelief at her behaviour. At her age, and with her seniority in the job, it was totally absurd even to have considered embarking on any kind of relationship with a married junior officer. And a much younger one at that. Even a one-night stand would be trouble. In fact, perhaps particularly a one-night stand.

She had considered it, though. Very seriously. And she couldn't help wondering if Phil Cooper would have accepted her invitation had she issued it. Something, maybe that goodnight kiss, light though it had been, made her pretty sure that he would have done.

On the fifth floor she stepped out of the lift and made her way along the corridor into flat number 12, trying desperately to concentrate only on her work, which was after all currently rather important, and to think just of what needed to be done the next day on the Richard Marshall case. But it was no good. Phil Cooper would not go away. She could see his face far too clearly, feel his hand on her arm and his lips on her cheek. And as she undressed for bed she realised that she was feeling distinctly horny. It had been some months since she had had sex at all, and then it had been little more than a one-night stand with an old flame.

Karen liked sex a lot. But she had never seemed to be very good at relationships, or indeed at picking the right man. Phil Cooper was most definitely not the right man.

'What you need is a cold shower, my girl,' she told herself sternly.

She had, however, no intention whatsoever of taking one. Instead she preferred to curl up in the warmth of her lone bed and imagine that Phil was there with her. She knew she shouldn't, that she was entering into dangerous territory, but she couldn't help it.

'Well, a bit of fantasising won't do any harm, will it?' she muttered, as if finding a need to justify her actions even to herself.

She knew all too well what lay at the root of the problem. She laughed too easily with Phil Cooper, much too easily. That night the laughter had been so very welcome. And when she laughed with a man like that, somehow it always did something to her heart. She pulled the covers up around her and in the warm and private darkness of her bed she gave in to all her fantasies.

'To hell with it,' she muttered. With one hand she shoved a protesting Sophie off her usual sleeping place on top of the bed, as she did not really wish to share this moment with a cat. With the other she reached between her legs. And as the pleasure spread through her body there was no way that she could stop herself imagining that it was Phil Cooper touching her and driving her wild.

Nine

In the morning Karen woke with a hangover accompanied by a strong sense of foreboding which she couldn't quite explain to herself. She just didn't feel optimistic about the day or about anything much really. The euphoria of the night before had completely evaporated along with the happier effects of the alcohol. She was now left with the residuals, and it wasn't a good feeling.

She jacked herself out of bed and made for the shower. Her head ached. Her mouth felt like a cross between an ashtray and an old sack.

Oh, God, she thought, remembering what she had so nearly done the night before. And indeed what she had done – admittedly, all alone.

As she brushed her teeth she considered the tasks facing her that day. The biggest and most problematic was that she had to go and see the chief constable at headquarters in Exeter.

Karen neither liked nor respected Harry Tomlinson, and she was quietly confident that the feeling was mutual. She thought the chief constable was a small-minded pedantic little man more interested in politics than policing. And she had a fair idea that he considered her far too much of a maverick, too much of a free spirit, not enough of a stickler for rules and regulations. She also reckoned he was enough of a dinosaur still to be prejudiced against women police officers in senior jobs.

She peered at her somewhat red eyes in the mirror. Her mouth still tasted disgusting so she decided to give her teeth a second brushing. It didn't help much but three cups of tea lifted her slightly. Unusually she gave the cigarettes a miss. She didn't think her throat or her lungs could take any tobacco that morning. She had no idea how many she had smoked the night before, but she knew it was a lot.

She kicked her favourite designer trainers out from under the bed and began to rummage amid the obligatory pile of clothes covering the little Victorian nursing chair while she decided what she was going to wear that day. Reluctantly she knew she must take the Harry Tomlinson meeting into consideration. It would help if she didn't antagonise him just by her appearance. Karen justified her usual extremely casual look – her much-loved trainers, baggy shirts and jackets, roll-up cotton trousers, sometimes even jeans – by saying that she was, after all, a detective. Detectives were supposed to blend. Detectives were supposed to fit into the communities in which they were doing their detecting. Neat little business costumes and high heels were not only dated but set women who wore them apart from the vast majority. Anyway, she managed to force a grin even though it hurt, she didn't like those sorts of clothes. It didn't suit her to be dressed up like a dog's dinner, and she knew it. It made her feel old, too. She liked young funky clothes, slightly off the wall. One of her favourite pairs of trainers appeared at a glance to be made of plain white canvas, but was actually covered with tiny silver spangles which danced and glittered as she walked.

However, for the chief constable Karen knew she must attempt to look the part of a detective superintendent – or rather the part as Harry Tomlinson saw it.

She delved into the back of her wardrobe and emerged with a dark grey linen trouser suit of the permanently crumpled look she favoured for practical reasons as much as anything else – not quite the tailored outfit Tomlinson would prefer but something of a compromise – and a cream T-shirt. Trainers, she told herself sorrowfully, would never do, so she plunged into the assorted shoes piled high in the bottom of the wardrobe and eventually found a pair of tan-coloured suede mules with small built-up heels which she reckoned Tomlinson might almost approve of and which she could just about bear to have on her feet. Then she gritted her teeth and prepared for war, which is what her meetings with the chief constable were inclined to resemble. Picking up her bag she rummaged in it for her car keys and only then remembered.

'I don't fucking believe it,' she said aloud.

Until that moment she had completely forgotten that she had left her car at the police station. It had seemed such a good idea the night before. But then, so had quite a lot of activities which most definitely would not have been. Now it seemed she had drunk so much that she was suffering from alcoholic amnesia.

Still cursing colourfully she grabbed the phone and dialled the number of her local minicab firm.

'What do you mean, twenty minutes?' she cried frantically. 'I need a car now. Right away. All right, all right. Just do your best, will you?'

Her head was beginning to ache. This really was a wretched start to the day. Karen slumped into a chair. She had no choice but to wait. Perhaps a black coffee would help. She hurried into the kitchen and checked her watch for the umpteenth time. Unfortunately she could not turn the hands back.

It was five minutes past eight. Her appointment with the chief constable and the locally based CPS chief prosecutor was for 9 a.m. She had planned to allow an hour for her drive to HQ at Middlemore thirty-five miles away. There was all that holiday traffic to contend with, too. All too often in the summer, particularly in the mornings and evenings and even more so in the days close to a bank holiday, the first stretch of the journey, the road between Torquay and Newton Abbot, could be jammed solid. She realised she would now be lucky to have half an hour to get to Exeter, and that was never going to be enough. Why, oh why, did she always contrive to put herself at a disadvantage?

There was absolutely no way she was not going to be late.

The cab made it in fifteen minutes, not twenty. But the five-minute reprieve did not help much. It took ten minutes to get to the police station. That could have been a much longer journey on a bright sunny August morning in one of the nation's holiday capitals, but it still didn't help.

By the time Karen had retrieved her car it was 8.35 a.m. She was in deep lumber. She was about to put herself on the back foot, that was the worst of it, and how she hated that. The traffic at least moved after a fashion all the way to Newton

Abbot, but it was a crawl. And although she broke every speed limit on the brief stretch of the motorway-standard A38 leading to Devon's ancient county town, she did not arrive at the Middlemore HQ until 9.15. By the time she reached the CC's office, having run across the car park and along the corridors, it was nearly 9.25, and she was sweating, flushed, out of breath and generally in a state of dishevelment.

'Go straight in,' said Tomlinson's secretary. 'He *is* waiting for you.'

The emphasis was heavily on the word *is*. The bloody woman didn't quite sniff as she spoke to Karen, but she actually did contrive to look down her long nose.

'Thank you so much,' Karen responded icily.

She thought she probably disliked Tomlinson's secretary, a neat-looking creature, superior in manner, with a geometric yellow haircut, every bit as much as she disliked the man himself. The secretary was of that extremely irritating species who had taken on an aura of self-importance even more highly developed than that of her employer.

She knocked on the door to Tomlinson's office. His voice boomed at her.

'Enter.'

Karen reflected that it was like something out of Oscar Wilde. *Enter* indeed. Who did the bloody man think he was?

She entered.

Tomlinson, a small trim man, every bit as neatly made and turned out as his secretary, was sitting at his overly large desk directly facing the door, cup of coffee in his hand, immaculately shiny-shod feet propped up on the desk before him.

The chief prosecutor, James Cromby-White, with whom Karen had had many previous dealings, all too many of them tricky to say the least, was sitting to Tomlinson's right in one of the squashy black leather armchairs which lined the chief constable's spacious office. He grunted a greeting at Karen, but made no attempt to rise. As he was grossly overweight, a man of moderate height of five foot seven or eight maximum, weighing in at around eighteen or nineteen stone, Karen reckoned, he probably had great difficulty manoeuvring himself out of the low-slung chairs.

However, Harry Tomlinson, a deceptively agile little man, swung his legs off the desk and positively bounced to his feet as Karen closed the office door behind her.

'Ah, Detective Superintendent, you've decided to grace us with your presence after all, have you?' he boomed.

'Sorry, sir,' said Karen, who already had her excuse to hand. 'Car trouble, I'm afraid. . . .'

She may as well not have bothered to prepare herself. Tomlinson wasn't even listening. Instead, the diminutive police chief pointedly tapped the face of his watch with the fingers of his right hand.

'Time, Detective Superintendent,' he told her. 'Time. Time and discipline. The very key to policing. If you can't discipline yourself, how can you expect to discipline others?'

Karen winced. She couldn't believe that the bloody man was giving her a dressing-down as if she were a badly behaved schoolgirl, in front of Cromby-White, the leading light of Devon and Cornwall's Crown Prosecution Service. Her head hurt. Her hangover was still raging. What she wanted to do was to square up to Tomlinson and tell him a few home truths – like, with the hours she worked and the pressures she had to carry, it shouldn't really be the end of the world if she got herself wrecked occasionally and on this occasion had been a few minutes late for a meeting. To Tomlinson, of course, such a thing was the end of the world. And this was not a day for confrontation. Karen wanted and needed a result.

She saw that both men had her Richard Marshall report to hand. All that mattered was that she got the go-ahead to charge the bastard. She could not allow herself any self-indulgence.

'You're absolutely right, sir, and I really am very sorry,' she said, making no attempt to elaborate on her carefully crafted excuse. She was aware of James Cromby-White looking mildly surprised. Her intrinsic lack of respect for authority was well enough known, after all.

Tomlinson, too, looked surprised. He would certainly not have expected that kind of response from her. Indeed, she thought, he may have been deliberately trying to wind her up, to make her react in the confrontational way she had been tempted towards, to make her put herself at a further disadvantage. He was, after all, a prime operator when it came to political manoeuvring.

Whether or not that had been the CC's intention, Karen's meek reply, even though it had nearly choked her, might, she thought, prove to be her first halfway intelligent move of the day. Tomlinson seemed instantly appeased. She knew well enough how he liked servility – or respect for your superiors, as he would no doubt phrase it.

'Good, I'm glad to hear it,' he said. 'Right.' He consulted the watch he had so pointedly tapped. 'As we have lost almost half an hour of the time I can give to this meeting I suggest we get on with it. OK? James and I are both familiar with what is going on, Superintendent. No new developments since you filed this report, I don't suppose?'

Karen had completed her report of Marshall's arrest and interrogation to date just before leaving Torquay Police Station the previous evening and e-mailed it to the chief constable.

'No, sir.'

'And still not any joy from interviewing the man?'

'Not really, sir. Marshall's a pretty cool customer, as you know, or he wouldn't have got away with what he did for this long.'

'Indeed. So the question is –' Tomlinson glanced towards the top CPS lawyer who was so far giving nothing away. '– do we have enough to charge him?'

'I'm sure we do, sir,' said Karen quickly, determined to have her say before Cromby-White started to point out the shortcomings of the prosecution case so far. 'We have a body that we can already identify beyond all reasonable doubt as that of Clara Marshall, chiefly because we have found her Rolex watch. We know that Marshall had the means to dump a body at sea, in that he had a boat and is an experienced sailor. It is possible that this case may have been reopened eventually simply on the grounds of time, even without bodies. It would, after all, be without precedent I think for a woman and two children to disappear in the way that Clara Marshall and her children did and then to be discovered safe and well after this length of time. But we now have much more than that. We have a body at last, and don't forget we have witnesses who saw Marshall take his boat out and set off on a course towards Berry Head at around the time of his family's disappearance.'

'That's all very well, Karen,' said the chief constable. 'I admit that superficially we now have a decent case but the evidence is still circumstantial. If only Marshall would crack. Do you think there's any chance of that?'

'What, after twenty-eight years?' Karen realised as she spoke that she probably sounded challenging, something she had been trying so hard to avoid. She couldn't help it. What did Tomlinson expect, for God's sake? There was something about his manner which always made it difficult for her to maintain professional distance, and with this case and her involvement in it she was finding it even more difficult.

'I don't see why not, if he's properly handled, of course. Everyone has a cracking point. Even the Richard Marshalls of this world, Karen.'

Tomlinson's eyes were narrow. His use of her Christian name might have appeared on the surface to be conciliatory, a gesture of friendship and informality, but Karen merely found it patronising. She had little doubt that her chief disliked her every bit as much as she disliked him. She thanked God that he was due to retire the following year because she did not know how long she was likely to survive having such a tricky relationship with her chief constable. Tomlinson had been a stopgap appointment, given the job largely because of his political expertise and his instinctive knack for avoiding controversy and maintaining the status quo.

Karen had adored his predecessor, John Mason, a visionary high flier who had reached the office of chief constable at the age of forty-two but had died, completely unexpectedly, of an aneurysm five years later. However, Mason's fresh and liberal approach to policing had not always met with approval in high places. He had opened all manner of cans of worms which nobody quite knew how to deal with after his untimely death. Tomlinson, Karen was well aware, had been almost a safety measure. This was a man who stuck so rigidly to the book it was difficult to work out whether or not he ever had a truly original thought of his own. Tomlinson was not about taking risks, he wanted every case he embarked on to be copper-bottomed even though he knew perfectly well that was impossible, and particularly so with a case that had been around as long as this one and was already so high-profile.

Karen took a deep breath. This was about control, about remaining calm and reasoned. She had not made the best beginning. She had ground to regain.

'You're absolutely right, sir,' she began, repeating her earlier response, one which she knew full well the chief constable never tired of hearing. 'Some kind of confession would be the ideal, and that's what we are all still hoping for. I have given instructions for Marshall to be interviewed continuously, within the rules of course,' she added hastily. 'But I don't think we can rely on this man breaking, I really don't. He's as cool as they come, sir. I think we have to be prepared to go with what we've already got, and it's certainly a hell of a lot more than we ever had before.'

Tomlinson seemed mildly mollified, but still unconvinced.

'What we have, Karen, is a pile of very old bones,' he said. 'And no possibility of getting any verifiable DNA from them, I understand.'

'I am confident that our identification is already quite solid enough without DNA verification,' countered Karen defiantly.

'Well, that's as maybe. But shouldn't we at least wait until we get word from London confirming how long ago that body was dumped in the sea?'

Karen couldn't believe her ears. 'That would mean letting Marshall go, sir,' Karen replied, rather more sharply than she had intended. 'It'll be weeks before the isotopes of those bones can be established.'

The chief constable sniffed in a derisory fashion. 'I don't even know what a bloody isotope is,' he said, with a brief laugh in the direction of James Cromby-White. This called for the kind of chummy male-bonding response which Karen noticed, somewhat to her surprise, he didn't get.

'It's two or more species of a chemical element that have the same atomic number and nearly identical chemical behaviour but differ in atomic mass and physical properties, sir,' rattled off Karen, who'd looked it up in a reference book the previous afternoon. She actually understood the nature of an isotope or how its establishment actually determined age no more than the chief constable did, but she couldn't resist the self-indulgence of supplying him with her recently gleaned textbook definition.

'Oh, very well,' he muttered, and Karen was pretty sure she heard Cromby-White struggling to stifle a giggle.

'You're always in a hurry, aren't you, Detective Superintendent?' the chief constable continued.

Karen made no comment. She did not think a reply was called for. The chief constable was obviously in one of his obstructive moods, which was pretty much true to form, she reckoned.

'Did it not occur to you that it might be better to wait until we had all our cards in our hand before arresting Marshall?' he asked crisply.

'I considered that we had quite enough evidence already, sir, and I still believe that,' she answered. 'The media were already speculating about the identity of the recovered remains and I didn't want to give Marshall the opportunity to do a disappearing act.'

The CC grunted again. 'What if it turns out that the body was only dumped in the sea ten years ago? We've no way of telling so far, have we? What then?'

Karen gritted her teeth. 'I don't think that's going to happen, sir,' she persisted. 'Don't forget we also have the watch. And I consider that to be quite conclusive—'

'Ah yes, the watch,' Tomlinson interrupted, waving a hand dismissively. 'A watch that could have been dropped overboard independently of the body. Nothing conclusive about it, surely, Karen? A watch that, in my opinion, I'm afraid we have yet to prove absolutely belonged to Clara Marshall.'

'Well, I think we have already done that, sir,' said Karen, forcing herself to be patient, not her foremost quality. She was, she knew, in danger of losing it. Help came from a corner she had always previously regarded as unlikely.

'I'm pretty much content with the identification as it stands, actually,' interrupted James Cromby-White suddenly. 'We have a precedent with the records of a Rolex watch being used to identify a murder victim. That alone, I think, would be enough. And yes, if you accept that the watch was Clara Marshall's, and the sale of it from that dealer in Inverness does, I feel, establish that beyond any reasonable doubt, then there has to have been one hell of a lot of coincidences for those remains to be of anybody but her. I think even the lowliest hack lawyer could convince a jury of that one. With or without any further verification, it is my opinion that we do probably already have enough to go ahead.'

Karen shot the chief prosecutor a grateful look. He responded with a small shake of his head.

'Don't run away with the idea that I'm ecstatic about this case, Karen,' he said. 'But I do think we have one at last.'

'Well, it's your call, ultimately, James,' said Tomlinson, who liked nothing better than passing the buck. 'Are you really happy to go with it?'

'I don't think happy is quite the word, Harry. It's a quantum leap from accepting that the remains found in that wartime wreck are those of Clara Marshall to convicting her killer. But we do know Richard Marshall had the means, we do know he went out in his boat at the appropriate time, and we have all that other old circumstantial evidence against him including the lies he was continually caught out in and the fact that almost all of his wife's clothes and belongings were found at their house. And of course, most damning of all, certainly until these remains were found, no word of his wife or children for almost thirty years.'

James Cromby-White paused.

'So? Can we go ahead? Can I charge him?' Karen was champing at the bit.

The chief prosecutor looked directly at her. 'Karen, do not think for a moment that I want Marshall to continue to get away with this terrible crime we all believe he is guilty of, any more than you do. But as you know, my foremost concern with almost any case is twofold. I have to weigh up the chances of success and then consider whether or not it is in the public interest.

'In this case it has to be in the public interest to prosecute Marshall. It is reasonable to assume we are never going to have a stronger case, and we do not want a treble murderer cocking a snook at the law-enforcement agencies of this country, we really don't. But, and I must stress this, prosecuting Richard Marshall on what we've got will be risky. Just like Harry, although I do think we should go ahead, I really would prefer it if we could strengthen the case considerably.'

'I would like to charge Marshall today,' said Karen flatly. 'Apart from anything else, there is just a chance that if he is actually charged after all this time we might get something out of him at last. Perhaps he might be shocked into giving something away.'

Karen didn't actually think that was very likely. But on that particular morning, when she felt so near and yet somehow so far from finally bringing Marshall to justice, she was prepared to say almost anything in order to get her way. There was a pause which seemed like for ever to her. Eventually James Cromby-White hauled himself out of his chair rather more efficiently than Karen would have thought possible, and walked over to the window. When he spoke again he had his back to both Karen and Tomlinson, and he did not turn round.

'Charge him,' he instructed briskly. 'But don't stop working on it, aye? We'll need everything we can dig out on this one. You should have your team checking out every possible angle again and again and again. OK?'

'Absolutely OK,' said Karen, grinning at his not inconsiderable rear view. Obese though he was, she could cheerfully have given the chief prosecutor a big sloppy kiss.

On the way back to Torquay Karen felt almost exultant. She knew it was ridiculous. There was still a long way to go. But at least the first hurdle had been safely manoeuvred. She called Phil Cooper to give him the news and asked him to pass it on to the rest of the team.

'But tell 'em to keep up the pressure, Phil,' she said. 'This case is far from watertight, as you know. Keep on interviewing that bastard Marshall. Harry Tomlinson says everybody has a breaking point. Let's hope he's right.'

'He probably is, boss,' said Cooper. 'But we're not allowed to torture our suspects, are we?'

Karen chuckled. The man always had that effect on her, the ability to lighten the moment and to make her laugh. That was what had driven her into such dangerous areas the night before, and she somehow felt she couldn't finish the conversation without referring to that.

'How did you feel first thing, Phil?' she asked.

'Bloody awful, boss,' he replied. 'How 'bout you?'

'Terrible. And I was late for the CC because of it.' Briefly she told the sergeant the story of how she had forgotten that she had left her car at the station.

'Well, you got the right result none the less, boss,' said Cooper.

'Thank God, and for once old fatso himself deserves a thank-you, too,' Karen replied.

'See you soon then, boss.'

'Uh, yes.'

But something else had been weighing on Karen's mind. She decided that this was her opportunity to deal with it.

'I'll be another hour or so though, Phil,' she continued. 'Something I've got to do on the way. Then as soon as I get back we'll charge the bastard.'

She swung the car through the porticoed entrance of the Old Manor nursing home, and was immediately overwhelmed by her usual reluctance to proceed any further. It was not just guilt and distress which stopped her visiting her mother more often. Nor was it really pressure of work, although that was what she used as an excuse.

Karen had an almost pathological sense of foreboding about seeing Margaret Meadows in such a place. On more than one occasion she had driven to the Old Manor, sat in her car outside for as long as thirty or forty minutes, and then just driven away, totally unable to make herself go inside.

On this occasion, however, she had an extra incentive to carry through her intentions and pay her mother a visit – all the old questions that were still bugging her, so many of which she felt her mother could have the answer to inside her poor lost head.

Karen parked to one side of the gravelled driveway, refusing, just for once, to dwell on her mother's sorry condition. She forced herself to approach the big front doors, locked as always, and rang the bell. They couldn't leave the doors open because some of the residents wandered, or so they said. Karen hated the place, hated herself for leaving her mother there, and hated herself for neglecting her while she was there.

Margaret Meadows was only seventy-two years old, very young to be suffering from severe dementia. But the illness had started to develop in her mid-sixties and she had now been at the Old Manor for two and a half years.

She was in the big day room, surrounded by other residents in a similar state, all of whom seemed unable to do anything with their lives any more, other than to stare endlessly into the middle distance with blank unseeing eyes. Margaret Meadows was sitting in her wheelchair, slumped forward over one steel armrest. Karen felt another stab of guilt. She always seemed to be like that when she visited, rather than in the comfortable electronically-reclining armchair Karen had bought her. The staff invariably told her that she had either just been put in the wheelchair or was just about to be lifted out of it. Karen did not feel she was in a position to argue. She had complied with strangers in order to look after her own mother. She had in effect washed her hands of this sometimes so charming, always so vulnerable, woman whom she knew, whatever else, had always loved her.

Therefore she did not consider able to question much of the treatment her mother received. Or maybe that was a cop-out, too. Karen wasn't sure. Margaret Meadows had lost the ability to walk, for no apparent reason really, but in the way that people suffering from dementia are inclined to – Karen knew that it was as if they forgot to walk as well as forgetting so much else – and the various regulations covering what nursing staff could and could not do in their daily work sometimes had rather cruel results. Karen supposed that she understood why they could not be expected to manually lift her mother around, even though Margaret Meadows was so small and slight, but she hated the thought of her being lifted in and out of her bed and her chair by a mechanical hoist. The last time she had visited, Margaret had had an angry black bruise on her forehead. The staff had explained that she had knocked her head while fighting with the hoist.

The very thought of it made a little bit of Karen shrivel up and die.

She braced herself, leaned forward and touched her mother's arm. Margaret Meadows did not move. She had never been a big woman, but it seemed to Karen that she had shrunk considerably since she'd been in the Old Manor. Karen stroked her hair. It was still soft and pretty and, with the help of a hairdresser, retained much of its natural pale gold colour. Karen's mother had always been fussy about her appearance, except when she was into a heavy drinking bout, of course, and Karen paid for her to have her hair done twice a week. Such a small thing, when she knew there was so much else that she should do but didn't.

Not for the first time she noticed that her mother was wearing somebody else's clothes. However much she complained to the nursing staff this happened repeatedly. On this occasion Margaret Meadows was wearing a blouse Karen did not recognise.

Abruptly her mother sat up. Karen noticed then that not only was the blouse not hers but that two of the buttons were missing. You could clearly see her breasts, hanging low and encased in an inadequate bra.

Karen felt the tears welling, and fought them back. She had no right to cry. This was, after all, her fault, she felt. She was not equipped to look after her own mother, and she knew it, but that didn't make her feel any better about not doing so. It wasn't just the demands of her job and her desire, her need even, to have a life of her own. It was more than that. She was just not able to do it.

Margaret Meadows looked up at her daughter. Her eyes were very dark, surely much darker than they had been when she was well, and very bright. She wore no make-up but her cheeks had a pink and healthy shine to them. Her body, though emaciated with premature senility, was agile, and she still contrived to move in her chair in a quick, almost youthful fashion. Often she sat with her legs curled up in positions Karen thought most people half her age would probably be unable to achieve.

'Hello, Karen,' she said. 'Have you come to take me home?'

Karen clenched her fists behind her back. The tears nearly broke through. Tears of guilt every bit as much as of pity. She mustn't let them happen. She had on one or two previous occasions been unable to stop herself crying, and her mother had been bewildered and upset. This was, after all, only what her mother said to her every time she visited. She should be used to it by now. But she knew she would never get used to it. The words cut through her, cold and sharp as a knife, every time.

'Yes, darling,' she lied. And she hated herself for the lies. Hated herself for making a fool of her mother.

Margaret Meadows nodded contentedly and slumped back over the arm of her chair again. Visits were all too often like that. Her mother asleep in some contorted uncomfortable position, and Karen sitting quietly immersed in her own silent guilt.

She knew that when her mother woke again, in just a few minutes probably, she would either have forgotten what she had asked or would simply ask it again. The only replies you could give Margaret Meadows were those that she wanted to hear, the ones that would keep her quiet and moderately contented. If Karen had told her that she had not come to take her home, Margaret Meadows would have been distressed. And Karen knew that as long as she told her that was what she was going to do, all would be well. She never actually made a fuss about going with Karen. Indeed, she hardly knew where she was, and when she talked about home she was invariably referring to the little North Devon seaside village where she had been brought up. All the intervening years had disappeared into the indecipherable mists within her head.

Karen knew all that. It didn't make any of it any better. Didn't make what she felt she had done to her mother any less terrible. She knew that she had not really done anything to her mother. She knew that she was not responsible. She knew that she was not capable of coping with her mother in this state. She knew that she had done her best. And that at least she cared, cared deeply. It made no difference. The pain was a stabbing feeling in her heart, the pain was a contraction in her gut, the pain was inside her head, and ran through every vein in her body.

She was the only person in the world her mother still recognised and called by name, and sometimes she found herself actually wishing that this was no longer so, and that made her feel even guiltier than ever.

Margaret Meadows started to stir again. She sat bolt upright in that sudden way she had and stared directly at her daughter. Then she gave a small weak smile. Karen felt like jelly. She forced herself to smile back, reached out and took her mother's hand in hers. But what she wanted to do was to run. To take off. To hightail it out of the Old Manor and never return. Not ever.

'Have you been to see Mummy and Daddy?' asked her mother abruptly.

'Yes,' replied Karen immediately, embarking on another lie.

'And are they all right?'

'Oh yes, they're fine.' Karen concentrated on smiling at her mother. Her grandparents had died almost twenty years earlier. Once she had told the truth, and reminded her mother that they were dead. Margaret Meadows had burst into tears and had sobbed uncontrollably until one of the nurses had come to the rescue by telling her that her daughter had made a silly mistake. Of course Mummy and Daddy were alive and well.

After that Karen had allowed herself to become immersed in the web of deceit which invariably seems to surround dementia sufferers. More often than not it is centred on kindness, its purpose only to keep the sufferers at peace within their troubled minds. It was still deceit, though. It was still lying to the people you were supposed to care most about. But the alternative was to create turmoil inside already tormented heads.

Karen stroked her mother's hand.

'Do you remember Richard Marshall?' she inquired casually. It was, after all, however much she tried to convince herself that she also wanted just to visit her mother, the question she had come here to ask that morning. The first of so many questions concerning that time so long ago that she would like to ask.

Her mother stared at her blankly. Then her face acquired that look of panic which Karen was accustomed to, and which hurt her so much. It was the look she got whenever she was challenged, however mildly, when she was asked even the simplest of questions. Karen understood. She had seen enough of it now, with her mother and the others. It happened when her mother felt she should know something but then realised that she didn't.

'Richard who?' asked Margaret Meadows, her face contorted with the strain of trying to make her brain work, a brain that no longer did anything she asked of it.

Karen squeezed her hand tightly. 'It's all right,' she murmured, trying to sound soothing. 'It's all right. You don't have to remember him. You don't have to remember anything.'

Ten

Back at the station Karen formally charged Richard Marshall. She had been greatly looking forward to doing so, but the man gave her little satisfaction. She had no idea what his true feelings were, as he gave so little sign of them. If charging him might weaken him in the way she had suggested to the chief constable and to James Cromby-White, then so far there was no indication of that. Marshall had let his mask slip once and he wasn't going to do it again.

'You will appear at Torquay magistrates' court some time tomorrow to be formally charged,' she said. 'I would suggest you contact a solicitor before then. If you do not have one you wish to represent you, we can provide you with one.'

'I'll bet you can,' said Marshall.

'Take him back to his cell,' she said to the two uniformed constables who had brought Marshall into the custody suite where the procedure had been formally recorded by the sergeant in charge. Marshall looked back over his shoulder as they led him away.

'You'll never make it stick, Karen. You do know that, don't you?' he remarked casually.

'Detective Superintendent to you,' she responded sharply, and made no other comment, her face expressionless as she watched him disappear down the corridor to the cells.

'What do you think, boss?' asked Phil Cooper. 'We will make it stick, won't we?'

Karen smiled wryly.

'Are you asking me for reassurance concerning the legal processes of this country, Detective Sergeant?' she asked.

Cooper grinned back. 'Sorry, boss. I should know better, shouldn't I?'

'Yes,' said Karen. 'You damned well should.'

Back at her desk Karen slumped into her chair. She suddenly felt very tired. She realised that she was experiencing an immense sense of anticlimax, and she supposed that she should not be overly surprised by that. The buzz of the past few days could not continue indefinitely.

Now came the time for waiting, even though they were still working at building the case against Richard Marshall in every way possible.

She remembered Bill Talbot then. She had failed to ring him back as promised to rearrange their cancelled meeting. Not only did she owe him that – Bill had been very much her mentor during the years they had worked together – but also if there was anybody who might be able to delve into the past and come up with something, anything, a bit extra that might be used against Marshall, it could well be Talbot.

Also, this was the call she had been looking forward to. Talbot was just going to love the news she had for him, and she wanted to deliver it personally before the release of a statement which she had already authorised the press office to issue later that day.

Her old boss did not disappoint. Talbot actually gave a whoop into the telephone when she told him that Marshall had been charged minutes earlier.

'Look, if you want to meet up in The Bell tonight for a drink I'll tell you the whole story. There were actually one or two moments when the bastard's smirk slipped.'

Talbot chuckled. 'Can't wait to hear about that,' he said. Then in a quieter voice he asked: 'Is it going to stick, Karen?'

'God, I hope so,' she replied. 'It's not copper-bottomed, but it's strong. Any jury with half a brain between them really should send him down.'

'Right, no chance then,' responded Talbot.

'Don't even say that in jest.'

In spite of that ironic final exchange, she felt much more cheerful and positive after speaking to Talbot and launched herself with energy, if not with enthusiasm, into her remaining tasks of the day, almost all of which involved her least favourite activity, dealing with paperwork.

Bill Talbot was waiting for her when she got to the pub and had already been there some time judging from the inch or so of beer which was all that was left in his pint pot. She was not surprised. This was as big a day for him as it was for her – maybe even bigger, since Talbot had headed the until now unsuccessful Marshall investigation for much longer than she had.

He asked her what she was drinking, ordered the bottle of cold Bud she requested and another pint for himself, then suggested they retreat to a quieter and more private corner of the bar where they could talk quite freely.

First of all Karen cheerfully related the story of Marshall's arrest. She had just moved on to describe to a thoroughly understanding Bill Talbot, who had himself suffered in this way all those years before, the so far unenlightening series of interviews that had been conducted with Marshall, when she became aware, in that inexplicable way that people do, that she was being stared at.

Swinging around in her chair she spotted John Kelly standing at the bar. It was undoubtedly his gaze that she had felt boring into her back. And as soon as he caught her eye the reporter began to walk towards her and Bill.

'Congratulations, Detective Superintendent,' he said with a smile. 'I thought I might find you here.'

'Typical,' said Karen. It was, too. Kelly had a quite unfathomable knack of seeking out anyone he wanted to talk to when he was on a story, even if they didn't want to talk to him. Or perhaps particularly if they didn't want to talk to him, Karen reflected wryly. He certainly always seemed able to find her, anyway.

'Can I buy you a celebratory drink?' Kelly continued.

Karen opened her mouth to refuse – this was one occasion when she really didn't want Kelly's company and she was quite sure that Bill Talbot wouldn't want it either – when the retired detective butted in.

'Thanks, John, mine's a pint,' he said, to Karen's astonishment.

She then accepted the offer too, ordering another Bud, and, as the reporter made his way to the bar to buy the drinks, she turned to Talbot.

'I didn't know you even knew Kelly,' she remarked.

Talbot smiled. 'He was raising hell in Fleet Street during most of my time on the job, but I remember him as a cub reporter cutting his teeth on the old *Torquay Times*. And our paths have crossed a few times since he's been back here on the *Argus*. Anyway, he's up to his neck in the Marshall affair. He's suffered because of it, too, just like so many of us, and that's a bond, really. This day will have meant a great deal to John Kelly. He won't have liked the idea of Richard Marshall walking around the world a free man any more than you or me, Karen, would he?'

Karen was puzzled. She knew, of course, that Kelly had been employed by the *Torquay Times* at the time Clara Marshall and her children disappeared, and that he had worked on the story back then. But Talbot seemed to be referring to a greater involvement than that.

'What are you getting at?' she asked.

'Don't you know?' Bill raised his eyebrows in surprise. 'I thought you two were close.'

'We are. Ish. But I don't live in the bloody man's head, thank God.'

Before she could learn any more Kelly returned with the drinks. He was balancing his own tomato juice – Kelly was a recovered alcoholic whose only hope of leading a halfway normal life was not to touch drink at all – somewhat precariously between Talbot's pint and Karen's bottle of Bud. Just as he reached the table the glass of juice slipped from his grasp, thick red liquid splashed over Karen's cream T-shirt and her grey linen trouser suit and the glass dropped on to the hard tiled floor smashing into many pieces and sending a further shower of red upwards.

Involuntarily Karen jumped to her feet, brushing ineffectively with one hand at the red stains which seemed to be spreading all over her clothes.

'Oh, shit,' said Kelly. 'God, I'm sorry.'

'Just get a fucking cloth or something, will you?' responded Karen. She couldn't believe it. The grey linen trouser suit was one of her few outfits that could be considered suitable both for meetings with the chief constable and court appearances.

And her cream T-shirt, which was actually rather a good silk one, was unlikely ever to recover from its tomato juice soaking.

'Oh, fuck,' she continued. She might be a top detective but she was also a woman who loved good clothes, and she took a lot of trouble over her appearance whatever the chief constable might on occasions think of her apparel.

Kelly returned with a cloth. The barman joined in with another cloth, and a major mopping-up operation began. Karen was sponged down as effectively as possible, the table wiped over and the pieces of glass swept up off the floor.

By the time she resumed her story of events of the past few days – rather more cautiously now that a reporter was present, even though he had immediately assured both her and Talbot that their entire conversation would be in confidence – her former boss's rather intriguing reference to Kelly's involvement in the Marshall affair had passed into the mists of time. It was not mentioned again.

The trial began at Exeter Crown Court five months later, fast-tracked through according to the stipulations of the Nairey Report which a couple of years earlier had put an end to prisoners on serious charges being held on remand for sometimes as long as one or more years.

Police inquiries had continued, of course, but little or no additional evidence had been acquired. Indeed Karen had spent most of those five months heading up an investigation into a white-collar building society fraud, which had seemed very dull and tame compared with the Marshall affair.

And, as Karen had always feared, the prosecution's case had not been strengthened by any revelations from Richard Marshall who had stood firm throughout the time he was remanded in custody in Devon County Prison at Exeter, and had not given an inch. The London forensic laboratory had, however, established from the remains recovered from the sunken E-boat that the body had been deposited in the sea between twenty-three and thirty-three years earlier which, although also not conclusive, did add some weight to the identification evidence. It was surely beyond all reasonable doubt that Clara Marshall had finally been found.

One way and another, Karen, although not overly confident, had at least been extremely optimistic when she had
escorted Sean Macdonald to the courthouse, so dramatically
set within the medieval walls of Exeter Castle. For a start, she
and the whole force had been pleased that Mr Justice
Cunningham was trying the case. This was a man she had
encountered many times before, a red-robed judge not given
to much liberalism of thought. Indeed it seemed that he
regarded most acts of a liberal nature, certainly within the
processes of the law, to be acts of supreme folly.

As the lead counsel for the Crown, a youthful looking QC
called David Childs, imported from Bristol, made his opening
statement. Karen reflected that he seemed to be a sharp enough
operator. A lot sharper than some of the CPS counsels she'd
encountered, she reckoned. Karen also thought, to her relief,
that Marshall's QC, although obviously extremely capable, did
not seem in any way exceptional.

The positive identification of the remains recovered from
the sea as being those of Clara Marshall was fairly swiftly
established, as indeed it should have been given the evidence
produced, but there was no such thing as certainty in a court
of law. Karen, sitting at the front of the court just behind the
prosecution legal team, breathed a sigh of relief. The first
obstacle had been successfully negotiated. Everything hinged
on that positive identification. Without it, she felt, the police
case would almost certainly have collapsed.

At least the prosecution's case was simple and straightforward, always some sort of advantage when dealing with a jury.
It rested on two premises, the first of course being that the
court should accept that Clara Marshall's body had at last
been found, which it thankfully had. And secondly, that the
court should accept that the weight of evidence against Richard
Marshall, although circumstantial, was such that he was,
beyond all reasonable doubt, guilty of murdering her.

On the fourth day of the trial, Marshall was called as the
first witness for the defence. He stood very upright in the dock
wearing a navy-blue blazer and what appeared to be some sort
of regimental tie. Karen registered automatically that his style
of dress had not changed at all with the passage of time. She

could still remember from her childhood, albeit vaguely, that he almost invariably wore those kinds of clothes. And as usual, on the surface at least, he seemed perfectly cool and collected as he gave his version of events leading up to the disappearance of his wife and children, a story Karen was all too familiar with and one he invariably told convincingly.

She watched nervously as Childs began to cross-examine Marshall. 'You were seen taking your boat out to the deep water off Berry Head soon after your wife was last seen, and now finally, and against the odds, Clara's body has been pulled out of the sea there,' Childs asserted. 'I put it to you that you quite callously killed your wife because she was in your way. And that you then unceremoniously dumped her body in a place from which you did not expect it ever to be recovered. Is that not so, Mr Marshall?'

'No, sir, it is not.'

Hours of interviewing Marshall had led Karen to feel that she had got to know him just a little. And as Childs continued with his dogged line of questioning, she could see, to her immense satisfaction, the tension building up in the accused beneath his outwardly ever calm demeanour. There were stress lines etched in the heavy folds of flesh around his mouth and his hands trembled almost imperceptibly as he gripped the edge of the dock before him. Karen doubted if anyone else in the courtroom would notice that, but she noticed. Then she corrected herself. There was one other person who might notice.

Discreetly Karen glanced over her shoulder to sneak a look at Marshall's girlfriend from Poole, Jennifer Roth, whom she knew was sitting up in the public gallery. Jennifer was smartly dressed in a pinstriped grey trouser suit, her chestnut hair pulled back from her pale face in some kind of a band. And that face, set almost stonily as she stared straight ahead, gave little away. Maybe she had learned the knack from Marshall, thought Karen, as she returned her full attention to the proceedings.

The trial lasted only nine working days, a short time for a murder case. And when he gave his summing-up, Mr Justice Cunningham left little doubt about his own view. Mr Justice Cunningham did not like the idea of murderers walking free.

'It may be, members of the jury, that the weight of evidence presented here in this court, despite the fact that much of it is circumstantial, is such that you will feel you have no choice except to find the defendant guilty,' he pronounced, ensuring that his own opinion on the matter was made abundantly clear.

Things were starting to look good, Karen thought. And so it proved to be. The jury were out for less than half a day and duly recorded a verdict of 'Guilty'.

A surge of pure adrenalin coursed through Karen's body. Still sitting just behind the CPS team, she turned at once and looked up to the public gallery. Sean Macdonald was right in the front. He seemed very still, but she saw that there were tears running down his cheeks. She had seen his eyes mist over before, but she had never actually seen him cry, not even in the worst moments. His mouth was moving, and Karen, although she could not hear him and was no expert lip-reader, somehow knew exactly what it was that Mac was saying to himself over and over again.

'Thank God. Thank God.'

On the other side of the court Phil Cooper was considerably less restrained. The sergeant stood up and punched the air excitedly.

'We've got the bastard,' he shouted across to Karen who, only with a great effort of will, managed to prevent herself from responding in kind.

Mr Justice Cunningham looked at Cooper disapprovingly, but the hubbub in the court was so great as the verdict was delivered that he probably had not been able to hear the exact words, and with a bit of luck he didn't know Phil was a policeman as he had not been required to give evidence. This was a courtroom, not a football match, and police officers were not supposed to behave like that, but Karen felt pretty much like joining in. It was one hell of a day.

Karen leaned back in her seat, the relief washing over her like a warm bath as she listened to Cunningham sentence Marshall to life imprisonment, the statutory sentence for murder. She turned her full attention to the man whose dreadful crimes had haunted her for so long. And to her immense satisfaction, as sentence was passed, he slumped forward in the dock and buried his head in his hands. The aura of smug self-satisfaction that was so much a part of him had finally departed. For good, she hoped. Even with full remission it was reasonable to think that Marshall, now aged sixty-four, might die in jail. Karen sincerely hoped that would prove to be the case.

The big man kept his hands over his face as he was led away down the steps which led directly from the dock to the courtroom cells. His nickname so far could have been Houdini, but surely even he knew that he was finished at last.

Karen's attention was then drawn once again to Jennifer Roth, sitting at the front of the public gallery a few places to Mac's right. The young woman was again smartly dressed in the same grey trouser suit that she had in fact worn almost every day, with her long chestnut hair drawn back; she had been in court throughout the trial, not missing a minute. Her face was even paler than usual. She had turned quite white and she looked totally stunned. As the court rose and all the people sitting around her started to get up and make their way to the doors Jennifer Roth remained in her seat. She made no attempt to move. Instead she sat quite still, a bit like Mac, staring straight ahead.

Karen watched her for several seconds before joining the crowd pushing its way out into the historic old courtyard where once upon a time hundreds of men and women had been summarily executed upon the command of the notorious Hanging Judge Jeffreys and his like. It was a bitter January day but, although her breath formed mist in the freezing air and she was wearing only a light jacket, Karen did not feel cold at all. The elements meant nothing to her that day. She was elated. So it seemed was almost everyone else. All the police officers present had broad smiles on their faces. And so did the press, many of whom, like John Kelly, predictably the first reporter at Karen's side, had also waited a long time to see Richard Marshall go down.

'Great, fucking great!' exclaimed Kelly.

Karen grinned at him. He was irresistible sometimes. For a journalist who had once been one of the most feared and respected of Fleet Street reporters, Kelly had retained an extraordinarily childlike quality. His enthusiasm was contagious. He was a man who had an ability to communicate second to no one she had ever met. She knew that was what reporters were supposed to do – but it was somehow different with Kelly.

Maybe his own life story was what it was all about. Kelly had a chequered past. He had reached the heights of his chosen career, been the darling of Fleet Street for many years, and then, thanks to his own weakness, mostly drink and drugs, had sunk so low that he actually ended up living on the streets before returning to work in the local press in the town where he had been born and brought up. There was a lot more to Kelly than was apparent at first sight. You could not doubt that he was genuine somehow. That he cared.

The reporter reached out with both hands and grabbed Karen by the shoulders. Meanwhile Cooper and two uniformed officers were ushering her forwards. Karen knew she should pull away from her old friend, but she didn't. Kelly was in this too. Kelly had also wanted this day. Badly. She could see it in his eyes. She remembered then what Talbot had said that night in the pub just before she had been drenched in tomato juice. He had said Kelly had his own reasons for wanting to see Marshall go down. She almost asked the journalist about it, there and then, as they stood together in the ancient courtyard. Then suddenly the rest of the press corps were upon them and there was a chorus of requests, some sounding like demands, for a comment.

'How do you feel now, Detective Superintendent?'

'Are you satisfied with the result, after all this time?'

'Can you make a statement please, Miss Meadows?'

Suppressing her euphoria, Karen looked around frantically for the Devon and Cornwall Constabulary press officer. She needed somebody to take control of this lot. Gloria Smith was also pushing her way through the crowd, something she had considerable experience in doing and was, fortunately, rather good at. Gloria was a small woman equipped with sharp elbows and a voice even bigger than her somewhat extravagant blonde hairdo.

'OK, Karen?' she asked.

Karen nodded. It had been prearranged that she would give a statement outside the court. Pretty standard procedure, in fact. Although, she thought to herself, she might not have been quite so keen had Marshall not been convicted.

'Right, quieten down you lot,' bellowed Gloria so effectively that Karen involuntarily started away from her and the press corps shut up at once. 'Detective Superintendent Meadows will make a statement on behalf of the Devon and Cornwall Constabulary.'

Karen took in the assembled throng, the reporters waving their notebooks and tape recorders, the photographers rattling off frame after frame, the TV cameramen standing firm, their cameras balanced on their shoulders, sound booms thrust towards her face. She didn't feel nervous. For once this was a statement she wanted to make. She had done her share of apologising for the perceived shortcomings of the Devon and Cornwall Constabulary. This time her confrontation with the press was sheer unadulterated pleasure.

'It has taken us almost thirty years to bring Richard Marshall to justice,' she said. 'But at last, today, justice has finally been done—'

She was interrupted by a muffled cheer. It was unusual for the press to respond in such a way, but although members of the public, standing at the back of the gathered newsmen and women, had probably instigated the cheer, some of the press had joined in. Certainly John Kelly had done so.

'Justice has been done for Clara Marshall, and by default for Janine and Lorraine Marshall, and for their family, notably Clara's father who has believed for many years that his daughter's killer was walking the streets a free man, yet had no choice but to live with it.

'Justice has also been done for generations of Devon and Cornwall Constabulary police officers, who have refused to give up. We have put a monstrous killer behind bars. I am just one of a dedicated team who have waited a very long time for this day.'

There was the merest hint of a catch in Karen's voice. She hoped nobody would notice it, but she was sure John Kelly would. She glanced at him. Kelly was staring straight at her, making no attempt to write in his notebook. She knew he wouldn't need to. He would remember every word that she had said. He had always had a brilliant short-term memory and the ability to report verbatim without notes, as long as he did so quickly. In this case, so important to all of them, Karen reckoned he'd remember every detail for a long time to come. She could see that he was as moved as she was.

She made herself remember her job and her rank. 'That's it, ladies and gentlemen,' she concluded briskly. 'Thank you for your interest.'

The press did not back off, of course. Karen was well enough aware that they never knew when they had had enough. Their attentions switched to Sean Macdonald who had finally left the court and was standing, a little uncertainly it seemed, a few paces behind Karen. But the older man seemed mentally and physically unable to say much at all. Unusually for someone who was normally so articulate, he stumbled over his words. However, what he did manage to say was possibly the most moving part of the whole day.

'I'm able to bid a Christian farewell to my daughter at last,' he said quietly. 'And I've seen the man who murdered her punished for his crime. It was all there was left, all I've had to live for all these years. But nothing will bring my Clara back, nor her beautiful daughters, my grandchildren. . . .'

Then the tears started to come again. Karen ushered him towards the waiting car.

'C'mon, Mac,' she said. 'I'll take you back to the Grand.'

Phil Cooper pushed through the crowd just as they were climbing into the car and hurried across to them, his progress hampered by a pronounced limp. Karen knew that the sergeant had picked up a nasty injury to his left ankle during a rugby match, but if Phil was suffering any pain he certainly wasn't showing it. His eyes were bright, his face flushed. He looked absolutely delighted.

'We're all going back to the boozer, boss,' he said. 'This one calls for a real celebration. And you, Mac. You're included. You'd be very welcome. . . .'

The Scotsman wiped the back of one hand across his eyes, rubbing away the tears, and managed a wan smile.

'I know I would, and I thank you for that, young man,' he said. 'I thank all of ye, and I'd be glad if you'd pass that on to the rest of your lads and lassies. I thank you for everything that you've done. But I'm not in the mood for drinking, I'm afraid. I want to be alone with my thoughts tonight.'

'I understand, Mac,' said Phil, his voice gentle, and he reached out with one hand to touch the Scotsman lightly on the arm. Phil really was quite a sensitive bloke, for a burly rugby-playing cop, Karen reflected not for the first time.

'You'll come though, boss, won't you?' he continued.

'Wouldn't miss it, Phil,' Karen responded. She was actually not as keen on these kinds of communal boozing sessions as she had once been, but she knew she really had to be seen taking part in this one. It was, however, her avowed intention to stay a scant hour or so and drink just a couple of beers.

Good intentions, like promises, are all too easily forgotten.

It was a good do, a particularly good do. Somebody even done a fairly impressive quick phone round, it seemed, following Marshall's conviction. A number of Devon and Cornwall Constabulary veterans, now in retirement or working elsewhere, turned up to drink to Richard Marshall's ultimate demise, most notably Bill Talbot, who made a beeline for Karen as soon as she walked in.

'Congratulations, Detective Superintendent,' he said, reaching out to shake her hand. 'You've achieved what I failed to do for more than twenty years.'

Karen smiled and shook her head, denying the compliment.

'I had a little help, Bill, help you didn't get,' she said. 'From a chance diving expedition, from the elements, from an old shipwreck. Oh, and from the Rolex watch company.'

Bill grinned at her. 'Ah yes, the Rolex watch company – fast becoming a stalwart ingredient of the British legal system.'

He leaned forward and kissed her on the cheek. He was in control – Karen had never known him not to be, he was that sort of man – but she could tell that he'd already had several drinks. She didn't blame him. She didn't blame any of them. And glancing around the gathering of happy-looking policemen she knew it was going to be difficult, after all, for her to show the forbearance she had promised herself she would. Good results, certainly on this scale, were all too few and far between.

'Champagne?' inquired Bill, gesturing towards a magnum sitting in a bucket on a table just behind him. 'This is a celebration, after all.'

She hesitated for only a split second. 'Why not?' she asked. And as she took the first welcome sip of the icy cold bubbly liquid she reflected that it was a whole lot more interesting than a couple of beers.

She stood talking to Talbot for the best part of half an hour. She had liked working for him, more than that, she had learned so much of what she knew from him, and he had been one of her greatest supporters in her career; instrumental, she was well aware, in the speed of her promotion through the ranks. Also, she always enjoyed his company socially, and this was a very special night for both of them.

Everyone in the bar seemed to want to have a drink with her, which was par for the course. It had been a team effort through and through, but she was after all the senior investigating officer. Champagne was the order of the day. And when she finally considered going home, and checked her watch she realised that a good two hours had passed in a blink. She also realised that she had probably already drunk the best part of a bottle of champagne. Her car would have to remain in the station car park overnight again. It was not something she made a habit of, and in fact it would be the first time since that Indian meal she had shared with Phil Cooper on the day they had arrested Marshall the previous summer.

Special occasions called for special arrangements, she told herself as she made her way to the bar. But she wasn't keen on drinking any more in the assembled company in case she made a total fool of herself in front of her team. She had seen that happen often enough with senior officers, and knew all too well what good sport it always was for the rank and file. She was therefore determined to remove herself while still in reasonable shape.

'Steve, get me a taxi will you, darling,' she called to the landlord, raising her voice above the hubbub.

'What? You can't go yet. We're only just getting going,' said a voice in her ear.

Karen turned to find Phil Cooper right by her side. She had hardly seen the detective sergeant all evening. He had been ensconced at one corner of the bar with his rugby-playing colleagues. In one hand he carried yet another bottle of champagne and in the other an empty glass which he filled and held out towards her.

'Go on, have one more,' he said. 'You don't get too many days like this in this job.'

It was true. Without protest Karen accepted the glass and took a deep drink. She had already drunk enough to be highly susceptible to further temptation.

'You're right about that, Phil,' she said. 'This one's in a class of its own. I'll drink to that.'

She raised her glass and looked inquiringly at Cooper, who reached across the bar and lifted a pint glass of clear liquid to his lips.

'May the bastard stay locked up for ever,' he pronounced, as if making a toast.

Karen muttered: 'Hear hear,' followed by: 'What on earth's that you're drinking?'

'Lemonade,' muttered Cooper almost apologetically. 'That bastard on the Met team who crocked me last week did a really good job. He raked his studs right down my leg when he decided to stand on my ankle. The weals he left behind just won't heal and we've got the big cup game next Saturday. Doctor's put me on antibiotics. If I drink they won't work properly and the rest of our team will tear me to shreds.'

'Good God, when will little boys grow up,' grinned Karen. 'And now you have to sacrifice a bloody fine piss-up for the good of the police rugby team. Ra, ra, ra! It's tragic, that's what it is. Absolutely tragic.'

Cooper grinned back. 'I'll make up for it after the match,' he said. 'It's not too much of a sacrifice, actually. This is just such a great day I can get drunk on the atmosphere in here, I don't need any alcohol.'

Karen glanced down ruefully at her glass.

'Wish I could say the same,' she said.

'Don't worry, boss, I'm only trying to convince myself. Here, have a drop more.'

'What? You're not trying to get me drunk, Detective Sergeant, are you?'

Cooper put the bottle he had lifted down on the bar, and stood to a kind of mock attention.

'Would never even consider doing such a thing, ma'am,' he said, his face set, mouth fixed in a straight line.

Karen giggled. Here we go again, she thought. The dangers of laughter.

'You know, Phil Cooper, you're not a bad guy for a copper,' she heard herself say.

'And you, Ma'am, are not a bad guy for a copper, either,' he responded.

Karen's giggles developed into full-blown laughter then. Good God, she thought, I'm standing here in a bar full of half-drunk policemen flirting with my number one sergeant. This will never do, it really won't. With a tremendous effort of will she attempted to pull herself together and be sensible.

'You're good company, Phil, but I must go,' she said, then called across the bar once more. 'Steve, I need a taxi, could you give 'em a shout for me.'

Yet again the landlord, Steve Jacks, a retired policeman who in any case always had a habit of doing things his own way and at his own pace, did not seem to hear her.

Karen leaned over the bar. 'Steve, Steve,' she called.

Jacks, serving demanding customers as fast as he could, waved an impatient arm, his gesture saying that he would be with her as soon as he could and not before.

'You're not really going, boss, are you?' inquired Cooper.

'Yes, I am, before I fall over or something and make a complete prat of myself.'

'Oh yeah, boss, but when you make a prat of yourself you do it so beautifully. I mean, don't be a spoilsport. The lads all look forward to it.'

Karen grinned again in spite of herself. 'You're a cheeky bugger, Phil Cooper.'

'Yeah, but I'm lovable with it.'

Suddenly Cooper looked about twelve. Yes, thought Karen, you are lovable, actually, and that is the problem.

Aloud she said: 'Bollocks. You're a police detective – and with a very high opinion of yourself, too, it would seem. . . .'

At that moment Steve finally approached.

'What's it to be, Karen?'

'Can you get me a taxi—' she began.

'No need,' interrupted Cooper. 'I really should go now, too. In any case, lemonade starts to pall a bit after the fourth pint. You're on my way, boss. I can easily drop you off.'

Karen hesitated for just a second. Something told her she should say no. On the other hand to do so would be almost to admit that she had certain thoughts about Cooper that she knew she shouldn't have. And a lift would be very convenient.

'Oh, fine, all right, Phil, thanks,' she muttered, gesturing to Steve Jacks that she wouldn't need a taxi after all. The landlord who, both during his days in the force and now that he was running the local nick's favourite boozer, had always had a disconcertingly supercilious way of looking as if he knew something others didn't, raised one eyebrow but passed no comment.

'Right then, boss, I've just got to go to the gents. Car's across the road. See you outside, shall I?'

'Right.' Karen realised that Phil was actually executing a deliberate manoeuvre here, so that the two of them would not be seen leaving the pub together. He was, of course, completely sober and therefore well able to contrive such a plan. She suspected she might not have been able to think it through.

Somewhat gratefully she followed his obliquely issued instructions, but as she waited outside the thought occurred to her that by deliberately avoiding being seen to leave together Phil was actually indicating that there really might be some significance in their doing so.

Could he possibly have been fantasising about her in just the way that she had about him, she wondered? Could that good-night kiss which had consolidated her fantasies really have meant something, after all? She didn't know the answer. She did know that she should put all such considerations firmly out of her mind.

Eleven

In the car Cooper was his usual relaxed and funny self. If he shared any of Karen's somewhat inappropriate and turbulent feelings, he gave absolutely no sign of it.

Karen did not know whether to be relieved or disappointed. She was aware that she was a little drunk, and that Cooper was completely sober – which could, of course, explain everything. During the five mintues or so it took to drive from the pub to her apartment block, Cooper talked animatedly about the Richard Marshall case. He said nothing of a remotely personal nature, and even seemed to avoid any more of the mildly humorous banter which had become pretty much the norm between them.

Gratefully, Karen followed his lead. She didn't want or need this thing to develop. It could only lead to trouble for both of them. And when the car pulled to a halt outside West Beach Heights she opened the passenger door straight away and started to climb out.

'Many thanks—' she began.

But she was not allowed to finish her sentence.

Moving very fast Cooper switched off the engine, threw his arms around her, pulled her firmly towards him, and kissed her full on the lips. It was what she had wanted for some time now. It was also the forbidden fruit. And in addition she had been taken totally by surprise. Instinctively she tried to pull away from him. He continued to hold her tightly, to press his lips on hers. He was a big strong man. For a few seconds she thought he was not going to let go of her. She was both excited and disconcerted.

Then, as abruptly as he had grabbed her, he did let go of her, and backed right off.

'Christ, I'm really sorry, boss,' he said. There was a catch in his voice and she noticed that he was trembling.

She rubbed a hand over her mouth as if wiping him away, and sat back in the passenger seat.

'I'd say you were drunk if I didn't know you hadn't been drinking,' she remarked evenly.

'I am just so sorry, boss,' he repeated. 'I don't know what came over me.'

'No.'

'Look, I'd better go. I do realise that was really out of order.'

'Yes.'

She didn't know what else to say. She couldn't use her normal defence mechanism, make a joke of it, she just couldn't. She opened the door and stepped out of the car. This time he did nothing to stop her.

'Good-night then, see you in the morning,' she muttered. She suspected her face had turned bright red. God, it was so embarrassing. She was absolutely certain she was the only detective superintendent in the country, if not the world, who blushed so readily.

'Yeah, good-night, boss.'

She shut the door and turned away. But she had only walked two or three steps when she heard the whirr of a car window opening and Cooper's voice call out.

'Boss.'

Expectant in spite of herself, a kind of hope burgeoning up in her regardless of her fine intentions, she turned round smiling.

'I'll understand if you report me, boss, I really will.'

'Oh, for God's sake, Phil. . . .' she began.

Then suddenly it was all too much for her.

'Oh, for God's sake,' she repeated. But this time she was talking to herself.

She strode back to the car, flung open the passenger door, and reinstated herself next to a bewildered-looking Cooper.

'If you must know, I've wanted you to do that ever since we had that Indian meal the day we arrested Marshall,' she blurted out.

'Have you, boss?' Cooper was sitting very still, as if afraid to move.

'Yes, I fucking well have. But I don't think I can continue to have this conversation with you if you insist on calling me boss.'

Cooper grinned. He really did look like a little boy. He leaned towards her again, reached out to put his arms around her.

'No,' she said.

This time, although looking a little bewildered, he pulled away at once.

'No,' she repeated. 'Not here. I'm too old for necking in a car park. Let's go inside, shall we?'

She had always considered Cooper's wide grin to be one of his most attractive features. As she spoke it cracked his face wide open. She felt herself melt. She knew she was entering highly dangerous territory. She could not stop herself. And neither, it seemed, could Phil Cooper.

'Whatever you say, boss – I mean, Karen,' he replied.

He jumped on her as soon as she closed her front door behind them.

He caught hold of her by the shoulders, spun her round and pressed her against the wall, pushing himself into her. She could feel his hardness against her. Then he pulled away, sank down on to his knees and began scrabbling at the zip fastening of her trousers.

'Fuck, I want you,' he breathed, as he buried his head in her.

She let out a small cry, part pleasure, part surprise. This was not what she had expected at all. Cooper was mild-mannered and funny, a gentle family man – although she tried not to think about that. This was not how she had thought he would be.

He had come at her like an animal. And she found that she rather liked it. She was immensely excited by him. His hands were tight around her bum, his fingers digging into her. As he used his tongue on her he made small grunting noses. He was eager. The word that came to mind was rather an old-fashioned one. He was rampant.

She started to move with him. She was a woman who liked

175

the niceties of lovemaking, she did not fantasise about sex in dark alleyways or forbidden places where lovers might be discovered in embarrassingly compromising situations. That was not Karen's way at all. She liked warm comfortable beds and, to be honest, warm comfortable men. Her liaison with Cooper seemed to be turning out to involve neither.

He was handling her quite roughly. Something inside was beginning to turn over. Then he bit her. Not hard, but enough to drive her wild. She started to scream then. She couldn't believe it, but she was screaming. She could feel the climax building up inside her.

He pulled away from her again then, quite abruptly. She groaned in disbelief, slumped against the door. Then he reached up, caught hold of her hands and pulled her to the floor beside him. She half-fell down there, her legs hobbled by the mess of her trousers and knickers which were now wrapped around her ankles. There was a ripping sound as he tore them off her with one hand, then with the other he pushed her legs open. Somehow or other he had already managed to remove the clothing from the lower part of his body. With a low animal moan he threw himself forward on to her and entered her straight away.

The sensation was extraordinary from the start. Every nerve end felt raw. He clamped his mouth on hers as he began to move in her. She could smell and taste her own juices spread all over his face. She found it unbelievably sexy. He was an aggressive eager lover. She was aroused to the point of bursting. The climax when it came was more than great pleasure, it was an overwhelming relief. She knew she was screaming again as she moved beneath him, her legs wrapped around his neck. She couldn't help it. And she couldn't stop. Not for anything. If the chief constable had walked in, she wouldn't have been able to stop. If a fire had broken out, escape would have had to be delayed until she had finished. It had been a long time. Such a long time. Her body was crying out for release.

Great waves of pleasure swept over her, died away, then returned. It was the ultimate orgasm. She couldn't remember experiencing one like it.

Then just as her waves finally started to fade away to nothing she felt it begin to happen for him, too. His movements became more and more urgent. She was totally aware of his body exploding inside her.

Afterwards, they lay in a sweat-drenched heap, their clothes and limbs in a tangle, their breath coming in short sharp gasps for several minutes before either of them spoke.

It was Cooper who uttered the first memorable words.

'I'm really sorry, boss,' he said.

Karen burst out laughing. Straight away and without preamble, much the same way as the sex had been between them, really.

'Phil, I just do not believe you,' she spluttered. 'You've just fucked me rigid, gone at me like some wild animal, and at the end of it you've said sorry and called me boss.'

He started to laugh, too. Then he touched her face lightly with one hand.

'Do you have a bed here?' he asked, his voice still light with the laughter.

'Oh, yes,' she replied.

'And do you think you might like to take me to it?'

'Yes, I rather think I would.'

'Good.' He kissed her very gently on the lips and drew away at once.

'I want to hold you close to me, Karen,' he said, and there was an urgency about him just as great as the sexual urgency had been earlier, but of a very different sort.

'I want to hold you so much.'

Before they could climb into bed they had to turf off a disgruntled Sophie who was already lying spread-eagled on top of the duvet, waiting patiently for her mistress to finish whatever it was she had been doing in the hall.

'Love me, love my cat,' muttered Karen.

'My pleasure,' Cooper responded. He stayed until almost three in the morning. And as she watched him prepare to leave, a great sadness overwhelmed her. She was suddenly starkly aware that she was embarking on the age-old routine again. An affair with a married man who sneaked away from wife and work to be with her, and then in the early hours sneaked away from her, dressing in the dark, averting his eyes, trying to avoid the reality of his behaviour.

They had made love once more, and that time it had been exactly that, real lovemaking, slow, gentle and intense, quite unlike that first desperate animal fuck. But mostly he had held her, very close and very gently, just as he had said he wanted to. And she had held him back. She had clung to him.

She tried not to show what she was thinking as she watched him tuck his shirt into his trousers, fasten his tie and pull on his jacket, but she knew that she was afraid. She was somehow quite sure that this would not turn out to be a one-off fuck, another one-night stand. It had been too special. For her, anyway. She studied him as carefully as she could in the dimly illuminated room, which was lit only by the moon shining in through the windows. She couldn't see his face properly. Maybe for him it was just a bit on the side, a bit of fun. How could she tell? She knew him as a copper, as a workmate, as a drinking companion. She didn't know him in this way at all, not as a lover, as a man who could be a bull one minute and the gentlest, most cuddly of creatures the next.

He walked towards her then, sat on the bed, leaned over her and touched her hair. It was a full moon out over the bay and the light from it was shining directly on to the bed. She could see his eyes quite clearly as he came close to her, but she wasn't sure at all what she could see in them. It couldn't be love, not yet, and half of her hoped that it wasn't. She could imagine all too vividly the trouble that lay ahead of them.

She realised that it wasn't going to stop her, though. Nothing could. If Cooper wanted to see her again, to continue with whatever it was that they had started, there was absolutely no chance of her finding the strength to turn him away.

'You have no idea how much I want to stay with you,' he said softly.

Well, she had heard that before. But this time she believed the man who was telling her. Believed him absolutely. She did not reply. His next words surprised her, though.

'Will you sleep?'

She nodded, touched that he gave a damn. 'I expect so. I should.'

178

She stretched her limbs, pushed her neck and shoulders deep into the pillows. Her body felt wonderfully relaxed, sated, fulfilled. It was her mind which was racing, which might keep her awake, remembering the pleasure, fretting about what it could lead to.

'Yes, but it's not just that, is it? It's what's going on in your head.'

She was amazed. Could he read her thoughts? He smiled down at her, and his eyes were full of caring and concern. Her heart flipped. She hadn't known anything like this, not in all her life. She really hadn't, and she might as well admit it, to herself even if to nobody else.

'Shall I put you to sleep?'

'What?' She laughed again. He could make her do that so easily. It was uncanny. 'What do you think I am?' she asked. 'A sick dog that needs putting out of its misery?'

He kept smiling. He had such kind eyes.

'No, I think you're a wonderful, sexy, loving woman whom I don't want to leave, and I want to make sure you don't lie awake worrying about things when I've gone.'

'Ah,' she murmured. 'I'm not sure I can guarantee that.'

'I know,' he said. 'But maybe I can help.'

She glanced at him, puzzled.

'Are you comfy?'

'Umm.' She was, too, gloriously so.

'OK, snuggle down then, pull the bedclothes up around your chin, and I'm going to put you to sleep.'

He was talking to her as if she was a child, she realised. It was all rather peculiar. And the most peculiar thing was that she loved it. It seemed very natural, too.

'Now, I'm going to kiss you on your fringe,' he said, and he did so. 'Then I'm going to kiss your eyelids, then the tip of your nose. And then your lips. Just very lightly. Then your eyelids again.'

She reached up and smoothed his hair from his eyes.

'I'm not a baby, you know,' she protested hopelessly. 'I'm a detective superintendent.'

'Maybe tomorrow you will be again,' he said. 'But not right now. Right now you're my big baby.'

And when he left the warm glow that had earlier enveloped her body had engulfed her entire being.

Cooper smoked five cigarettes in between waking up the following morning and leaving for work. He had almost given up smoking, too. But, by God, he had never needed cigarettes more. His head was spinning. He couldn't believe what he had done. He couldn't believe what he was feeling.

He sat at the breakfast table ignoring the toast his wife had made for him. His mug of tea remained untouched. He knew that Sarah was watching him uneasily. After a few seconds she reached for his mug, stood up from the table where she had been sitting opposite him, emptied the cold tea down the sink, returned to the table and poured him another hot fresh mugful.

He made no comment, even though he was aware that he should at the very least manage a thank-you. But somehow he could not muster the energy to deal with life's mundanities. And he certainly had no interest in food or drink.

He lit yet another cigarette from the stub of the previous one.

Sarah reached across the table again and this time put her hand on top of his.

'Is something wrong, love?' she asked quietly.

Cooper shook his head and struggled to produce something which remotely passed for a smile of reassurance. He was aware, however, as his face stretched into a bizarre kind of grimace, that he had failed dismally.

Sarah gave his hand a little squeeze.

'Is it the Marshall case, love?' she asked. 'I know how it's upset you, with our girls and all. But I thought you'd got the result you all wanted, at last.'

Cooper made a real effort. 'We have,' he said. 'An absolute blinder. Against the odds, too. No, it's not that. Just office politics. You know how it is.'

'No, I don't. Not unless you tell me.'

Cooper pulled his hand away from her touch. He just couldn't proceed with this kind of conversation, not this morning, not after what he'd done the previous night.

'I wouldn't want to bore you with it,' he said.

'Since when have I been bored with anything that concerned you, Phil?' his wife asked. With just a note of reproach in her voice.

It was quite justified reproach, too, he reflected. They'd been married for eight years and Sarah had always been there for him. She'd always been more than his wife and the mother of his children. She'd always been there for him in every way. She was his best friend, his absolute confidante. He had always told her everything. Until last night, that is.

He couldn't bear the way she was looking at him, with that slightly puzzled, bewildered expression in her eyes. He thought it was possibly the first time she'd ever looked at him like that. After all, he'd never given her cause before. They had always been so close. He was aware that she believed that she knew him through and through. That he had no secrets from her. And she would have been right, too. Until just a few hours earlier.

He forced himself to smile at her properly and gave her hand a reciprocal squeeze before taking his gently away and rising out of his seat. He forced himself also to make the kind of response he knew she was waiting for.

'Never, darling,' he said. 'Never. But it's nothing, honestly. And I can't talk to you now, anyway. I'm late already.' He glanced at his watch. 'In fact, I'm going to be seriously late if I don't go this instant.'

Her puzzled look turned into simple anxiety then.

'You give too much sometimes, Phil,' she said. 'Nobody can work the sort of hours you do without something breaking. I mean, whatever time did you come in last night, for a start?'

He turned away because he couldn't bear to look her in the eye. Sarah was a heavy sleeper and she invariably went to bed well before midnight. She was a woman who needed her sleep and, after all, she was up every morning not long after six in order to be ready to get the children off to school and then to go to work herself. Sarah was a primary school teacher. Their joint incomes, although neither was that great alone, meant that they enjoyed a good lifestyle. They owned their own four-bedroomed house in Paignton. They each drove a car. They holidayed abroad. Earlier that year they had taken the girls to Disney World in Florida. They'd had a ball, too. Phil and Sarah still enjoyed each other's company hugely. And that had been a big component in the success of their marriage so far. Phil, although he was disinclined to admit it at the nick or on the sports field, had always enjoyed being with the woman he married more than with anyone else in the world.

It did not come naturally to him to deceive her. Thanks to Sarah's sleeping habits he had been able to creep in at 3.30 that morning without disturbing her, and it was far from the first time that he had arrived home in the middle of the night that way. Indeed it was something of a habit. His was one of those sorts of jobs. It was not, however, his habit to arrive home in the middle of the night having climbed out of another woman's bed.

Already he felt consumed with guilt. A guilt made all the worse because, in spite of Sarah's concern about his out-of-character behaviour, he was well aware that the last thing on her mind was the remotest suspicion that he may have been unfaithful to her. He had known he would be able to get away with it. He knew he would almost certainly be able to get away with it for some time to come, should he choose to follow that path. And that made things even worse, really. The kind of trust that there was between him and Sarah would take a lot of shaking. But he dreaded even the thought of what might happen to either of them if it was shaken.

He reached for his car keys which, upon his eventual arrival home the previous night, he had deposited on the shelf above the fridge where he always kept them. Funny how the same habits of everyday life continue even when you are rocking the core of it to the very foundations, he reflected obliquely. Even the thought of that made him feel quite nauseous.

He struggled to make his voice sound normal when he finally replied to her question. He didn't think he could manage a specific lie, and thanked God that he would almost certainly not have to produce one. Sarah would not push the point. It wouldn't occur to her that she had any reason to do so.

'Not a clue,' he said, feeling like a complete rat. 'Best not to think about time sometimes, particularly when all it does is make you realise how little sleep you're going to get. You were blotto, though. As usual.'

He grinned at her. He was trying desperately to behave normally, not to give a hint that anything out of the ordinary had happened at all. He leaned forward and pecked his wife on the cheek, affectionately ruffling her curly red hair as he did so.

'Oh, Phil, why do you always mess up my hair?' she asked, and she pulled away just as she always did. She smiled, though. It was part of the routine of their life together. He played with her hair. She grumbled about it even though he knew she rather liked it. And somehow it cut right through him to the quick.

'If I stopped messing up your hair, would you miss it?' he asked suddenly, and he could feel tears pricking.

Her eyes softened. As usual he could see the love in them. 'You know I would, you big softy,' she said.

His grin came more naturally then, but it still hurt. He touched her hand one last time before heading for the door.

'See you tonight, love,' he called over his shoulder.

'And try not to be so late,' she responded. 'Tell the miserable sods that if you don't get a decent night's sleep you won't be able to work at all.'

He laughed as he shut the door behind him, knowing that she would expect him to. There was always plenty of laughter between the pair of them. But as soon as the door was closed he stopped laughing and an expression of almost physical pain wiped the smile off his usually genial face, giving him a grim and haunted look.

He couldn't do this, he thought to himself. He really couldn't. Most of the men he knew seemed able to sleep around and have affairs without a second's thought. It just wasn't in Cooper's nature.

He climbed into his car and slammed the door swiftly and noisily behind him, as if trying to shut off the worries of the world outside. For a few seconds he slumped back in the seat reflecting on the troubled path he had set out on. Then he made a resolution. The only possible one.

'Right, that's it,' he muttered to himself as he started the engine. 'I'm sorry, Karen Meadows, I really am. But last night will have to be not only the first time, but also the last.'

Karen's alarm woke her at 6.45 a.m. as usual. And she woke with a smile on her face. It was not, however, long-lived. The memories of last night's glorious lovemaking, that wonderful instant closeness to a man she really liked and cared about was one thing. The reality of the situation, of embarking on any kind of relationship with a married, much younger junior officer, was quite another.

Plus, her head ached and her mouth felt like a dirty ashtray again. Good sex does not stop you suffering the effects of a hangover, she reflected wryly.

With a great effort of will she dragged herself out of bed and into the bathroom. 'Oh, shit,' she muttered to herself as the entire flat seemed to wobble before her eyes.

The condition of her head was still distinctly poor and her mood remained mixed as she drove to the station. Her body felt absolutely great. But she didn't like to think about any of the possible consequences of the previous night's activities. It had, however, been special. Very special. She had no doubt about that.

It was another cold grey January day, but one good thing about winter in a holiday resort was that there were few tourists about and without them Torbay's traffic usually ran reasonably smoothly. Her journey to the police station took a scant five minutes in a mini-cab that she had ordered after this time remembering that she had abandoned her car. As the cab pulled into the station yard, while she was still trying to make some sort of sense of the way she was feeling, she caught a glimpse of Phil Cooper arriving. Swiftly she climbed out of the cab, paid the driver, and waited for Phil to park.

He did not seem to see her. Clapping his arms around himself as if they would protect him from the wintry chill of the morning, he walked straight towards the back door of the station. She called out. She couldn't help herself.

'Phil,' she shouted.

His stride faltered, he seemed to hesitate, then he turned to look directly at her.

'Uh, good morning,' he said flatly.

She did a double take. This was not the Phil Cooper of yesterday. She feared at once that he was already regretting their brief liaison. His face was flushed. There was a look in his eyes that she could not quite recognise but she was pretty sure that it involved panic. The wide face-splitting grin she found so attractive was conspicuous by its absence. Indeed, he did not smile at her at all.

'Good morning,' she responded uncertainly. And after that she didn't know what to say at all. Phil Cooper simply squared his big shoulders and turned away. She nearly called after him again. She wanted desperately to say something about the previous night. Just to mention it, just to acknowledge what had happened between them – indeed, to acknowledge that anything at all had happened between them, would have been, at that moment, enough.

She did not do so, however. Instead, filled with foreboding at the prospect of the day ahead, she followed the detective sergeant slowly into the building. She worked closely with Phil Cooper all the time, and she wasn't at all sure how she was going to be able to cope. Although so well fulfilled physically, she had felt uncertain and anxious about what she had allowed to happen, or rather what she had actively encouraged to happen, from the moment she had awoken. However, the grim reality of meeting Cooper for the first time after their sex session, which it now seemed to her must be all he regarded it as, had been far worse than anything she had imagined.

She had anticipated a certain awkwardness, she had been well aware that this rash escalation of an excellent professional relationship into one which was both physical and, for her at least, emotional too, was likely to present both of them with a daily quandary. But suddenly, and with devastating clarity, she realised what she had seen in Phil Cooper's eyes just seconds earlier. It had been hostility.

Karen's heart sank. She felt ice forming in the very pit of her belly. She recognised that feeling, too. She was in the process of getting hurt again. She clenched her fists, forced herself to hold her head high and walk briskly. Had she not built an emotional wall around herself all these years? Did she not know how to deal with let-downs like this?

It seemed pretty darned certain that their liaison had not been at all special for Phil Cooper. She cursed herself for behaving like a fool yet again. Just because he was not known in the station as a womaniser did not mean that Cooper didn't have a lively private life which he had somehow contrived to keep exactly that. More than likely she had been just another conquest for him. He had shagged the boss and that was that. The look he had given her, the way he had turned away from her, left Karen in little doubt that he wanted no more to do with her.

She sighed. Would she never learn? Phil Cooper was a married man. A bit on the side was one thing, but no fleeting episode of extramarital sex would be allowed in any way to threaten his domestic tranquillity. Phil had already, with his body language alone, made that perfectly clear.

Karen felt a tear or two rising. She reminded herself that she was a senior police officer, a top detective. It made no difference to the way she felt. Inside the brittle wall of professionalism she had created around herself, she remained a woman. Inside, she was a human being. She longed for love and affection. She longed for a relationship with someone which made life worth all its battles, made every minute of work, worry and pain, one hundred per cent worthwhile because of this one person you would do anything for.

Karen had seen a film once, starring Helen Mirren, a film about the IRA, the kind of movie she usually disliked intensely. There had been one line in it, uttered by the then young Jon Lynch, which had moved her intensely.

'Would you die for me?' he asked.

That's what she had wanted all her life. She wanted somebody she would die for. Somebody so close that there was really no point whatsoever in living without them. Somebody who would die for her, too. Maybe it was what everybody wanted. Karen didn't know.

She bit her lip and clenched her fists, so tightly that she dug her fingernails into the palms of her hands. She did it deliberately. She much preferred physical pain to the dull ache she was beginning to get in her heart. Particularly when she was about to start a day's work amid a load of chauvinistic policemen, the vast majority of whom, she was sure, regardless of their surface camaraderie, would like nothing better than to detect signs of weakness in her.

For most of her life she had kidded herself that she neither needed nor wanted a long-term relationship, that one-night stands and occasional romps with past lovers were quite sufficient. It was, of course, a lie. A lie to herself. None of that had ever been, nor would ever be, enough.

She was, however, Detective Superintendent Karen Meadows. Successful, popular, competent, in charge of herself and others. She forced a bounce into her stride as she marched into the building, slamming the door behind her, and called a cheery greeting to the two uniformed constables standing by the custody suite.

'This is it,' she told herself. 'This is all there is, and all there's ever going to be for you, Karen Meadows. So you may as well make the best of it.'

By the time she reached her office no casual observer would have suspected that there was anything wrong with her at all, nor suspected for one moment that she was anything but utterly content with the life she had built for herself. Nobody would ever have guessed the misery which that day lay like a lump of ice-cold stone somewhere in the depths of her belly. Nor would they ever have guessed just how easily this tall, tough, together woman could be hurt.

She had, after all, spent very many years cultivating her own personality, building it into a pretty darned impressive act. And she remained absolutely terrified of what might happen if she ever let that act drop.

Twelve

The bombshell dropped just after midday. Karen no longer had to put on an act. All thoughts of anything except the crisis she was suddenly presented with were completely wiped out of her head.

Phil Cooper, usually in and out of her office all the time, had somehow avoided coming near her all morning. It was Tompkins, his somewhat morose appearance most appropriate on this occasion, who gave her the news which was to add the final absolutely disastrous touch to an already grim day.

'Marshall's bird is in the front office asking for you, boss,' he said. 'She won't talk to anyone else, won't even say what it's about.'

'Jennifer Roth?' Karen queried, unnecessarily perhaps, but she was almost hoping it might be somebody else, maybe an old girlfriend. There was something about Jennifer Roth and her blind faith in Richard Marshall that had made Karen uneasy from the moment she first met the young woman, and she was immediately anxious about what had brought Jennifer to the police station.

'The same, boss,' said Tompkins.

'Well, you'd better show her up then, hadn't you?' Karen spoke in a level voice and hoped that she appeared cool and in control. As seemed to be her wont, Karen was desperately trying not to display her true feelings.

But the moment the veteran detective constable had left the room Karen rose from her desk and began to pace around, like a wild animal in its cage. Logic told her that there was nothing Jennifer Roth could say or do which could change the events of the last few days at Exeter Crown Court which had led to Marshall finally being brought to justice for the murder of his wife and sentenced to life imprisonment. But she couldn't help worrying. And although less than five minutes passed before Tompkins led Jennifer Roth into her office, it seemed far longer.

Karen looked her up and down. Jennifer's long hair was no longer held back in a ponytail, but instead hung in greasy unkempt strands. She was wearing grubby denim jeans, stained trainers and a sweater with holes in the sleeves. She had certainly made no effort with her appearance, and her eyes were red-rimmed and swollen. She looked rather as if she had not stopped crying since the court case had ended the previous day.

Her face was still very pale. There were dark smudges below her eyes, partly shadows etched in her rather fine skin and partly the remains of yesterday's eye make-up, Karen thought.

She let Jennifer stand uncertainly just inside the door for a few seconds before ushering her to a chair. She then sat in her own big black leather job behind the desk. Under normal circumstances Karen would have taken one of the low chairs on the other side of her desk, right next to Jennifer. But these were not normal circumstances. Until minutes earlier the detective superintendent had believed that the Richard Marshall case was, at last, over. The man was never now likely to stand trial for the murder of his children, but he had at least finally been brought to justice for killing his wife, and the end result would in any case be just the same. With a bit of luck Marshall would spend the rest of his life in jail, and he only had one life, however many murders he was convicted of. But now, suddenly, Karen was no longer sure it was over after all. So she preferred to sit behind her big mahogany-finished desk and on a chair which was slightly higher than the one she had offered the other woman. If she had thought it would have done any good, she would have refused to see Jennifer Roth at all. But that course of action could only ever have resulted in more trouble. And trouble, she was somehow quite certain, was going to be the only outcome of this visit.

'Well, Miss Roth, what can I do for you this morning?' Karen began briskly.

'I came to tell you that Ricky didn't murder his wife and children,' Jennifer Roth began.

For just a split second Karen almost relaxed. This was, after all, what Jennifer Roth had been saying, over and over again, ever since Marshall was arrested.

'You are entitled to your opinion, but as a court of law and a jury of his peers have decided otherwise, your opinion is irrelevant,' said the detective superintendent sternly. She was determined not to give an inch on this one, whatever Marshall's girlfriend threw at her.

'It's not an opinion, it's a matter of fact.' Jennifer Roth glowered at Karen. She had about her that stubbornness which Cooper had remarked on right at the beginning. She was extremely determined. Like Marshall she had an arrogance in her. And she had a temper. Cooper had seen that, too, and made a note of it in his reports.

Karen leaned back in her chair and, putting on a performance which belied her true feelings, as she so often did, adopted a nonchalant unconcerned manner. 'And what exactly is this matter of fact?' she inquired, sarcasm heavy in her voice.

'Ricky could not have done it. I know he didn't do it. And that is a fact,' said Jennifer Roth.

'I'm afraid you'll have to do better than that, Miss Roth,' Karen responded.

The other woman looked at her levelly enough, but her lower lip still had a tremble in it. She was genuinely upset. Karen had thought all along that there was no doubt that Jennifer Roth genuinely loved Richard Marshall. She had thought that when she had seen Jennifer in court every day, and she thought it even more now that Marshall had been found guilty and imprisoned. It was remarkable, really. The man was a monster and yet he could still inspire this kind of devotion. He had done it all his life with women – she strongly suspected that he had done it with her own mother – and he was still doing it. Remarkable, infuriating and quite unfathomable, thought Karen.

Jennifer Roth did not respond for several seconds. Then, as if maybe aware that Karen had deliberately orchestrated the seating arrangements so that her visitor was at a disadvantage, she wriggled in her chair so that she was sitting as tall as possible. Her blue eyes bored into Karen's, so much so that the superintendent had to make a real effort not to look away.

'I know Ricky could not have murdered his wife because I was there.'

Jennifer Roth spoke very quietly, putting no particular emphasis on any of the words. When you dropped a bombshell like that you didn't need to, reflected Karen obliquely as she stared long and hard at the young woman, trying to make any kind of sense of her words.

Karen's brain was buzzing. Was Jennifer Roth mad? Or was there some other logical explanation? Something much more dangerous to the safety of the conviction so recently obtained. All kinds of thoughts raced through Karen's head. As ever she fought the demons of doubt inside her to ensure somehow that when she spoke again she appeared calm and controlled and unflustered.

'How could you have been there?' she asked, her voice as expressionless as Jennifer Roth's had been.

'I was there because Ricky is my father,' Jennifer Roth announced, almost casually. 'My real name is Janine Marshall.'

Karen was dumbfounded. This was unbelievable. This was potentially catastrophic. She found herself studying Jennifer Roth closely, trying to work out if she could see a resemblance with the man who had just been jailed for murder, and also trying to see if she could detect any trace of the child she had known only briefly so long ago. Jennifer was every bit as pale-skinned as she remembered both of Marshall's daughters to have been. Karen stared into the young woman's eyes. She also remembered how the little girls had both had their father's very clear, very light blue eyes. Jennifer's eyes were blue all right, but much darker and murkier, certainly not nearly as bright or as clear as Marshall's still were. They could so easily have changed as she grew older, of course. The detective superintendent could really reach no conclusion at all based on Jennifer Roth's appearance. She was exceptionally tall, just like Marshall, and had the same air of arrogance about her, that was for sure.

Karen shook herself mentally. She was being ridiculous. This wouldn't get her anywhere.

'Together with the rest of the world I understood that you were Ricky's girlfriend, his lover,' she countered.

Jennifer uttered a little snort. 'People believe what they want to believe, don't they?' she sniffed. 'I'm thirty-one years younger than Ricky, but when I moved into his flat the entire world just assumed we were lovers. Ricky said he was flattered. And it was much easier to go along with it. Much safer too, under the circumstances.'

'And what particular circumstances are you referring to, may I ask?'

'Ricky told me you lot had never left him alone, you were always after him, and you might come after him again at any moment. And if you did, well, I was supposed to have disappeared, wasn't I, along with my sister and my mother? It was much safer to leave things like that.'

'Was it indeed?' inquired Karen. 'If one half of what you say is true, why on earth didn't you speak out before?'

'Ricky wouldn't let me. He said there was no need. He said I had gone through enough. He said there was no real evidence against him and that he was sure to be acquitted without me rocking my boat, as he put it. But when he was sent down, well, I was left with no choice, was I? I can't let him spend the rest of his life in jail for something he didn't do, can I? He'll be angry with me, I know. He didn't want me to suffer, and he didn't want to blacken Mum's name either, he said.'

Karen tried desperately to think straight, to return to the basics of policing, to pick up on detail and allow small points to clarify the big ones.

'Why should anything you have to say blacken your mother's name?'

Jennifer opened her eyes very wide then, as if in surprise. 'Didn't I say?' she inquired. 'I thought I'd said. It was Mummy who tried to kill us, Lorraine and me. She tried to kill all of us. It was Mummy who killed herself. Daddy had nothing to do with it at all.'

Karen called in Tompkins again then, and arranged for Jennifer Roth to be taken to an interview room for formal questioning on tape. This was very serious indeed, and she wanted no loopholes in procedure. The eventual outcome could so well be Marshall's reprieve. If that appalling end was achieved

Karen wanted at least to be sure that it was not down to any basic errors in policing.

Once the three of them were installed in an interview room Karen gestured for the tape recorders to be switched on, sat down opposite Jennifer Roth and began the formal interview.

'First of all I would like to ascertain for the record that you are Janine Marshall,' began Karen.

Jennifer nodded.

'Please say your answer out loud for the tape recorder,' instructed Karen.

Jennifer Roth did so.

'Now, could you tell us the events of that Sunday in June 1975 which led to the death of your mother and sister?'

'Not my sister,' said Jennifer. 'Only my mother. Lorraine's alive.'

Karen did a double take. This was getting more and more curious. If Lorraine Marshall was also alive, where the hell was she? She turned her attention back to Jennifer Roth.

'Just tell me what happened, everything,' she said.

Jennifer Roth leaned back in her chair and half-closed her eyes as if trying to transport herself back into another time. Her voice sounded far away when she spoke.

'Mummy and Daddy had had a terrible row that day,' she said. 'They were always rowing, usually about money, sometimes about other women. Oh, I know I was only five, but kids do pick up on things. Parents never seem to realise it, but they do. Mum was violently jealous of Dad. Completely without reason, but she was totally neurotic, of course. . . .'

Jennifer Roth paused. Karen smothered a wry smile. Without reason? Half the paperwork in the Marshall file involved reports on the multitude of convoluted liaisons with women in which Marshall had become embroiled over the years. Including bigamy. He was not capable of monogamy, that was for certain.

Jennifer began to speak again.

'Dad was out, I don't know where – it was Sunday of course, I think he may just have been down in the harbour working on his boat or something – but he phoned home and he and Mum had this particularly awful row. Mum kept shouting at him. Screaming at him. Accusing him of being with another woman. She told him that if he was going to behave like that she would take us away from him. Permanently. He could have whatever life he wanted, but he couldn't have us. Then she slammed the phone down on him and grabbed Lorraine and me and took us into the garage. . . .'

Jennifer paused, put one hand to her forehead. She was frowning, trying to concentrate.

'It's hard, so hard to remember it. I've blocked it out for all these years. . . .'

Her voice tailed away.

'Take your time,' said Karen softly. 'Just take your time.'

Jennifer nodded. 'Can I have a glass of water?' she asked.

'Of course.' Karen gestured to the uniformed constable at the door, who immediately left the room.

'Do you want to wait?' she asked Jennifer.

'No, I want to talk. I want to get it out of my system, I really do, it's just, it's just so painful to make myself remember. . . .'

Karen tried to look understanding. It wasn't easy. She so wished this wasn't happening. Never mind Jennifer Roth's own boat, or Janine Marshall or whoever she really was, at the very best this young woman was going to seriously rock the boat of justice. At worst she could turn it right over and sink it.

'Mummy took Lorraine and me into the garage,' the woman who claimed to be Marshall's daughter continued. 'Lorraine was crying. She was the oldest. Only a year but I think it made a difference. She always got really upset when Mum and Dad rowed. I was just bewildered mostly, that's the limit of my memory of it, anyway. I don't think I had a clue what was going on. Lorraine seemed to. Lorraine knew. Dad's always said that. Lorraine knew. She knew exactly. That's why it was more terrible for her than for me.'

Jennifer just stopped talking then, stopped dead, almost as if she had no intention of continuing.

'What did Lorraine know, Jennifer?' Karen prompted, and it seemed a very long time before she got a reply.

'She knew that Mummy was going to try to kill us. She knew.'

Karen studied Jennifer carefully. The more the young woman spoke of the tragic events of so long ago, the more she seemed to acquire a childlike voice, and childlike mannerisms. It was a bit spooky. Karen felt a shiver run down her spine.

'Mummy took us into the car and talked to us. She was trying to calm Lorraine down. Lorraine was clinging to her. She was frightened. I clung to Mummy, too. I didn't know what was going on but I didn't know what else to do. Mummy held us and kissed us and then she told us we were going on a journey with her, that it would not be an easy journey, not a nice journey at all, but we'd all be together always, and that would make it all right.

'Then I started to feel sleepy, and then I don't remember anything for a bit until I woke up in Daddy's arms. Daddy was shaking me, asking me if I was all right. Asking me if I knew what had happened.

'I didn't know. I didn't know until years later, in fact, not until I found Daddy again. I'd blocked it out, like I told you. It was so terrible I just shut it out of my head. Mummy had attached a hose-pipe to the car's exhaust and she had tried to kill all three of us. But Daddy had been so frightened by what she had said to him on the phone that he came home straight away, and he arrived just in time to save Lorraine and me. We were both unconscious, but Mummy was dead already. Daddy said it was because she was bigger than us and the gas had risen so that she had inhaled much more of it more quickly than us.'

Karen sighed. There was something about the way Jennifer Roth was talking that made her not doubt for one moment that the young woman was telling the truth. Or at the very least what she believed to be the truth.

'So why didn't your father call the police, call an ambulance, tell the truth?' she asked.

Jennifer shrugged. 'Because with his record nobody would have believed him, would they?' She sounded perfectly together and grown-up again. Her voice, with its public school accent, had once more acquired that note of sarcasm, that hint of arrogance which almost made Karen angry with herself that she had not recognised her as her father's daughter.

'Jennifer, Richard Marshall had a criminal record, yes. But for bigamy and fraud. It's a huge jump from those sorts of crimes to murder. I really can't see any reason why he should have been under any more suspicion than any other man in those circumstances.'

'No?' Jennifer Roth's voice was heavy with sarcasm. 'What about the boy he killed?'

'I'm sorry?' Karen had no idea what Jennifer Roth was talking about.

'When Daddy was still at school he hit another boy so hard that he killed him. It was a playground fight. It was an accident. At the time nobody found out exactly who had hit the dead boy and so no charges were brought against anyone. But Daddy knew that if there'd been an investigation into Mummy's death all that would have come to light. He knew he'd be a suspect.'

'If your mother died in the way you have told us, Jennifer, I think any investigation would have been able to prove that.'

'Daddy didn't think so. He told me that the row with Mummy had started in the morning in their bedroom and that she'd flown at him and started to hit him and he'd grabbed hold of her by the arms to keep her off. That's all he did. Daddy was never a violent man.'

Karen studied her carefully. Jennifer was being totally ingenuous. She was apparently as completely under the spell of her father, if indeed he was her father, as had been all the other women in his life.

'But he knew there'd be bruises on Mummy. He reckoned the police would think he'd forced her into the car. And us. That he'd done it. He was sure of it.'

'You don't think he could have been lying when he told you all this?'

'No, no, I don't!' Jennifer Roth shouted the words.

'Look, Jennifer,' Karen persisted. 'We have investigated your mother's death. We prosecuted your father, if he is your father, and he was convicted. But I don't know anything about him having killed anyone when he was at school. That's never come to light at all.'

'Yes, but we're talking nearly thirty years ago, aren't we? If

Daddy had called the police when he'd found Mummy dead back then it would all have been different. He was certain the police would find out about the boy he'd killed.'

'A missing persons inquiry was launched a year after whatever occurred in your house on that Sunday in June, 1975. It never came to light then either.'

Jennifer Roth made a dismissive noise. 'That whole investigation was a mess, wasn't it? The police never got anything right. Everybody knows that now. But Daddy wasn't to know then that they'd all be so incompetent, was he? Daddy thought they'd find out what he'd done at school and he'd be labelled a killer.'

Jennifer looked triumphant. Karen leaned back in her seat, perplexed. She didn't know quite what to say.

'Looks like Daddy's been proven right, anyway,' Jennifer continued. 'You lot kept on going after him for twenty-eight years. And he didn't do anything. He really didn't do anything.'

'Even if he didn't kill anyone, he certainly did something,' Karen told her bluntly. 'At the very least he illegally disposed of his wife's body, didn't he? Your mother's body, if you're telling the truth. And that alone is a serious offence.'

'I don't know anything about that,' responded Jennifer rather prissily.

'We found your mother's body at sea, as you well know, wrapped in a tarpaulin and bound in chains. Surely you must accept that it is highly unlikely anyone but your father would have put her there.'

'I don't know anything about that,' Jennifer repeated. 'He never told me what he did with Mummy's body and I never asked him. I wasn't surprised, though, when that skeleton was discovered. It was important that she wasn't found, you see. So what better place than the Atlantic Ocean. It was only through freak circumstances that she was ever found.'

Jennifer spat the words out.

'You seem very detached when you talk about your mother. Didn't you love her?'

The question went off at a tangent, but Karen couldn't resist asking it. She was rewarded somewhat by the fleeting expression of surprise in Jennifer's eyes.

'I must have done, once,' she answered obliquely. 'But I barely remember her. She did try to kill me, you know. Any feelings I might have had for her as a kid were part of what I tried to shut out. And if you think about it at all, well, knowing that someone tried to kill you, even if it is your mother, does rather put you off loving her.'

It seemed to Karen that Jennifer was looking down her nose at her as she spoke. Certainly her voice had acquired a definite note of superiority. She remembered that Cooper had remarked on her snootiness when he had interviewed her at the very beginning.

Karen sighed. 'And so?' she inquired. 'Where have you been for the past twenty-eight years?'

'I was adopted,' replied Jennifer in that rather smug voice again.

'You were what?'

'Ricky said that there was no way he could keep us, not after he started telling people that our mother had walked out on him,' she began.

It was strange, Karen thought, how different her voice and her manner became depending on whether she was referring to Marshall as 'Daddy' or 'Ricky'. She was now, once again, quite grown-up and together.

'Ricky said we were too young to be asked to keep a secret, and he was also terrified of the effect that what had happened might have on us. He thought that the best thing to do was to encourage us to forget it all. Children do have short memory spans. But he thought if we stayed with him we would have to live with it all for ever. And I think he knew what the future was going to hold for him, that he would be hounded wherever he went.

'He found two childless couples who were desperate for children. The sort that don't ask questions. There are always plenty of those, you know. He agonised about splitting us up. It was more difficult to place the two of us, and he knew there would be publicity sooner or later and we'd be more likely to be spotted and to have to live through it all again, become immersed in it just the way he didn't want us to be.

'But that wasn't the real reason he split us up. No. He

wanted us to forget. He wanted us to have new lives. That's why he never contacted us. And he thought we would always remind each other, wouldn't be able to help ourselves. He thought that apart, with new caring parents, we'd forget more easily. Maybe even be able to forget altogether. That's more or less what happened to me. There was always something in the back of my mind, but for many years it was buried inside my head.'

'Jennifer, for a start I don't think it's ever been that easy to arrange adoptions in this country . . .' Karen began.

'Oh, not the way you mean,' interrupted Jennifer. 'Not officially. I suppose Dad just gave us away, really. And he fixed everything. I think he even arranged all the papers that were needed like a new birth certificate. You know Dad. He's always been very resourceful.'

Karen sighed again. Yes, she knew 'Dad'. Just a bit. And he was certainly quite resourceful enough to have been able to acquire false birth certificates for his children. Karen concentrated hard on all that she had been told. On the face of it, Jennifer's story had holes in it you could drive a bus through. There was a great deal that needed to be checked, including the very basic premise that she was indeed Marshall's daughter – although Karen would somehow have bet a month's salary that she was. And there were a great deal more questions to be asked, including one that had been festering away in Karen's brain ever since Jennifer had arrived at the station that morning.

'Look, if all that you say is true, why on earth should your father, if that's what he is, care about blackening your mother's name?' she asked.

'Because he loved her, of course,' Jennifer Roth replied swiftly. 'He loved her in spite of everything. He didn't want it known that she'd tried to kill her children. He said he'd rather stand trial himself. That it was the last thing he could do for her. Dad was always like that, you know.' The voice went child-like again. 'He loved Mummy very much, only she didn't seem to understand that. She kept getting at him, accusing him of things he didn't do. But he just carried on loving her, even after she . . . after she tried to kill his children. Even after he lost us too, even after he was arrested, he was still loyal to her.'

Karen stared at her. There was no sign at all that Jennifer Roth was being anything other than totally honest and straightforward.

'How do you know all that?' she asked suddenly.

'What do you mean, how do I know?' The now familiar belligerence shone through yet again. 'I know because of all that he's told me and all that I know he's done over the years. He did everything out of love. That's the sort of man my father is.'

Jennifer was positively glowing with pride.

'You have a very high opinion of him, don't you?'

'Yes, I bloody well do,' Jennifer responded aggressively. 'He's remained the same nice, kind, gentle man right through all this, and I don't know how he's done it, to tell the truth.'

'And your sister, Lorraine? Does she share your high opinion of your father?'

Jennifer shrugged her shoulders.

'I've no idea,' she said. 'I haven't seen her since Daddy gave us both away, and I have absolutely no idea where she might be.'

'Are you sure she is alive?'

Jennifer hesitated. 'I suppose not. But I'm sure she didn't die along with my mother, if that's what you mean. Of course I am. And I'm absolutely certain Daddy didn't kill her.'

'You mentioned something about finding your father again?'

Jennifer Roth nodded. 'Yes. I always knew I was adopted, although it turned out it wasn't a legal thing at all. I suppose it couldn't be. Not that that made any difference, they were good people, they were good parents. I was brought up in Cheshire, I understand they moved there to start a new life, so that nobody would ask questions about my sudden arrival. We had a lovely home, I had a pony, they sent me to a good school. Looking back I think they were always trying to make things up to me. . . .'

Jennifer's voice tailed off.

'Were good people?' Karen queried swiftly. 'What do you mean by that?'

'They were in their late forties when they took me in. They both died of cancer within a few months of each other about five years ago. They'd kept in touch with Ricky, although I'd not seen him – he thought it was better that way – and I found some letters. Then I tracked him down. I had dreams, you see, I remembered bits of things. I needed somebody to tell me about my past.'

'So what you are saying happened that day in 1975 is not really your own recollection, it's what Richard Marshall told you happened, isn't it, Jennifer?'

'No,' Jennifer was emphatic. 'It's not. It's what I remember. I needed something to jog the memories I'd buried, that was all.'

Karen felt like bursting into tears. She could barely believe what she had heard. She continued to stare at Jennifer Roth. The young woman's jaw was set at a very determined angle. She seemed disconcertingly sure of herself, and totally sure of the extraordinary story which she was suddenly presenting as fact.

And there was one undeniable fact. If she did indeed prove to be Richard Marshall's daughter, then there was at least one murder it had always been believed he was guilty of which had never been committed by anyone.

Thirteen

Cooper thought the door to the incident room was going to be torn off its hinges when Karen stormed through, long lanky Tompkins, morose to the point of embalmment, following meekly behind. Cooper had never seen her so angry. And he had a fair idea his behaviour that morning had something to do with it. He also realised that the appearance of Jennifer Roth on the scene was almost certainly what had really upset the detective superintendent. Together with the rest of the team his eyes were riveted on Karen. They all knew that she had just finished interviewing the young woman, and it was pretty darned obvious that the results of the interview had not pleased her at all.

'Right, let's have some hush, shall we?' she shouted, quite unnecessarily as the incident room had fallen into nervously expectant silence the moment she had entered.

'We have big big trouble, boys and girls,' she went on, still speaking much more loudly than she needed to.

Cooper already knew that there was another gentler softer side to Karen – she had shared it with him during their so brief time together. He also knew that she was a woman who did not like to let her real feelings show. She had plenty of front, as his mother would say, and she knew how to protect it. But the detective superintendent looked as if she had been really thrown by whatever it was that she had learned from her meeting with Jennifer Roth. And, rather typically, her feelings were taking the form of what appeared to be blind fury.

Her next words made Cooper understand exactly why.

'Jennifer Roth claims she is Richard Marshall's daughter – not his fucking lover but his fucking daughter.'

Cooper felt as if he had been kicked in the gut by a mule. This was an absolutely devastating revelation. He felt Ron

Smiley's eyes burning into his back. It was he and Smiley who had interviewed Jennifer Roth, established her role in Marshall's life. Or so they had thought. Cooper felt sick. But there was worse to come.

His senior officer did not even glance at him. Indeed it seemed to Cooper that she quite pointedly avoided doing so. She looked almost everywhere else as, still standing in the middle of the incident room, she briefly related the story Jennifer Roth had told her – how Clara Marshall had tried to kill her daughters, but succeeded only in killing herself, and how Richard Marshall's only role in the affair had been to prevent the truth being revealed, and to secretly dispose of his wife's body.

When she stopped talking the silence in the normally bustling room was all the more pronounced. Nobody moved, let alone spoke. But at least the act of telling the story seemed to have calmed Karen Meadows somewhat. After she had finished she sat down on the edge of the nearest desk and folded her arms.

Cooper could feel all the blood draining from his head. It was blindingly obvious that this evidence could overturn the whole case against Richard Marshall. He didn't need to hear what his boss had to say when she spoke again.

'So if Roth is telling the truth then it would seem there is at least one murder Marshall is not guilty of,' Karen concluded. 'Her very existence is a rather strong piece of evidence in Marshall's favour.'

There was heavy irony in those last words. She stood up again then, quite abruptly, and rounded on Cooper, pointing at him, arm outstretched. She was no longer shouting. Her voice was calm, but there was ice in it.

'Which begs the question, Detective Sergeant Cooper, why did we not find out who Jennifer Roth was? You were in charge of checking her out, you were the one who first reported that she was Marshall's lover. I want to know how that could have happened. And I want a full and detailed report on my desk before this day is out.

'I've seen some pretty fine examples of incompetence during my time in the force, Cooper, but this just about takes the biscuit. You have almost certainly made fools of the entire fucking force and you may well be responsible for Richard Marshall having grounds for appeal and almost certainly getting off. I do hope you are proud of yourself.'

Phil Cooper said nothing. There was nothing to say. He felt his neck and face begin to burn and hoped to God that he wasn't going to blush, something he hadn't done since he was a teenager. He knew Karen Meadows was right in everything she said. Absolutely right, and even though he didn't see how anyone could have spotted the truth beforehand, if there had been a monumental cock-up then he had to take the blame for at least a big chunk of it. The bloody woman had told him she was Marshall's live-in, for God's sake. How was he supposed to have known she was his bloody daughter? If, indeed, she was. But Karen wasn't even waiting to make sure before give him the bollocking of his life, and in public, too.

Cooper struggled to keep control, but the more he did so the more he could feel the blush developing, spreading from his neck right up his face and to his hairline. He cursed under his breath. He knew that he had turned bright red, which made him feel even more of a prat. Even if the worst-case scenario was proven, he couldn't believe that Karen Meadows had chosen to speak to him like this in front of everybody. Not after what had gone on between them the night before.

He winced. He was actually well aware that, professional though Karen was, their nocturnal liaison was almost certainly responsible for the level of anger she had specifically directed at him. Or to be absolutely accurate, he suspected, it would not have been so much what had happened between them in bed, as the way he had behaved that morning.

Oh, fuck, he thought. He continued to say nothing, but instead attempted to outstare her. Unfortunately that was difficult to do when you knew your face had turned beet-root red. Karen's eyes, still blazing with anger, bored into his. Cooper was no match for her in that sort of mood. Within seconds he was somehow forced to drop his gaze and he even bowed his head slightly, all too painfully aware of the sounds of embarrassment emulating from the rest of the team, ranging from nervous coughing to elaborate feet shuffling.

Karen turned her back on him then, almost as if dismissing him.

'Right, so let's get to business and see what we can do to turn this disaster around yet again,' she said.

'Jennifer Roth has agreed to have a DNA test. That's the first step, although I have to say I believe her already. I wish I didn't, but I do. Tompkins – get that organised straight away, will you?'

'Yes, ma'am.'

In spite of his distress, Cooper almost managed a smile at that. Tompkins, like all of them, invariably called the superintendent 'boss', and in a very casual way, too. Karen Meadows was not the sort of high-ranking police officer who either expected or required formality. Normally she had an easy authority about her, and commanded respect – even, albeit grudgingly, from the most chauvinistic of coppers – in a friendly although very professional way which did not really have anything to do with deference to her rank. But that morning DC Tompkins, a man of considerable experience after all, was quite understandably taking no chances with his superior officer's temper. Ma'am was the correct form of address. So ma'am it was.

Karen spent another two or three minutes directing the rest of her troops. She organised one team to check out the information Jennifer Roth had given her about her upbringing in Cheshire and the couple who had adopted her, legally or not, and another to launch a search for Lorraine Marshall, although she was painfully aware that there was little more to go on concerning Lorraine's whereabouts than there had been previously. Were both sisters really still alive? Karen had no idea. She wasn't at all sure she wanted to find Lorraine. The safe emergence of a second sister might well make Marshall's conviction all the more unstable, particularly if Lorraine came up with the same story.

When she eventually returned to her office Karen slammed

the door shut behind her with almost the same kind of force she had earlier exhibited in the incident room.

'Oh, fuck,' she muttered to herself, unwittingly echoing Cooper's response.

She knew she had been right to reprimand Cooper. It may or may not have been his fault and it probably wasn't. He had none the less been responsible for a key part of the investigation, and his failure to come up with absolutely vital information could now have disastrous repercussions. However, she also knew that the way she had gone about it had been all wrong. She had rebuked him publicly and in a very personal manner, and she was honest enough with herself to be well aware of what had triggered off her extreme anger with the detective sergeant – and it was something nobody but her could take responsibility for.

She had jumped into bed with a married junior officer regardless of the consequences – consequences Cooper had already made all too clear. His manner towards her that morning left her in little doubt that he wanted nothing more to do with her, and that he already regretted what had passed between them. She was quite sure that their working relationship would never be the same again. That friendly easy camaraderie was lost for ever. She had blown something good and replaced it with an out-and-out mess.

Typical, she thought. And what a day to choose. This was an all-round disaster day.

Heaving a big sigh she picked up the phone to inform the chief constable of all that had happened. For several seconds she sat with the receiver in her hand before ultimately forcing herself to dial the number of the Exeter HQ. Harry Tomlinson was going to be delighted, and he did not disappoint her.

The chief constable's reaction, although predictable, was more extreme than anything Karen had yet encountered in her dealings with him. He went through the roof. Previously he had always niggled, been sarcastic, been pompously self-righteous, huffed and puffed a bit. But Karen had never known him really lose his temper before. It wasn't Tomlinson's style. And being on the receiving end was not a pleasant experience at all.

'If there's ever been a sloppier example of policing than this, then I've never heard of it, Detective Superintendent,' he stormed.

Karen winced. For once she could not find fault with the CC's judgement and she had no answer for him. She had said much the same to Cooper, after all. The only problem was that she was the senior investigating officer and the buck stopped with her. Which Harry Tomlinson went on to point out.

'Be sure of one thing, Superintendent, if heads are going to roll over this mess, mine will not be among them.'

'Absolutely, sir,' said Karen. She would always have expected the CC to offer up any of his officers as a sacrifice in order to save his own skin. But on this occasion she could not entirely blame him.

By the time she left for home that night she felt utterly beaten. And she was quite convinced that the worst was still to come.

The wait for the DNA tests seemed like for ever even though it was only six days. When they eventually came through everybody's worst fears were realised. The tests proved positive DNA matches for Jennifer Roth both with Richard Marshall and with samples taken from the skeleton recovered from the sea, the skeleton which had been proven beyond all reasonable doubt to be the remains of Clara Marshall. This time the mitochondrial DNA, evident only in the female line, extracted from her bones was able to do its job, even though it unfortunately confirmed the result Karen had been dreading. Jennifer Roth was the daughter of Richard and Clara Marshall, just as she claimed. The solicitor she had employed, for whose services she would, to Karen's further annoyance, almost certainly get legal aid, immediately filed an application to the Criminal Case Review Board for the right to take Richard Marshall's case to the Court of Appeal in London.

Karen felt a sense of impending doom. She really didn't see how she and her team were going to wriggle their way out of this one. Any halfway decent lawyer would now be able to tie the prosecution case in knots. It was true that Marshall had never been charged with murdering his children, that the only charge against him had been for killing his wife, but none the less the disappearance of all three members of his family without trace had been fundamental to the prosecution's success. And now one of the daughters presumed killed along with her mother had turned up, not only alive and well, but singing the praises of her father and prepared to give evidence in support of his innocence.

Jennifer Roth's whole story of her unorthodox adoption and the death of her adoptive parents checked out. A false birth certificate had indeed been obtained for her – no doubt by the ever devious Marshall, Karen reckoned, just as Jennifer had suggested, but she knew she would never be able to prove that either – and Jennifer Roth's doting substitute parents had painstakingly built a new identity for her around it. No trace of Lorraine Marshall was found and Richard Marshall refused to give any information on her alleged adoption on the grounds that he did not want the completely new life he believed his elder daughter to have to be upset in any way.

Karen was convinced that Jennifer's evidence was at least highly suspect. She believed that the young woman was severely disturbed, but Jennifer Roth had no history of any mental illness, and although Karen would have loved to have been able to make her see a criminal psychiatrist she had no way of forcing her to do so and, naturally, Jennifer turned down the suggestion that she might like to seek psychiatric guidance in view of her traumatic childhood experiences and the effect they may have had on her.

It was all an absolute disaster. And to make matters worse, as soon as news of the appeal, on the grounds of new evidence, broke, the press were on to it like a kennel full of terriers, sniffing and nipping their way to yet another series of splash headlines on the Marshall case.

No details of the appeal were released, of course, but Torquay Police Station, in common with most, Karen thought, leaked like a sieve. One of the first and most disconcerting press calls she received, on the very day that the appeal was announced, was, predictably enough, from John Kelly. It shook her into a stupid reaction.

'I just want you to tell me that what I've heard is wrong,' he began.

Karen found herself playing cat and mouse with him. She had little choice.

'And what might that be?' she inquired, trying desperately to sound unconcerned.

'As if you don't know.'

'Kelly, I do know that you think you're the greatest fucking hotshot newspaper reporter who ever walked this earth, but the information you glean from the various low lifes you hang out with is not always fucking sacrosanct.'

She regretted the outburst as soon as she had made it.

Kelly did not respond in kind. There was a pause, and when he spoke again his voice was very quiet and strained.

'I heard that Jennifer Roth is claiming to be Richard Marshall's daughter,' he said simply.

Karen sighed. She still didn't know how to deal with this, but she was, in spite of her display of anger against him, glad at least that it was Kelly who was on the line with it, and not some anonymous flash young hack from London.

'Look, John,' she began, her voice as quiet as his now and the use of his Christian name was not usual for her. 'Look, even if that were true, you couldn't print it, an appeal's been filed—'

Kelly interrupted her.

'I do know the law, Karen. I am aware of all the implications. And I can't think of anything more likely to get that bastard's conviction overturned. I just want to know for myself. It's important to me. . . .'

His voice tailed off.

Karen sighed again. She'd always trusted Kelly and he'd never let her down yet. She'd only rounded on him out of sheer frustration, and she hoped he knew that, because she wasn't going to tell him so. That would be going too far.

'It's true, and it's indisputable,' she admitted. 'We've had DNA tests done.'

'Ah.' Kelly sounded as down as she felt. 'Thanks, Karen. I did need to know.'

He'd rung off then, abruptly, leaving Karen feeling slightly puzzled. Why was it so important to Kelly, she wondered? Why did he need to know? This was a seriously great story, of course, and John Kelly had been involved from the very beginning. But Karen felt there was more to it than that. She remembered again Bill Talbot's words in the pub, about how much it mattered to Kelly. But the reporter had shown no inclination whatsoever to share his motivation on this with her. She made a mental note to phone Bill Talbot that evening and ask him what he had meant.

Meanwhile, now that the DNA results had dealt their irrevocable blow to everything the police and the CPS had tried to achieve, Karen did her best to concentrate on the case as a whole, and to endeavour to think of ways in which they could come up with something, anything else in order to block the appeal. It was going to be an uphill struggle, she reckoned. In a vain attempt to keep her team's spirits up, she did not allow them a moment's respite in which to dwell on the consequences of the potentially disastrous new developments. Instead she threw work at them. She insisted that all the old records be studied and dissected yet again, every witness, however peripheral, re-interviewed, every jot of evidence scrutinised for the umpteenth time.

It turned out to be true that a schoolmate of Marshall's had been killed in a playground accident, but the coroner's verdict at the time had been accidental death and the new inquiries shed no further light on the affair. But fifty odd years later, that was not really surprising, Karen reflected. However, almost thirty years ago, when Marshall was first arrested, a similar investigation may well have produced very different results, just as Jennifer had suggested.

Karen even got on to Interpol and had Marshall's former lover Esther Hunter re-interviewed in Canada where, having a Canadian father and therefore dual nationality, she had gone to live when she and Marshall had split up about five years after the disappearance of Clara and the girls. Esther, while being another of Marshall's women who apparently believed totally in his innocence, had also always claimed that she knew absolutely nothing about anything, which was why she had not been called to give evidence at Marshall's original trial.

And she proved no more able or inclined to help now than she had been at any previous stage. None the less, it all kept the troops busy.

She also made herself go to the Bell occasionally after work, particularly if there was a special reason, like PC Brownlow being promoted to sergeant. She knew that most of her team would be there that night. Brownlow was a popular young officer, and she felt it was important for morale and solidarity that she joined the troops, all of whom were feeling pretty beleaguered.

Phil Cooper was already there when she arrived, but he didn't look capable of joining in any kind of celebrations. Instead he was sitting morosely alone in a far corner beyond the pool table, a pint of bitter and a whisky chaser in front of him. When he saw Karen walk into the bar he got up at once and made his way across the room to her.

She was mildly surprised. After all, not only had he made it perfectly clear that he wanted no more to do with her person-ally following their night together, he had also, since she had blown him out publicly over the Jennifer Roth thing, avoided all direct contact with her as much as possible. He had got on with his job, but also tried to keep his distance. She really didn't expect him to come near her ever again, and was still trying to get her head around a way of dealing with their working relationship at least. She certainly didn't want any sort of confrontation with him in the pub, and she began to push her way through the crowd in order to both get to the bar and to avoid the detective sergeant.

He was too quick for her. He cut her off easily, even though just as he approached her he bumped into a chair and slopped beer down his shirt, narrowly avoiding spilling it over Karen too. He stumbled quite heavily as he recovered himself and it was then that Karen realised that, in spite of the speed with which he had moved, Cooper was already a bit drunk. His face was flushed and he was sweating.

'I just wanted to say I was sorry, boss,' he muttered, swaying gently as he stood before her. His words were very slightly slurred.

'What about?' she asked briskly.

He looked slightly uneasy then, but continued none the less.

'About Jennifer Roth, of course,' he said.

'Of course?' she queried obliquely.

His unease seemed to develop into full-blown bewilderment then. That was all right. Karen had no wish to discuss the other matter in the station pub, if indeed there was any point in ever discussing it at all.

'Ah yes, Jennifer Roth,' she went on, causing Cooper to look all the more flustered.

'Don't worry about it, Phil,' she said, her voice heavy with sarcasm. 'Any fool could have done it.'

She brushed past him, knocking against him as she did so. She hadn't actually meant to have another go at him, certainly not in the pub, but she hadn't been able to stop herself. She told herself he deserved it. The whole case, the case they all cared so much about, was up in the air again. She knew it wasn't all Phil Cooper's fault, but she was looking for a scapegoat, someone she could blame as well as herself. And, of course, although she tried not to think about it, Cooper had hurt her, really hurt her, by backing off in the way he had following what really did seem to have turned out to be just a sordid one-night stand.

She strode past him to the bar, ignoring everybody else who spoke to her, although she was well aware of their curious stares, and ordered a double Scotch. Then another one.

An hour or so later Cooper approached her again, by which time she suspected she might be a little drunk herself, too. She was talking to a uniformed sergeant nearing retirement age who was being particularly gloomy about his bitter disappointment at the prospect of this man they had all wanted behind bars for so long winning his appeal. Cooper pushed his way between them.

'I just wanted to say I'm sorry about the other thing, too, boss,' he said.

Karen shot him a withering look. 'I was having a private conversation, Cooper.'

The uniformed sergeant, however, no doubt picking up on the atmosphere between the two detectives, backed away at once leaving them more or less alone in the crowd.

'Look, I just wanted to say sorry, boss,' Cooper repeated.

'Sorry for what exactly?'

'You know boss, w-what happened . . . you know, what happened between you and me . . . and everything . . .' Cooper seemed unable to get the words out. Whether this was caused by embarrassment or alcohol, Karen did not know.

'Don't worry about that either, Phil. I was beginning to think you weren't aware that anything had happened at all, and that's probably the best way to keep it. I'm sure you've been quite right to do so.'

Phil's alcoholic flush began to turn into a proper blush then. Karen hadn't realised until recently that Cooper was inclined to blush when he was embarrassed, much as she did. The first time she had seen it had been, of course, when she admonished him on the day that Jennifer Roth had revealed her true identity.

The DS moved closer to her, looking anxiously around to make sure nobody else was listening. Even though she had been drinking heavily since she entered the bar, she was quite overwhelmed by the sour smell of beer and whisky on his breath.

'Look, Karen, I'm really really sorry—' he began in little more than a whisper.

'So am I,' she interrupted, but he wasn't to be put off.

'Look, Karen, I just couldn't carry on with it. I'm married, it's my wife, you see, and the kids, and you're the governor, it's all too much—'

'Really, Phil.' Karen treated him to her most withering look. 'And that's all new, is it?'

'Sorry, boss?'

Cooper was obviously not at his quickest on the uptake. The alcohol had thoroughly dumbed him down, it seemed.

'I mean, your situation is new, is it? You have only acquired a wife and family since you spent half the night fucking me, have you? Because quite obviously you wouldn't have done so had you already been a husband and father, would you?'

Cooper's blush deepened. He had turned bright red right into the collar of his shirt now, and he seemed to be looking around the room even more frantically to reassure himself that nobody was listening.

Karen slammed her drink down on the bar and left, aware of even more curious glances as she headed for the door, but well past caring. She had to get out. She didn't trust herself to stay. Not with several large whiskies inside her.

The next day she went to visit her mother again at the Old Manor nursing home. She hadn't been for weeks. The effort required to make herself do so became increasingly greater. Sometimes she wondered if her visits helped anyone.

Unusually, Margaret Meadows was sitting in an armchair looking relaxed and comfortable, which made Karen feel marginally less guilty. But only marginally. Her greeting to Karen was the same as ever. And none the less gut-wrenching for its familiarity.

'Have you come to take me home?' she asked.

'Not until later,' replied Karen. The same lies. The same bending of the truth. The same desire to run and run. To go anywhere in the world, to never ever have to put herself through this again. She didn't run, of course. Instead she sat down next to her mother and took hold of her hand, stroking it. Margaret Meadows, apparently forgetting her request to go home, smiled at her daughter and promptly fell asleep, her head lolling forwards on to her chest. Karen resisted the urge to try to rest it on a cushion. Such ministerings invariably merely left her mother distressed.

So she just sat there quietly holding her mother's hand and tried to think happy thoughts which, in that nursing home, and with both her personal and professional lives causing her distress, was pretty difficult.

After a few minutes her mother snapped awake, quick as a flash, in that way she had a habit of doing.

'He wasn't going to stay with that hairdresser woman, you know,' she said suddenly. 'It was me he cared about. Always.'

'What, darling?' Karen was startled. Was her mother really saying what she thought she might be?

'But there were scratches,' she went on, spitting the words out as if they were something she wanted to get rid of.

'What scratches, darling?' Karen asked.

'Scratches,' repeated her mother. 'His face had scratches.'

'Whose face?'

'Him, him.' Her mother sounded impatient. With the finger of one hand she tapped the copy of the *Daily Mirror* which lay open in her lap. Karen still paid for her to have a daily paper, even though it was a very long time since she had seen Margaret Meadows respond in any way to a newspaper, let alone attempt to read one. The displayed page carried a picture of Richard Marshall.

'I didn't tell, though. I couldn't tell. Not on him. I loved him.'

Karen felt as if she had been poleaxed. She had more than once over the years tried to ask her mother about her part in the tragic events of all those years ago. It had never got her anywhere. And in recent years she did not think that her mother even knew what she was talking about.

'Richard Marshall had scratches on his face?' she inquired softly.

'I've just told you, scratches.' And with that Margaret Meadows raised her right hand to her face and stroked both cheeks as if showing where the scratches had been.

Karen made herself study her mother dispassionately. At that instant Margaret Meadows seemed perfectly alert and lucid.

'Was that the night he came to see you, the night he brought the little girls around?' Karen asked, remembering vividly all over again her own half-view of the proceedings from the top of the landing.

'What?'

Karen looked deeply into her mother's eyes, trying to decipher what lay within her confused head.

'Was that the night he came to see you, brought the little girls around?' She repeated the question in as calm a fashion as possible.

'Who?'

'Richard Marshall?'

'Who?'

Karen squeezed her hand more tightly. Margaret Meadows' eyes had acquired the frightened bewildered look her daughter knew so well, the look that indicated that she didn't understand what she was being asked, that she didn't understand anything very much and remembered even less.

Karen tried one more time.

'You remember Richard Marshall,' she prompted, pointing at the photograph of him in the newspaper still lying open on her mother's lap. 'You looked after his children when his wife disappeared.'

And you had an affair with him, too, she thought obliquely. An affair neither you nor I ever told anyone about. And apparently, even after he moved Esther Hunter into Parkview, you carried on believing in him, carried on covering up for him.

Her mother glanced down briefly at the paper, then screwed up her features into an expression of pure anguish. 'Richard who?' she asked, her brow creased into a deep frown.

'It's all right, darling,' muttered Karen. 'It's all right. Just forget it.'

She knew, however, that her mother already had forgotten it. If Margaret Meadows had been as lucid as Karen thought for just a few seconds, then she was no longer so. She was quite sure that her mother had been telling her that Marshall's face had been scratched that fateful night. Quite sure. But the moment had passed.

That, and anything else she might know, was once more locked inside Margaret Meadows' troubled head.

And the one thing her daughter was certain of was that nothing would be gained by passing on the half-delivered message to anyone else. Not now. It was far too late. Margaret Meadows could never be a witness. She could not even give a statement. The best thing that Karen could do, for her own sake as well as her mother's, she knew, was to keep quiet. Just as she had for nearly three decades.

Richard Marshall was given leave to appeal and his case came up at the Court of Appeal in London's Strand three months later. Karen accompanied Sean Macdonald, just as she had done at the trial. She felt that she could do no other. However, she had few doubts about the eventual outcome, she could really see little alternative to Marshall being released. The appeal proceedings were every bit as much of an ordeal for her and for Mac as she had expected.

Jennifer Roth appeared under her given name of Janine Marshall, although Karen, hard as she tried, could not think of her as that. Indeed, when she gave her evidence it was a bit like watching a ghost talk, Karen thought. She was, however, both clear and succinct. She repeated almost word for word what she had already said in her statement to the police – that her mother had tried to kill her and her sister Lorraine before succeeding in killing herself, and that, far from harming his family her father had done what he thought was the best thing to do, albeit misguidedly.

The prosecution counsel, David Childs again, did his best to cast doubt on her testimony, pointing out, as Karen had tried to earlier, that the young woman must have been deeply scarred by her childhood experience and would undoubtedly benefit from psychiatric help in order to work through the minefield of her memories. But Jennifer, speaking quietly in her nice public-school accent, was extremely convincing. David Childs also attempted to explore the aspect of Jennifer's, or Janine's, missing sister. Jennifer merely insisted that she had never known where her sister was and had no wish to upset her life by involving her again.

Richard Marshall took a similar attitude, just as he had done in further statements made since the intervention of his younger daughter.

'I lost touch with my elder daughter Lorraine a few months after I placed both girls with families,' he said. 'I believe that her adoptive parents took her abroad, but I don't even know that for sure. And I never tried to find out. Although I was more than happy that Janine's new family were prepared to keep in touch with me and tell me how she was getting along, I understood the attitude of Lorraine's family. I told both families more or less the truth. But the girls had to be protected. That was why I acted in the way that I did. I didn't want them to grow up with the stigma of being my daughters, living in the shadow of their mother's disappearance. Although it hurt me, I was and am happy to think of Lorraine growing up without that shadow. She may even have shut the whole thing out of her mind, I don't know. But she has never tried to contact me, and I respect that. I have no intention of revealing even the names of her adoptive parents or any details that might identify them in this court today or to anyone at any time. And I honestly don't even know the name Lorraine uses now.'

Marshall sounded extremely sanctimonious and sure of himself. Technically, of course, he could have been prosecuted for withholding evidence, both initially the fact that Janine was alive and now the names of Lorraine's alleged adoptive parents. In practice, the CPS had decided that any such prosecution would merely make matters worse and allow Marshall to appear even more saintly. In any case, he had been charged only with the murder of his wife, and not of either of his daughters.

'I may have done the wrong thing, My Lords, I realise that now,' Marshall continued. 'But the action I took all those years ago was because of my children. I wanted them to have the chance of a fresh start.'

He bowed his head and wiped one hand across his eyes as if brushing away tears. Karen wanted to slap him, not for the first time. She tried to convince herself that the three appeal judges would see through him. To her horror, although not totally her surprise – he was so plausible and he did have one hell of a witness on his side – this did not seem to be the case.

She watched the proceedings with an increasingly sinking feeling. Marshall was good, very good. He would not have stayed a free man for as long as he had were that not the case. She also felt sure that nobody in the court, including the judges, would doubt that Jennifer believed absolutely what she had said.

And she was right. Richard Marshall's appeal was upheld and his conviction quashed. He walked out of court a free man.

There was a muffled cheer from the public gallery. Karen glanced up in surprise. She found it impossible to imagine Marshall having friends, but obviously he did, or maybe it was friends of Jennifer up there. The rest of the court, including Karen, sat in a kind of grim stunned silence. And it was somehow all the worse for Karen because of that extremely disconcerting visit to her mother. She was so certain of what her mother had been trying to tell her, and coming from someone in full possession of their wits it was the kind of evidence that could swing a case. Coming from Margaret Meadows in her condition, however, it was worse than useless. Karen had always wondered if the police investigation would have taken a different, more positive, course all those years ago if she had revealed to anyone that her mother had had an affair with Marshall, and she had always told herself that it would have led nowhere. Now she could no longer kid herself about that. Her mother had seen scratches on Marshall's face the day after his wife was last seen, Karen was sure of it. And if that had been disclosed back in 1975 or even '76, maybe, just maybe, it could have led to Marshall being put behind bars years ago.

Karen's load of guilt was heavier than ever. Her head ached. The muscles at the back of her neck had knotted and tightened like little cords of coiled wire. She could feel Marshall's eyes on her as he walked from the dock. She tried not to look at him – she knew that was what he wanted – but she couldn't help herself. Marshall was smirking at her. His lips curled unpleasantly. She struggled to keep her gaze level, to show no emotion.

Marshall raised both eyebrows quizzically. Then he lifted his right arm in what was at first a clenched fist of victory, and then developed into a Churchillian V for victory salute – all the while looking directly at Karen.

She was incensed. She couldn't believe the cheek of this man. She stood up quickly, turned away from him and marched out of the court. She wanted to get outside before he did. She didn't think she could stand watching him perform in front of the assembled press whom she knew would be outside clamouring for a statement.

There was indeed a large group of them gathered on the wide pavement, but this time Karen refused to speak to them at all. She knew her thunderous look was not good PR. But she did not see how it was possible to put any kind of PR spin on anything that had happened that day. As far as she was concerned it had been a disaster.

Only as she pushed through the press on the way to her car did she remember Sean Macdonald.

'Damn,' she muttered to herself. But she just couldn't leave without saying something to the Scotsman whom she liked and respected so much. She swung around and saw him making his way slowly out on to the pavement, his head bowed. She walked quickly towards him.

'I am just so fucking sorry, Mac,' she began.

The strain showed clearly in Sean Macdonald's face, in the heavy lines around his mouth and the red rims around his eyes. For once he really looked like an old man.

'Not as sorry as me,' he said.

'No, I know.'

'It's all right, lassie. I don't blame anyone. He is just such a slippery bastard. I told you, didn't I? Like an eel. You think you have him in your grasp, but you don't. None the less, it seems impossible that he's got away with it again.'

'You still don't have any doubts, do you, Mac?'

'No, none at all. He murdered my Clara. I'd stake my own life on it.'

'But,' Karen made her voice gentle, 'that's your granddaughter who just got him off. Your granddaughter whom you thought was dead.'

'Aye, I know, and I have no explanation at all. Maybe she's more her father's daughter than her mother's, but I don't believe that either. Nobody could be as evil as him, nobody.'

'I don't think she's evil, Mac. I think she's brainwashed. Unfortunately, that's neither an accepted medical nor a legal term.'

'I know. I just can't feel she's really my granddaughter, not after what she's done.'

'You haven't seen her at all, have you, not since we found out who she was?'

'No.' Mac shook his head quite violently. 'I just couldn't bring myself to see her, not knowing that she was probably going to be instrumental in getting Marshall off.'

'Do you want to see her now?'

'No. I know it's not fair, I know she must be under his spell in some way, or that she really is mentally disturbed like you think but can't prove, Karen, but I can't forgive her.'

'I hope you can forgive me, Mac?'

Sean Macdonald smiled weakly.

'Oh, lassie, there's nothing to forgive you for. You've never given up, none of ye have, and I'll always thank you for that.'

'What are you going to do now?'

'Oh, I'm straight off back to Scotland. I need some thinking time.'

'I don't blame you.'

He grabbed her by the arm, pulled her towards him and stared directly at her.

'I'll not give up, though, Karen. I promise you. I'll not give up until I've got justice for my Clara. And if I can't do it through the law I'll do it another way.'

Karen put her hand on his and squeezed.

'Mac, you've always worked with us. Never against us. Don't change now.'

Mac gave a small derisory sniff. 'I've learned a lot about policing and the legal system of the United Kingdom since this nightmare began, Karen. There's nothing you can do now, is there? Whatever happens now he's got away with it. The law of double jeopardy is still in place, in spite of all the talk from politicians. He can't be tried again for murdering my daughter. He's made fools of us all.'

'It may be possible to try him for Lorraine's murder one day.'

Mac sniffed again. 'What, with no body and him claiming she's alive and well? We couldn't make a murder charge stick even with my Clara's remains finally lying in a morgue.'

'Well, maybe you're right, but double jeopardy will change, Mac, and it won't be long now either, I don't think. Then maybe we can have another go. There could be other charges, too. The illegal disposal of Clara's body for a start . . .'

'You're an optimist, Karen Meadows, or rather, you're pretending to be. I don't think you really are inside. I've learned enough about the CPS over the years. They'll never want to go ahead on that one, and as far as the chances of trying him again for murder, well, even if the law does change you'll need substantial new evidence, and what on earth is going to be turned up now, after all this time? We had an extraordinary piece of luck with this, with the divers finding her body and the watch and all that. It still wasn't enough, was it? And do you know, if it wasn't for DNA, I would believe that Marshall had invented the whole scenario, persuaded Jennifer Roth to make up a story and give evidence on his behalf. I really would. He's capable of it. Well capable.'

'I know how you feel.' As she said it Karen realised the words were a mistake.

'Do you?' snapped Mac, his anger, she felt, directed at her for the very first time. 'No, Karen, you don't know how I feel. None of you do. I have lived with the loss of my daughter and the knowledge that the bastard who killed her has remained a free man for the last twenty-eight years. Out there enjoying his life when he'd taken my Clara's life away from her. Now, just as I thought he had been brought to justice at last, just as I thought that at least I could say farewell to my daughter in peace, in the knowledge that her death had been avenged, now I have to live with the knowledge that Richard Marshall is going to be a free man again thanks entirely to the evidence of a young woman I have to accept is my granddaughter, the granddaughter I thought he had also killed. No, Karen, you have no idea how I feel. Not even you.'

'I'm sorry,' Karen began, feeling more inadequate than ever. She wasn't quite sure what she could possibly say next but in any case she was interrupted by the hubbub behind her. Richard Marshall and the young woman she had been forced to believe was his daughter had walked out of the court. The press, having totally lost interest in Karen once she had made it clear she wasn't saying anything, were all around them like flies around a honey-pot. A couple of dozen motor drives whirred – the Nikon choir was in full mechanical voice – and a group of reporters, written press and broadcasting, were yelling their questions.

Marshall's lawyer stepped forward and raised a hand for silence. 'My client has a brief statement to make,' he announced.

Then a beaming Richard Marshall, holding a smiling Jennifer by the hand, began to speak.

'This is a great day for me and for British justice,' he proclaimed. 'I have been hounded by the police for three decades.

Wherever I went to try to escape from them, they followed me. They have never stopped persecuting me because of a crime I did not commit. I have always proclaimed my innocence, through everything, but nobody ever believed me.

'It took the courage of my beautiful daughter . . .' He paused then, turned to Jennifer, hugged her demonstratively and kissed her on the cheek, at which point she kissed him back and clung on to him like the little girl Karen thought she so often resembled.

'It took the courage of my beautiful daughter for my innocence to be finally and irrevocably proven in this court-room today.'

Karen turned away then. She couldn't bear to watch what she felt was a carefully stage-managed little scene. She found it quite nauseating.

Hurriedly she hailed a taxi to take her to Paddington Station. She had had enough. She just wanted to go home and hide. But as the taxi pulled away she was vaguely aware of DS Cooper, who had this time been called as a witness to give evidence concerning his inquiries into Jennifer Roth, running across the pavement.

'Boss!' he yelled. 'Hey, boss, hang on a minute. . . .'

'Just drive on,' she instructed the cabbie, who being a London taxi-driver of many years' experience had not, in any case, hesitated. She didn't want to talk to anybody. There really was nothing to say. She had rarely felt so totally and utterly desolate. And she wanted to talk to Phil Cooper less than anyone else.

Fourteen

He phoned her on her mobile just as she arrived home.

'Boss, I just wanted to say how bloody sorry I am.'

Not again, thought Karen. She wanted to scream. Arguably the most important case she had ever dealt with had fallen apart. Richard Marshall was free again. She was not in a good mood. In fact, she was in a foul mood. Apart from anything else, she reckoned that if anyone should shoulder more than their fair share of blame, it should be her, not Phil Cooper. She wasn't telling him that, though. Her personal feelings continued to overshadow her professionalism in her dealings with the detective sergeant. Their brief time together had meant too much to her, far too much. But she wasn't telling him that either.

Instead she railed at him, as had become something of a habit, almost a way of getting rid of her frustrations. In as much as anything could.

'What the fuck are you after, Phil? Absolution?'

'No, boss. Look, it's not that. I know I fucked up, but I think anybody would have done. There were no clues, honestly.'

'We've been over that. Over and over. Save it, Phil, I'm not interested.'

There was a brief pause. Then when he spoke again Cooper was no longer apologetic verging on servile. Instead he sounded cold and determined.

'Where are you, boss?' he asked.

The question took her so much by surprise that she answered it.

'I've just arrived home. Why?' she asked, adding almost as an afterthought: 'And what the fuck's it got to do with you where I am, anyway?'

'Because I've bloody well had enough of this,' Cooper

snapped. 'I've driven back and I've just got to Torquay. I'm coming around to see you right now, whether you like it or not. I'm ten minutes behind you.'

And with that the line went dead.

'Oh, fuck,' muttered Karen. She was too weary for this, she really was. She knew somehow that Phil Cooper did not really want to see her to talk about the case, in spite of how important it was to both of them. No, Cooper had another agenda. And, just like before in the pub, when he had said he was sorry, she had not been at all sure what he was apologising for. His professional or his personal conduct. It was all so confused, somehow.

Karen went into the kitchen, rummaged in the fridge for an open tin of cat food and fed a loudly meowing Sophie who had been demanding sustenance ever since her mistress had come through the front door. Then she switched on the kettle and put a tea bag in a mug. A cup of tea would have to do. She badly wanted an extremely strong drink, but didn't dare have one. Her brain was in too much of a whirl.

The doorbell rang little more than five minutes later. Either Cooper had been a lot closer than he'd let on, she thought, or he'd driven like a madman.

She was still holding her mug of tea in one hand when she opened the front door to him. He looked flushed and angry. He didn't wait for her to ask him in. Instead he pushed his way past her.

'Right,' he said. 'Let's get a few things straight here, shall we? I'm as thoroughly pissed off as anybody is about this case going pear shaped – but there's no way I carry the whole fucking can. And you don't think that either, otherwise you'd have me on a report.'

He was pacing the room, shouting at her. In spite of herself she was almost amused. He was so angry and so determined. Very macho, she thought obliquely. She'd never seen him like this before. It was a bit of a revelation. None the less, she kept the act up.

'Would I?' she inquired laconically.

'Yes, you fucking well would, and you know it. You also

know that the reason you keep blowing me out all the time and doing your best to make my life a fucking misery has nothing whatsoever to do with this case.'

'Do I?'

'Will you stop being such a fucking smart-arse?' he almost screamed at her. 'Of course you fucking do. And so does half the bloody nick by now, I shouldn't wonder, with the way their minds work and the way you've been fucking well behaving.'

He sat down abruptly. Again without being asked.

Karen was taken aback. Cooper was a mild-mannered man. His language was usually nothing like as colourful as hers. She had rarely even heard him swear before. As ever, though, she did not intend to let her true feelings show.

'Have you been drinking?' she asked, realising as she did so that she was continuing to handle this every bit as badly as she had done ever since the night she and Cooper had gone to bed together.

Cooper looked up at her, the anger still flashing.

'No, I fucking well haven't,' he stormed. 'I've just driven back from London, for Christ's sake. Do you think I'm barking mad? We don't all have to be pissed out of our fucking minds in order to show a hint of genuine emotion, you know.'

To her astonishment she saw that there were tears in his eyes. She sat down opposite him. Something about the rawness of him made her want to be honest for once. To tell the truth rather than to cover it up with that act she had so perfected.

'I'm sorry,' she said, running her hands through her hair, trying to make sense of it all. 'You're right, of course. I didn't know how to handle what happened between us, and how you were with me afterwards. I guess . . .'

She hesitated. What she was about to admit was quite monumental for her.

'I guess I was hurt.'

His eyes opened wide.

'You were hurt?' he queried.

She managed a wry smile. 'Don't sound so surprised. Women don't particularly like being fucked stupid and then ignored. Not even policewomen. It doesn't make us feel very good.'

'Is that what you thought?'

'Yes. Except it isn't "what I thought". It's how it was.'

He shook his head vigorously. 'No, no, honestly no, I just didn't know how to deal with it, either,' he stumbled. 'It wasn't that way. It really wasn't. And I intended to explain, eventually, I really did. But when you kept turning on me, when you kept bawling me out in front of everybody, well, I just thought you didn't want to know. Honestly I did.'

He paused. She said nothing. She didn't know what to say.

'So I decided tonight, that I'd had enough. That I couldn't take it any more. That I was going to tell you . . .'

His voice tailed off. She was curious.

'Tell me what?' she prompted.

He didn't respond for a while. She stared at him, genuinely puzzled. Her first thought was that he was going to tell her that he'd applied for a transfer or something similar – that he no longer wanted to work with her or be with her in any way. And she realised that she wouldn't like that at all. Even baiting him the way that she knew she had over the last three months had given her a certain twisted satisfaction, had scratched the itch that was inside her. She didn't like the idea of losing him for good, even though he had never been hers. Except for one brief night. And only part of a night at that.

She felt the tears welling. This would never do. As ever she fought to show nothing, to keep her expression blank. Her mind was still intent on exerting control – over her tear glands as well as her body language – when he spoke again.

'To tell you, to tell you . . . that I'm in love with you,' he said.

Karen was dumbfounded. She had not expected this. In fact, it was the last thing she had expected. She was not a woman with a high opinion of herself when it came to men and their feelings for her, or the effect that she had on them. Indeed, she was not a woman with a high opinion of herself in any area. Even when it came to the career in which she had been extremely successful, Karen did not consider herself a success. She was always plagued with doubts. Her whole persona, the way she was when she went out in the world, was so much based on pretending. It really had not occurred to her, given his behaviour towards her following their one-night stand, that Cooper cared about her one jot, except maybe as a senior officer who could affect his future prospects in the job.

She stared at him in amazement.

'I thought it was you who didn't want to know,' she stumbled. 'I thought I was just a quick lay, and that you regretted it the next day. That's how you behaved, or that's how it seemed to me, anyway. Indeed, that's how you've been behaving ever since.'

He shook his head. She thought he looked a bit like an overgrown puppy dog that knew it had misbehaved badly and was craving affection, wanting to be stroked and made a fuss of.

'I knew I was in love with you the moment I touched you,' he said. 'I guess I was in love with you before, actually, but I didn't realise it. The night I kissed you after that Indian meal, for a moment I thought you were going to ask me in then. I wanted you to so much. But I just didn't dare do anything about it. And then when you did, well, it was beyond anything I could have expected, beyond anything I'd ever known.'

He began to cry then. To weep unashamed tears. His shoulders shook. Big sobs racked his body.

'I really am in love with you,' he muttered through the tears.

She got up from her seat, went across and sat next to him. She wrapped her arms around him, this big strong man. He buried his head in her shoulder and just carried on weeping.

It was several minutes before he stopped. She did not try to say anything. Instead she just held him very tightly, her whole body encouraging him to let his feelings out. He certainly seemed better at doing so than she was, she thought. And she warmed to him even more because of it.

Eventually he pulled away from her, wiping his face with both hands. His eyes were red and swollen and full of anguish. She didn't think she had ever witnessed such an instinctive outpouring of raw emotion.

'I'm sorry,' he said.

'No,' she responded gently. 'I'm very very flattered.'

He pulled even further away, the pain in him all the more apparent.

'Is that all? Just flattered? What about you? What do you feel?'

'I – I don't know,' she said. She thought that she did know well enough. In fact, she knew that she did. But old habits die hard. It was not in Karen's nature readily to open her heart.

'You don't know?' He sounded quite distraught.

'You've given me a shock, Phil,' she went on, trying to be lucid, to be logical, to cool the situation a little. 'I mean, you're a copper. And a married one. I actually know nothing about your personal life. I don't know if you're happy, I know nothing about your marriage or your family. I am well aware, though, how so many of the blokes in the job are. I'm privy to locker-room gossip. I'm another cop. I know how they talk about women, particularly the married ones. How they talk about their wives. How they talk about other women who are stupid enough to let them into their beds. Most of them have no intention of rocking their marital boat, that's for certain. They just like a bit of variety. And they're quite inclined to boast about it. They're into one-night stands, because that way they don't get any extra problems. I thought that's what I was to you. Just a one-night stand. I thought you made that perfectly clear. I thought maybe that was how you lived your life. That you liked to play away from home occasionally but that was all. And that in the cold light of dawn you backed away – particularly from me, a woman you worked with, a woman who is a senior officer.'

It was quite a speech for Karen, and it was the truth. Phil Cooper looked as surprised as she had been earlier. He shook his head.

'Is that really what you thought, boss?'

'Phil, for Christ's sake, will you stop calling me boss? Under the circumstances it makes me feel even worse.'

Cooper managed a wry smile. 'Sorry,' he muttered, for the umpteenth time. He took a big white handkerchief from his trouser pocket and blew his nose noisily. The handkerchief had been neatly pressed and folded, by his wife, no doubt. Only men who had wives who did that sort of thing for them were likely to carry carefully ironed real cloth handkerchiefs around with them.

She watched in silence, determined not to get too carried away. The handkerchief had been a timely reminder. Whatever he said, whatever he professed to feel for her, he was still a married man who had shown great reluctance to follow up their night together.

It was a minute or two before Phil began to talk again, his voice quite calm now. 'I'd better tell you about me,' he began. 'I'm not like the others.'

Well, that was original, she thought, trying desperately to remain at least a little cynical.

'You see . . .' He looked uncertain, sounded as if he couldn't get the words out. 'You see, I met my wife when we were both very young. She was sixteen and I was seventeen. We were both virgins. We became best friends and eventually lovers and before either of us knew where we were we were married. I was barely twenty. Neither of us had been to bed with anyone else.'

Another pause. Karen waited again.

'The thing is, Karen, that was still how it was until you, until us . . .'

He really couldn't get the words out. Karen was confused. He couldn't possibly mean what he seemed to mean, could he?'

'I don't quite understand,' she said. 'What are you trying to tell me?'

'I'm trying to tell you that you are the only woman I have ever been to bed with except my wife. I've always been faithful to her. But it's not something you let on to in a police station. Most of the guys would think that there was something wrong with you.'

With a different sort of man Karen might have thought this was a chat-up line. There was, however, absolutely no chance that Cooper was being anything other than devastatingly truthful. She somehow did not doubt that for one minute. And she could see that he hadn't finished what he was saying. She waited in stunned silence for him to continue, to drop a further bombshell, maybe.

'I don't mess around, Karen. I never have and I never will. This thing that happened between us, it didn't happen by chance. It wasn't a game. I don't know about you, I can't guess about you. You keep things so close to your chest. But for me it had been building up for some time.

'I tried very hard not to let myself do anything about it. I didn't know how you felt but I bloody well knew how I felt. I knew it was important before it happened, and when it did happen, well, it was probably the most momentous thing in my life. I've never felt anything like it, Karen. Yes, OK, I told myself afterwards that it must never happen again. But I just knew in that instant when we first touched how special we were, that there was something between us that I may well have been looking for all my life.'

He stopped. He looked uncertain now, perhaps regretting already that he had said so much. Karen touched his face, then took his hand and squeezed it in a gesture of reassurance. No, not a gesture. She wanted desperately to reassure him, to bring him comfort. The time had come even for her to be honest. She had tried not to admit to herself what she really felt. In the face of this extraordinary outburst of emotion, this extraordinary display of trust in her, this candid declaration of love, she could do nothing, for once in her life, other than be totally honest about the depth of her feelings.

'It's all right, Phil,' she said. 'It's the same for me.'

'Really?' His voice was very small.

'Really. From the beginning of "us". As you say, maybe even from before that. But I thought it wasn't like that for you. When you didn't want to speak to me the next morning I didn't know what to do. I was devastated. You had really hurt me and I just wanted to hurt you. That was why I kept sniping at you. I am sorry.'

'Don't be. I understand. I can see how it must have looked.'

'Yes, well. Why, though? Why couldn't you at least have talked to me the next morning?'

Cooper gave a little grunt.

'I'd just sent my children to school. I'd just had breakfast with my wife. I don't cheat, Karen. I don't do it. It might seem old-fashioned, but there it is. When I saw you in the car park I just wanted to take you in my arms. But I couldn't. I just didn't dare respond at all. So I decided I had to try to walk away. Turn my back on you. It was all I felt capable of.'

'Guilt, then? That old friend.'

'No.' Cooper sounded mildly surprised at his own reply. 'I didn't feel guilty. I don't feel guilty. I don't think it comes with this particular territory, not when you're being absolutely honest, not when you're being true to yourself.' He managed a small smile. 'Fear more than guilt, I think.'

'And are you still afraid?'

'Terrified.' This time he beamed at her, that big wide smile which seemed to have done something permanent to her heart-strings.

'Me too,' she said. There was a warm glow inside her, though. She knew she was possibly about to embark on a dangerous journey, but she could not help herself.

'I do feel the same. I felt it from the beginning as well. I think I love you, too, Phil.'

He stared at her for a few seconds, then wrapped his arms around her and kissed her full on the lips, long and hard. It was fast and passionate. Just like the first time he had grabbed hold of her. She felt a kind of shudder run through her body. She didn't know what it was. She had never felt it before.

'Did you – did you feel that?' she stumbled.

'Yes, oh, yes,' he murmured into her ear.

'So, what was it?'

'I have no idea. I think the earth moved.'

'What, with just a kiss?'

'There's something special between us, Karen. Something rare. Something I can't stay away from any more, can't waste. That's why I'm here tonight.'

'I know.'

He kissed her eyelids and her nose and her lips very lightly, all the while stroking her hair, in much the same way as he had when he'd put her to sleep like a child that first night. She was equally moved. She dissolved into his arms.

'Will you take me to bed now?' he asked.

'Is that what you really came for?' She was aware of a certain edge to her voice. An edge of uncertainty, an edge of suspicion. But then, it was new for her to really trust someone, particularly in this situation. She couldn't help questioning still, just a little.

He kissed her eyelids again.

'No, that's not what I really came for,' he said. Then he grinned, lightening the moment. 'Well, it's certainly not all I came for. I love you, Karen Meadows, detective superintendent of this parish. I really love you. I wanted to tell you all that I've told you, and now I'll settle just for holding you if you want. It's more than enough. It really is.'

Karen pulled his mouth on to hers and kissed long and hard, savouring the flavour of him, breathing in his scent.

'Don't you dare,' she whispered into his ear. 'I don't think it's enough for me. Not nearly enough.'

'So what do you want me to do about it?'

'I want you to fuck me. And I don't care whether we do it in bed or right here.'

He was on her then. Every bit as urgent as before. Once again he was not as she had expected as a lover, even though she didn't know quite what she had expected, or even if she had expected anything. He ripped at her clothing and at his own. He had a way of crawling all over her, or that was how it seemed.

His mind, as well as his body, seemed to enter hers. She felt the shudder again, a kind of internal and quite uncontrollable shake starting somewhere in the abdomen and stretching both ways at once, down to her toes and up to her head.

She asked him again if he felt it, and he said that he did. Cried out that he did, and that he was loving every moment of it.

When the first time was over they instinctively followed the same routine as before. They went to bed, once again having to remove a prostrate Sophie who hissed angrily at Cooper, no doubt seeing him merely as an unwelcome intrusion, and lay close and tight together before making love again. Whatever they did, whether it was just lying together or making love, they seemed to fit so well. Everything fitted so well. They didn't talk much. Perhaps they had said it all, perhaps they didn't dare say more. Karen wasn't sure. She knew this was earth-shattering. She knew it wasn't just that flush of first lust. She really knew that, was absolutely sure of it. And after they had finally finished she fell asleep in his arms. It felt wonderful. Sleep engulfed her with a kind of sweet ease that was entirely new to her.

She woke with a start when she felt him ease away from her, unfold his arms, try to slide out of bed unnoticed. She noticed, of course. It was impossible for her not to. She felt as if she were joined to him at the hip. If he twitched, if he hiccuped, if he sneezed, if he stubbed his toe, she would know. And she certainly knew that he was planning to leave her.

She watched him dress, smooth down his hair, pull on his trousers and his shoes, button his shirt, fasten his tie around his neck. Then he came to her and sat on the edge of the bed.

'I'm so sorry I have to go,' he murmured.

'I know. I've heard it all before.'

He winced. 'This is different, Karen. This really is different.'

'I know,' she said. And she did know, too. It didn't help, though, not at that moment. He was going to go just when she needed him most.

He leaned forward then, kissed her fringe, and her eyelids, and her nose, her chin and her lips and said, like before: 'I'm putting you to sleep now.'

He almost succeeded, too. She watched him leave the room through half-closed eyes. She was nearly asleep. Then, when she heard the front door slam in the distance, she seemed to be slammed into full wakefulness again.

It had been quite a day. The horrible experience of being in court and seeing Richard Marshall freed, and then the extraordinary thing that had happened between her and Phil Cooper – and it was extraordinary, she had no doubt about that – overwhelmed her.

She rolled on to her front, buried her face in the pillows, and sobbed her heart out.

Fifteen

The following day reality hit even harder. Karen never liked mornings very much. This was one of the hardest mornings of her life. Knowing what was ahead of her made it even more difficult than usual to drag herself out of bed. Sophie, who had returned to her favoured corner of the duvet as soon as Cooper had departed, yawned luxuriously. Karen was too preoccupied even to give the cat her usual morning stroke.

She peered at herself unenthusiastically in the bathroom mirror and splashed cold water repeatedly on her swollen eyes. Karen's face did not recover quickly from tears, which was one of the reasons she tried to avoid them.

The events of the previous day had been monumental. And as she brushed her teeth with only a poor attempt at energy she realised that she was unsure exactly what had had the most devastating effect on her, Richard Marshall walking free or Phil Cooper confessing his love.

She felt rather as if both her head and her heart belonged to someone else, and someone else she didn't know, at that. Her elderly neighbour Ethel was putting her rubbish in the chute again when she left for work.

'And how's my favourite policewoman this morning?' Ethel inquired cheerily.

'Fine, thanks,' replied Karen absently, not at all inclined towards banter for once, as she walked slowly towards the lift, head down, lost in her own thoughts, but none the less aware of Ethel's curious eyes following her.

When she arrived at Torquay Police Station it took a monumental effort of will for her to put on her usual act. She made herself stride into the station with her head held high, to appear self-confident and in control. And just like getting out of bed in the first place that morning, it was as hard as she had ever known it to be. Every officer she encountered that morning looked subdued.

She considered that it was very much part of her job to lift their spirits, to help them move on, indeed to drive them forwards. They all had work to do, after all. She just had to make herself forget that she was a human being, too. She reckoned that was the only way she was going to get through what lay ahead.

There would be an inquest, albeit an informal one, into the whole Marshall affair, and as the senior investigating officer she was the one who would ultimately have to carry the can. Indeed, the chief constable, with whom she had a meeting she was not looking forward to that afternoon, had already made it clear that he wasn't going to. The morning passed in something of a daze until it was time for her to set off for Exeter HQ. She had to get over that particular hurdle before she could even attempt to look to the future in the way she was already encouraging those around her to do.

Even though she made absolutely certain that she arrived on time, and had dressed as conservatively as she could manage, Harry Tomlinson indulged in no social niceties at all before launching into an all-out blistering attack. His earlier huffing and puffing reached a crescendo of outrage.

'All our worst fears have been realised, Detective Superintendent . . . total waste of the taxpayer's money . . . more like a bloody circus than a murder investigation . . .'

There was much more of the same, and Karen had little choice but to stand and take it. Anyway, she felt that she deserved it. And in a weird sort of way she felt slightly better for suffering the sackcloth-and-ashes experience of her meeting with Tomlinson. The chief constable did not, in any case, take things beyond personally displaying his severe displeasure. Karen was not formally rebuked and she was also left feeling fairly certain that she would not be the recipient of any disciplinary action. Indeed, there was no reason why she should be. The only flaw in the operation which she had led had been the failure to establish that Jennifer Roth was Marshall's daughter and not his lover, and logic dictated that most investigations would probably have missed that, based on the information available at the time. However, Karen remembered only too well how she'd rounded on Cooper after Jennifer Roth had revealed her true identity, and her show of temper had not been entirely caused by what she had felt at the time to be his rejection of her. She had been genuinely furious with him, with or without justification, for his part in a potentially disastrous blunder. Now that the feared disaster had happened, Marshall was a free man again, and Karen and her team had been made to look stupid, even if they hadn't actually been stupid. The chief constable's response was only a part of it. As senior investigating officer, even with no official reprimand to her name, she knew very well that the mud was going to stick for quite some time.

Whether or not any one individual was really to blame, it was still a fact that she had presided over just about the biggest and most public failure in the history of the Devon and Cornwall Constabulary.

Karen dealt with it all by trying to put the Marshall case out of her head and getting on with whatever else was on the books. It was a big ask. She never seemed to quite succeed. There were constant reminders, for a start.

Just over two weeks after the successful appeal, The *Sun* newspaper carried a major series on the affair: 'MY THIRTY-YEAR ORDEAL BY MAN CLEARED OF MURDERING HIS WIFE. HOW THE POLICE NEVER GAVE UP PERSECUTING ME. I WAS INNOCENT BUT THEY WOULDN'T LEAVE ME ALONE.'

They had bought up Richard Marshall. He was a free man, properly acquitted in a court of law, and there was nothing in any kind of editor's code to stop them. Karen and everybody she knew in the force was devastated. It was truly sickening stuff. Sean Macdonald called from Edinburgh more than once. He, too, was sickened by the series.

'This is the final straw,' he said. 'It's like having your face rubbed in the dirt. There must be something else we can do, something else you can do, Karen.'

'If there is, Mac, then I don't bloody well know what it is. The CC has more or less said we have to write it off. To let the fuss die down. To be honest, I can't think of any alternative myself. We are all deeply upset.'

'She wasn't your daughter, Karen. I'm just not prepared to let it go. I can't let it go. Not when we were so close, not when Marshall was actually convicted and sent to jail. To see him walk free after that has been just too much to bear.'

There was an edge to Sean Macdonald's voice that Karen didn't like at all.

'Mac, you must leave it to us. If it is ever possible to do anything again we'll jump on him straight away. Right now I just don't see it, that's all. But you mustn't try to interfere. You'll only cause trouble for yourself, and you don't deserve more trouble, you really don't.'

'Karen, I have left it to the police for nearly thirty years, and it's got me nowhere. My daughter's killer is still a free man. Her death has still to be avenged. That's wrong, Karen, that's very wrong.'

'I know it is, Mac.'

There was nothing else she could say except that. Nothing else she could do except agree, and maybe apologise yet again.

It was Mac who finished the conversation quite abruptly, and very nearly hung up on her. Karen was left with a distinctly uneasy feeling. She hoped Mac was not going to do anything stupid, not attempt to take the law into his own hands. She didn't give a damn about Richard Marshall. But if Mac did anything outside the law he'd be sure to be caught. However, he was no criminal, and he was also eighty-three years old, she reassured herself. She was being silly. Mac would not step out of line.

All day, that first day of the *Sun* series, she was aware of a certain atmosphere in the station. Officers gathered in clusters, pointing at sections of the story and muttering about it. And away from the whispering groups they all seemed much quieter than usual. There was very little banter going on. Even the air they were breathing seemed heavy with a leaden silence.

Cooper appeared to be sunk most deeply of all into grim despair. She spotted him in the corner of the canteen at lunchtime, sitting with his head in his hands. A copy of the *Sun* was open on the table in front of him.

'Can I join you?' she asked.

238

His face lit up at the sight of her – that was how it was between them – but then swiftly fell again.

She sat down opposite him, only narrowly resisting touching his hand. She was vaguely aware of a number of pairs of eyes fixed on them and a bit of whispering going on. Station gossip had been inevitable, of course, but she reckoned there was little doubt that word was getting around, and it was doing so considerably quicker than she had expected, even in a police station. Their body language was partly to blame, she thought, firmly clasping her hands together in full view on the table before her. Whatever the reason, she suspected that the vast majority of officers at Torquay nick already at least suspected that there was something going on between her and Cooper. It was not a comfortable situation.

She ignored the buzz of interest which her sitting with him had provoked, and so did he. She considered it likely, however, that Cooper was so preoccupied he did not even notice.

'You look happy,' she said. It was an inane remark. All the more so because she knew exactly what was troubling him.

'Ecstatic,' he said.

'It wasn't your fault, Phil,' she said quietly.

He grunted. 'That's not what you said before.'

'No, well, I had a hidden agenda, didn't I? I was pissed off with you. You were right, though, right when you told me that nobody else would have picked up on who Jennifer Roth really was either. And even if we had known, well, we would have been forewarned I suppose, and maybe we wouldn't have gone ahead with the original prosecution. But there is no way we could have done anything more about securing a conviction, not up against her evidence.'

Cooper looked grey and drawn. There was no sign of that face-splitting grin she so adored.

'That's all right for you to say, boss. I messed up, whatever way you look at it. It was my responsibility. I was supposed to be checking Jennifer Roth out, and what a balls up I made of it. I still can't get my head around it, that's the trouble. And then you read crap like this. . . .'

He gestured at the the *Sun* spread out before him. She noticed that his hand was shaking. His frustration suddenly got the better of him. He picked the paper up, screwed it into a ball and threw it across the room against the nearest wall. Everybody in the canteen turned to look. Cooper seemed oblivious.

'It's the last straw, boss,' he said, unconsciously echoing Mac's words. 'Nothing's changed. There can't be anybody who doubts that Marshall killed Clara and his elder daughter, can there? And God knows what he's done to Janine's head, or Jennifer, or whatever she calls herself now. What has she gone through, what's he done to her, for God's sake? She believes the bloody man's innocent, she really does, I'm sure of it. How can that be? She and her sister were about the same age as my kids when it happened. . . .'

Cooper paused, shot her an anxious look. After that second time they spent together, when he told Karen that he had always been faithful to his wife, they had never discussed her again, and neither did he ever talk about his children. It was part of a kind of unspoken deal between them.

'It's all right, Phil,' she said.

He half-nodded. 'Well, I think of them, I think of something like that happening to them, of one of them being killed, of the other one being screwed up somehow, screwed up for life. That's what happened to Jennifer, there's no doubt about that. And when I watch my kids playing or eating their tea or something, I get this vision. . . . I just can't bear it. . . .'

Phil looked down abruptly. 'I'm sorry, I guess I'm a bit wound up about everything right now.'

That was an understatement, thought Karen. She studied him anxiously. She knew how torn apart he was. She knew he didn't know what to do, and that his personal dilemma was adding greatly to the stress he was experiencing at work. She also knew that what there was between them was just as important to him as it was to her. She did not doubt that for one moment. They were both in a state of turmoil, but she actually thought his was probably worse than hers.

It was so obvious that his personal feelings were all mixed up with his feelings of failure over Richard Marshall. He really was deeply upset. It hurt her to see him like this. She wanted to reach out and take him in her arms. She almost always wanted to do that. But in this instance more than ever. She could not, however, do so in the police canteen. Not if she wished to survive. She compromised by reaching out under the table with one hand and squeezing his knee.

'I do understand, Phil,' she said.

He managed a wan smile. 'I know you do, Karen,' he said quietly. The use of her Christian name, something he usually avoided at work, further indicating just how troubled he was. 'But even that doesn't always help.'

She could see the pain in his eyes, and it made her feel terribly sad.

He looked over his shoulder then and glanced around the room, as if checking out, a little late, she thought, whether anyone was listening to their conversation. Then he spoke in a whisper.

'Can I come round this evening?'

She nodded. She couldn't say no, and he knew it. That was the way it had been since the night of Marshall's appeal, and that was the way it would continue. Phil Cooper, the man who didn't cheat on his wife, had become rather good at it, it seemed to Karen.

Most days he seemed to find an excuse to spend at least some time with her. She had given him a key to her flat. If they weren't able to be together at night, she became accustomed to being woken by him early in the morning when he had sneaked away from home to come to her. More usually, he would spend at least a couple of hours with her, often more, after work. Occasionally he would stay for the whole night. Karen had no idea what he told his wife, but she accepted totally that he was experiencing genuine anguish. There was absolutely no question of her not believing that. And so was she.

She was, of course, well aware that one day they would have to confront the reality of their situation. Fate would probably play a part, she thought. It often did in these situations. Meanwhile she was happy to be an ostrich. Well, happy was something of an exaggeration. But there were only two alternatives. One was that they should stop seeing each other, and the other was that Cooper would take the initiative and tell his wife. The first was definitely not an option, and she somehow suspected that it never would be. As for the second, well –

although their present situation was far from ideal, she accepted that quite probably neither of them was ready for that second option yet. Apart from anything else, in love as she was, Karen was also aware of the implications on her career if this professionally dangerous relationship blew up in their faces. And her career was all there had been in her life for a very long time. She did not take lightly any threat to what she had achieved through sheer hard work and determination. Her recent promotion to detective superintendent had very nearly not happened because a previous case she had led had threatened to go catastrophically wrong. Now already she was facing another tricky time in the job, and she knew darned well that she was lucky not to have found herself in much bigger trouble.

Politics, as executed by Tomlinson, a master politician if nothing else, had been her saviour, she suspected. The chief constable and those who pulled his strings at Westminster, had, she reckoned, decided that to take matters further, and certainly to delve into any kind of witch-hunt concerning blame in the Marshall affair, would serve merely to draw further attention to it and cause more mayhem than already existed.

Karen was, however, almost certainly in a more vulnerable position than she had ever been before.

John Kelly, too, found himself more upset than he had expected to be by Marshall's release. It bugged him. It really bugged him. He didn't like to think about the reasons why this case mattered so much to him. Kelly had allowed himself to be brought down both by events around him and by his own behaviour often enough in the past.

Like Karen Meadows, he forced himself to put on a brave front. He made himself concentrate on other aspects of his life – his work with the *Argus*, his son Nick, Moira, the woman he lived with who was always so patient with him – rather than dwelling on a situation he could do nothing about.

However, just over three weeks after the *Sun*'s serialisation of Richard Marshall's story, Kelly made one of his increasingly rare trips to London for a farewell party for the newspaper's veteran crime correspondent, Jimmy Finch.

Kelly enjoyed his occasional forays back into a world he had long ago left, but this time he had an ulterior motive. Finch's swansong had been to mastermind the Marshall buy-up. Kelly wanted to talk to him about it. He couldn't resist the opportunity. The case was on Kelly's mind all the time, however much he tried to deny it. He knew that Finch would have spent a lot of time with Richard Marshall and, knowing the reporter's habits, he would almost undoubtedly have gone drinking with him.

The party was held at a wine bar not far from the *Sun*'s Wapping offices and just around the corner from the Tower Hotel where Kelly booked himself in for the night. There was a good turnout, mostly other journalists, but also quite an impressive cross-section of police contacts, not to mention a villain or two. Finch was old school, the reporter's reporter who also managed to walk the tightrope in his speciality, thus maintaining the trust of his connections on either side of the law while at the same time somehow or other managing to keep his extremely demanding tabloid editor happy. He was a popular man, big, brash and genial, his lifestyle evident in both his girth and his flushed features.

Jimmy Finch, already showing the signs of having had a considerable amount to drink, greeted Kelly, his equal in height but certainly not in bulk, with an enthusiastic bear-hug, and led him straight to the bar.

Kelly found that there were more old friends at the bash than he might have expected, and enjoyed the evening in spite of not being able to drink himself. He did not, however, forget his hidden agenda.

Quite deliberately he waited until the early hours of the following morning before contriving to get himself involved in a conversation with the by then extremely well oiled Finch about the Marshall buy-up. The other man had a selection of the usual kind of tales, ranging from the machinations of extracting every jot of the story from Marshall to how the opposition were shaken off, and naturally Jimmy Finch was the hero of every one.

Kelly gave him his full attention, chuckling appreciatively in all the right places, before asking casually: 'So what do you think then, Finchy, did he do it or not?'

'Completely innocent, old boy,' replied the veteran crime man. 'As told to the Currant Bun, and you'd never doubt Britain's greatest newspaper, would you?'

Kelly grinned. 'There speaks one of the few men in Fleet Street to work to full retirement age and be looking forward to a hefty News International pension,' he said.

'Dead right, Johnno.' Finch was on the whisky now. His diction remained surprisingly clear – he was, after all, well practised in the arts of coping with copious quantities of alcohol – but his flushed features had turned almost purple. Although the temperature in the air-conditioned wine bar was still pleasant enough there was a film of sweat on his forehead and cheeks. He was breathing heavily. Kelly wondered obliquely how long Finch would actually live to enjoy his generous pension. And as he gently returned the other man to the question he so wanted to hear answered, he reflected that there were some advantages to not drinking, like having a brain still in working order at the end of a night like this one, for a start. Kelly's history of alcoholism had nearly destroyed him twice, and he was absolutely sure that he wouldn't survive a third time. It was actually plain blind fear that kept him sober while all around him drank. He ordered himself a Diet Coke and Jimmy Finch another large whisky without asking him whether he wanted it, lining the glass up on the bar alongside the two already waiting there. Flattery, Kelly thought, might be the answer.

'Come on, Finchy,' he coaxed. 'Don't forget I first worked on the Marshall affair back in the seventies. I'm dying to hear what you think. Knowing you, you've got an opinion. And you're not often wrong, mate, either. If the police had just a handful of guys as sharp as you, we wouldn't have half the cock-ups.'

'You're right, you're absolutely right, Johnno,' responded Finch with a gravity that suggested that Kelly had imparted some extraordinary truth rather than indulged in a buttering-up process which the sober Finch would at once have recognised for what it was.

'So go on, then, waddya think?' Kelly persisted. 'Has justice been done or not? C'mon, Solomon. Let's have your wisdom.'

Finch puffed up his chest self-importantly. It was that time of night. That time in his career, too. He leaned close to Kelly, everything about him conspiratorial. His breath stank of beer and Scotch. Kelly, born-again teetotal, albeit only because he had no choice, had to force himself not to recoil.

'Actually, the bastard more or less told me he'd done it,' he said.

Kelly felt a numbness that began in his belly and spread slowly throughout his body. It was a bit like a morphine injection except that it did nothing to relieve the tension in his neck and shoulders.

'What do you mean?'

Finch leaned even closer. 'Well, you know how smug he is. I asked him if he really didn't know where his other daughter was. He just sort of leered at me. "Oh, I know all right," he said. So I asked him if he was still in touch, in spite of what he'd said in court.

'"Don't be stupid, Jimmy," he replied. I could see it then, in his eyes. He'd had a few, you understand, we both had. But I was holding it better than him. More practice.'

Kelly didn't doubt it. Finch paused to take a deep swallow of his whisky. His hand was steady and he swayed only slightly as he lifted the glass. Kelly had no idea how much Scotch he'd drunk but he knew the old crime reporter had previously been on champagne for most of the day – and he was still functioning, although admittedly a little sluggishly.

'Then I just asked him, outright, just like that, straight.'

Finch took yet another drink.

'Asked him what, Finchy?' prompted Kelly.

'"Did you do it, Richard? Did you kill her then, after all, her and her mother?" Just like that I asked him.'

Finch looked even more pleased with himself, nodded his head sagely and seemed uninclined to say any more.

'So what did he reply, Finchy?' Kelly prompted again.

'He said: "Is the Pope Catholic?"'

'He said what?'

'"Is the Pope Catholic?"' Finch repeated. '"Is the Pope fucking Catholic?"' And he smiled. 'You gotta hand it to him, Johnno. That man has balls. Whatever else he is, by God, he's got balls.'

And with that Finch threw back his head and roared with laughter. It seemed a very long time before he stopped. This was one man who was completely untroubled by his involvement, albeit briefly, in the Marshall affair. Typical bloody tabloid hack, thought Kelly, conveniently forgetting for a moment his own turbulent tabloid past.

'So did you tell anyone about this, Finchy?' he asked, trying to sound casual. 'Did you tell the police?'

'Are you frigging joking, Johnno? You've been out in the sticks too long, mate. We had a major story running.'

'Yes, of course,' replied Kelly very seriously. 'But we are talking murder here—'

'Bollocks,' interrupted Finch. 'None of my bleedin' business.'

'The murder of a young woman and her child, Finchy,' Kelly persisted. 'The solving of a twenty-eight-year-old mystery. Wouldn't that be an even bigger triumph for the old Soaraway?'

'It's in the too-difficult file, mate,' responded Finch. 'Richard Marshall's been up before the appeal court, for God's sake, and the three wise men said that he'd been unjustly convicted and was innocent. Who am I to argue? Anyway, I didn't have a tape on, it was late at night in the boozer. Who'd believe it?'

Kelly looked the other man up and down. Drunk or sober, like him or loathe him, Jimmy Finch was a pro through and through.

'I do, mate,' he said. 'I believe it.'

Mid-morning the following day Karen received a phone call from John Kelly, who told her that he was calling from the train on his way home from London.

'Wondered if you fancied a bite to eat tonight?' he inquired. 'It's been a while. It would be good to catch up. Anyway, I've something to tell you.'

Karen accepted promptly. She was almost grateful. She knew Phil would not be able to see her at all that night. He had muttered something apologetic about a play at his daughter's school. She didn't like to think about those aspects of her lover's life. It was enough that he could not be with her.

It would be good, she thought, to spend time with Kelly. Their long friendship meant that they were easy with each other. He was one of the few people in the world she didn't have to put on an act with. In addition, Kelly had said he had something to tell her. Kelly wasn't a time-waster. Kelly knew how to give as well as how to take. And although his approach had been very casual, there had been something in his voice that had set her antennae waggling. Immediately she wondered if it had anything to do with the Richard Marshall case. It still weighed heavily on her mind, and she knew that it was important to Kelly, too. She might even find out why it was so important to him. There was certainly no doubt that Kelly cared. That had always been one of his problems, she thought wryly. He probably cared too much.

Kelly suggested The Drum at Cockington, a pub in one of Devon's prettiest thatched villages, which she had always liked in spite of the vast numbers of tourists who flocked to it. And he offered to pick her up in a taxi and take her there.

'You may as well take advantage of me,' he told her. 'As an enforced non-driver I don't have any choice. Let me give you a lift in my cab, then at least you can have a drink.'

Karen agreed with alacrity. So much so that she slightly worried herself. She did seem to be drinking more and more lately. A combination of the ups and downs of the Marshall case and her intense affair with Cooper seemed to be leading into what she knew was increasingly dangerous territory. She had always drunk for fun before. Nowadays she was all too often drinking to forget, or simply because she felt she needed alcohol.

Her anxiety, however, was merely fleeting. She had put it firmly out of her head by the time she and Kelly arrived at the Drum, and she gratefully ordered a large gin and tonic.

It was a fine May evening and she had enjoyed the brief taxi ride to picturesque Cockington which was yet to drown under the sea of another summer's tourist wave. Things began exactly how she had hoped, with Kelly regaling her with old newspaper stories. Some of them Karen had heard before. It made no difference. Kelly was a great natural storyteller.

They ordered steak-and-kidney puddings, individually

cooked so that they arrived with their crusts unbroken, thus giving off a quite mouth-wateringly aromatic burst of steam when you dug your fork in. She drank red wine with the meal. Kelly stuck to mineral water. Karen half-considered joining him. Then she told herself it would be a waste of his chauffeuring offer.

It was only when they had both ordered coffee that Kelly became serious.

'Look, Karen, I've got something to tell you,' he began. 'I don't know that it will do any good. But, well, you know I feel every bit as strongly about Marshall and all that has happened as you do, don't you?'

'I know you're involved, Kelly, yes, I do.' She looked at him quizzically. 'As for who cares most – well, it's not a competition.'

'Don't be tricky,' he instructed.

She grinned at him.

He leaned back in his chair, and took a deep swig of his coffee before continuing. Karen knew him well. She guessed he was wishing it was a large Scotch. He had once told her that he didn't think he would ever stop missing alcohol.

'I was up in London last night for a farewell do for one of my few remaining mates in The Street, Jimmy Finch,' he began. 'Ended up having quite a conversation with him. . . .'

He paused, glancing at Karen to see if she registered the significance of what he had just told her. Karen looked blank. She didn't have a clue who Jimmy Finch was.

'He's the *Sun* man who handled the Marshall buy-up.'

Light dawned. Karen was interested now, all right.

'Surprised you didn't know the name from his byline—'

'Just get on with it, Kelly,' muttered Karen. 'Only journalists notice bylines. I'm surprised you haven't learned that by now.'

Kelly pulled a face at her.

'Anyway, he was full of it,' he began. 'It is the crime story of the year, after all, if not the decade, even if the *Sun* getting it was down to their cheque-book rather than the skills of their journos. There was an element of gloating at first, but he's sound, Jimmy Finch, and a bloody good reporter. . . .'

He told her all of it then. And although in many ways his story merely added weight to what she already believed, it was a whole different ball game to hear that Richard Marshall had actually damn near made a confession. Albeit in a pub after a skinful. There were, however, a number of points which bothered her.

'The man's not talked in almost thirty years,' she said. 'He's been interviewed again and again by some of the best in the business, he's been cross-examined in court, and he's stayed tight as a drum. Why on earth would he put himself at risk like that?'

'I don't think he saw any risk, and the bastard's probably right, isn't he?'

'More than likely.' Karen sighed. 'I don't know if there's any point, but this Jimmy Finch, if we looked him up would he go on the record with this?'

Kelly shrugged. 'I doubt it,' he said. 'Finch is a wily old hand. He knows the law inside out, and unlike prats like me and you, I suspect, he knows better than to ever get personally involved. He's always just done his job like a sensible fellow. And if he and his newspaper go on record to say that Marshall has confessed, they put themselves in the wrong, don't they? Newspapers aren't supposed to pay money to criminals for anything, let alone a pack of lies about a murder. It's a tightrope, Karen, and the Jimmy Finches of this world know exactly how to walk it.'

Karen nodded. She knew the type well enough. 'In any case, there's no evidence, is there?' she said. 'You've told me he didn't tape what Marshall said.'

'No chance. Marshall would never fall into that trap, even out of his brains.'

'No.' She drained her red wine. 'I'll think about it overnight, Kelly,' she went on. 'But I really don't know what we're going to be able to do about it, if anything.'

The reporter shrugged again. 'Neither do I,' he replied flatly. 'I just thought you ought to know, that's all.'

'Thank you.' Karen stared at him hard. 'There's something else I'd like to know, Kelly. Why do you care so much about this one? You must have a reason.'

Kelly smiled. 'Not really. I just go back a long way with that bastard Marshall, same as you do.'

He spoke easily enough, but Karen was somehow quite sure there was something he wasn't telling her. The something that Bill Talbot had hinted at all that time ago in the pub. She made a mental note to call Bill the next day and find out exactly what her old boss had been getting at.

First thing, though, she had another call to make. As soon as she got into her office she phoned the chief constable and passed on everything that Kelly had told her.

'I just wanted you to be aware of this development, sir,' she told him.

She could see no way that any action could sensibly be taken, but apart from anything else she was beginning to learn to play politics. Just a little. And about time, too, she reflected. She had a personal situation which might turn sour on her professionally at any time, and she had already had a very narrow escape over the Marshall affair. It could have ruined her career, and it still promised to do it little good. A good start in her determination not to let anything like it happen again was to try to improve her relationship with the CC, and at least keep him informed of everything, keep him up to speed at all times. That way triumphs and disasters were both at least partially shared and it was a lot less easy for the likes of Harry Tomlinson to make a scapegoat of her at will.

None the less, the chief constable's response was exactly what she had expected.

'Hardly a development, Karen,' he responded. 'Even if this confession is kosher, we have no proof. And we don't even know if the journalist is prepared to go on record. Isn't that the sum of it?'

'More or less,' she replied unenthusiastically. Put like that – and Harry Tomlinson would put it like that, of course – it did all sound a bit of a waste of time. She had, however, known that before she began her conversation with him.

'Karen, even if this Jimmy Finch is prepared to go on the record about everything he was told, for God's sake, indeed even if he had taped Marshall's confession, well, the first question must be, is it a confession? "Is the Pope Catholic?" A good barrister would soon sort that out.'

'Well, sir, maybe, but surely everyone understands the expression. It means you're stating the obvious. It means, yes, of course.'

'It's ambiguous, at the very least. But, OK, even if you accept that, it still gets us nowhere. Not at the moment, anyway. Double jeopardy is still in place. You don't overturn a six-hundred-year law overnight.'

For once, Karen had to agree with her chief. And for once he was not even being his usual pompous belligerent self. Indeed, he sounded quite regretful. Perhaps some memories of what it was like to be a policeman did lurk in the recesses of his highly political brain after all, thought Karen. She also reflected that he'd been almost friendly. It seemed that her new approach, her expressed desire to keep her boss informed, had been remarkably effective. She and the CC finished their phone call on the best of terms, which, for them, in any situation let alone under the recent strained circumstances, was a real result, and Karen made a resolution to share her innermost thoughts with him more often. It was not, however, a resolution that she realistically expected to be able to stick to for long.

Rather strangely, her conversation with the chief constable had cheered her up. Perhaps sharing the burden, even with Tomlinson, did work after all. She found herself chuckling as she picked up the phone to call Bill Talbot. The retired detective did not answer. Nether did his wife. And neither was any kind of message service connected.

Karen replaced the telephone receiver on her desk and told herself that was fate. She would not bother Talbot again. What difference could John Kelly's reasons for being so interested in the case make to anything, anyway? Particularly now. Talbot was probably being melodramatic. Kelly's professional thirst alone was enough to drive him on with any story, as she knew perfectly well.

There really was nothing more anybody could do about Marshall. It was infuriating, but that was that. The best thing for her and everyone else involved, including poor Sean

Macdonald, was to try and forget all about it, to move on and get on with their lives. Hers was becoming quite complex enough without dwelling on the past. Apart from anything else, she needed to concentrate on her relationship with Phil Cooper and make sure that she was in charge of it rather than the other way round – although she feared it may already be too late for that.

Her priority had to be the future. She could feel her life spiralling out of control and she didn't like it. She needed to do some concentrated thinking, and not let her brain be entirely led by her heart and her body. She did not need the ghost of Clara Marshall, nor the ghost of a lost daughter she was equally sure had been murdered, to continue to haunt her. She had to exorcise them. And she also had to abandon the near obsession with bringing Richard Marshall to justice which she had harboured more or less throughout her career.

It was over, she told herself. For better or worse, it was over.

Part Three

Sixteen

Karen was, of course, completely wrong. It wasn't over at all.

Five weeks later, Richard Marshall was found dead in the apartment he still owned at Heron View Marina, Poole. He had been shot through the head with a single bullet from a revolver. No attempt had been made to conceal his body.

Karen received the news by telephone from Dorset CID. It seemed that the alarm had been raised by the local postman, delivering a package, who had noticed that the front door to the flat was standing very slightly ajar. And when there was no reply from inside, after he had knocked several times and called out, he attempted to push the door fully open. It moved only three or four inches before he could push it no further. Something heavy seemed to be preventing it from opening. Peering through the gap, the postman had seen the body of a man lying just inside the hallway.

'Oh, fuck,' muttered Karen to herself. And afterwards she sat very quietly and all alone in her office for several minutes. Her first reaction was shock. Pure shock. Her second, hard as she tried to prevent it, involved a certain sense of pleasure. She was glad Richard Marshall was dead. She couldn't help it. She experienced a very strong feeling that a kind of justice had been done at last.

For just a moment she indulged herself, allowed herself to revel in the knowledge of his sudden violent death. She hoped also that whoever had killed him had made sure that Marshall was quite aware that he was about to die, and why. She hoped he had known fear, just as his victims must have done. She hoped that when he had looked death in the eye he had been absolutely one hundred per cent aware that his end had finally come.

Karen sat with her fists clenched and her eyes closed,

savouring the thought. After all this time, after all this heartache, she just couldn't help it.

Then, abruptly, her mind switched track. The police detective in her swung into action. 'Whoever had killed him.' That was the rub. It was now her job and that of the Dorset police to find Marshall's killer. And that thought brought her firmly back down to earth. She was suddenly acutely aware that Richard Marshall's death could only be welcome if it did not create another victim. And there was little doubt that was exactly what it would do. Indeed, Marshall's murderer was almost certainly a victim already, and probably about to become an even greater one.

She turned her attention then to the question of the identity of Marshall's killer. It just had to be someone who had suffered because of the crimes they all believed he had committed. It would stretch credibility even to consider any other motive.

Top of the list, Karen was well aware, had to be Sean Macdonald. Karen knew that. And she didn't like the idea one little bit. Sean Macdonald, of whom she had become so fond. Sean Macdonald, who had made it quite clear that he'd had enough of British justice, and had virtually threatened to take the law into his own hands.

She reminded herself again that Sean Macdonald was eighty-three years old. None the less he was a fit man and a volatile one. And a man who felt deeply aggrieved on behalf of a daughter whose killer had never paid the price for his crime. Until now, perhaps.

She picked up the phone again and called Inverness. Mac's answerphone clicked in. She tried twice more and on the third attempt left a brief message. Then she called Inverness police and asked them to go around to Sean Macdonald's address. After that she gathered her troops around her.

By the time she walked into the incident room it was obvious that the whole of CID and quite probably the whole of the nick knew that Richard Marshall had been murdered. Tompkins and Smiley were giving each other five in one corner. Everybody in the room seemed to be on their feet, laughing and talking. A bottle of whisky was hastily stowed in a drawer as she entered. She pretended not to notice that, but the rest of it had to be attended to.

'Right, that's enough,' she called. 'We're going to a funeral here, not a bloody wedding.'

'Yeah, but it couldn't be a better funeral, could it, boss?' responded Tompkins, to a general muttering of approval. He was looking almost cheerful, which was actually quite difficult for him.

'You think not, Chris?' Karen inquired icily. 'Between us and Dorset we have to find out who murdered Richard Marshall. And that's where this all goes pear shaped.'

There was more muttering, of a different kind.

'I've got Inverness checking out Sean Macdonald,' she went on.

'Oh, fuck,' interrupted Tompkins, no longer appearing at all cheery.

Karen smiled grimly. 'Oh, fuck, is dead bloody right, Chris,' she said. 'Mac has to be our number one suspect and I don't like it any more than I know any of you will.'

She paused, aware that they were all quietening down now, growing thoughtful, which was exactly what she wanted. She was after as much thinking as she could get. She wanted to jerk their brains into action every bit as much as her own.

'Right,' she said. 'We need to get to Poole and check out for ourselves what's happened. Chris, I want you and Ron with me on that.' She nodded towards Smiley. 'You came before, you know the set-up, and you, too, Phil.' She waved one hand at Cooper who had been resolutely keeping an extremely low profile. 'And we'll take two cars.'

As she said that she was aware of somebody giggling but she wasn't able to identify who it was. In any case, she was in no position to do anything about it. Instead she headed for the door, but she didn't shut it before overhearing a whispered: 'And no guesses who's riding with who,' again from someone unidentifiable, followed by a louder: 'Fuck off, wanker,' from Cooper.

Outside in the corridor she leaned briefly against the wall. 'Damn,' she muttered to herself. She'd already had quite enough to worry about even before the discovery of Richard

Marshall's body. Her affair with Cooper was now an open secret. And she didn't know what to do about it. She couldn't give him up. She just couldn't. And yet she feared that she was courting disaster by continuing with such a potentially dangerous relationship.

She travelled with Cooper in his car, which was exactly what everybody expected her to do. But she couldn't help herself.

'No point in disappointing the troops,' said Phil with a grin as he opened the passenger door for her. She grinned back. Just the prospect of being alone with him in his car for the best part of three hours made her feel warm inside. At least he seemed not quite as troubled by the part he had played in Marshall's conviction being overturned as he had a while ago. She suspected that knowing that Marshall was dead had made him feel better, even if he was concerned, like her, about who had killed the man.

He drove with one hand on the wheel, and the other, for most of the time, on her knee. It was companionable. It was easy. That was how it was between them. As if they were joined at the hip. She glanced at him as they made their way out of Torquay and headed towards Exeter. He seemed to feel her eyes on him and turned and smiled. She loved him. She really loved him. And she knew he felt the same. How could she walk away from him?

She was indulging herself, just enjoying the feel of being with him, relishing his company, when their brief few minutes of peace were shattered by the insistent ring of her mobile phone. She answered promptly. This was not a time when she could expect peace.

'Sergeant Craig Brown, Inverness,' said a distinctly Scottish voice. 'I have some information for you concerning Mr Sean Macdonald.'

'Yes?' Karen could not stop an anxious note creeping into her voice. She really was fond of Macdonald, and there was something about the Scots policeman's words which made her think she wasn't going to like what he was about to tell her.

'We have so far been unable to contact Mr Macdonald,' continued Sergeant Brown. 'But we have talked to neighbours who said that they last saw him three days ago loading a suit-case into his car and nobody seems to have seen or heard from him since.'

'I see.' Karen had been right. This was not what she wanted to hear.

'There's more,' said Sergeant Brown. 'On the grounds that he is being sought in connection with a murder inquiry we gained a warrant to enter Mr Macdonald's home. It seems that he must somehow or other have managed to acquire a gun. We found empty ammunition packets in the dustbin, of the type that would contain bullets for a 45-calibre handgun. We are still searching the house but so far have not found the gun itself. I'm afraid, Detective Superintendent Meadows, that it seems reasonable to assume that Sean Macdonald took the gun with him wherever he may have gone to.'

'I see,' said Karen again. She wasn't surprised. Mac was an old military man. She had suspected he might still have contacts who could supply him with hardware if necessary.

She ended the call and briefly told Cooper the news, then she called back to Torquay Police Station.

'Get on to Dorset and tell them Macdonald is now defi-nitely the number one suspect,' she instructed. 'And put out an alert nationwide. I want him found, and I want him found fast.'

As she ended the call she turned to Cooper.

'Oh, shit,' she said. 'I really don't want to put Sean Macdonald in jail.'

The crime scene had been more or less dealt with by the time they got to Poole. Richard Marshall's body was on its way to the morgue in the nearby hospital for a post-mortem. The scenes-of-crime officers had already done their stuff.

The officer in charge, Detective Inspector Gordon Crawley, reported fully to Karen.

'Marshall was shot point-blank in the forehead,' he said. 'Classic entry-and-exit scenario. Small hole in the front of his head and the back of it damned near blown off. We found the bullet lodged in the plaster of the wall just behind the spot where Marshall would have been standing.' Crawley gestured with one hand to an indentation in the cream painted wall. 'One of our guys is a bit of a weapons expert. Was able to tell right away that the bullet was from a 45-calibre handgun, a Browning or something like that.'

Karen looked around the hallway of the small neat apartment and through open doors to the bedroom, living-room and kitchen beyond. Nothing seemed out of place. But then Marshall had been a very organised man, you had to be organised to get away with what he had got away with for so long.

'There's no sign of a struggle at all,' Crawley continued, as if reading her mind. 'It looks as if chummy opened his front door and got it straight in the head, of which there is not a lot left, as you will see if you stay on for the post-mortem tomorrow.'

Karen winced. Partly at the news that it was a 45-calibre handgun that had been used, the same specification as the ammunition found in Sean Macdonald's house, and partly at the thought of attending an autopsy on a body with most of its head blown off. She had done it before. She had learned long ago to toughen up and deal with such gory situations. That did not mean, though, that she liked it.

At the same time the thought occurred to her that she would be able to stay overnight with Cooper, and they didn't get many opportunities to spend the whole night together.

Then she promptly gave herself a mental telling-off. This was too serious a matter to allow herself to start thinking about her sex life. And she suddenly remembered that nobody had mentioned Jennifer Roth at any stage.

'She's not here any more,' explained Crawley. 'She and Marshall lost their jobs at the marina when he was first arrested, but of course he owned this flat. And he would have made enough money from that newspaper article to keep everything going, I imagine.'

He glanced towards Karen as if looking for confirmation. She nodded briefly.

'We understand Jennifer – or Janine, I suppose I should say – recently took off to London looking for work,' Crawley continued. 'She may even have lined up a job to go to. Certainly she's not been seen around here for weeks, not since quite soon after the appeal, in fact. But we're on the case, ma'am, I can assure you.'

Karen then gave Tompkins and Smiley instructions to co-operate with the Dorset police in their search for Jennifer and anything else that they could help with which might speed up the investigation.

'I don't want any cock-ups caused by lack of communication,' she told them. 'DI Crawley is willing to let you have the run of his incident room, and before you head off back home I expect you to know the Dorset operation inside out. No more mistakes, got it?'

Together with Cooper she left the flat then. They stood for a while looking out over Poole Harbour. It was a very different kind of day from the one the previous August when they had come to the marina to arrest Marshall. Different in every way. A light drizzle was falling. The sky was leaden and grey. It wasn't cold but Karen found that she was shivering a bit.

Abruptly she turned to Cooper. 'Got your toothbrush?' she asked.

'Always keep one in the car,' he responded.

'Good, 'cause I haven't got mine,' she said. 'I'll need to borrow yours.'

'I can think of nothing I'd like more, Detective Superintendent,' he replied.

Using Cooper's name they booked into the Hilton in nearby Bournemouth, a hotel Karen had rather liked when she had stayed there once before while on an antique-hunting weekend, with a former boyfriend and fellow enthusiast, around the many antique shops of nearby Boscombe.

She and Cooper treated themselves to a double room with a big balcony overlooking the sea. And as usual there were things they did because of the illicit nature of their relationship which Karen didn't like to think about much and which they avoided discussing. Using Cooper's name was one of these. She knew all too well that he needed to tell his wife where he was staying. He needed an address, even for one night away from home. She didn't need to tell anyone anything. All Karen had to do in order to free herself for the night was to call her neighbour, Ethel, and ask her to feed Sophie the cat. Everyone she worked with had her mobile number and that was the only method of contact necessary.

Cooper did briefly express anxiety about the cost of the room, which was considerably more than he was likely to be able to reclaim on expenses. Karen would have none of it. She knew he spent very little on himself, and had no wish to increase his guilt by insisting that he spend money he would normally spend on his family – which was something else she didn't want to discuss with him, not when they could be together all night in what turned out to be a rather good hotel with twenty-four-hour room service.

'It's on me,' she told him shortly.

He didn't argue. Instead, as soon as they had shut their bedroom door he took her by the hand and led her to the bed where they lay together, fully clothed, for almost an hour, just savouring their closeness.

'I can't get over how good this feels,' she murmured.

'I know.' And he kissed her hair and her eyes and her nose in that unique way he had which almost turned her from lover into child.

They ordered steak and champagne on room service. The earlier drizzle had cleared completely and, although it was now mid-June, it turned out to be an unusually warm night for England in early summer, so they took the opportunity to eat outside, sitting on the big balcony watching the stars and the lights of Bournemouth. The town's two theatres, the Pavilion and the Pier Theatre beyond, blinked at them. The Isle of Wight ferry, which looked a bit like another theatre floating in the sea, was moving slowly across the horizon. It was a magical view.

Karen had had an idea in the back of her head that, with so much more time than usual to be together, this might be their opportunity to talk about their relationship, about where it was going, if indeed it could ever go anywhere. But, as she and Cooper sat together hand in hand, looking out over the seaside town to the ocean, she found that all she wanted to do was enjoy the moment and preserve its memory intact. She didn't want to talk about their problems or what the future might hold for them. She wanted to concentrate on the present. She wanted to be an ostrich. She was head over heels in love. She wanted to pretend that everything was perfect, as, just for one night, in this seaside hotel, it was. Absolutely perfect.

After they had eaten their meal and drunk their champagne they went back to bed and this time they undressed and made love. Their love-making was at the stage where it seemed to get better every time. As far as Karen was concerned, she believed that it was simply because she had never cared so much about anybody.

'It's the same,' he said suddenly. 'It's the same for me.'

She hadn't even spoken. She knew he was right, though. That's how it was between them. They thought and felt the same things at the same time. Often they didn't need to speak at all. She considered it to be quite remarkable.

She reached out for him and drew him to her. He felt so good. He smelt so good. He tasted so good. She realised she was becoming aroused again. Naturally he was, too. At the same time, at the same pace. And they were just beginning again, in a very leisurely fashion, when there was a loud knock on the door.

Automatically they pulled apart.

'Who the hell's that?' Cooper asked.

Karen checked her watch. It was almost midnight.

'Could be room service wanting our tray,' she suggested. 'The waiter did ask us to put it outside.'

'At this hour?'

'Well, I don't know. Just stay here, they'll go away.'

She pulled him close again, and as she did so there was another equally loud and rather more insistent knock.

'Oh, fuck,' he said. 'I don't think we double-locked the door. I'd better have a look.'

He climbed out of bed, ambled over to the door, still naked, and peered through the security peep-hole. At once he recoiled, almost as if he had been attacked.

'Oh, my God,' he whispered.

'What is it? What's wrong?' Karen sat upright in bed, sensing his alarm.

He turned to her.

'It's . . . It's . . .'

He was interrupted by another insistent hammering. Then a voice called out.

'Phil, Phil, I know you're in there with that bloody cow. Open this door, Phil.'

'Oh, my God,' repeated Cooper.

Karen realised at once that it must be Cooper's wife who was out there in the Hilton's fifth-floor corridor. She had no doubt at all, even though Cooper seemed incapable of putting a coherent sentence together. She jumped out of bed, reaching to pick up her clothes which she had unceremoniously dropped on the floor.

'Phil, Phil, open the door!' came another shout from outside. 'Now!'

It was a command. And to Karen's horror Phil appeared to be about to obey. He reached for the door handle.

'Don't!' Karen shouted. 'Don't open it. Tell her you'll meet her downstairs. Tell her anything. Just don't open it!'

It was too late. Meekly, Phil Cooper, the husband who had never cheated before, opened the door. His wife pushed past him into the room. Karen watched it all happen as if it were a movie being screened in slow motion. Automatically, she tried to cover herself with the bundle of clothes she now had in her arms. Her shirt and trousers were both in a tangle. She couldn't sort them out. She felt both pathetic and vulnerable and was quite sure she looked it, too.

Phil Cooper just stood there, still holding the door open, also still stark naked. He seemed to be completely in shock. So was Karen – they were, after all almost always in sync. Sarah Cooper walked towards her. Karen had only seen photographs of Cooper's wife before. She had never met her. She was as pretty as she looked in the pictures Cooper had shown her, before they had begun what now seemed to be their ill-fated affair. But her red hair was dishevelled and you could see from her eyes that she had been crying. Her face was contorted with hatred as she approached Karen.

'You bitch!' she screamed. 'You bitch! I know exactly who you are and I'll get you for this. I'll ruin you. You'll see.'

For a moment Karen thought the other woman was going

to hit her, and she wouldn't have altogether blamed her had she done so. Involuntarily, she took a step backwards. Her nakedness made her feel quite defenceless.

But Sarah Cooper was not that interested in Karen, it seemed. Instead she swung around to face her husband.

'And you. . . !' she began, still screaming. 'As for you, I never want to see you again as long as you live. You are not my husband any more, you bastard. You are no longer the father of my children.'

She ran back across the room, then, to Cooper and slapped him just once across the face. He flinched, and still seemed unable to find any words.

'I am going to make absolutely sure that you never see the children again,' she stormed. Then she pushed past him and out through the door he was still holding open. He let go of it at once and lurched across the room to pick up his clothes, which were also all over the floor.

'I have to go after her, I have to go after her,' he gasped, his voice sounding strangulated, as he struggled into his trousers and shirt.

Karen just watched in silence. There was nothing much she could say and it was pretty obvious she was not in any case going to be given a chance to say it. Cooper seemed almost to have forgotten she was there.

Once he was dressed, after a fashion, he picked up his car keys from the bedside table and took off at a run. In fact, he was in so much of a hurry that he actually opened the door and left the room without speaking to her again. She stood trembling with shock. She had a pain in her stomach. She felt as if she had been abandoned in another universe. This was Phil, the man she loved more than she had thought possible. And, now that he had been confronted by his wife, he did not even have time to give her one small word of comfort.

Just before closing the door, however, he put his head back around it.

'You'll cover for me tomorrow, won't you, Karen?' he asked.

'Of course,' she replied glumly. She had tried to put irony into her voice, but he didn't even notice.

He was gone almost at once. She stood for a few seconds

more, the events of the last few minutes racing through her brain. She feared that she was well enough aware of what it all meant. Phil's reaction had spoken for itself. He was a family man. She had known that. His family had been everything to him until she came along.

And if it came to a choice between her and his children, there was going to be no contest at all. She supposed she had always known that, really. Now she was absolutely certain of it.

She let her clothes fall to the floor again and threw herself on to the bed where so recently she and he had made love so splendidly. And so lovingly.

'You really are a bloody fool, Karen Meadows,' she muttered to herself.

Then, not for the first time during her brief relationship with DS Phil Cooper, she buried her head in the pillows and sobbed her heart out.

Seventeen

In the morning Karen made herself rise early. She showered, brushed her teeth and scrubbed at her red swollen face. She ordered breakfast and she asked reception to arrange a hire-car. She had, after all, been abandoned without transport. But her job now was to forget the ordeal she had been through.

She had an important post-mortem examination to attend. She had a murder inquiry to run. She was Detective Superintendent Karen Meadows. She was not destined to have a man in her life, to have a family, to have a relationship that meant everything to her – unlike, it seemed to her, just about everyone else that she knew. It was as simple as that. Her destiny was her work and nothing else, she told herself. And that was a mess now, too.

She found she couldn't eat the scrambled egg and bacon she had made herself order. The tea, however, was welcome. She was on the second cup when her mobile phone rang for the first time that day. She guessed who it was even before checking the display panel.

'Hello, Phil,' she said flatly.

'Karen, I'm so sorry about everything,' he said. Cooper's voice sounded unnaturally high-pitched and had a definite quaver in it.

'I just don't know what to do,' he went on.

'I think you've done it, Phil.'

'Karen, I didn't have any choice. I had to go after her. Sarah's my wife. She's the mother of my children. I can't lose my children. I really can't.'

'Fine.' Karen didn't really want to hear any of this. She had, in any case, already known it.

'How did it happen, anyway?' she asked. 'Why did she come to Bournemouth?'

'She told me she'd had suspicions about you and me for some time. I thought I was being so bloody clever, but apparently I wasn't at all. She said that it was the way I was behaving, the hours I was keeping, even the way I spoke about you, that made her start wondering. Sarah and I have been together a long time. She knows me very well. When I called and told her I was staying overnight at the Bournemouth Hilton she told me she somehow immediately guessed that I was sharing a room with you. So she simply phoned the hotel and asked if Mr and Mrs Cooper had checked in. The reply was all the confirmation she needed.'

'And she came all the way to Bournemouth just to check it out?'

'I suppose so. She said she still couldn't quite believe it, she had to see for herself. So she took the kids round to her mother's and drove straight here.'

'Well, she certainly saw for herself, all right. What now?'

'God knows. I was in too much of a state to do or say anything sensible last night. And she was in a state, too. But she's not having any so far, that's for sure. She made me sleep out in the car last night.'

'Right.' Karen took note of the self-pity in his voice. He had yet to even ask how she was feeling, what she might be going through. Apart from anything else, Sarah Cooper, with or without justification, had threatened to ruin Karen, and Karen had taken that threat absolutely seriously. It would be extremely easy to carry out. All the woman had to do was contact the Devon and Cornwall Constabulary top brass and let them know what had been going on, that a detective superintendent had been having an affair with a married junior officer, and Karen would be in very serious trouble indeed. This was not, however, what was foremost in her mind. She felt as if her emotions had been hit by a bulldozer, and the bulldozer just kept crashing on and on.

'Look, I can't work today, I really can't,' Phil continued. 'I've got to try to sort this mess out.'

So that's what I am, thought Karen, a mess.

Aloud she said: 'OK, don't worry. I'll say you were called home urgently because of family sickness. All right?'

'You're a brick, Karen.'

'Aren't I, though?' Her sarcasm was actually directed at herself rather than him.

'Well, thanks anyway. Look, as soon as I've got to grips with this I'll get back to you, OK?'

'Of course.' She couldn't believe it. He sounded as if he were in a business meeting. Get back to her? Good God!

'Oh, and Karen, I think I left my watch behind. Could you bring it with you?'

'Sure.' She'd noticed it on the bedside table earlier, and his tie was still lying on the floor.

He rang off then, barely saying goodbye. Karen sat looking at her phone for a moment or two. Her hands were trembling. It had been like talking to a stranger. Phil was now going to attempt a reconciliation with his wife, she assumed. And he seemed to just take it for granted that she would accept that. She *would* accept it, too, of course. In any case, what choice did she have?

She gathered up her briefcase, shoved her phone in her pocket, and hurried out of the room. All she could do was switch her mind off Phil Cooper. She didn't have time to think about her feelings any more. And in any case she was too frightened to do so.

The post-mortem examination brought no surprises. Richard Marshall's estimated time of death was between ten and twelve hours before his body was found. So he had been killed the previous evening, and his condition indicated that the handgun with which he had been shot had been fired at close range. His body showed no signs of any other injury.

Karen found that she was completely dispassionate as she watched the proceedings. The truth was, she had grudgingly to admit, that although it was, of course, useful to exchange views with the Dorset policemen present, and to know at first hand the thoughts of the pathologist, she might not have bothered to stay over for the inquest at all had it not been for the opportunity to spend a night with Cooper. And look how that had turned out, she reflected wryly.

Not even the gory sight of the decimated remains of Richard

Marshall's head moved her. Although she had become extremely good at steeling herself at post-mortems, Karen didn't think anyone ever got completely used to the sight of mutilated or decayed bodies. However, on this occasion she was completely unmoved. Whether or not this was due to her complete lack of any kind of compassion for Marshall or whether it was simply that she was still numb from the events of the previous night, she was not sure. A bit of both, she supposed.

As she walked to her car she received a second call on her mobile, this time from DC Tompkins back in Torquay.

'We've found Sean Macdonald, boss,' said Tompkins, sounding almost excited. 'He was on a fishing trip, staying in some remote Highlands hotel. Apparently he saw on breakfast news this morning that Richard Marshall had been found dead and immediately phoned here for you.

'Inverness are checking it out but the hotel have already confirmed that he's been there for four nights. He admits that he did buy a handgun, from some old army pal apparently, though he won't say how, of course, and that he did consider seeking his own revenge on Marshall. But he says he couldn't go through with it. The gun was in the boot of his car. He said he was planning to throw it into some deep water somewhere. If you ask me, boss, he still hadn't quite made up his mind whether to have a poke at Marshall or not. He was still hedging his bets. There was ammunition with the gun, but the Inverness boys say that if Mac had tried to fire the thing he may well have ended up killing himself. It turned out to be an old Second World War Smith and Wesson, would you believe? They're having it checked out by forensic, but they don't reckon it's been fired in twenty years, let alone two days ago.

'So it looks like Mac's in the clear, boss, whatever he may or may not have intended. Of course, it was illegal for him even to have the gun in his possession, but Inverness have indicated that, taking all the circumstances into account, including Mac's age, they'll probably settle for a formal caution on that.'

'Thanks, Chris.'

Karen felt relief wash over her as she climbed into her hire-car. Having to arrest Sean Macdonald might well have proved one thing too much for her to cope with, she thought.

She started the engine and switched on Classic FM. It was her favourite driving and thinking station. She wanted to concentrate hard on where this latest development left the new murder investigation. If Sean Macdonald was no longer the main suspect, then who was next on the list?

Suddenly another thought struck her. She was still in the hospital car park, heading for the exit. Abruptly she pulled in to her left on to a wide section of pavement and stopped the car. Then she fished in her handbag for her phone again.

There was somebody she hadn't heard from. She dialled another mobile phone number. The phone was switched off. All she got was a message service. She didn't leave a message. Not yet. Instead she dialled the number of the *Evening Argus* back in Torquay.

The news desk told her Kelly wasn't there. He was off sick.

'Was he in the office yesterday?' she asked.

'Oh, yes,' responded the young news-desk assistant help-fully, apparently finding nothing curious in such a query. 'Well, he was in first thing but then he went home because he said his tummy bug was back. He'd been off the day before, you see. . . .'

Karen felt her heart start to beat faster. She made another call then, to Kelly's home. His partner, Moira, answered on the fifth ring. She sounded sleepy. Karen remembered then that Moira was a nursing sister who worked nights at Torbay Hospital. She didn't feel guilty about waking her, though. This was far too important.

'Is John there?' she asked.

'Uh, no, he's working.'

The warning bells rang at once. His office had said he was off sick. Moira said he was working. This didn't look good. Unless Kelly, a man with a bad track record with both women and wine, was up to his old tricks, of course. Karen didn't think so.

'You don't know where he's gone, do you?' she asked as casually as she could.

'He's working on the Marshall story. I'm surprised you haven't caught up with him. I would have thought he'd have been chasing you, actually.'

'He has,' Karen lied swiftly. 'I missed his calls. Now his mobile's switched off. Between you and me, I've got something for him. Something we can help each other over. But I need to get to him fast. Do you know exactly where he is?'

'Well, no. He left in a hurry yesterday morning. He woke me up halfway through my day's sleep, too, phoning to say there'd been a development and he had people he needed to see on the Marshall case and he didn't know when he'd be back. I guessed he was going to Bournemouth, and then, well, when I heard on the news later about Richard Marshall I just assumed he'd had one of his tips. . . .'

For a moment Karen felt hope rising. 'So was he at home the previous day, then?'

Her hope was swiftly squashed. 'Oh, no. He was out on the story all that day as well, Bournemouth then, too, I assumed. I think he told me so. Oh, I'm not sure. . . .'

Moira Simmons' voice tailed off. Karen could sense the other woman's sleepy brain beginning to turn over. She was not quite as ingenuous as the *Argus*' young news-desk assistant, who must surely, Karen thought, be very new to his job.

None the less, she persisted a little more. 'Have you heard from him since he left yesterday morning?' she asked.

'Yes, he called late afternoon to say he would be away overnight. . . .'

Moira Simmons sounded really concerned now. Karen ended the call abruptly before Moira could start to question her. She realised that she must have put all kinds of thoughts into the woman's mind, but that wasn't important. All that really mattered was to find out where Kelly had been for the last two days and what he had been up to.

Karen had that sinking feeling again. First Sean Macdonald, now Kelly. What was it with this case? It was just too close to home, it really was.

She fiddled in her handbag again and fished out a cigarette. She really needed one. Again. Tomorrow she would definitely give up. Then she made another call. This time to Bill Talbot.

To her relief her old boss was at home and answered his phone straight away.

She didn't waste time with small talk.

'Bill, do you remember you mentioned to me in the pub once that John Kelly had a special reason for being so interested in the Richard Marshall case? Can you tell me all about it, please?'

'Sure.' Bill sounded puzzled. 'Hey, what about the news, though? That bastard Marshall's got his at last. Couldn't believe it when I heard. You won't find it necessary to look too hard for whoever took him out, I hope.'

Karen had neither time nor inclination for those sort of sentiments. She ignored him totally on that issue. Instead she persevered with the purpose of her call.

'Bill, please, tell me about Kelly.'

'Oh, yes.' Talbot sounded disappointed. He'd wanted to enjoy the moment, no doubt, to share it with a kindred spirit.

'Well, it's all about Kelly's mother, really,' he went on. 'Angela Kelly taught Marshall's girls at primary school. Well, actually, she was the headmistress, and a bloody good one at that, I'm told. It seems that the day after Clara Marshall was last seen the eldest Marshall girl, Lorraine, told Kelly's mother that her father had got rid of her mother—'

Karen interrupted there. Light had suddenly dawned. 'I knew about the headmistress, it's in the files, and I'm not at all sure I didn't hear it gossiped about at the time. But I had no idea she was John Kelly's mother. I'd missed that completely.'

Karen cursed herself. She felt she really should have known.

'Do you know the rest?' Talbot asked.

'Well, I know that the headmistress always blamed herself, thought that if she'd reported to the police what the little girl had said that she might have saved both children. She had no reason to blame herself, of course – what Lorraine Marshall said was just the sort of thing kids do say when their parents' marriage is on the rocks.'

'Indeed,' Talbot continued. 'But that was not the end of it, I'm afraid. It played on Angela Kelly's mind. I talked to her myself, you know, when the shit finally hit the fan the year after Clara and the girls disappeared and when we first arrested Marshall. She kept saying over and over again: "Lorraine told me her father had got rid of her mother, she told me her father had got rid of her mother. She told me that and I should have understood. I should have done something."

'Mrs Kelly always believed that it was because she had confronted Richard Marshall and told him what his daughter had said that he then killed his children as well as his wife. And she couldn't forgive herself for having been taken in by him, for believing him when he said that Clara had first left him, then returned for the girls. I remember that I couldn't console the woman at all. And neither, it seems, could anyone else. Six months later she killed herself. She took an overdose. And her family, John included, never had any doubts at all over why she did it. . . .'

Talbot paused there. Karen felt a chill in her spine.

'Oh, my God,' she whispered.

Talbot began to speak again. 'Well, as it's turned out Marshall certainly didn't kill both children. That's one thing we do know, because at least one of those girls is still alive. Ironic really, isn't it, Karen?'

Karen did not reply. She was lost in her own thoughts, and they were extremely disturbing ones.

'Karen?' There was both curiosity and anxiety in Talbot's voice now. He had started thinking too, it seemed. 'Karen? Are you there? You don't think Kelly had anything to do with it, do you? Surely not. . . .'

Karen interrupted him then. She wasn't going down that road. Not yet. Not with anyone. Not even with Bill Talbot.

'For God's sake, Bill. I've had people going through all the files on this case over and over again. How could they have missed the headmistress's suicide? Was it there? Was it properly recorded?'

'Well . . .' Bill sounded disconcertingly unsure of himself. 'Yes, it must have been. Everything was. It's just that the inquiry was so disjointed. After we launched the initial investigation, and then had to let Marshall go because we didn't have enough on him, well, everything went pear shaped really. People kept coming up with theories, with their slant on things, you know how it is . . . you've moved on to something else by then—'

She interrupted again. 'Bill, are you trying to tell me that Mrs Kelly's suicide and its probable cause wasn't properly recorded?'

'No, of course not. It must have been. It's just that there was so much, and so much after the event, if you see what I mean—'

'No, I don't bloody see what you mean, Bill,' Karen stormed. 'No wonder this fucking investigation has made the Devon and Cornwall Constabulary a laughing stock. Problem is, I just got the tail end of it and now I'm the one taking all the shit full in my face.'

She pushed the end button then. She knew she'd been unfair, really, but she couldn't help it. The whole investigation had been a series of disasters from the very beginning, at least one of which she shared the blame for, and nothing seemed to be changing. But this was another development which hit her hard personally. She cared about Kelly. Not only that, she had to admit to herself, too many people knew of her close friendship with him. In fact, before her relationship with Phil became the focus of station gossip, she knew there had always been talk of her and Kelly having an affair. That had actually never been the case. None the less Kelly was already a suspect character.

Not that long previously Karen had been instrumental in arresting John Kelly and of actually charging him with a murder during the investigation of another case, which she had always considered never to have been satisfactorily resolved. And that had been the case which had at one stage threatened to scupper her promotion to detective superintendent, or worst, at least partly because of her association with Kelly. Kelly had fallen under the spell of the mesmerising Angel Silver, the high-profile widow of a rock star. And although he had been proven innocent before the case had even got to court and all charges had been dropped, he had only got himself into such a situation because of his tendency towards allowing his emotions to take control of him. It was true that his behaviour then had probably been accentuated by excessive use of drink and drugs, and, as far as Karen knew, Kelly was now clean, but none the less he had shown little self-control over anything much over the years.

Karen took yet another cigarette from her packet and lit it with the glowing end of the first. She inhaled deeply.

She had to admit to herself that if there was one man in the world who she knew was capable of acting in a thoroughly out-of-character way because he had allowed his feelings to run out of control, it was John Kelly. Fond as she was of him, she had believed before that under certain circumstances he could be capable of murder. She still believed it. And with his healthy list of criminal contacts Kelly was another man who would have no trouble at all getting hold of a gun if he wanted one.

She picked up her phone again and called Torquay Police Station.

'I want a national alert put out on John Kelly,' she said. 'I want him found. And I want him found fast.

'And if he won't co-operate, if he won't come quietly, I want him arrested on suspicion of murder.'

Eighteen

It did not prove necessary to arrest John Kelly after all.

Karen arrived back at Torquay Police Station just as the call came through from the Met. Kelly had turned up at Hammersmith Police Station less than an hour earlier. He had wanted to report the discovery of a body. The body of a young woman believed to be Jennifer Roth.

Karen felt yet again as if she'd been punched in the stomach. What was going on here? The whole scenario was becoming more and more complex and confusing by the second. What on earth had happened to Jennifer Roth? How had she died? And why had John Kelly of all people, a Torquay-based reporter, found her body in West London? She and the entire might of two police forces hadn't even had a clue where to find Jennifer Roth.

She grabbed the phone from the hand of the detective sergeant who had taken the call.

'Detective Superintendent Meadows,' she announced in a loud clear voice which she hoped would indicate to whoever was on the end of the line that she was in charge and which, as ever, totally belied the way she was feeling.

'DS Farthing, Hammersmith,' came the response.

'Right, DS Farthing,' commanded Karen, 'I want you to start at the beginning and tell me everything that has happened.'

'Well, it's a bit confused still, ma'am,' began the detective sergeant. 'But one thing that is straightforward is that a young woman, whom it seems is almost certainly Jennifer Roth, was found lying in a pool of blood in her own flat with half her head blown off and a handgun by her side.

'This chap John Kelly came in here to say he'd found her. He was in a dreadful state, and he still is. Could hardly get the words out. He kept saying: "She's topped herself, she's topped herself." Now that could be the case, but we just don't know for sure yet what happened.

'Anyway, one of our lads, who recently transferred to the Met from down your way, remembered Kelly at once from that big case you had a couple of years back involving that rock star's widow, Angel Silver. He also remembered that John Kelly had actually been charged with murder at one point, so we reckoned we could at the very least have a suspect character on our hands. Then we realised who Jennifer Roth was, and who her father was – and, well, we thought we'd better get in touch with you guys at once.'

Karen took a deep breath and did battle with herself to stay calm.

'I'm grateful for that,' she said. 'You still have Kelly, I presume?'

'You bet, ma'am. We're holding him for questioning. That man's going nowhere till we are quite sure we know how Jennifer Roth died. For a start it looks pretty certain that he broke into her flat this morning. Or if he didn't somebody else did. A window's been smashed round the back. We've got the SOCOs there, of course, and our pathologist, so we should be getting some basic facts soon. Meanwhile we're getting a doctor in for Kelly. Whatever he may or may not have done, he's in total shock and we just can't get any sense out of him.'

'Right,' said Karen. 'I'd really like to talk to John Kelly myself, if that's all right. I have a history with Kelly; I think I'd stand a better chance than most. Can you square it with your governor?'

'Shouldn't be a problem, ma'am. He knew I was calling you guys and agreed it was the best thing. To tell the truth, this John Kelly has actually been asking to speak to you, and he doesn't seem willing to even attempt to talk to anyone else. You'd better fax over a request in writing, for the record, but I can promise you that'll just be a formality. Any help you can give with sorting this lot out would be greatly appreciated. You can move the crime scene down to Torquay if you want.'

Karen chuckled. 'We have quite enough crime scenes of our own, thank you very much, Sergeant,' she replied. She glanced at her watch. 'I'll get the fax organised, then I'll be on my way. Should be with you by about six, I'd hope.'

She rang off then and turned to Tompkins.

'Right, Chris,' she said. 'You're with me again and you're driving. I've done enough of that already today. And by the time this day's over I'm going to be out on my feet, I reckon.'

They arrived at Hammersmith Police Station, just off the main shopping street, at ten past six. Pretty good timing, Karen thought. She'd been just ten minutes out. But then she had been pushing Tompkins to drive to the limit all the way.

DS Farthing came to meet her almost as soon as she walked into the front office. She immediately expressed her gratitude to him for the speed with which he had contacted the Devon and Cornwall Constabulary and for the way in which he had arranged for her to join in the operation. That kind of co-operation between the Met and a county force was rare indeed. Under the present happy circumstances, Karen didn't make a point of that, of course. But then she didn't need to. She and DS Farthing were both experienced long-serving police officers. They knew the score.

Karen didn't feel she had time for any preamble. 'I'd like to see Kelly straight away if I can,' she said.

'No problem, he's in an interview room already, waiting for you.'

Karen raised both eyebrows. This was co-operation of an unprecedented level. She could only assume that the Met in Hammersmith had more work than they could cope with, because they were certainly content to unload all they could of this case.

Kelly was sitting at a table in a small windowless interview room, looking much the same as he had when she had last seen him in a similar situation. Rather disconcertingly, his eyes seemed to be somewhat glazed. She did not treat him to the courtesy of any preliminary greetings. Instead she sat down smartly opposite him, gestured for the uniformed constable already in attendance to switch on the tape recorder, and began.

'Right,' she said. 'Let's start at the beginning. How did you come to find the body of Jennifer Roth?'

Kelly looked startled, as if he had expected a different, more sympathetic approach, perhaps, from his old friend. Well, that was tough, thought Karen, because he certainly wasn't going to get it. Kelly seemed to be beginning to make a habit of this kind of thing. He had put her at risk professionally before, and she wasn't going to let him do it again. He may have done her a big favour once, but that was a very long time ago, and it was a favour which she felt had been called in on more than one occasion already.

She noticed that Kelly had not shaved that day, that his eyes were red-rimmed, and that his hands on the table before him were trembling. He was staring hard at her. For a moment she thought he was going to ask her for some sort of favour. Then he just seemed to slump in his chair, and at the same time he began to speak.

'I travelled up to London yesterday as soon as I heard the news of Marshall's death,' he said. 'I had to see Jennifer straight away. I took the train to Paddington and then the tube back to Hammersmith. I went to her flat but there was no reply. I tried a few times, then I booked myself into a pub round the corner that does B and B. I had her phone number and I kept calling. I even called in the middle of the night. Still no reply.

'So this morning I went around to the flat again and when I still couldn't raise her I decided to break in and have a look. I was worried, and I was right to be, it seems. I felt responsible, you see, I had a dreadful feeling that I knew what might have happened. And I also had a dreadful feeling it was down to me.'

Kelly paused and wiped the back of one hand wearily across his eyes. Karen did not speak. She had no intention of putting him out of his misery.

'As you probably know now, it's a basement flat in one of those big old terraced houses just off the North End Road,' Kelly continued. 'I went round the back and broke a pane of glass in the kitchen door. It only had a Yale lock so once I could get my hand inside all I had to do was open it. Some security, eh?'

'Get on with it, Kelly.' Karen had no more time for diversions than she had for social niceties. She was deliberately brusque even though she knew it was only nervousness which had made him make the remark about security in the first place.

'Well, I went into the flat and I called out for her and then I just went through the rooms. I found her in the bedroom. . . .'

His voice tailed off. He looked as if he might be about to be sick. He ran his tongue around his lips.

'Can I have a glass of water?' he asked.

Karen nodded and gestured to the uniformed constable to do the honours. She was, however, not in the mood to show a great deal of compassion for Kelly. God knows what mess he had managed to get himself in yet again, but this time she was determined she was not going to join him in it.

'She was spread-eagled across the bed. That damned gun beside her. I can't remember when I last saw so much blood . . .'

Kelly stopped again.

Karen was not going to give him an inch.

'Go on,' she instructed.

'She'd blown her fucking head off, hadn't she?' Kelly leaned back in his chair, closed his eyes and grasped his head with both hands, covering his face. For a moment Karen thought he was going to pass out. She still showed him no mercy, gave him no encouragement. Instead, once again, she waited in silence for him to continue to speak.

'I didn't need a doctor to tell me she was dead, that's for sure,' he said eventually. 'I dialled 999, and the rest you know, I expect.'

'The rest I most certainly do not know. You are aware that the Met regard you as a suspect, I suppose?'

'Yes, and they're dead right to,' responded Kelly instantly. 'I am responsible for her death, I reckon.'

Karen sighed wearily. 'Not again, Kelly,' she said. 'We seem to have been down this road once before, I recall. Will you please stop playing games with me, and tell me in plain English what exactly you mean by that remark.'

Kelly leaned forward and bowed his head over the table. Karen could see the tension in him. His hands were trembling even more. Under different circumstances Karen might have felt sorry for him, but the way things were she had neither time nor inclination for any sympathy at all.

'Well, if it hadn't been for me, if I hadn't done what I did, I reckon she'd still be alive—'

'For Christ's sake, Kelly,' Karen interrupted in a stentorian roar that caused both Chris Tompkins, and the young Met constable who had just returned with the requested glass of water, to look extremely startled. She was aware that she was conducting this interview in a far-from-textbook way, but she couldn't help it. This was John Kelly, after all.

'All right. All right.' Kelly knew perfectly well what was required of him, Karen suspected, and from his demeanour it seemed that he might at last be prepared to give.

'I've been in touch with Jennifer Roth for some weeks, well, since just after I went to Jimmy Finch's retirement do, actually,' he said, glancing at Karen rather sheepishly. She feared that she could guess what was coming next, and she also had a dreadful idea that she knew exactly where it was leading.

'Go on,' she prompted for what seemed the umpteenth time.

'Well, she'd already moved from Poole to Hammersmith. I tracked her down through the marina office. She'd left a forwarding address, simple as that.'

Karen shut her eyes briefly, then opened them again. She wondered how long it would have taken Dorset CID to think of that. And she should have arranged for such a simple inquiry herself, too.

'She'd found herself a job in an office,' Kelly went on. 'A surprisingly good job, she said, but I think she also wanted to get away from her father, at least for a bit.

'Anyway.' He stopped and glanced at Karen. 'You know what I'm going to say, don't you?' he asked.

Karen thought that she might. She wondered if Kelly was ever going to stop playing games. And she also wondered if it was really just nerves that was making him behave like this or if he was covering something up. Mind you, she reckoned, if he was, then it was probably only his own thoughtless behaviour.

'Kelly, for Christ's sake,' she said yet again.

He continued straight away then. 'Well, I sought her out because I wanted to tell her what Jimmy Finch had said about Marshall confessing to him.'

'You did what?'

'I told her that Marshall had more or less confessed to killing her mother,' Kelly repeated a little sheepishly. 'Not just about her mother's death, but also implying that he'd killed her sister, too.'

'Terrific,' said Karen. 'Absolutely terrific. And how did she respond to that, as if I couldn't guess?'

'Look, I actually had a purpose in telling her what I did.' Kelly was on the defensive now. 'I'd got the name of this doctor who was an expert on Recovered Memory Syndrome. You know about it?'

'Of course.' There'd actually been a conviction based on the highly controversial condition the previous year up in Merseyside which involved a young girl witnessing her father kill her mother in 1978. The girl, by then a twenty-nine-year-old woman, underwent intensive counselling sessions including hypnotherapy which had allegedly caused her to recall scenes that she had previously blanked out of her mind.

'Well, I suggested to Jennifer that she should see this doctor and undergo therapy, so that if she had any doubts at all about her memory of what happened she could at least be reassured. Well, that was the way I put it to her. . . .'

Kelly paused. Karen smiled tightly. 'Reassured' was a word that slipped rather too easily off the tongue of a one-time tabloid hack, she thought to herself. This time she waited a little more patiently for Kelly to start talking again.

'She listened to me but she didn't seem all that keen; then she called me to say that she had made an appointment. I think she just wanted to talk to someone. Also, when you and the prosecuting counsel had all gone on about how she could have been disturbed as a child and that her memory, prompted by Marshall, might not be one hundred per cent, I think something did seep through even though she wouldn't have it at the time. I think she already had her doubts and I provided her with a way of putting them to rest. Or at least that's what she hoped would happen.'

He paused and glanced at Karen as if he was looking for reassurance now.

'If you ask me, she so desperately wanted a father, a real father, that she willed herself to believe in Marshall, and that meant that she had to believe everything he told her about what happened with her mother and her sister. Marshall played daddy to her from the moment she rediscovered him, and she didn't want it to end. By God, she didn't.'

He stopped again. Karen studied him appraisingly. Sometimes she just could not believe the way Kelly behaved, the way he meddled.

'Psychiatrist yourself now, are you?' As she spoke she realised this was not the first time she had made that remark to him. But she had never been so serious before.

'Obviously not,' he replied very quietly. 'I made a real balls up of it. It's true what I said before, all right, whatever you make of it. She's dead because of me. I am responsible.

'Two days ago now she phoned again and she said that she'd had several sessions with the shrink I'd recommended and that she had successfully recovered her memory, and that this time she was absolutely certain that she remembered everything correctly. She said she wanted to tell me all of it. But she wouldn't talk on the phone. Said she wanted to meet me face to face. So I dropped everything and took the train to London.'

Kelly coughed drily and reached for his glass of water. Karen was intrigued now.

'Why you, do you think?' she asked more gently.

'She said I'd provided the key to her memory and maybe I could tell her how to use it.' Kelly smiled. 'Those were her exact words, come to think of it. Quite poetic really. I don't think she knew who to turn to, actually. She had no friends worth mentioning and no family apart from Marshall.'

'What about going to the police?'

'Under the circumstances she didn't think the police could help. Not this time round, as she put it.'

'Under what circumstances?'

Kelly smiled grimly. 'Look, you don't have to listen to me telling you anything second-hand,' he said. 'I've got it all on tape.'

'You have?' In spite of herself, Karen could feel the excitement welling up in her.

'Yup. I did an in-depth interview with her at her flat the day before yesterday. Then afterwards I went back home to decide what to do with it, what to do next, what I could do next. It was pretty tricky stuff, as you can imagine. Then I heard the news yesterday morning that Richard Marshall had been killed. I couldn't believe it. I hadn't expected her to do anything like that. I really hadn't.'

Kelly covered his face with his hands.

'Anything like what, exactly?' Karen was being very careful.

'Well, I just knew at once that she'd killed him. That she'd killed Richard Marshall. I just knew it. I mean, if he'd been my father I'd have killed him.'

Yes, but not everyone is quite such a hothead as you, thank God, thought Karen. Aloud she said nothing. Instead she waited again for him to resume speaking.

'I knew she'd done it so I just got myself to the station and caught a train straight back here. I didn't know what to do when I couldn't raise her. It was during the night that I began to think she was probably dead, too. That was why I broke into her flat this morning.

'And I was proved right, unfortunately. She was dead. Stone dead. Half her bloody head blown off. And I'll bet you, I'll bet you everything I've got, that you'll find the gun that killed her also killed Richard Marshall in Poole.'

By late afternoon the next day the Met were satisfied that Jennifer Roth had indeed almost certainly killed herself. The regional Home Office pathologist reported that the angle of the gun indicated a self-inflicted wound. Initial forensic evidence also backed up the suicide theory. And the gun used, a Browning 45, was also almost certainly the weapon used to kill Richard Marshall in Poole.

Kelly, who had been held overnight at Hammersmith Police

Station, was released into Karen's custody, enabling her to take him back to Torquay. She couldn't wait to hear that tape which, for reasons that defied her, he had left in the drawer of his desk at home. His explanation was that he thought the content so explosive that he didn't want to carry the tape around with him.

In the car on the way down the M5, Karen's mobile phone rang and a familiar number flashed on to the screen. It was Cooper. For a moment she considered not answering it. She glanced at Tompkins. It was a filthy day again for the time of year. The rain was tipping down and the detective constable was frowning in concentration as he peered through the curtains of misty water being formed by the heavy traffic all around him. In the back seat Kelly, who had earlier grumbled that he had not slept for one minute during his night spent in a police cell, was snoring gently.

Karen let the phone ring several times before finally pressing the receive button.

'Yes,' she said curtly.

'Karen, I've got to talk to you—'

'This isn't a good moment. I am in the middle of a murder investigation.'

'Look, Sarah has said she'll give me another chance if I apply for a transfer. It's not what I want, but I'm just terrified of losing the kids—'

Karen interrupted again. 'I think it *is* what you want, actually.'

Something in her voice attracted Tompkins' attention. She was aware of him briefly shifting his attention from the busy motorway and glancing at her curiously.

'I'm sorry, Karen. Look, it needn't be permanent. I don't want to lose you, honestly. But for the moment I think it would be for the best. She's also said that if I do that she won't take any action about you.'

'That's big of her.' The words slipped out. Tompkins looked around again. Like most of his colleagues Tompkins, in spite of his taciturn appearance and manner, was a natural-born gossip. Karen knew that all his inner antennae would be waggling by now.

Cooper was still speaking. 'I just don't know what else to do, it's all such a mess. . . .'

His voice tailed off.

'That's absolutely fine,' said Karen. And she ended the call.

Tompkins said nothing, as usual, but Karen had a small bet with herself that he had guessed who was on the end of the phone and was currently speculating colourfully about what might be going on. No doubt the incident would be reported fully back to Torquay nick ASAP.

By the time they reached Kelly's house Moira had left for night duty at the hospital and the three of them had the place to themselves. Without preamble the reporter produced an audio cassette which he began to play on the big living-room stereo system.

Karen sat on a hard chair by the window. She didn't feel like making herself comfortable.

Jennifer Roth's voice filled the room. It was a good sound system. The result was extremely eerie. It was surreal. This was a voice from the dead. A voice Karen remembered so well and already associated with dropping bombshells. But never before a bombshell on this scale.

Kelly stood, leaning against the wall, over by the kitchen door. His head was bowed and he was stroking his forehead with the fingers of one hand. Tompkins perched on the edge of the sofa, hands on his knees, all ears, more alert than Karen had ever seen him before, she thought.

'*I just wanted to tell you what happened, John, because I know now, beyond any doubt. I really know. And I'm talking to you like this because I want to put the truth on record,*' said Jennifer's voice on the tape. She was speaking very deliberately.

'*Thank you for trusting me,*' replied Kelly.

Karen shot him a mildly disgusted look across the room. Kelly had the grace to look ashamed. He had been using his 'I'm a nice journalist, you can tell me anything' approach, and Karen was all too familiar with it.

'*I have now completed six therapy sessions with the psychiatrist, Dr Huxtable, who you recommended me to,*' continued Jennifer. She was speaking almost without expression, the tone of her voice very flat, her public school accent less noticeable perhaps than usual.

'*I was more inclined to go to him than you may have realised. I'd been having these dreams. I had them as a child. As a very young child. They were never clear. They were shadowy. I had a vision of being in another house, of a lot of shouting and screaming. Of dreadful things happening but I somehow wasn't sure exactly what. All the while I was being brought up in Cheshire I knew perfectly well that I'd had another life. But I shut everything out because I wanted to escape from the things that happened in my head whenever I tried to sleep. My adoptive mother told me that I was just having nightmares. They were such good people, my new parents, Carol and Michael, they looked after me and loved me and they helped me blot out the past. I have no idea what they knew, more than likely the same story Richard Marshall was to tell me later, after Carol and Michael died.*

'*It was then, when I was sorting through all their papers, that I came across letters from my real father. From Richard. He had obviously been keeping in touch with Carol and Michael, wanting to know about me. It was wonderful for me to find that I still had a father, my natural father, and that he had cared about me all these years.*

'*I wrote to him and he wrote back to me at once. He came to see me in Cheshire and talked to me about it all and explained what had happened when I was five, how our mother had tried to kill us all, he told me what had led him to give me away. And my sister Lorraine, he said. Suddenly it all made sense, the violent dreams, all of it, and I suppose what he told me was what I wanted to hear. Or as near as was possible, anyway, given that my mother was dead and I'd lost my sister. He seemed so kind and gentle and everything he said expressed concern for me.*

'*I believed him wholeheartedly. And then he told me about this new job he had in Poole and the flat and everything and asked me if I wanted to live with him there. It was like another dream to me, but a good dream for a change. He said the police had never stopped hounding him, that he wanted to protect me from all that, so it was better just to let people think I was his girlfriend.*

'*We were happy together. He was rebuilding his life, I think, after breaking up with his latest woman. He was honest enough about* that side of himself, too. He said he had a weakness for the ladies. He said that had caused all of his troubles. He even told me about his fraud conviction, and he said he'd only done what he'd done then because he'd got into financial trouble when he'd been trying to run two families. I suppose I believed what I wanted to believe. Because I had always wanted something like that, to find my real father or mother again, to get to know them.

'I thought I did know him, too. When he was arrested I believed in him absolutely, and when I came forward after he was convicted I still believed in him. A lot of what the police and the lawyers said, though, about my being disturbed by what had happened to me as a child, did get through to me. Because I knew that none of it was clear, whatever I said, none of my memories were clear. They were all hazy around the edges.

'Then, after my father won his appeal, I began to get the dreams again. The dreams I couldn't understand. That's why I thought it might be best to move away from him for a while. I started looking for work elsewhere. I had been an office manager before, and I was rather good at it. I found a new job quite easily and moved here to Hammersmith. I didn't tell my father about the dreams. I didn't want to face up to them, I suppose. But they began to get worse and worse.

'So when you told me that my father had confessed more or less, to that crime reporter on the Sun, it really got through to me. And then when you explained about Recovered Memory Syndrome and suggested I see Dr Huxtable, well, I wanted to do it at once even though I didn't admit it either to myself or to you, John. I hadn't talked to any other journalists. I'd never heard of RMS – I don't read the papers a lot – I just wasn't aware of it. For the first time in my life I could see how it might be possible to open a window into my past.'

Jennifer paused, and Karen could hear a swallowing sound as if perhaps she was taking a drink of something. When she started to talk again there was a definite catch in that flat well-educated voice.

'Dr Huxtable just talked to me at first and then put me into hypnotherapy. We started to have results almost at once. I began to remember things in bits. It was like the dreams but this time I knew, just knew, it was what had really happened. I didn't have any doubts at all.

'Suddenly I remembered it all so clearly as if it was yesterday. It was like I was five again, like I was there again.

'Our mother hadn't tried to kill us in the car in the garage, neither had she killed herself. No. . . .'

Jennifer's voice broke completely. Karen could hear muffled sobs, and the young woman was still crying when she continued to tell her story.

'There was a terrible row. Lorraine and I were playing in our room upstairs but there was so much noise that we crept out on to the landing and then downstairs to see what was happening. We lived in a hotel, of course, and there were guests, but they wouldn't have heard anything because the guest bedrooms were all in the new extension. Mummy and Daddy were in the kitchen. They were shouting at each other, screaming. Then Daddy caught hold of Mummy around the neck and started shaking her. She made this awful sound. This gurgling noise. I can hear it now, I can still hear it. I just turned and fled upstairs, but Lorraine was always braver than me. She ran into the room and I could hear her shouting at Daddy to stop.

'Then after a bit Daddy came upstairs with Lorraine in his arms. She was still in tears but she was fairly calm. Daddy said everything was all right and Mummy was fine. Lorraine and I just huddled together because we were frightened. Then a little later he came back and said that Mummy had been very cross with him and she'd gone away and he was going to take us next door to the neighbours because he wanted to go after her and find her.

'Even Lorraine was too frightened to say much that night but at school the next day she kept telling the teacher that Daddy had got rid of Mummy. I think that's what she said. I think those were her exact words.

'We went back to the neighbours' house after school that day but early the next morning Daddy came to fetch us. He said that Granny would be coming to look after us. I couldn't take any of it in, really. Then he said we could have the day off school as a special treat. I still don't remember much about that day. We stayed indoors, I think, until bedtime. And I do remember that when he put us to bed Lorraine kept asking him what he'd done to Mummy. Why had he hurt Mummy? Where had he put Mummy? I just clung to him, though. I don't think I even wanted to know what *was going on. I sensed that I had lost one parent, I suppose. I really didn't want to lose another.*

'Eventually I fell asleep. And I have no idea what else happened that night. But in the morning Lorraine wasn't there. Her bed was empty and I never saw her again.

'Daddy said he was taking me to live with some kind people for a while who would look after me until he'd found Mummy and Lorraine. He kind of suggested that Lorraine was with Mummy, I think. I was too young to understand, to question anything.

'He took me to Carol and Michael. They had wanted children all their lives. They looked after me and cared for me and helped me forget, I suppose. So I blocked it out. That's what kids do. Sounds incredible but it's very common with small children faced with something terrible, Dr Huxtable told me. They just shut everything out.

'Without his help, without learning about Recovered Memory Syndrome from you, I would never have remembered all this. Never have known the difference between my nightmares and the truth.'

Kelly's voice broke in.

'Are you quite sure of this, Jennifer?' he sounded stunned, as indeed he might, thought Karen. Whatever he may have suspected, whatever any of them may always have believed, hearing it first-hand after all these years was something none of them would have thought possible. It was a total shock to Karen, too.

'Oh, yes, I'm quite sure. I can see it so clearly. It's absolutely real to me. I can see our father bringing Lorraine upstairs and trying to tell us everything is all right. I can even see the scratches on his face, angry weals down both cheeks. Mummy must have tried to fight him off, but he was always such a strong man. . . .'

Jennifer completely broke down in tears then. Karen found that her own hands were trembling, just as Kelly's had been in Hammersmith Police Station. She remembered what her mother had said. 'Scratches, he had scratches on his face.' The tape was silent for almost a minute before Jennifer's voice filled the room once more.

'Lorraine wouldn't stop accusing him. I have no doubt at all that he killed Lorraine, too. But not me. I survived because I didn't really question our father, I think. Didn't question him at all, in fact. Also, I think I'd always been his favourite. I was a complete

daddy's girl. I didn't want to believe he'd done what he'd done, so I just didn't accept it. And I was only five.'

Kelly's voice came on the tape. *'What now, Jennifer?'* he asked. *'What are you going to do? What do you want me to do? We should go to the police, you know.'*

Kelly no longer sounded like a journalist doing an interview. It was as if he had been overwhelmed by the magnitude of what he had just learned. And Karen could understand that well enough.

'There isn't any point in going to the police, is there?' It was a rhetorical question from Jennifer. *'My father has successfully appealed against his conviction. He cannot be tried again. I know the law might change one day, but that's how it is at the moment. In any case, would I be believed? It was my evidence, the evidence of my alleged memory, which let him walk away a free man, wasn't it? I doubt what I have told you would ever stand up in a court of law. I don't know what I'm going to do yet, Kelly. But I want you to take this tape away with you, so that the truth is on record. And I want you to get it published if you can.'*

Kelly had said something about doubting that any paper would dare publish such stuff about a man who had been declared innocent by the Court of Appeal, and Jennifer had simply responded: *'You'll do your best, though, won't you? I know you'll do your best.'*

Then the tape ended. Karen realised she had been holding her breath for the last couple of minutes. She let it out in a whoosh.

'Jennifer did know what she was going to do though, didn't she, Kelly?' she said.

Kelly nodded and smiled grimly. 'She knew, all right. I'm sure of it. She'd already decided that she was going to kill Richard Marshall. And right after I left her she drove to Poole and shot him. God knows how she managed to get hold of a gun, but she was a lot more resourceful and together than she looked, that young woman. She was, after all, her father's daughter.

'When I got the tip the next day that Marshall was dead I just knew at once what she'd done. So I took off back to London again to confront her, to make sure, I suppose. But . . . but, she was dead.'

Karen stood up with a jump. 'You'll never learn not to interfere, Kelly, will you?' she asked.

'I might after this,' said the reporter. 'I can't say I'm sorry that Marshall's dead, but I am sorry about Jennifer Roth.'

'Too late,' said Karen. 'It's too late for that. Dead bodies follow you around, don't they, Kelly?'

The reporter stared hard at her. He looked despairing.

'This was the last thing I wanted,' he said. 'I feel as if I am to blame.'

'You are to blame, Kelly,' Karen said flatly. 'You bloody well are to blame.'

Epilogue

Four months later, on a crisp clear autumn day, Karen stood on a Scottish cliff-side looking out over the sea to the Isle of Skye. They were just outside the little Scottish coastal town of Plockton, known both for its palm trees, an unlikely vegetation in the Highlands made possible only by the presence of the Gulf Stream, and as the setting for the TV series *Hamish Macbeth*, about a dope-smoking copper.

It was a long time since Karen Meadows had smoked a joint. As she surveyed the scene being quietly played out before her, its melancholy made her head long for the escape that would bring.

Sean Macdonald, wearing a big iron-grey overcoat, was standing on the edge of the cliff, surrounded by a small group of dark-clad friends and relatives. In his hands he held a small cast-iron urn which Karen knew contained the ashes of the granddaughter he had never known. Not since she had been a very small child, anyway.

Months earlier Mac had tossed the cremated ashes of all that had remained of his beloved only daughter out over the water in the same place. It was where the old man so often came to fish, where he found peace. Now he was going to throw his granddaughter's ashes to the winds.

A loan piper began to play, the notes of his bagpipes wafting eerily into the air, as Mac slowly removed the lid of the little urn with one hand and lifted it up high in front of him. The wind caught the ashes even as he began to tip the urn. A little cloud drifted out over the sea.

There was a lump in Karen's throat. And when Mac turned around to face the small group standing behind him, she saw that there were tears coursing down his face. Throughout all the heartache of almost thirty years it was only the second time she had ever seen the Scotsman cry.

The big bearded man standing to her left, a fishing chum of Mac's, touched her arm lightly and passed her a small silver flask. It contained a fine single malt, rich with the peaty taste for which the malts of that area of the Scottish Highlands are famous.

Gratefully, Karen took a deep drink. It didn't change the world in quite the way that a joint would have done, but it sent a glow into her belly and somehow made her feel alive again.

This was one case she was not sure she would ever entirely get over. And she was not the only one. A week after finding Jennifer Roth dead, Kelly had resigned from the *Evening Argus*. He had been vague about what he was going to do with his life, and neither did he seem to know what he was going to live on.

'I do know that I don't want to have anything to do with journalism any more,' he'd told her. 'I'm just too bloody good at it, that's the problem. Always have been.'

He hadn't been boasting. Far from it. Just stating a fact. And Karen knew exactly what he meant. Kelly was too good. That was why he was always getting entangled, that was why he was always getting sucked into other people's lives. He couldn't resist taking that one step further, like telling Jennifer Roth that Richard Marshall had confessed to murder.

Karen could barely imagine just how desperate Jennifer Roth must have been to do what she had done. DNA and forensic evidence had now proved beyond doubt that she had indeed killed her father and then taken her own life. Karen thought Jennifer had probably already been deeply disturbed by the traumas of her childhood and the half-formed memories which had always floated around her head. Then, when she finally came to know the truth, thanks largely to the interference of John Kelly, she had cracked.

Karen turned her attention back to the present as Mac began to walk towards the cars parked on the cliff road. The rest of the group automatically stood back to let him pass by. When he drew level with Karen he paused and looked directly at her.

'If only I hadn't been so bitter,' he said. 'If only I'd gone to her. I blamed her for speaking up for her father. I didn't understand. I could have saved her, at least. But now I've lost them all.'

'It wasn't your fault, Mac,' she said, instinctively grasping the old man's hand. 'You weren't to know.'

'I wanted Marshall dead.' Mac spat the words out. 'I've wanted Marshall dead for so long. But I never imagined this. Never imagined her killing him. I just wish I'd found the courage to do it myself. I should have killed him. I should have done it myself.'

Mac spat out the last few sentences.

'At least it's over,' Karen said, desperately seeking words of comfort, any words of comfort. 'At least it's finally over.'

Mac snatched his hand away. 'No,' he said. 'It'll never be over for me. Not until I'm dead myself.'

He strode away from her, his powerful steps belying his age. The tears pricked at the back of Karen's eyes.

Her mobile phone rang, cruelly breaking into the moment, as she watched him go. She hadn't realised it was still switched on. Automatically she answered it.

The caller was Phil Cooper, who had recently been transferred to the Avon and Somerset force at Bristol – a transfer he had requested himself, just as he had indicated to Karen that he might, They had not been alone together since that ill-fated night in Bournemouth.

'Look, Karen, it's no good, I can't go on like this. It just isn't working. I can't carry on without you. I really have to see you. . . .'

She dropped the mobile away from her ear, and as she held it loosely against her hip she could still hear his voice, but not what he was saying. After a few seconds she pushed the off button.

Then she turned to the big bearded fisherman still standing alongside her.

'Have you got any more of that malt?' she asked.

He passed her the flask. She took a deep long pull, relishing the burning sensation as the fine whisky trickled down her throat, and trying desperately to shut everything else out of her head.

296